W9-DBW-488

While She Was Sleeping

Also by Suzanne Forster in Large Print:

Husband, Lover, Stranger

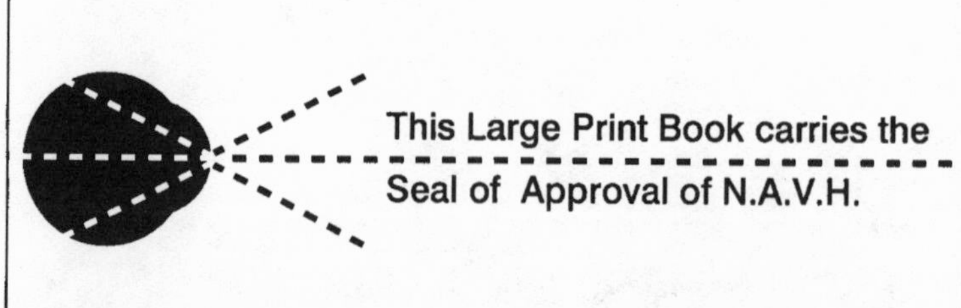

While She Was Sleeping

Suzanne Forster

This is a work of fiction. Names, characters, places, and incidents either are the product of the author's imagination or are used fictitiously, and any resemblance to actual persons, living or dead, business establishments, events, or locales is entirely coincidental.

Published in 2003 by arrangement with The Berkley Publishing Group, a member of Penguin Group (USA) Inc.

Wheeler Large Print Compass.

The text of this Large Print edition is unabridged.
Other aspects of the book may vary from the original edition.

Set in 16 pt. Plantin by Ramona Watson.

Printed in the United States on permanent paper.

Library of Congress Cataloging-in-Publication Data

Forster, Suzanne.
While she was sleeping / Suzanne Forster.
p. cm.
ISBN 1-58724-558-2 (lg. print : hc : alk. paper)
1. Police — Washington (State) — Seattle — Fiction. 2. Women — Crimes against — Fiction. 3. Seattle (Wash.) — Fiction. 4. Homeless women — Fiction. 5. Police artists — Fiction. 6. Witnesses — Fiction. 7. Large type books. I. Title.
PS3556.O7443W47 2003
813′.54—dc22 2003062117

While She Was Sleeping

National Association for Visually Handicapped
serving the partially seeing

As the Founder/CEO of NAVH, the only national health agency solely devoted to those who, although not totally blind, have an eye disease which could lead to serious visual impairment, I am pleased to recognize Thorndike Press* as one of the leading publishers in the large print field.

Founded in 1954 in San Francisco to prepare large print textbooks for partially seeing children, NAVH became the pioneer and standard setting agency in the preparation of large type.

Today, those publishers who meet our standards carry the prestigious "Seal of Approval" indicating high quality large print. We are delighted that Thorndike Press is one of the publishers whose titles meet these standards. We are also pleased to recognize the significant contribution Thorndike Press is making in this important and growing field.

Lorraine H. Marchi, L.H.D.
Founder/CEO
NAVH

* Thorndike Press encompasses the following imprints: Thorndike, Wheeler, Walker and Large Print Press.

Prologue

July 10, five minutes to midnight

She would never know what it was that stirred her from sleep. The faint creak of a door hinge? A shadow thrown by the moonlight? She was trained to pick up the obvious sounds of intrusion, but this was something more insidious. She could feel the breathing presence of another human being. His nearness. His body heat.

His cruel, cruel intentions.

There were no night-lights. She couldn't sleep unless it was as black as a cave, but her senses had pricked. Someone was in the room with her.

Her blood turned to ice, and her thoughts leaped feverishly. *He's come back for revenge. It has to be him because the alarm hasn't fired, and no one else knows how to get in. My God, what kind of crazy nerve does that take?* They'd fought before he left. She wanted to break it off with him. They worked together, and it wasn't safe anymore, not for either one of them. But he knew her weaknesses, and he was playing on all of them.

At his hands, revenge *was* sweet.

Excitement trickled like sweat on a glass of ice water. She wasn't supposed to want this. No one was supposed to want this, but especially not her. She was a guardian of the public safety. She lived by a rigid standard of conduct, and it had to be that way. *Zero tolerance*. But her imagination was already spinning, sucking her into the miasma. Her mind was morbidly fascinated with its own dark corners. She had to look, even knowing what waited there.

The sound of ripping fabric gave her a painful start. She didn't want to be tied up tonight, but there was no way to stop him. He dropped like an executioner's axe, his hands barely touching her as he sealed off her mouth with duct tape. The glowing black mask he wore made his face look ghoulish.

She wasn't imagining anything. This was happening. He was there, and he was going to rip all control away from her. God, she was lost. The helplessness would send her swinging in a mad arc between terror and ecstasy. It would fill her with guilt and shame and wonder. She had never understood how restraints could free her, but they did. Nothing else on this earth could make her shiver like water and take whatever form she was given.

A knee pressed into her solar plexus, forcing the breath out of her. God, it hurt!

He pinned her to the bed while he duct-taped her hands in front of her, one wrist on top of the other. She couldn't even move her fingers. Normally he would have used ropes and tied her to the bedposts. By now he would have touched her or whispered something evil in her ear, their code language.

She struggled to get up and felt a hand on her forehead, shoving her back down. It smelled strongly of leather. Was he wearing gloves? He'd never done that before, either. How far was he going to take this? The tape adhered to her mouth like liquid steel. All she could do was moan.

"Don't speak," he hissed. "You're not allowed to speak to me. Do it again, and I'll kill you right here in your bed."

She quieted immediately. This was not the time to fight. Her intuition was telling her that this was not the lover she played dangerous games with. Or if it was, he wasn't playing games any longer. He meant her harm. She couldn't ID him from his voice. He spoke too softly. But something was seriously wrong.

"You learn quickly, Sharon. I thought you might."

He knew her name! Who *was* he?

Her mind slowed, and she began to think strategically. She didn't want to strike out blindly, and it was too late to use her legs. He'd already taped her ankles, and now he was lifting her to a sitting position, probably to blindfold her eyes. She felt the chill of leather sliding across her bare skin. He was wearing a leather jacket, maybe leather pants. She could hear the soft swish as he moved. That was the sound that had awakened her!

She twisted out of his hands and got a look at the bedside table. Her gun and her badge were there, but it was the clock she needed to see. It was midnight! *This couldn't be happening. It had to be a nightmare.* She was working on a serial abduction case, trying to apprehend a leather biker who the press was calling the Violator. He broke into women's homes at midnight, kidnapped, drugged, and tortured them. She was going to be number four, but he would never let her live, not once he discovered she was the detective on his case.

Or maybe he already knew. Maybe that's why he was here.

She lurched forward and collapsed under the weight of his body. He held her down until he'd secured the blindfold, then he dragged her off the bed and onto her knees. Thank God, she had on clothing. She slept in sweat pants and a tank top. The Violator's MO was to dress his victims like bikers and abduct them on the back of his motorcycle. She'd been trying to trap him for months. How had he trapped her? Who let him in?

"You need to be taught a lesson, Sharon," he whispered. "Class starts now."

Her head fell back, and she felt the sting of something wet and cold in her nostril. A nasal spray? Was he drugging her? One of those new date rape concoctions? A heavy object dropped over her head — a helmet — and the face mask snapped shut, sealing her in her own dark hell. Her breath whistled sharply in her ears. Abruptly she was jerked to her feet, and the tape that held her ankles was cut free. He had a knife. But he wasn't releasing her. He was letting her participate in her own destruction. *He was teaching her a lesson.*

The whistling turned into the deadly roar of a motorcycle.

Chapter 1

"Exactly what *is* your problem with women, Sadler?"

If sarcasm were bullets, Russ Sadler would have had several holes in his back. He stood facing the interior windows of the police chief's oak-paneled office, looking down the hallway, where a couple of Seattle's finest were drinking vending machine coffee and probably debating the grittier points of a murder case. Russ couldn't hear them, but what else would homicide detectives be doing, besides deflecting bullets from a superior.

His superior just happened to be Kate Townsend, the newly elected chief, and she was shooting to kill this morning. Could be the pressure she was under. There was a nut on the loose, abducting women right out of their beds, and he'd just turned killer. Kate had the entire city up in arms. But she was dead wrong when it came to Russ's problems.

He didn't have a problem with all women. It was just *one*.

"I don't want her on the Violator case, Kate. That wouldn't be asking for trouble. It would be begging."

He turned to face his superior and got the full force of Kate Townsend's displeasure. Her cropped gray hair bristled like an angry hedgehog's. She was tallish, solidly built, and her intelligent blue eyes fired both barrels.

"You don't get a vote in this decision, Russ. A former partner of yours is dead, and we have a dangerous serial assailant at large. We need her."

"I always get a vote, Chief."

The homicide badge in the breast pocket of his black knit shirt was his vote. He could set it on Kate's desk at any time and walk out. But that didn't have to be said. She knew it.

Russ had casually folded his arms across his chest, but there was nothing casual about the geometry of his stance. The hard right angles of his head and shoulders said a forklift couldn't have moved him, which meant Kate didn't have a chance, despite the fact that she was fierce, formidable, and about the same age as his mother.

"Sure, you can quit." Kate swiftly negotiated her massive oak desk and came halfway across the room before she stopped, hands planted on her hips. Light blazed from the window behind her, haloing her stocky frame. Seattle was in the midst of a record-breaking heat wave, and when the late afternoon sun hit the Public Safety Building head-on, the dreary offices lit up like a torch.

"You can take the coward's way out and walk," she said, ignoring the intercom that was buzzing on her desk. "Let Sharon's killer go free if that's how little her death means to you. But how are you going to feel when he kills again?"

Quietly, Russ said, "Be glad you're not a man, or you'd be on the floor now."

Kate didn't blink. She was too well-trained for that, but the room fell silent. With a slight nod, she acknowledged that one of them had crossed the line, and it wasn't him. Within seconds she'd returned to her desk.

Russ hadn't just seen red at Kate's suggestion that Sharon Myer's death meant nothing. He'd smelled it, tasted it, and inhaled it like fire. Sharon had been his partner once, and her death had — was — destroying him. Three days ago, near dawn, a security guard had found her denuded body, lying in a city park in the Crown Hill area in north Seattle. She'd been suffocated and left on a greenbelt in public view, wearing nothing but a disposable medical examining gown.

What distinguished the case from other serial crimes was the pristine condition of the body. There wasn't a mark to be found on her pale flesh, other than the expected signs of lividity, caused by pooling blood. But every follicle of body hair had been shorn away, including her heavy red tresses, her eyebrows, and even her eyelashes.

Russ hadn't slept since.

He'd been the one to officially ID her at the coroner's office, and it had drained all the color out of his vision. Like most homicide cops, he dealt with death on a daily basis, but this was personal. Images of Sharon's chalk white, hairless corpse screened through his head like a television news flash. Kate should have known how he felt, and if this was a guilt trip, it was unconscionable.

The jacket of her tan pantsuit was draped over the back of her chair. She slipped it on and tugged it into place, efficiently smoothing the lapel.

"I'm damn glad I'm not a man, always have been," she said, looking him straight in the eye. "And don't be so sure who would have been on the floor."

Russ didn't smile, but he thought about it.

"Exactly what *is* your problem with Jennifer Nash?" she asked.

Other than the fact that she was the woman who taught him everything he knew about commitment phobia?

Russ walked back to the windows. Problem? Yeah, you could safely say that he had a *problem* with Jennifer Nash, but that had nothing to do with why he wanted her off the case. No one in the department, Kate included, knew anything about his personal history with Jennifer, and he intended to keep it that way. This was strictly professional. Kate was blundering into a minefield, and he needed to make her see that.

Jennifer Nash was a forensic sketch artist who'd made a name for herself with her eerily accurate sketches of suspects. She'd also stirred up plenty of controversy with her unorthodox methods of interviewing witnesses, but all the fuss had eventually paid off. Her sketches had broken several big cases for the FBI, which had made her a sought-after consultant, as well as something of a media darling. If the case had an eyewitness and there was a sketch involved, the news shows were clamoring for Jennifer Nash to be their guest expert. As for Jennifer, she seemed more than eager to sell her "method" as the answer to modern criminology.

That was the problem. Nobody had the patience for solid investigating anymore. They wanted sketches, Amber Alerts, and neighborhood justice. Russ wasn't saying that approach didn't work. It often did, depending on the case. But hot new trends didn't always sit well, especially with the veterans on homicide squads. And neither did Jennifer Nash sit well.

"Bottom line, she's not a team player," Russ said. "She has an agenda. Nothing major, she just wants to change the entire face of crime scene investigation."

Kate's eyebrows lifted. "Isn't that a bit extreme?"

"That depends on how you define extreme. She insists on being the first one to interview the witness after the preliminary police report is done. She's also fanatical about not contaminating witnesses by exposing them to composite catalogs or lineups, and with the results she's had, people are bound to take her seriously. I know how passionate she is about this cause of hers, Kate. If anyone's extreme, it's her.

"Just keep this in mind," he cautioned. "If you bring her here and accept her conditions, you might as well turn the investigation over to her. Are you willing to give up that much control? *I'm* not."

Kate shrugged. "If she can get the bastard's face plastered on television sets across the country, who cares? It could break the case."

The chief had begun to sift through the material on her desk as if she was searching for something, but she glanced up long enough to give Russ a scrutinizing look. "This is about the case, isn't it, Russ? About catching Sharon's murderer?"

"What else would it be about?"

A guy's heart, his soul, his belief in mankind?

By his best count, Russ hadn't seen Jennifer Nash in twenty-seven months and eleven days, and if their paths never crossed again, it would be too soon. In the annals of male–female relationships, there seemed to be countless blunders a man could make to earn a woman's undying scorn. There were only a couple a woman could make to earn a man's: ditch him at the altar, which had to rank in the top ten of a man's most vulnerable moments, or deprive him of his vital body parts, à la Lorena Bobbitt.

Jennifer was halfway there.

They'd worked together in the downtown division long before she got famous. He'd been a beat officer at the time, patrolling one of the city's heaviest crime areas, and she'd been doing sketches to pay her way through grad school. The attraction had been instant, mutual, and so powerful it couldn't have been anything but star-crossed. A blind man could have seen that the odds were against them. They had too much in common. Both were compulsive workers with little to no success at long-term relationships. But Russ was too busy being distracted by the sparkle in Jennifer's voice to notice. Everything about her shone. He'd been dazzled by nothing more than a woman's misty smiles and bubbling laughter, and that wasn't like Russ Sadler.

He'd never let anyone in the way he'd let her in, and he'd paid dearly for it. Men dying on the battlefield had bled less. After she walked out on him, he'd wound the tourniquet so tightly, he'd lost all feeling. It had left him numb inside, deadened. But at least he had her out of his system. After two years, he was clean and sober. And now, what did they want to do but fly her back from wherever she was to consult on a case. *His* case.

Over several dead bodies.

Kate fanned herself with a notepad, creating a stiff breeze that riffled her salt-and-pepper bangs. "The department's in trouble, Russ, and like it or not, there's no one else I can turn to now but Jennifer."

"I don't like it, Kate."

"Well, that makes two of us, but you're not the one who has to answer to the public and the press, not to mention the city council." She pointed at him. "This isn't an office, Russ. It's a pressure cooker."

"And you think Jennifer's arrival will calm things down?"

"No, I think she'll distract the press, draw their fire."

Or create a media frenzy, Russ thought. He knew all about Kate's pressure, but she knew nothing about his. There were things he couldn't tell her about this case. Things he couldn't tell anyone. Sharon Myer had not resisted her abductor. The other three victims hadn't, either, but that didn't surprise him. The assailant struck at midnight, when his targets were asleep. They were already bound and gagged before they were alert enough to resist. But Sharon was a cop. Cops didn't sleep the way other people did. They were like new mothers and vagrants, vigilant for any unfamiliar sound. Even if her alarm system had malfunctioned, she should have been awake before an intruder penetrated her bedroom, awake and holding a gun to his head — the one she kept by her bedside.

There was always the possibility that a drug had been used. The new date rape drugs were out of the system within six to twelve hours, so forensics wouldn't have found any evidence. But the other victims reported being drugged before they were released rather than when they were abducted, and in Sharon's case, there was an eyewitness who saw her attempt to resist the abductor on the street, while he was putting her on the bike. That was enough reason for everyone else involved to dismiss the idea of a known assailant, but Russ hadn't. He couldn't. Maybe the Violator had resorted to drugs because Sharon was a cop, but there was still something missing. She was too good a cop to let anyone get the drop on her like that. No, when a victim didn't resist, it was usually because he or she knew their killer. Russ couldn't get that thought out of his mind.

Kate was fanning herself again. "We're *all* under pressure, okay? I think you should know that your partner's been talking. He's not happy with the way you're prioritizing."

"Partner? What partner would that be?"

Technically, Russ and Sharon Myer had been partners until Russ was made acting lieutenant several months ago — and ended up spending most of his time behind a desk. Sharon was paired with Kent Wright, an ambitious cop whose partner had retired, and Russ, whose new duties included making such assignments, never bothered to make one for himself. It had worked beautifully until he asked to be relieved of his administrative duties to work on the Violator case, which was what the serial abductions, and now Sharon's murder, were being called.

Kate put him in charge of the entire operation but insisted he take a partner, like everyone else. Kent Wright just happened to be available, and it was a done deal.

Kate was unwavering. "Your *partner* thinks you're holding back, Russ. He claims you're dragging your feet and being selective about the information you share with him. The word he used was *secretive*. Are you being secretive, Russ?"

Russ would have been secretive with Kent about the time of day. He didn't trust the guy on principle. As for holding back, Russ was guilty of that, too. Yes, he was stalling. He had a reason. The same reason he was stalling with Kate.

He threw up a flare to distract her. "Kent has a top gun mentality. He sees me as his competition, not his partner. If he could aim his gun, he'd shoot me out of the sky. That doesn't make for a good working relationship."

"Make it work, Russ. That's your job."

He hadn't expected her to cut him any slack. This was the biggest case Seattle had seen since the Green River Killer, and the media was all over it. They'd been critical of the way things were handled from the beginning, starting with the fumbling of some potential evidence in the very first strike. As of this morning, there was a feeding frenzy over rumors of an eyewitness to Sharon's abduction. Russ had given strict orders to his people to withhold that information for the witness's protection, but someone had conveniently leaked it.

Someone from the department, he'd concluded, and he would have bet his left lung who it was — and thrown in the right to sweeten the pot. He hadn't said anything to Kate because he didn't operate that way. He wasn't a squealer, unlike Kent Wright. Russ did things differently, as Wright would find out.

"Tell me where you're at," Kate said.

She wasn't inquiring about his mental health. "The BMW motorcycle's a match," he told her. "It's hell getting prints when the weather's this dry, but based on the tire tread, it's the same bike that was used in the first two strikes."

"Three out of four? Not bad. What about the SUV?"

Kate was referring to the second strike, one that occurred last summer, where the tread of a sports utility vehicle was found at the site where the victim was left. They'd analyzed it and done a DMV cross-check against BMW bike owners, but had come up with nothing.

He shook his head. "The dump site was clean. We're focusing on the motorcycle, rechecking DMV records, dealerships, repair shops. I'm tracing Sharon's last steps, and my *partner,* Kent, is running comparisons of the crime scene data to make sure we're dealing with the same guy. We know that all three victims prior to Sharon were held for seventy-two hours in some kind of trailer before they were released, probably a single-wide, based on their accounts. They were blindfolded and drugged, but all reported being kept in a closet-sized bedroom with drapes for doors, and being taken to a head in the back of the trailer when they needed to relieve themselves."

"A head in the back? Is that typical?"

"We're checking that out, too. He took them to the trailer and left them there, still bound and blindfolded, for a few hours before returning. Two of the three women noticed a powdery substance on their hands while he was gone. The other didn't notice it until he ripped the duct tape off her wrists. Unfortunately, he cleaned them up before he released them, so there were no traces of it left."

Kate frowned. "Something to do with the depilation?"

"He didn't depilate them until the last day. That was their farewell present." Now for the bad news. "None of them knew where they were geographically. Their estimates of the motorcycle trip varied from forty-five minutes to over an hour, which means the trailer could be almost anywhere in western Washington. I need somebody to check that out. Hell, I need an army to check that out."

Kate's expressive voice was mildly scolding. "I don't have any more people, and Sherlock Holmes couldn't break this case without a sketch of the suspect. That's why we need Jennifer Nash. We don't have any evidence!"

"We don't have any evidence that will hold up in court. Yet."

Russ wasn't yielding any ground. It was a fight he couldn't afford to lose, but they both knew that what Kate was saying was true. Seattle PD was known for its strange cases, but this one might be the strangest. Local single women were being snatched from their beds in the dead of night. The Violator targeted redheads exclusively, shaving all the hair from their head and body because it was the "source of their sinfulness."

Russ had come to think of it as a rite of purification. The Violator also lectured the women and humiliated them to frighten them out of their "wanton ways." He called them names — temptresses and tramps — and warned that he was going to teach them a lesson they would never forget. Russ doubted they would.

Before the Violator released his victims, he gave them drugs to impair but not completely erase their memory of the events. Whether he wanted them to be living examples of correct moral behavior to the world, or he simply didn't want them to forget him, he was smart enough to ruin their credibility on the stand, should the case ever come to trial.

And so far, with the exception of tire treads and some cotton fibers found in Sharon's throat, he hadn't left any forensic evidence. But as Russ had discovered over the years, sometimes no evidence *was* the evidence.

"We have one eyewitness, albeit a lousy one," Kate admitted. "A homeless woman who saw Sharon being taken from her apartment and got a brief glimpse of the guy's face when Sharon dislodged the visor of his helmet."

"You're being *way* too optimistic, Kate. We don't have an eyewitness. The woman was on painkillers that night. She was not only running from the scene, she was a block away when she fell and knocked herself out. If a convenience store clerk hadn't seen her and called 911, we wouldn't know she existed."

"Her description of the Violator matches everything we know about him. Why would she claim to have seen the abduction if she hadn't?"

"You tell me. She babbled one story to the paramedics, probably in a state of shock, but by the time our guy got there, she'd changed it. She couldn't remember her own name when I questioned her, and our sketch artist couldn't get anything from her, either."

"Which is exactly why we need Jennifer. If the woman actually saw the suspect, Jennifer will get to the image that's hidden in her subconscious. That's what she does, Russ. She dives for buried treasure, and I can guarantee you that Jennifer Nash's involvement will give this investigation some credibility. It will also work wonders to calm the public's panic and get the press off our back."

"Then call her in. Let her have at it."

Kate's smile was fleeting. Her mouth tightened. "Ah, but that's where you come in. I can't give her the department's stamp of approval," she admitted, "because that has to come from you. I just run the place, and until these people come to know and love me, I'm going to need your cooperation. You're the local hero, Russ. They look up to you."

She picked up the notebook and sent her bangs flying again.

If Russ was surprised by Kate's admission, he didn't let on. He wasn't quite the Eagle Scout she'd made him out to be, but he'd been with the department since his Academy days — over twenty years — and he'd built some strong alliances in that time.

It had also hit Russ what was going on. They weren't just asking him to work with Jennifer Nash, they wanted him to rescue her ass. God, what a position to be in. The woman lived or died by his decree. *Off with her head.* Two years ago, he would have made a deal with the devil to have that kind of power over her. Now his needs were simpler. He was free of her, and he wanted to stay that way. It would be much more pleasant for everyone concerned.

"I can't help you, Kate."

She gave him a sharp glance. "If there's a problem between you and Jennifer Nash, you need to put it behind you, Russ. It's getting in the way."

It *was* behind him, and he intended to keep it that way.

"Hold on a minute," Kate said as she went back to searching her desk.

Russ's pager went off, and the annoying bleat was music to his ears. A fire alarm would have been music. He pulled the remote from his jeans and checked out the number and the message. "It's Junior. Urgent."

Kate sniffed. "I can't imagine what Junior Gordon is urgently in need of, besides a beer. Hey, wait!"

Russ was almost out the door before she called him back. She'd found whatever she was looking for on her desk, and she was beckoning him.

Russ went reluctantly.

Big mistake.

"It's Sharon," she said, handing him the official department photograph of a triumphant young woman who'd just fulfilled her dream to make detective. "She needs to go up on our fallen officer's wall, and you were her first partner. It's more fitting that you do the honors than me . . . or Kent, for that matter."

Russ couldn't look at the photograph. The hope in Sharon's clear blue eyes and her shining smile haunted him. Maybe he hadn't given Kate enough credit. This was a low blow, and a premeditated one. He could hardly refuse, and that was her plan. He took the picture and muttered a thank-you, which apparently inspired her to land another kidney punch.

"The only thing that matters now is catching Sharon's murderer, whatever it takes to do that. I know you must agree with me," she said. "Will you give Jennifer a call and talk to her? Strategize with her and let her know she's welcome? I'd like to get her up here tomorrow."

"Yeah, sure, tomorrow."

"Russ, I'm serious. We're not going to be friends if you buck me on this."

"I've been getting along pretty well without friends up to now."

Kate looked a little stunned at his bluntness. *She'll get used to it* was his next thought, equally blunt. Okay, it was a flaw.

Russ's arms were folded over the tight pink scar that crisscrossed his forearm. He'd sustained the knife wound months ago, but it still ached, and he could feel it throbbing against his wrist. Extremes of weather made it worse, and it didn't get much more extreme than today. The mercury had hit the century mark by noon.

Kate had drawn herself up. "All right, fine," she said, "but you've been warned. She's going to be involved in this case, with or without your blessing."

Somebody should warn Jennifer, he thought as he turned to leave. She was the one walking into the mortar fire. It wasn't just him who had a problem with her way of doing things. He doubted there was anyone in the department who wanted her tromping all over their investigation, except possibly their new chief, who had her own credibility issues. Someone should warn both of them.

Chapter 2

Russ took the back stairs. He preferred them to the building's creaky elevators, even though Kate's office was on the tenth floor, and Junior ran the crime lab, several flights down on the second floor. On his way down, Russ stopped by his own office on the fifth floor to drop off Sharon's picture. He put it in the out box on the credenza behind his desk.

Russ found Junior in his cubicle, deeply engrossed, but not in work. He was tilted like a ladder against his desk, munching from a bag of Doritos Extreme and watching the Home Shopping Network on a wall-mounted monitor that was supposed to be providing surveillance feed of the lab.

"What's up?" Russ asked.

Junior gave him a blank stare. "Nothing's up. Why?"

Russ tapped the pager in his hand. "You beeped me. This thing says urgent."

"Oh, yeah, right." An indolent grin lit Junior's cherubic face.

Russ was always reminded of Norm Macdonald, the *Saturday Night Live* alumnus, when Junior grinned. His friend had the same lazy eyelids and don't-give-a-damn attitude. Very little motivated Junior to move a muscle except the gory minutiae of a good homicide case — and now, possibly, home shopping.

"I was upstairs on ten, checking out the new coed bathroom. Whose idea was that, anyway?" Junior's voice tended to rise slightly at the end of his sentences, as if to hold you in suspense until he finished. "I mean *there's* a situation fraught with the potential for abuse, right? Ever watch *Ally McBeal*? Somebody has to make sure no one's fornicating in the stalls or stealing toilet paper."

Russ glanced at his watch. "Is there an end to this story?"

"I saw you in Kate's office," Junior hastened to explain. "Didn't look like you were having fun, so I figured you might need to be sprung."

Junior held out the bag of Doritos, which Russ ignored. The scar on his arm prickled and burned. "Kate wants to call in Jennifer Nash."

Junior's eyebrows lifted. "Jennifer Nash? Are you talking about our Jenny, the sketch artist? The *Jenn* Girl? The *Jenninator? Jennarama?* She was hot, Russ."

"Stick with the chips," Russ advised. "That's all the heat you can handle."

"Jennahlicious," Junior murmured.

"Maybe you and your crime lab goons

could concentrate on getting me some usable evidence," Russ suggested, "instead of monitoring coed bathrooms and drooling over inaccessible women? Like a set of prints that doesn't disappear into thin air?"

Russ was referring to fingerprints that had been lifted from one of the crime scene bedrooms but had never made it to the lab. No one ever figured out what happened to them, including Junior, who was generally meticulous to the point of being fanatical about evidence collection. It was the first abduction, before anyone realized they were dealing with a serial assailant, which had made it low priority, compared to the attention the case was getting now.

The odds that they were the Violator's prints were slim, Russ knew. He didn't leave prints. But what if he'd been careless that one time?

"Hey, everybody's entitled to a screwup."

Russ blinked at Junior's choice of words. "Right, but it's one a lifetime, not one a week. What about the stuff on Sharon's nightstand that never got bagged? The first officer at the scene said there was some kind of book, a diary —"

"Someone was hallucinating. There was nothing on her nightstand but a table lamp, a clock radio, her badge, and gun. Other than that, her apartment was so bare she could have been living in a hotel room. I was there, dude. The whole damn crime lab was there."

Russ had reason to think Sharon kept a diary, and he'd scoured the crime scene himself looking for it. She'd told him about it when they worked together, confessing that she kept track of her love life solely to remind herself that she didn't make good choices where men were concerned. The diary could be important, and Russ intended to find out what had happened to it, but he would do that quietly — and on his own.

Russ's stomach rumbled. Junior's munching was driving him nuts. The noise made him feel hollow and queasy, maybe because he hadn't eaten since breakfast. Yesterday.

"Thanks," he said, helping himself to a handful of chips.

Nacho-flavored heat exploded in Russ's mouth as he bit down on one of the crunchy red-and-gold triangles. His stomach growled with pleasure, and his taste buds roared to life. "I had no idea Doritos were this good."

Russ plucked the bag from Junior's hands and headed for the door.

"Hey," Junior called after him, "did you watch *Sex and the City* last night? The hot one — I forget her name — hit the rack with a midget. Do you think women like that really exist?"

Russ made a sound. Maybe it was a growl. He wasn't sure. He was trying to kill a smile. He'd forgotten Junior's other obsession: getting a date. Russ could remember being that way, obsessed. Thank God he wasn't anymore.

By the time Russ reached his office, he'd already made a mental note to reinterview Myrna Simone, the witness to Sharon's abduction, and to do it before Jennifer Nash arrived on the scene. He might get something useful, and once Jennifer began her interview process, he would undoubtedly be locked out of his own case.

Jennifer was going to accuse him of contaminating the witness anyway, since Myrna Simone had already been handled in the traditional way, which included preliminary questioning by the investigating officer and more extensive questioning by Russ. Simone had also worked with the department's sketch artist, looking at lineups and going through catalogs of facial features. Jennifer wasn't going to be happy about any of that, but Russ figured if he was paying the price, he might as well get the goods.

He dropped the crumpled Doritos bag in the wastebasket and cast a wary eye on the wilting plant that sat on the credenza behind his desk. In the last couple of days the ficus had begun dropping leaves, most of them as yellow as the cracks in the linoleum floor.

"You're not going to die on me, too, are you?"

Russ cleared his throat and turned away. He didn't have a clue what to do at that moment, so he began searching the paper piles on his desk, wondering how the hell he was supposed to save a small, dying bush. That was the reason he'd hired a plant rental service for his home. But Sharon had asked him to baby-sit the plant while she took some time off. She hadn't made any elaborate travel plans. She just wanted some R&R, but it was a vacation from which she never returned, and somewhere in this rabbit warren of an office were the instructions she'd given him before she left. She'd written them out and read them aloud to be sure he understood. But in all honesty, he'd pretty much forgotten about the plant until the morning he got the call that they'd found her body. No one even knew she'd been abducted until then. And now it was too late.

"Too late?" he heard himself saying. "Sharon is gone, Russ. This is a plant you're talking about."

Nevertheless, his chest felt tight when he took a breath, as if his ribs were caught on something. Even when Sharon had walked into his office with the ficus in her arms and announced that she was going to entrust her precious baby to him, he hadn't understood why she was doing it. Did he look like Mr. Green Jeans or something? Hell, he couldn't grow mold on leftover food.

She said it was because of the time he saved her life.

That didn't make sense, either. He hadn't saved her life. All he'd done was stop a kid who pulled a knife. They'd been investigating a domestic homicide, and when Sharon went to cuff the alleged perpetrator — a man under suspicion of shooting his girlfriend — one of the man's teenage sons pulled a knife and lurched toward her. That was how Russ sustained the cuts on his forearm.

The kid wasn't going to kill her. He wasn't trying to hurt Russ, either. He was scared to death and probably desperate to protect his dad. The cuts had occurred when Russ leaped to disarm him, but they were clearly accidental, and the boy had not been charged.

Sharon had proclaimed Russ a hero, over his vigorous protests, and when she walked into his office with the plant that day, she reminded him that in some cultures, when you saved someone, you were responsible for them the rest of their lives. But Russ would be glad to know that she was letting him off the hook. All he had to do was take care of her plant while she was on vacation.

Saying no was not an option, she informed him. He owed her one lifetime, and he should be damn glad she was only asking him to ride herd on a plant for a couple weeks.

And here he was. Riding herd on a sickly ficus, maybe for a lifetime.

He was supposed to have watered it, but she'd also cautioned him not to overwater, and he honest to God didn't know the difference. Was once a week too much, once a day, an hour? Yesterday he'd sprinkled it with the remains of a watered-down soft drink, but that had seemed to make it worse. She'd said something about plant food and misting, and she'd implied that plants liked to be talked to, but that was absurd.

"I'm not talking to a plant, okay?" He turned to the ficus, which meant of course that he *was* talking to it, but only to make a point. "So, if that's what you're waiting for, take a number."

It annoyed him that he cared. It was a *plant.* He didn't have time.

Still, something made him kneel by the small pile of leaves and examine them for bugs or other clues as to what was wrong. *When all else fails, conduct an investigation,* he told himself. It was the way men like him got through life, even when terrible things happened to people they cared about. They investigated. They never stopped investigating, and by the time they had the answers, sometimes, if they were lucky, the pain had eased enough to be bearable.

He slapped leaf stuff from his fingers and rose to his feet. This was getting ridiculous.

He had a sick plant on his hands, and the only solution was to give it to someone who knew how to take care of it. There were several Earth Mother types in the records section whose desks were crawling with plant life, but he didn't like the idea of seeing Sharon's ficus on someone else's desk. Besides, she'd made a last wish.

"I'm letting you off the hook. Just take care of my plant. . . ."

The ficus shivered, and more leaves sprinkled the floor.

"Frightening women and children isn't enough? Now you're harassing plants?"

Russ turned to see Junior standing on his threshold, grinning. Russ did not grin back. "Why are you here," he muttered, "when there are women in the bathroom you could bother?"

"I thought you might like a hot lead."

It was the only offer Junior could have made to keep himself from being evicted.

"The Violator isn't a man," Junior said, "it's a woman."

"How do you figure?"

Russ was more than a little suspicious of Junior's theories, but every once in a while he came up with something brilliant. Meanwhile, Junior was creating a chaise lounge out of Russ's two fold-up visitor chairs and making himself comfortable. He'd brought a paper cup of coffee with him, which he balanced on his knee. Russ caught a whiff of it on the way back to his desk and emitted a sound of disgust.

"Where'd you get that stuff?" he asked.

"From Starbucks."

"It's from our vending machine, and it smells like the inside of a wet cardboard box." Russ was trying to kick the habit, and he should have been glad it smelled like paper pulp. But he was a purist when it came to his caffeine addiction, and he deplored the machine-generated swill.

"Too bad coffee isn't somehow relevant in the Violator case. You have the nose of a bloodhound." Junior took a slug and grimaced. He swung himself up, walked over to the ficus, and tipped the cup as if to empty it.

"Stop!" Russ bellowed.

The other man leaped back, out of the splash range. Only droplets hit the plant. The rest went all over the floor.

Russ searched through his desk drawer and found some napkins. He dropped several of them over the spill to soak it up. Junior just stood there, sizing up the situation, including his friend's consternation. It didn't take him long. As soon as he noticed Sharon's picture in Russ's out box, he began to nod.

"Oh, I get it," he said. "This was Sharon's plant, right?"

Russ went thunderously quiet, but Junior

didn't seem to notice. He continued with his breakthrough theory. Stretching out on his chaise, he employed deductive reasoning worthy of Sherlock Holmes. "Not *just* a woman," he pronounced, "a woman deeply conflicted about her sexuality, who acts out by punishing her own gender. It's beautiful, right?"

Russ couldn't completely discount the idea. Junior had decided the UNSUB, which was police lingo for unidentified subject, was a woman because it explained much of the missing evidence. The victims were ordered to perform acts of autoeroticism, and then punished for their behavior. However, none of them was ever touched or molested during these acts. Also, no sperm was found on the victims' bodies or the paper medical gowns they were released in, despite the fact that a male perpetrator would most likely have engaged in some autoeroticism of his own during these acts.

"That's why the Violator never spoke above a whisper," Junior asserted. "It would have given away her gender, and she wants us to hunt for a man."

"Sharon had sex the night she was killed," Russ countered. "I just got the preliminary report from the medical examiner. There was no semen, but she was clearly penetrated, and roughly, by the bruising. Did your woman Violator do that?"

Junior was clearly uncomfortable with that news. Russ had been, too, but it couldn't be withheld much longer. Eventually the report would have to be made available to the entire task force, and there was a leak somewhere. He just hoped the press didn't get their hands on it.

"That's not the Violator's MO," Junior said. "She doesn't have sex with the victims. She punishes them for *being* sexual. Besides, Sharon wasn't abducted until midnight. Maybe she had sex with a lover. Maybe Sharon had a life."

"It wasn't the Violator's MO to kill them, either," Russ pointed out. "She — or he — released the other three victims. They were unconscious and drugged, but alive. Sharon was suffocated. According to the report, she choked on something that was stuffed into her mouth, possibly her own underwear. The medical examiner's office found cotton fibers embedded in her throat."

"An accident? Maybe the Violator was trying to keep her quiet?"

"Unlikely, based on the force that was used."

"Okay, but that doesn't mean it wasn't a woman. Sharon was taking some time off, dressed like a civilian. The Violator wouldn't necessarily have known that she was dealing with someone who could fight back. Maybe Sharon got killed trying to get away."

"Or maybe she got too close."

"Yeah?" Junior peered at him. "You think she was on to something? Have you looked at her reports, her notes?"

"I'm doing that now." Russ was going over them for the second time, forcing himself to look for anything that might yield clues to what happened that night. If Sharon was getting close to the Violator, the indicators would be there, embedded in the meticulous notes she took — or in her diary. Russ had to find it, too, and go over it as thoroughly as her case notes. It felt intrusive, an act that compounded the violation of her death, but it had to be done.

He changed the subject. "Woman or man, I think our Violator could be an investigator of some kind, maybe even a scientist."

Junior was with him on that. "She sure as hell knows her stuff. Other than this cotton residue you're talking about, there were no prints, no fibers, no fragments, no body fluids. Nothing to run DNA on and nothing found on the victims' bodies, including their own hair, which would have acted as a lint brush."

"So where was the mistake?" Russ asked. In his experience, an UNSUB made mistakes, and those mistakes tended to compound like interest, only negatively. The fact that this one had made so few had him thinking he was dealing with a professional.

"It makes sense that she would have a trained mind," Junior said. He was clearly intrigued with his own theory. He had an unwavering fascination for the arcane details of violent crime. His knowledge of murder and sexual victimization was encyclopedic, and he was eager to discuss the gory details of history's most infamous cases with anyone, including the women he took out, which was why he rarely had a second date.

"And speaking of trained minds . . ." He looked up at Russ. "How about Jennifer Nash? What do you think of bringing her in on this? You never said."

Russ had been thinking of little else. He would rather drink vending machine coffee than work this case with his ex-fiancée, but his personal feelings could not be allowed to dictate the decision. This wasn't about a lovers' feud. It wasn't even about personal justice, although all of the victims, especially Sharon, deserved that. It was about public safety and Russ's sworn duty. Somehow, in the last couple of hours, he'd come to realize that, but his conversion had nothing to do with anything Kate Townsend or Junior Gordon had said.

It was a damn ficus plant.

Chapter 3

She was a willow tree bending in a fierce wind, graceful and flexible, yet strong enough to spring back when the wind subsided. That was the image Jennifer Nash held in her mind as the taxi pulled up and dropped her off at the Washington Memorial Plaza on Fourth and Madison.

She opened the car door and swung around in one smooth motion, setting her shoes firmly on the asphalt. Fortunately, the cool black linen and white lapels of her new summer suit gave her an extra measure of confidence, and she needed that right now.

You can do this, Jenn. The victims you work with suffer traumas that make this little hurricane of yours look like a trade wind. Keep it in perspective. You're here for a reason, the best of reasons. There's a witness to be interviewed, a woman with a killer's face locked away in some cold, dark room in her mind, and you're going to help her find the courage to open that door.

That was what Jennifer Nash was good at: finding hidden faces, opening bolted doors, and peering into dark places. She saw the things witnesses were afraid to see and victims were afraid to remember. But there was another door that had to be opened while she was here, and that was going to be much harder to do. It might even be more frightening than staring into a killer's eyes as they materialized on her sketch pad. She was a forensic scientist now, but she was also a woman taking a journey home.

You have to tell him the truth, Jenn. It's time.

It was eight a.m. in Seattle, and the brilliant sunshine made the looming memorial to World War II veterans gleam like a massive black gemstone, perfectly set to catch the light. Protests and press conferences were held here, yet the plaza was also a place for contemplation and self-reflection. It occupied the heart of the city as surely as it looked into the hearts of its citizens. Jennifer had been one of those citizens not too long ago, and her heart had not borne the scrutiny well.

She pulled her sunglasses from her purse and slipped them on against the brightness. Incognito was better anyway, at least until she got inside. The plaza was actually the back entrance to the Public Safety Building, home of the Seattle Police Department.

"Are you Jennifer Nash?"

A young woman ran up, and Jennifer nodded before she saw the microphone in her hand. A reporter. Jennifer thought about smiling and moving on, but a flashbulb popped, and it was too late. She'd been caught.

“Have you been brought in to work on the Violator case, Ms. Nash?”

“I’m here to help, yes.”

“In what capacity? Sketch artist? Witness advocate?”

The woman was pumping her for information, and Jennifer had been briefed to say as little as possible. “In whatever capacity I can be most useful.”

Jennifer tried to move around the woman, but suddenly she was dealing with a small cluster of reporters.

Another microphone appeared, and a bearded man crowded close and shouted in her ear, “Are you aware of the controversy surrounding your involvement in the Violator case, Ms. Nash?”

It was a mobile cam unit from a local television station, and the reporter was apparently determined to get himself on the record, if nothing else. Jennifer had to say something, even if it was “No comment.” You didn’t blow off the press one day and expect them to enthusiastically circulate your sketch the next.

“Who called you to consult on this case?” he asked.

“I don’t know anything about a controversy,” Jennifer said. “I’ve been called in to interview a witness and produce a sketch that will help in the manhunt. I used to work here,” she added, hoping she hadn’t said too much. "I'm looking forward to seeing old friends and coworkers. Thank you."

With that she dodged the bobbing mikes and made her way toward the Employees Only entrance. The first part was true anyway. As far as old friends went, the only one in the division who might have welcomed her back with open arms was Sharon Myer, and tragically, Sharon was dead. When Jennifer got the news, she'd immediately called Kate Townsend and offered her services. She and Sharon had worked closely when Sharon was a sex crimes cop. In fact, Jennifer was the reason Sharon became a detective. She'd encouraged her to go for the promotion, and Sharon had encouraged Jennifer in her unusual interview methods.

Jennifer held herself perfectly straight as she crossed the stone plaza, but she could feel apprehension building. Publicity could be helpful for a case, but not in this situation. What she did was still considered controversial in some circles, and she'd had to fend off claims of grandstanding and publicity-seeking by those who didn't like her conditions.

She couldn't imagine that Russ Sadler was going to like her conditions. She couldn't imagine he was going to like anything about her waltzing back into his world and helping herself to his case. And nothing made her more apprehensive than that.

Jennifer had looked into many a killer's

eyes, whether they materialized on her sketch pad or peered at her from across a courtroom. None of them had ever frightened her in the same way that Russ Sadler's did. His eyes exposed her for what she was: a coward, as hungry for intimacy as she was terrified of it. They ripped through her heart and opened it wide for his inspection. No one had ever known who Jennifer Nash really was, including Jennifer. And there were some terrible things to know. With Russ, she would not have been able to hide.

"Quiet, everyone! I have an announcement to make."

Kate Townsend waved her arms, trying to subdue the throng gathered in the duty room. She was standing at the podium in front of a pegboard where the scheduling officer had posted that day's schedule, but the meeting she'd called had nothing to do with assignments. She was about to spring Jennifer Nash on the troops.

Russ Sadler stood in the back, alone, his eyes on the woman sitting next to the podium. He hadn't expected to feel anything when he saw her again. But apparently he still had some life left in him . . . or her ability to ensnare even a gun-shy ex-fiancé was stronger than he would have imagined.

His chest was tight. *Hell.*

It was difficult to forget those pensive pink

lips and her lightly freckled complexion. Her eyes were the same still green waters, but her hair was different. There had been red highlights when they were together, as if someone had poured essence of strawberry all over her and let it dry, shiny in the sun. Now it was a rich teak brown. Maybe she'd tinted it after she'd washed him out of her hair.

He almost smiled. Anyone reading his thoughts would have accused him of being bitter. But he wasn't anymore, just wary. He felt like a hit-and-run victim, and if he'd learned anything from the accident, it was not to cross against the light.

"First the bad news," Kate said. "We all know what that is. The search for Sharon's killer has stalled out. We have no suspects, no evidence, no substantial leads — or as they say in CSI, not a mother-hugging clue. That isn't quite the way they say it, but you know what I mean."

That prompted some chuckles, but not from Russ. He was still watching Jennifer, who had clasped her hands and was staring at them. She hadn't looked his way yet, but then she'd always been a little reticent. He'd actually found that appealing. There wasn't much he hadn't found appealing, except her exit.

"I can't do this, Russ, I want to, but I can't. I don't feel emotionally safe with you."

That was her opening salvo in the voice

mail he'd received the night before they were supposed to have met in Las Vegas and been married. A double homicide investigation had taken him out of state, and he hadn't seen her in a week, which may have contributed to her doubts about their elopement. But it wasn't the first time she'd expressed those kinds of fears. She thought they were moving too fast, and she wondered if *he* was ready. She even questioned his ability to commit, and maybe he'd given her some reason. He'd fought his feelings for her in the beginning, and his track record with women in general wasn't great, but that probably had more to do with the demands of his job and with his choice of partners rather than with his ability to commit.

"This is different," he told her. *"Those women weren't you."*

Maybe he'd never really understood what she was dealing with, but they had talked about her fears, and she had seemed more at ease afterward, even eager to go on with their plans, especially after he admitted that he was afraid, too. God, he'd never been in love in his life. He felt as if he was about to leap the Grand Canyon. But he hadn't been the one to chicken out.

"I'm not ready," she'd said.

Why hadn't he listened? What was it about her that made him want to pursue her, despite her warning signals? The fact that she ran? The fact that she was so breathless when he caught her? Or that she had touched him and, like rain, brought him back to life?

Why hadn't he listened?

"And now let me introduce you to the good news," Kate was saying. "Jennifer Nash is a miracle worker, according to the many people she's helped, and we're lucky to have her here. This year alone she's broken two of the FBI's toughest cases, and her success is partly because of the extraordinary bond of trust she's able to forge with witnesses and victims. They speak of her in glowing terms as compassionate, insightful, a loyal friend and defender — and devoted to the cause of helping them unlock their terrifying memories."

A real Girl Scout, Russ thought, forgetting for a moment that he wasn't bitter. It did fascinate him that the miracle worker who helped victims face their fears ran like a gazelle from her own.

Kate went on, apparently determined to rally the troops. She was overplaying her hand, in Russ's opinion, but she was the one who'd called this meeting.

"Jennifer Nash asked me if she could donate her services," Kate said, "and I took her up on it immediately. Right now Jennifer is our secret weapon, our best chance of apprehending Sharon Myer's murderer, but before I bring her up here, let's hear from someone else. I see Russ Sadler there in the back. He's worked with Jennifer, and I know he must want to say a few words."

Sandbagged, Russ thought. He was going to say damn few words, and he was pretty sure Kate wouldn't want to hear them. She was calling him out. That was one ballsy move when he could so easily have called her bluff, but to refuse would have been mutiny, and apparently he'd been chosen as the role model for office harmony and cooperation.

Flashing one of his famous scowls, he walked up to the podium and adjusted the mike.

"Loyal, trustworthy, and devoted?" Russ glanced down at Jennifer as he addressed the riveted crowd, and saw that her knuckles had gone white.

"It's good to know the chief has so much faith in our former colleague," he said. "I'm sure Jennifer is all those things: loyal, trustworthy, *and* devoted." *Unless you're foolhardy enough to fall in love with her.* "And I have no doubt that she's going to break this case wide open." *She's had plenty of practice breaking other things, like hearts.* "So here's to the secret weapon," he said. "I, for one, plan to give her all the support she so richly deserves." *I may not even pull her pigtails or break her crayons.*

"Now, enough backslapping," he said. "We've got a psycho out there, killing cops.

Let's get off our backsides and solve this case."

Russ got a standing ovation, and it was all Kate could do to quiet the crowd enough for Jennifer to say a few words.

Not that Jennifer wanted the honor. She wasn't any more thrilled about speaking than Russ had been. The metal chair creaked obscenely as she rose, but she covered with a quick smile that said everything was fine. She even thanked Russ warmly as he stepped away from the podium, although she couldn't bring herself to meet his gaze.

Her voice shook a little as she started talking, but she swiftly brought it under control. She'd faced hostile press conferences and dealt with difficult VIPs of just about every stripe, but none of that seemed as daunting — or as important — as winning over this crowd. Maybe because they represented her past mistakes. He, more than anyone.

"It's good to be back," she said to a room that had gone quiet. There were faces that she recognized and those she didn't. What surprised her was the uniformity. She didn't see open hostility, but there were no welcoming expressions, either.

"Sharon was a friend as well as a colleague," she said, "and I was lucky to know her. She was there for me when times were tough, and I'm here today because I want to help, and this is the only way I know how. A friend and colleague is gone, but there is a way to give meaning to the senseless tragedy, and that's by bringing her killer to swift justice."

A little steadier, she went on. "I think you all know my area of expertise. I'll be working with the witness to come up with a sketch of the killer's face, but if there's anything else I can do while I'm here, don't hesitate to ask me. Please, feel free to share your concerns with me and tell me how I can best help. I *want* to help."

She smiled, hoping to break the chill. "Thank you all for coming."

The response from the group was stony silence.

Jennifer felt her face go warm. Her composure seemed to desert her all at once. *She hadn't expected it to be this bad.* She glanced around for Kate but couldn't find her. Her only source of support seemed to have vanished, and if Jennifer could have arranged it, she would have vanished, too. Somehow she had to excuse herself and walk out of the room without tripping or doing something equally embarrassing. Falling on her face would get a standing ovation from this bunch.

She stepped back from the podium, and who did she turn and walk into but Russ Sadler. She apologized instantly and covered by reaching for his hand. Their fingers brushed, and he pulled back as if she were an open wire.

Jennifer pulled back, too. But his expression was the open wire. His face was as strong as she remembered, his jaw as tightly strung, his soul as wild. Somehow you knew that just by looking at him. His dark hair wasn't regulation length like the others. It had the depths and currents of a river.

If she hadn't known he was a detective, it wouldn't have surprised her to find him on the other side of the law . . . one of the faces she drew.

"I was looking for Kate," she explained. "I was going to thank her, but while I'm at it, let me thank you for your . . . kind words."

Some emotion struck at his mouth, twisting it for an instant. Just as quickly it was gone. Vanishing acts, she thought. People vanished. Emotions vanished. She had vanished. And now he couldn't see her anymore. Or wouldn't.

"Not a problem," he said evenly. "Kate had another meeting, but I'm sure you'll find an opportunity to thank her."

"Russ —"

His gaze stopped her cold. It was as swift as an ice pick.

"What?" he asked.

"Oh, nothing. It's nothing." *Nice to see you again, you look great, and all the other stupid things people say when they're trying not to say what they feel.* "I need to go through the police reports, of course, before I see your witness."

"Of course," he said. With that, he turned and walked out of the room.

She hadn't expected it to be this bad.

Jennifer didn't need to look at her watch. Thirty seconds ago it was five minutes after two in the afternoon, so it must be five minutes and thirty seconds after two now.

"A day for the record books," she announced to the empty interview room. "Jennifer Nash is a pariah among her peers, and now her witness is officially a no show."

Myrna Simone was supposed to have been there an hour ago. The appointment was scheduled for one, and Jennifer had been told to wait in an interview room on the tenth floor. She'd actually been closeted there since noon, partly to be by herself and to calm her nerves. She was still rattled over what had happened in the duty room, and she wouldn't be much good to a nervous witness if she was a nervous wreck. She had also wanted to go over the police reports to get a better sense of the case and how this particular witness had been handled.

Badly, in Jennifer's opinion. For her purposes, they'd done everything exactly wrong. In the last seventy-two hours, Myrna had been exposed to enough contaminating material to destroy any hope of accurately capturing what she saw. Jennifer's only shot now was to get past the layers of distorted images to the snapshot that the mind took and preserved of every event it witnessed. That was what her method was designed to do.

"But it can't happen if the witness doesn't show up."

She tapped the table leg with the toe of her shoe and talked to herself under her breath. If the room's ticking clock, murky green walls, and rock-hard vinyl furniture were getting to her, she could only imagine their effect on someone as agitated as Myrna Simone. She would have preferred to meet at the witness's home or anywhere they could have felt more at ease, but Myrna had been taken to a women's shelter nearby. For her own protection, they'd said, but it was probably because they wanted to keep an eye on her.

One of the media liaisons on the tenth floor had given Jennifer a sketch of the suspect done by the department's artist. Jennifer hadn't looked at it for the same reason she wouldn't have wanted the witness to look at composite catalogs of facial characteristics. Such things were highly suggestible to a traumatized mind, and it was clear that Myrna Simone was both traumatized and frightened, of the police, as well as the Violator. She may have been questioned too aggressively, probably about the painkillers she was taking. The police report said she didn't have a prescription.

Jennifer peeled herself off a rock-hard vinyl chair and went to the room's only window. It was sticky close in the room, and the window-mounted air conditioner was making suspicious gurgling noises. She wasn't sure it was working — or that it had ever worked. The Emerald City didn't quite know what to do with itself when things got hot. Women sat on park benches and pulled up their skirts to sunbathe. Men rolled up their pants legs.

"Another one for the record books," Jennifer said, meaning the heat wave.

She lifted her suit jacket at the shoulders to get some air circulating and felt a welcome swirl of coolness. The cell phone she'd left on the table was stubbornly quiet for once. She'd already put in a call to Kate Townsend's office, but Kate was out of the building at a meeting. Laurie, her assistant, had promised to find out what happened to Myrna, but that was a half hour ago, and she hadn't called back.

"We will not call Russ. We will not give him the satisfaction, Jennifer."

Moments later, her cell phone began to rattle against the table. She kept it on vibrate to avoid disrupting interviews. She scooped it up and flipped open the mouthpiece. "Jennifer Nash."

"Jennifer, there's a problem." It was Kate's assistant, Laurie. "The witness is refusing to participate in any more interviews. She claims the man she talked to yesterday confused her and made her cry."

"Who did she talk to yesterday?"

"I don't know. She couldn't remember his name, but she described him as having dark eyes, like an eclipse of the moon."

"An eclipse of the moon? What does that mean?"

"No idea, but she's pretty dramatic. She kept insisting he didn't believe her. She knew that because of the way he furrowed his brow."

Jennifer was concerned for the same reason the witness was. The Violator may have gotten a better look at Myrna Simone than she did at him, and if that was the case, they all had plenty to be frightened about. She didn't fit the profile of his victims, but that didn't mean he wouldn't see her as a threat who had to be eliminated.

"What about the shelter director?" Jennifer asked. "Wouldn't she know who the man was? She must have asked for his ID." Generally, there was very tight security at a shelter. The women there needed protection, and no one knew the location, except possibly the law-enforcement agency involved.

"The director was doing an intake," Laurie explained. "One of the volunteer workers said a detective came and took Myrna for a ride."

A detective. That was all Jennifer needed to hear. She knew exactly who it was. Apparently Russ Sadler wasn't satisfied with intimidating Myrna Simone. He wanted to make a hostile witness out of her, and he may have succeeded.

"I'd like to talk to Myrna myself," Jennifer said. "I'll go to the shelter, if necessary. I may be able to turn her around."

"I'll have to check with Kate on that."

"Thanks, Laurie, do that, okay? And give me a call at my hotel."

Jennifer was packing up her things, and grateful to be out of there, when she heard a loud rap on the interview room door. Her heart was off and running even before she looked up. Something had warned her who it was, probably the steady force of the knock. Or maybe she needed one more terrible thing to happen so that this day could officially qualify as one of her top ten worst.

As the door swung open, Jennifer released the breath she'd been holding. Her premonition was correct.

"Well, well, well," she said, "if it isn't the man who makes eyewitnesses cry."

Chapter 4

Jennifer braced herself as her nemesis walked into the room. That's what you did when you were about to take on Russ Sadler. You braced yourself. It was like getting in the ring with a world-class boxer, except that Russ rarely had to throw a punch. In his case, one well-directed glare was usually enough to stop a confrontation in its tracks.

He was an imposing SOB. It was a gift he had. Jennifer had seen his coworkers, men and women alike, clam up like POWs rather than risk his displeasure. She'd done it herself. But that wasn't how it was going to happen today.

"You intimidated my witness," she said.

"*Your* witness?"

"You frightened her so badly, she refuses to come in for the sketch. Do you know what you've done?"

"I know I spilled my coffee. *Sonova—*"

He quickly switched hands, shaking the steaming coffee off his fingers and doing an interesting little dance to avoid the shower. Whatever Jennifer had expected, it wasn't that she would be watching him dodge the spillage from the biggest cup of Starbucks she'd ever seen. He popped his fingers in his mouth, saving both his khaki Dockers and the floor.

She wasn't amused by his duel with the droplets, but that didn't stop her from watching. She was rooting for the coffee.

Apparently very little had changed with the ace homicide detective. He was still hooked on caffeine, although he'd been vowing to quit the stuff for as long as she'd known him. *He still dressed well, too.* The fashionably baggy black shirt and the khakis he was protecting were a touch more *GQ* than she remembered, and she was surprised to see short sleeves. He didn't normally wear those. Of course, Seattle didn't normally have three-digit weather.

"Answer my question?" she inquired icily. "If you're done playing with your coffee, that is."

He glanced up, his eyes as steamy hot as the dark brew. *This was what she'd expected.*

"I know exactly what I did," he said. "I re-interviewed the state's only witness to a brutal cop killing before you had a chance to deny me access to her. Now, *ask* me if I'd do it again."

It seemed the gloves were off, which was fine with Jennifer. She'd never put hers on. "I wanted a few hours with her. How is that denying you access?"

"I know how you work. You won't release

a sketch until the witness approves it, and with a mental case like Myrna, that could be never."

"It *will* be never if she won't submit to an interview. How am I supposed to do what I came here to do? My trip is pointless."

"Then maybe you should go home," he said.

Her frustration spilled out in a fiery sigh. "You're trying to drive me off. Admit it. This is your revenge."

The air conditioner gurgled obscenely. He seemed to find that, or her accusation, amusing.

"When I want revenge, Jennifer, you'll be the first to know. And please, give me credit for coming up with something a little more creative than co-opting a witness."

Next to him by the door was a moldering rattan umbrella stand with a wide rim, possibly for wet hats or gloves. Its very unsightliness brought an oddly human touch to the spare, institutional green room. Russ was using it for a coffee table, and as he set his cup down, Jennifer noticed what seemed to be a scar on his forearm. The lacerations looked fairly new, and her mind seized on the worst-case scenario, that someone had tried to stab him. It was also the most logical scenario. He worked in violent crimes, and he wasn't clumsy with weapons.

She didn't ask. Having her curiosity satisfied was not worth the risk of being blown off again. She liked to pace her rejections.

Grudgingly, she said, “What came out of your interview with Myrna?”

Russ looked her up and down, clearly surprised. It was a concession, and they both knew it.

“She’s highly unreliable,” he said, “and very reluctant. She told the officer who found her that she was homeless because she didn’t want to give out her address. She’s convinced the Violator saw her and he’s going to hunt her down and kill her, despite our having moved her to a safe location.”

Jennifer wasn’t surprised. She’d read the preliminary interview. Myrna was a sixty-five-year-old twice-divorced white female, who lived in a run-down apartment house in a seedy part of town. She’d worked as a waitress and a hostess but claimed that back pain from the birth of her only child, now an adult male with whom she’d lost touch, had disabled her and made it impossible to hold a job. Currently, she existed on her Social Security check and not much else, apparently, although that was barely enough to pay her controlled rent.

“I read the prelim,” Jennifer said. “It sounded like she was all over the place, contradicting herself and confused by the questions, or pretending to be. If she is abusing painkillers, then some of her concern about the Violator could be drug-related paranoia, but the mind plays tricks on all crime witnesses, even the sober ones."

Which is all the more reason you need me, she thought. It took time to get to that one still place at the center of the chaos. Time, patience, and the intuition of a stalker. But just like every storm had an eye, so did every human, even a frightened, elderly drug addict. Jennifer called it the true eye, and in her experience, it could see with photographic clarity what the mind refused to see. The image had been recorded. It was there, waiting for someone to coax it out of hiding.

Russ had fallen silent.

"What is it?" Jennifer asked. His arms were folded, and he was scrutinizing her as if she were under suspicion.

"When did you start wading through police reports?" he asked. "The usual procedure is to be briefed by the lead investigator."

Yes, but in this case, the lead investigator is you.

"I needed some time to adjust," she admitted. "Sharon's murder was a terrible shock, and then there was the press, and all the resistance to my being here — and just the fact of coming home."

Oh, and did I mention a hostile ex-fiancé?

He gave her a respectful second of silence, but just one.

"Are you done adjusting?" There was a hint of irony in his expression.

"Possibly. Why?"

"Because we're out of time. The Violator is beginning to walk and talk like a serial killer, and if he snatches another victim before we have anything on him, it's going to be wholesale panic. Having a sketch to circulate would help."

There it was, *his* concession. She wondered what it must have cost him. He didn't make allowances, and she couldn't imagine him relaxing that rule for someone who'd betrayed him.

I didn't betray you. I betrayed myself. You got caught in the crossfire.

The air conditioner spluttered, and the room's closeness felt overwhelming. Moisture sheened Jennifer's throat, but she didn't want him to see it. She would walk out of the room before she'd let him know what effect he was having on her. They had kissed in a room like this, behind closed doors. Kissed until she was sheened with moisture in other places, and it had happened in an instant. *It had happened when he'd looked at her.*

Jennifer couldn't bear that kind of responsiveness. She couldn't even bear to remember it. In a sharp voice she said, "If you want to worry about someone's adjustment, worry about Myrna's."

He was drinking coffee, carefully. "Myrna won't be a problem."

"Really? The last I heard, she was confused and crying."

"I suggested she say that for her own protection. I also told her not to talk with anyone unless she okayed it with me."

Jennifer blinked at him. "You told her not to talk with me?"

"I meant the press, who wouldn't be above posing as one of us to trick her into an interview. They know we have a witness, and they'd eat their own young to find out who she is."

"So what *did* come out of your session with Myrna?"

"Well, she thinks I'm, let's see . . . How did she put it? A lovely boy? And she tried to give me one of her scarves, said it was to remember her by. The woman could open a scarf store."

His deadpan was perfect. Jennifer actually admired that about him. He could have read *Macbeth* without inflection. And it wouldn't have surprised her if Myrna *was* all over him. Most women were. His brow was always furrowed in dark reflection, and he wore a perpetual scowl, but the man was fine.

Myrna had been right about his eyes, too, Jennifer had to admit. An eclipse would not have been too dark. And there was also the obvious sex appeal of his broken nose, which one naturally assumed had been sustained in the line of duty. Jennifer happened to know the truth. He'd bought himself a motorcycle in his college days, and he'd wanted to see what it could do. He found out when he hit some loose gravel and got dumped, just like any other guy. But no one wanted to believe that. Not with his mystique.

You wanted to ascribe courage and old-fashioned chivalry to a man like Russ Sadler, not a penchant for speed or a reckless disregard for his own safety, but in fact, he had all of those traits, and more. She was a witness, a reluctant witness.

"When do you want to see Myrna?" he was asking. "I'll set up the appointment myself."

He'd made his move. *Make yours, Jennifer.*

"As soon as possible, but there is one condition," she said. "The sketch has to be a strong one, and I've only got one shot at it. We can't release it and then change our minds and do another one. That would broadcast Myrna's confusion and work against us if we ever get the Violator to trial."

"Only *one* condition? You must be losing your edge, Nash."

Add sarcasm to his list of traits, she thought. *Right at the top.* "I don't want to do the interview here. That's my condition."

"This is our interview room. Where else would you do it?"

"Wherever the witness feels comfortable, and that's not going to be here, in a discount dentist's waiting room."

She wasn't a total slouch herself when it came to sarcasm.

She pushed one of the metal fold-up chairs out of her way, and it let out a *skreeek* that was still reverberating as she picked up her tote bag.

"This place is sterile and unfriendly," she said. "It's not conducive to the atmosphere of trust I need to create."

"Ohh . . . I see." He went to the opposite end of the table and pulled out a chair that made no sound at all. "You need to create an atmosphere of *trust.* And what would it take to accomplish that? A monastery? A chapel? A beauty salon?"

To her credit, she did not take the bait. "Possibly the shelter or the witness's own home. Even my hotel room would be better than this. The point is to distract her from the horrors of the crime she witnessed, not to remind her of them. We want her to feel safe, to open up and give us what we need."

His look said, *Open up the way I did?*

Jennifer sensed the flinch more than saw it. A muscle near his mouth twitched, and something inside her recoiled. She watched his expression go ice cold, and she stopped talking. *This must be how an eyewitness feels,* she thought. Suddenly she knew what it was like to watch a crime and to feel helpless; only in this case, she was the criminal.

"It has to be here," he said.

His voice was low and detached. The tone of it made Jennifer fear there was no bargaining with him. This wasn't about revenge. He'd said that, but she wasn't sure she believed him.

"Why?" she asked.

"Because I intend to be here when you do it."

"Why?"

"Myrna Simone is a lousy excuse for a witness, but right now she's all we have. If she can't get her story straight, then we can't use her, and we have to know that going in. On the other hand, something could come out in your session with her that could win us the case. I need to be here, and I need to have it documented on videotape — the entire session."

"No, Russ, *no.* Witnesses are frightened, they're vulnerable, and mostly they're suspicious of the whole process. It's not possible to gain anyone's trust with a detective in the room, much less a video camera."

"The camera isn't going to be obvious. She won't even know it's there."

Jennifer was already shaking her head. "*I'd* know, and I can't work that way. No, that's impossible." She hitched up her tote bag, intending to leave. "I'll go to Kate."

He stepped in front of the door, perilously close to blocking her way.

"I just came from there," he said, "and Kate agrees with me."

Jennifer couldn't believe what was happening. He'd cut off all her options, and the door he stood in front of was the least of it.

"We need you," he said, "but we can't lose this case because of you. Your methods are controversial, and we have to make sure the witness isn't being led and that her testimony isn't being unduly influenced by anything that happens in your session. Do you understand?"

She understood that they had no faith in her at all. She hadn't expected any from him, but that Kate should side with him? Kate was her only ally in this place.

"I won't do it." Her voice was scratchy and hot. She could hardly make it work. "You might as well ask me to assault the witness myself. It goes against everything I'm trying to do."

Jennifer had been videotaped many times, but it was for instructional purposes. This was surveillance. Even if it didn't affect Myrna, it would affect her. She couldn't work with him in the room, breathing down her neck, silently criticizing everything she did.

She walked around the table and straight at him. If he didn't get out of the way, they were going to collide.

He stepped aside but caught her arm as she walked by him. Jennifer stared at his hand in shock, and the air in her throat turned to fire. *This* was the open wire. His hand on her arm. The current was strong enough to electrocute.

"At least think about it," he said. "It's for everyone's protection, including yours. I'll have Myrna in here tomorrow morning at eight, and if you still don't want to do it, I'll call in one of our sketch artists."

She pulled away from him and strode through the doorway. Her head was spinning madly, and it was impossible to think beyond her next decision. She had two choices, the elevator or the stairs.

If she took the elevator, she would have to deal with the media. If she took the back stairs, she would be dealing with him again. They were the very steps where she'd first met Russ Sadler after coming to work for the division.

She vividly recalled that she'd been going down, and he'd been on his way up when they stopped to say hello, just one step apart. That had brought her almost to eye level with him, and her response had rivaled what happened just seconds ago. Jennifer had to reach out and touch the railing to ground herself. Attracted? He might as well have been a bolt from on high and she a defenseless lightning rod. *Spronng.* She'd never had a reaction quite like that before, and it was only the beginning.

With heart-stopping swiftness, they were involved in an affair that had to be kept secret because of their work situation. Fraternization among coworkers was discouraged, and neither wanted their private lives bandied about, anyway. Jennifer remembered being barely in control of her faculties at the time, and he had seemed pretty shell-shocked, too. Russ, the man who needed no one. The impenetrable black box. She had thought of him as a classic loner who subsisted on nothing more than the air he breathed; that was how self-contained he appeared. She remembered what it was like watching a man like that open up, watching him start to need things, *to need her.*

A few months later he had proposed to her on that stairway. Step 154. She had counted every one of them.

A strangled sound slipped out of her. She whirled around and searched the hallway, praying she wouldn't run into him coming out of the interview room. Where was the damn elevator?

He'd never thought of the motorcycle as an extension of himself. That was for easy riders and bike nuts. For him it was nothing but one big, screaming machine that cost almost as much as he made in a year and burned through more tire tread than a semi. But that was the price of respect when you couldn't get it any other way. It was like identity theft. When he rode down the street, curved forward like a springboard diver, he wasn't awkward and clumsy anymore. He wasn't a loser. The bike conferred its grace and power on him and turned him into one of the people he watched.

Not that he could ever be one of them, or even aspired to anymore. He'd pretty much reconciled himself to this, stealing what he could get of the dream. Some people didn't get that much. He was lucky. On a bike, he could pass. He could pretend. On a sizzling hot summer day, in jeans, a T-shirt and mirrored shades, he was cool.

He saw the blue and white convertible as he roared past the line of cars waiting to get on the I-5 north. The woman at the wheel had a scarf looped around her neck, and her long red hair bounced like an old-fashioned movie star's. But she was young and pretty and sunlight blinked off her dark glasses. He saw all that as he came up on her and whizzed by.

And then, in his rearview mirror, he saw her smile. Jesus, at him. She'd smiled at him!

He *could* pass. From a distance — and for a few seconds — even a woman like that had seen him as cool. A man worth a tilt of her rosy lips. He smiled back, knowing she probably couldn't see him — and that none of this would have happened if they'd met in any other way. On the street, he wouldn't have rated a second glance.

On an impulse, he took the next exit, doubled back, and came up on the freeway behind her. He hung back, letting a delivery truck be his cover, and when she pulled to the right and made a connection east, he followed her at a safe distance. Some miles later, she rolled down an off-ramp, her scarf flying. They were in farm country, and the traffic was sparse. But eventually they ended up on a rural road, the only two vehicles for miles, and she must have known he was behind her.

How could she not have seen him? And did she know what she was doing to him? His heart was working harder than the engine.

Her hair fluttered in the hot breezes, and she drove at such a leisurely pace, it seemed like an invitation. The thought that she might be luring him made him bear down on the accelerator. He didn't roar up behind her. That wasn't his style. He took his time, creeping forward and enjoying his advantage until he'd closed most of the distance between them.

She glanced in the rearview mirror, saw him back there, and continued on at the same pace.

Was she smiling? He couldn't tell. He hardly knew what to do next. Maybe he had the wrong woman. Maybe it wasn't even her. He hadn't thought to check her plates, but how many classic Chevy convertibles were rolling around western Washington, and how many women wore their hair like that? No, he couldn't have mistaken the hair. He'd never seen anything so red-hot and lush. It didn't look real.

He fell back, letting her pull away from him and wondering what to do.

She didn't look real. She was something out of a Hollywood movie, a classic, like the car. *American Graffiti.* Maybe he was suffering from heat stroke and she was nothing but a mirage.

His palms began to sweat, slicking the leather grips.

She stuck her arm out the window and wiggled her fingers. He had no idea what she was doing until he saw the little two-pump gas station up ahead. She was making a left-turn signal. She needed gas. Or something. What?

Him? Did she need him?

Laughter scalded his throat.

What was he thinking about? He couldn't try to pick up this woman. She would spot him for a loser the second he got off the bike. Women like her had antennas. They had "loser" radar, and when it went off, they turned into cold-hearted bitches. They hung out in groups, snickering and whispering about guys who didn't measure up.

There was a dirt road a couple hundred yards beyond the station. He sped past the convertible without looking, made a turn, and headed down the road. Rocks spewed in his wake. When he was out of sight, he stopped the bike and sat there, shaking.

Shaking like a fucking kid. He hated being weak. He hated the way he reacted to women. Maybe he just hated women. He didn't understand the power they had over him, how they could make him tremble with a look. Just once he wanted some beautiful creature to look at him without pity or contempt in her eyes. Like he was a human being. He wasn't asking for her undying love. Maybe just some basic decency and respect?

But who was he kidding? That wasn't going to happen. Not with a woman like her. She was born to laugh at guys like him, born to shoot them down.

And he was sick of hiding, sick of being afraid. Sick.

He began to walk the bike forward. As he left the cover of the trees and the sun struck his shoulders, he nudged the accelerator and began to ride for real. He hoped to God she was still there, because he was going back. He wanted to see the expression on her face when she looked up from her perfect little daydream of a life and saw a big black beast roaring straight at her priceless classic car. He wanted her to know she'd made a mistake.

Unfortunately, he wasn't to have that satisfaction. The Chevy was parked in front of the pumps where she'd left it, but the door was hanging open, and she wasn't anywhere to be seen. He didn't spot the bathroom until he'd walked around the entire building. It was the stench of ammonia that caught his attention first, and then a soft humming sound. Both were coming from a louvered window, apparently cracked for ventilation.

She was in there, and the door wasn't locked. He knew that without even trying the handle. Women like her never thought they needed to take the normal precautions, which was what made them such perfect targets. They believed their good looks got them a free pass. Being born beautiful was a state of grace that extended to the rest of their life, right? Who would hurt such a lovely thing?

Wrong. Oh, God, little girl, so wrong.

He eased the door open and saw her busily searching through her makeup bag, humming as she looked for something, probably the lipstick that turned her mouth into a cherry pink Valentine. He slipped into the hot, cramped room and ducked behind the barrier created by the outermost of two stalls, where he could see but not be seen.

He loved the feeling that came over him. Loved and hated it. He was trembling again, but this was different.

She pulled a brush from her bag and bent over, still humming. He expected to watch her comb out that luxurious mane of hair, and meanwhile it was interesting the way her short denim skirt hiked up the back of her thighs. Her legs were long, slender, and free of the dimples that plagued less fortunate females. That came with the package that set her apart. There were no visible flaws. Maybe it was being in the presence of perfection that made men shake.

He didn't know. He didn't care, because she did have flaws. She just hadn't met them yet.

Any minute now he would make the introductions. First he wanted to watch the hair ritual. She was tugging on it oddly, almost as if she were trying to pull it out of her head. He wondered if it was a strengthening exercise, like brushing, until he saw the hair actually fall to the floor. All of it. A heap of red the size of a small fox was lying on the stinking bathroom tile, and the woman bending over it gave out a sigh of relief and shook her head vigorously.

He ducked back as she grabbed the dead animal and came back up. Her own hair, a matted net of dark blond, was plastered flat to her head. Every ounce of energy drained out of him as he realized what had happened. She was wearing a wig. *A wig.* The joke was on him. She wasn't even a redhead.

She fussed with her own hair for a few minutes, lifting it with her fingers and making it short and spiky all over her head.

When she was satisfied, she wandered into the first stall and left that door hanging open, too, while she peed.

Somebody ought to drown her in Lake Washington just for that, he thought, *for being so fucking complacent and smug.*

He took a chance that she was too preoccupied with herself to notice him, and he slipped out of the bathroom. The stench of the place stayed with him as he loped back to his bike, but he didn't hear any screams or commotion, which meant he must have made it past her without being detected.

Several miles down the road, he was still trembling, but this time he knew why. "Shit," he muttered, "*shit,* that was close."

Engine noise drowned him out, and the wind blew away his words.

He hit the accelerator, desperate to reclaim the power. He could not be without the power. Not anymore.

Chapter 5

"TGIT, dude. Let's go!"

Russ looked up from his desk to see Junior poking his head through the foot-wide crack in the office door. He had on his beer drinking uniform, and he was ready to go do his duty. The billowy Hawaiian shirt and Foster Grant sunglasses were de rigueur for Tuesday afternoons, when a motley crew from the homicide unit headed across the street to Wahoo's.

"You coming?" Junior asked.

Wahoo's served beer for a buck and free fish tacos from five to seven. For Junior it was a pilgrimage to the Holy Land. Russ wasn't a regular, but he went when he could, which was not going to be tonight.

"Can't." He dropped his pencil on the yellow legal pad and rolled back his shoulders. "I'm in the middle of something."

Over his head would have been closer to the truth. The Violator strikes had started last spring, and there'd only been four, counting Sharon, but the paperwork that had accumulated was mountainous. There'd been several pairs of detectives assigned to the case, the latest being Sharon and Kent, and they'd each had their theories and leads. Eventually, Russ would review all of them, searching for the patterns they hadn't seen. But at the moment he was only interested in Sharon's.

At some point every good investigator came to realize what he or she was dealing with. Criminals were a dime a dozen, and most of them weren't very bright, or they would have considered the odds. Occasionally one came along who could laugh at the odds. Not just another garden-variety crook but a master planner. The cop who didn't recognize and respect this quintessential adversary made a mistake, sometimes fatal.

Tonight Russ was going through Sharon's reports, line by line, looking for that mistake. He wanted to know what point she was at, and whether or not she had recognized who she was dealing with. Did she have a suspect, even if she hadn't named him yet? Did she know the man who killed her?

Junior grinned. "Plotting your next abduction? I thought you liked redheads. Wasn't Jennifer a redhead once?"

Russ gave nothing away with his expression. Cherubic or not, Junior was one of those guys who loved to dance and jab and get as close as he could to inflicting wounds without actually drawing blood. Often he came too close. It was a strange male rite of bonding that was especially prevalent in law enforcement, Russ had noticed.

"I'm plotting *your* abduction," he told Junior. "They're either going to find you doing the dead man's float in Lake Washington or in the coed bathroom, wearing women's underwear. I can't decide which."

"How about they find me across the street, having a cold one? Come on, Sadler. It's Miller time!"

"Miller will have to wait. *Sadler* hasn't got time."

Junior actually stopped grinning. "You're too close to this case, dude. Way too close. Give it a rest."

The kid had a point. "Maybe when I finish up here."

"Yeah, right! You'll be here all night, trying to break this puppy before *she* does. I can't figure out what you're hooked on, the case or the sketch *artiste*."

Too close. "Get out of here, Junior," he growled.

Junior stepped back, swaggering a little, but ready to run. They both knew how it would come out in a showdown. They were roughly the same height and build, but at six two, Russ had a couple inches on him and at least twenty-five pounds. He also had the advantage of having come up through the ranks. He'd paid his dues, patrolling some of the city's heaviest crime areas, where you were either quick or you were dead.

He'd also done boot camp in hell — not the military, in this case, but his own home. His father was a Marine Corps captain, and Russ had had to learn about self-defense just to survive the old man's penchant for discipline, which could be summed up in one word: brutality.

"Don't be drawing hearts with her name in them now." Junior waggled his fingers as he left.

Russ let him have the last word. Junior's imagination was already working overtime, a dangerous thing with a mind like his. But it was probably too late for damage control. Russ was beginning to think he and Jennifer had not been very successful at keeping their relationship a secret, back then or now. Kate had picked up on it, too. Maybe everybody knew. Russ had visions of himself and Jennifer being as obvious as the heat wave bombarding the city.

Heat wave.

He sat back and closed his eyes. The chair groaned, and his head tilted back. It was almost a reflex. He wondered if he was smiling or frowning. It had been a long time since he'd allowed himself to think about the heat they used to generate with nothing more than an accidental glance. All they had to do was see each other unexpectedly in the hallway or innocently brush arms when they were discussing a case. A touch, a glance — and the tinder caught. It spat and crackled and burned.

He'd never understood the intensity. It was actually daunting, even for a man who faced death on a daily basis. Dying didn't scare him. She did. The feelings did. Still, he couldn't stop himself. It was such a beautiful fire, and nothing else had ever made him feel that way. Alive. Aware. Hungry to experience the sliding friction of being close to her. He was the fire, defined by his own oxygen-starved state.

No, he didn't allow himself to think like that. Not in years. What was the point in allowing himself to remember how ungodly much he'd needed her? Or how he hadn't been able to think about anything *but* her? He *didn't* allow it, but the memories swept through him anyway. They swept through him, and they burned.

Dead leaves crackled under the wheels of his chair.

The familiar pressure in his temples warned him a headache was coming on. He needed coffee, and probably some food, but there wasn't time. He had the grim task of laying bare Sharon's life — professional and personal. When he was done with her work, he would start in on her credit card charges, bills, and phone records. He needed to pursue this part of the investigation alone and without interference, but it wasn't easy holding his more passionate colleagues off.

He had Kent Wright drowning in DMV records, and he'd blocked Jennifer, which bought him some time, but he didn't know how much. He was reasonably sure she wouldn't get anywhere with Myrna, but Jennifer could not be underestimated. She had intuitive gifts. She opened people up to realities they didn't know existed. No one knew that better than he did.

But he didn't let himself think about that. *What was the point?*

He reached for the legal pad and pencil, where he'd summarized what he knew about the case so far.

1. UNSUB has obsession with redheaded women, possibly based on a mother fixation, although age range of victims, 25-34, doesn't support this. Hair color was the only obvious correlation between the victims found by the computer.

2. The strikes appear to be seasonal, occurring in the spring or summer months. The first three victims were held and tortured for seventy-two hours before being deposited in city parks, dressed only in paper examining gowns. They were found alive, but drugged.

3. The fourth victim was found dead of apparent suffocation.

4. Torture consists of bondage and forced autoeroticism, after which the victims are verbally chastised and punished by depilation of all body and head hair by various means, the most painful of which is hot wax.

5. UNSUB manifests deep-seated fears of women and female sexuality. Believes their red hair is source of their sinfulness.

6. Has pathological need to control and humiliate the victims, perhaps to compensate for fears.

7. Exhibits characteristics of a mission serial assailant. The first three victims were punished for their sexuality and taught moral behavior, but they were not sexually assaulted physically.

8. Sexual identity is probably fragile. Lack of sexual contact with victims may indicate fear, revulsion, or inability. Wears gloves at all times. More evidence for mother-figure fixation.

9. Engages in excessive risk-taking, even for serial assailant. Breaks into victim's home or apartment at midnight when victim is asleep, physically subdues, and

removes her. Victims describe suspect as large and powerful.

10. May have God complex. Wants victims awake and responsive. No drugs administered during abduction and torture. The unidentified drug given before release impairs but does not erase their memory of the events. The first three victims may have been released alive so they could spread the word of UNSUB's mission.

11. Compulsively meticulous and fastidious. A neat-freak biker? Highly skilled at eliminating and/or concealing evidence. This suggests medical, forensic, or law enforcement background.

The list went on, but Russ stopped to consider the last item. It didn't endear him to his colleagues, but he'd often thought that the best investigators could think like criminals because, except for a flip of the cosmic coin, they would have been the criminals. They had the intelligence, the predatory instinct, and, when necessary, the killing instinct. It was impossible to explain what put them on the right side of the law and the outlaws they hunted on the wrong side. There were plenty of criminals from good homes and loving families. Philosophers had been trying to figure it out since the birth of thought. Science and medicine had thrown their best at it.

He hesitated, studying the list again. Other than the last item, it was bizarre how much the profile made him think of his father, although fear was not an emotion he'd ever associated with Captain Chuck Sadler. And he could hardly imagine his dad on a motorcycle, abducting women. No, that wasn't the captain, but his father was certainly capable of control, humiliation, and preaching the gospel according to Chuck Sadler.

Russ hadn't been back to the Whidbey Island home where he grew up more than a handful of times in over twenty years, but he and the captain still spoke on Father's Day. *There* was a joke. His father was a parent straight out of a low-budget horror movie. He drank too much. He was overbearing and intolerant, and his need to shame and humiliate those he considered weak was legend. Russ had wasted a good part of his life hating the man. Now he wondered why he'd bothered, although every time he had any contact with the arrogant old bastard, he was reminded. You couldn't treat a kid that way and expect his undying love and devotion. Or a woman either.

Russ's mother had run away when he was ten, and Russ had sat down and wept. It wasn't the pain of missing her as much as the relief that she was free. He'd helped her get away, knowing he might never see her again. It was easier to lose her all at once than to watch her be killed by degrees.

Before she left, she warned him he might become his father's target, but he'd already learned to deflect the blows in a way that she never could. What would have destroyed her had hardened him. And years later, when he was out of his father's house and enrolled in the Academy, she contacted him by phone.

This time it was she who wept. Russ couldn't. Nothing touched that part of him anymore. But his chest tightened when they agreed to meet. He drove south to Vancouver, where she had a small home and a new life, though she had never married again. They talked for hours and promised to keep in touch, but when it was time for him to go, she asked him to keep her whereabouts a secret. She still didn't trust his father. Neither did Russ.

He rolled back to get up, and his chair wheels jammed in the pile of leaves.

Sharon's plant. He wasn't going anywhere. He was trapped, and the realization brought a sense of heaviness, even despair. His thoughts turned ironic, cynical. Apparently there was no escaping the evidence that life was a bitch. His one refuge was the investigation. There he could be cold and clinical, distanced, no matter who the victim was and no matter who he had to work with. He could close off his heart and open his mind. He'd done it all his life, and if anything accounted for his investigative skills, it was that.

It had also made him machinelike and cruelly efficient. He couldn't feel, but he could think — maybe outthink — *any* predator, even this one. That was a frightening kind of power, and he didn't know the price of invoking it, but he could think of one: his humanity.

A pulse of red light danced before his eyes. His head was throbbing, and his stomach was empty, queasy. He needed some food. More than that, he needed to get out of this office for awhile. He came out of the chair and grabbed his sunglasses. They were sitting on top of his computer, a pair of military aviators he'd had forever, maybe since his Academy days. Ice cold beer and fish tacos sounded pretty good right now.

Russ spotted the all-male contingent from the Public Safety Building as soon as he opened the saloon-style doors at Wahoo's. Chunks of mesquite-grilled cod sizzled on hooded grills, and tangy beer foamed from brass spigots, but it was the commotion coming from the bar that drew Russ's attention. His coworkers had commandeered the area, and they were having a good laugh about something.

There were about a dozen guys, most from the fifth floor, but a few from violent crimes and Junior's lab. Russ watched them trading quips and cracking each other up and was glad he came. He needed to push away the stink of dead leaves and dead bodies for awhile. He needed to forget.

As Russ approached the bar, he saw Junior hoist a mug of beer and make a toast. "To the famous sketch *artiste,*" he said. "May she trip over her high profile and sprain her drawing arm."

There were some uneasy chuckles before someone chimed in "Hear, hear!"

Several other mugs were lifted, and Kent Wright — Sharon's former partner and Russ's new one — offered dryly, "May somebody steal her colored pencils."

Junior took a swig of his beer and nearly spat it out. "Or dye her hair red, sic the Violator on her, and scare the living shit out of her."

That got a round of applause and more toasts. Somebody offered to buy her a one-way bus ticket back to San Francisco. Another suggested her time would be better spent sketching dirty pictures on the bathroom stalls for the entertainment of the occupants.

Russ didn't like the sound of anything he was hearing, maybe because he'd been thinking along the same lines they were. He tried to tell himself it was just a bunch of guys letting off some steam. No one had noticed him yet, and maybe that was just as well. He considered turning around and walking out, but something kept him there. He had a bad feeling about where this Jennifer Nash love fest was going.

"Hey, be nice." Junior mocked the others. "She's here to crack the case and save Seattle PD from disgrace. We're a bunch of fumblebutts, didn't you know?"

"Yeah, maybe *you're* a fumblebutt, Gordon. You're the genius who misplaces key evidence, like fingerprints."

"Someone made off with my evidence kit," Junior said sullenly. "It can happen."

"Speaking of the *artiste,* where is she? Nobody invited her to join us?"

The kid who broke in to ask the question was the department's new criminalist, a twenty-something who had all the charm of a high school class clown. Russ didn't know his name.

"No?" The criminalist pretended to be shocked, and Kent Wright grimaced. "Damn, what an oversight," Wright said. "We wouldn't want to her to feel unloved."

The class clown pretended to grab his crotch. "I love her, and I can prove it!"

Not a proud day for law enforcement, Russ thought. *Or the male gender.* He took a deep, tight breath and willed his heart rate to slow.

He didn't like the idea of bashing heads for several reasons, the main one being Kent Wright. There was enough strain between the two of them as it was. Nevertheless, things were getting ugly.

Russ calmly walked into the midst of the raucous, laughing group. He approached the bar and ordered a beer without saying a word. The joking ceased as the men became aware of him, and when he turned to face them, beer in hand, the laughter died, too. Maybe it was the blood in his eye.

Junior broke the silence. "Hey, dude," he said, grinning at Russ. "You solve the case yet?"

"Hell, yes, I solved it yesterday, didn't I tell you? It's all wrapped up with a bow." Russ set the beer on the bar without touching it. *I beat her to it,* he thought, realizing that he had wanted to sabotage her as badly as they did.

"Cool," Junior said. "Your turn to toast. How about a nice send-off for the *artiste?*"

"How about a send-off for you, Gordon?" Russ shot Junior an icy glare and then swept the rest of them with it. He wasn't angry anymore. And he didn't care that some of these men were colleagues and friends. It wouldn't have mattered who they were. When something unpleasant had to be done, Russ called upon a cold resolve that was unwavering. He didn't know where it came from. He was just damn glad it was there. It was the same kind of resolve that allowed you to take aim and squeeze the trigger. You didn't have to like it. You just had to do it.

He spoke softly, just to make sure they listened. "You guys are a joke," he said, "a joke and an embarrassment to the department. Maybe we should call a press conference and share our fear and loathing of Jennifer Nash with the whole city, since we're making her the butt of our humor in a public bar."

Kent Wright returned Russ's glare. "Hey, man, chill," he said. "It was harmless fun. Nobody meant anything by it."

"I *know* what you meant, Kent. I'd sell my soul to buy the woman a ticket back to San Francisco, but how's that going to help get us our guy? Jennifer is here to do a job, and we need to put our shriveled male egos back in our pants and accept that. She's smart, she's tough, and she can do what we can't."

"Make babies?" someone smirked.

"She's making babies out of you bums." Russ raised his voice. "I get the feeling some of you didn't get the message, so let me be perfectly clear. You're going to cooperate with Jennifer Nash if it kills you. Because if you don't, I will."

It wasn't necessary to elaborate further. His tone said the Violator would be a pussycat compared to him.

Off to Russ's right, Junior was waving and

trying to tell him something. He was mouthing words Russ couldn't understand. Apparently Junior wanted the teacher to call on him, but whatever his problem was, it could wait. Russ shook his head, but Junior kept right on.

"Everybody clear?" Russ said, ignoring him. "From now on, anybody who fucks with Jennifer Nash fucks with me."

"Russ!" Junior hissed. He made his way through the knot of men and bounded up to Russ. "Look behind you!" he whispered.

Russ turned to see Jennifer Nash standing in the doorway. He didn't know how long she'd been there, but from the startled expression on her face, she'd obviously heard every word he'd said.

Chapter 6

Russ's training had prepared him to make split-second decisions. Hesitation could be deadly. He had no doubts about when to draw a weapon and when to use it. But for a moment, staring at the woman in the doorway of Wahoo's, he didn't know what the hell to do. He saw the shock in Jennifer's eyes, the confusion, and realized with his own sense of shock that she appeared to be fighting emotion. Her eyes sparkled too brightly and her nose was red-tipped. Tears?

No, he had to be imagining that, and if he wasn't, he didn't want to think about what it meant. Not right now.

He had just made a complete idiot of himself defending her honor. And he was about to do it again. He had to get her out of this place. That was his overpowering impulse. He could see that she was off balance, but she wasn't likely to back down. She was gathering her forces, which meant there was a damn good chance she might decide to take them on herself, all of them.

Under normal circumstances, he had little doubt that she could handily put them in their place. But these weren't normal circumstances.

She'd suffered enough character assassination for one day, whether she realized it or not. He wasn't going to let her subject herself to any more. Not when he'd been one of the assassins.

The cluster of men were still eyeing him as if he'd lost his mind. Hell, that had happened the day he met the woman. He flashed them a look that said *Mind your own business,* and then he fished in his pocket and threw down a twenty for a beer he'd never touched.

Jennifer's eyes widened as he came toward her. She braced her legs, as if steadying herself. He hoped she wasn't gearing up to resist, because he was taking her out of this place, one way or another. But even as he strode over to her, he was grappling with his better judgment, and something much more powerful, the memory of pain that cut so deep it had left him fighting to breathe.

Walk right past her and out the door, you idiot. Just like she did. She ended it for reasons you'll never understand, and if you start it again, someone ought to shoot you with your own goddamn gun.

"Ready to go?" he said when he reached her.

When had he ever taken his own advice? He knew how to defend himself with a gun, but he had no feel for self-preservation when it came to her. It was all or nothing.

"Go where? I came for a taco. I want a taco."

If there'd been tears, she'd already blinked them away, and she wasn't going to be handled. He took her by the elbow anyway.

"I know a better place," he said.

"Where?"

"Your hotel. They have room service. Let's find a taxi and put you in it."

"You can find ten taxis," she informed him under her breath, "but you're not *putting* me anywhere."

Her eyes were so dark and sharply green, they stabbed.

"Agreed," he said, "I'm not putting you anywhere. You're humoring me, okay? Now, could we go outside where we can talk?"

That worked. He applied some pressure to her elbow, and that was the last thing she said until they were on the sidewalk.

The street traffic on Fourth was light but oddly pitched and noisy. Buses whistled by, and a small cluster of men arguing a few storefronts away added to the overall clamor. The pavement was so hot Russ could actually smell asphalt and road dust, a rare combination in the city. There wasn't the usual precip to mute sounds and tempers. There hadn't been in weeks.

"I could have handled myself in there," she said, drawing away from him. "You shouldn't have tried to stop me."

"I had to."

"Why?"

"I wish to God I knew." Brakes squealed, and Russ turned to look up Fourth Street at a delivery truck trying to make an illegal turn.

There was an edge to his voice that even he didn't understand, but his wish got lost in all the noise. When he turned back, Jennifer was hurrying away, and he wondered if she'd heard him. She was headed for the opposite intersection, her tote bag swinging and her high heels clickety-clicking on the cement.

Russ watched her for a moment with reluctant admiration and more prurient interest than he wanted to admit. The city might be hot, but she was hotter. She'd taken off her jacket, and the light linen shell she wore revealed the workings of a sheer bra. The back was pretty damn spectacular, so he could only imagine the view from the front. Her black skirt was short enough to show a dangerous length of leg, made even longer by sexy slingback heels.

Great shoes, he thought. *Great legs.*

His stomach dipped, and he reminded himself that he did not need these feelings. They might be the last thing he needed. Still, when she reached the corner, he loped up behind her and trailed her across the intersection.

"I guess this means you don't want that cab?" he asked when they reached the other side.

"I prefer to walk to my hotel. I need the air."

"I'll walk with you."

"Not necessary. It's only a few blocks."

"Necessary. There's a serial criminal loose in this city."

"*Not* necessary. He abducts local women from their homes at midnight. I don't meet his criteria."

"So far."

She reached back and fiddled with the neckline of her shell, lifting the damp material away from her neck. That bra was something. Or maybe the word was nothing. He wondered why she even bothered. When she was done with her blouse, she lifted her hair and cupped it to her head, letting the breezes cool her flushed skin. It was a nice move, feminine and graceful yet revealing. A taxi would have been air-conditioned, but it might not be a good idea to point that out. It was an odd feeling for a man with the reputation of intimidating his own shadow to find this woman slightly intimidating.

"Need any help with that tote?" he asked.

She switched the bag to her other hand, making him feel like a mugger.

They were heading up a steep hill, and she was going at a good clip. Maybe she'd trained on the San Francisco hills, but most visitors to the city found the going pretty rigorous. Russ didn't remind her of that, either. He simply kept pace and listened to her puff.

Nothing like the sound of a woman breathing hard, he thought.

They hadn't yet reached the top when she abruptly stopped and turned to him. "Why did you do that?" Her voice was light and raspy from her breathless climb. Her hair had not quite stopped swinging.

"Do what?"

"Stand up for me like that?" Her eyes welled up again, but only for an instant. She was stronger now, but so was the emotion.

"Somebody had to —"

"No, nobody had to, but you did. Why?"

So many reasons. He understood what it was to be an outsider, for one thing. "We need to be concentrating on catching a killer, not sabotaging each other. *All* of us need to do that."

"Oh . . . I see."

She was clearly conflicted, clearly struggling with something. Finally she released a breath and met his gaze. "You can videotape my session with Myrna," she said. "I'll agree to that as long as she's told. It would be a violation of her trust otherwise. And if you feel a two-way mirror is absolutely necessary, I'll go along with that as well."

He was surprised and pleased. He hadn't expected either concession, and he was trying to find words to tell her, but she'd already started up the hill. They climbed together for another moment or two before she stopped again.

"Can I thank you *now?*" she asked.

There was a glimmer of hope in her eyes, and he could feel the answering glimmer in his heart. That was why he had to quash it. Hope didn't heal. Hope destroyed. It was the most insidious and treacherous of emotions. She wanted to talk, maybe to explain and apologize again, but he couldn't let her. He could apprehend and arrest people. He could even take a life when it was necessary, but he couldn't let a woman say she was sorry.

What if she wanted another chance? What if she didn't?

The collar of his linen jacket was damp, but he couldn't take it off. He was wearing a shoulder holster and he could feel the leather straps tugging as he climbed. His existence was gray and without any real joy, but that wasn't as bad as the exquisite pain of having her in his life. The nine-millimeter automatic he carried was nothing. She was the dangerous weapon. There was no safety switch on Jennifer Nash.

"Just get me a face and do it quickly," he said. "I'll be a happy man."

She tried to smile. "One face coming up. No problem."

She didn't seem to want to look at him after that. The tension was thick and palpable, hanging with everything left unsaid. Maybe they'd both realized that it was over, and the last chance for this hope they'd felt had passed. The glimmer was gone. It had been snuffed out. But he had to make sure of that.

"You look whipped," he said. "Let's get you back to the hotel."

She gave him a quick nod, but he knew what she was thinking. He could almost read her mind. He had made an innocent comment that had nothing to do with her appearance. It was about her stamina, but she wouldn't take it that way. She would think that he no longer found her beautiful. Everything he said and did she would take personally and analyze and find painful meaning in it.

He had just ground the glimmer into the dirt. Under his heel and into the dirt. Now it was out, snuffed like a candle, and they were both safer. He was a hero, and she didn't even know it.

They started back up the hill, climbing in silence, but everything about the moment was deafening. Horns were beeping and overheated tires were squealing. In the distance, a siren whooped mournfully. It was quitting time, and hordes of working stiffs were trying to get home. Russ could escape the sounds of the emptying city, but he would never escape the sound of a woman breathing hard.

"For God's sake, Jennifer, quit lying around like a lovesick puppy. Someone choked the life out of your friend, and you're wasting your time, trying to communicate with a man who so clearly doesn't give a shit. Get your priorities straight!"

Jennifer was lying on her hotel bed, staring up at the ceiling and counting the slats in the air-conditioning vent. Across the room, housed in an armoire, the television blinked soundlessly. She'd turned it on to distract herself, then hit the Mute button almost immediately. That's when the battle with her emotions had begun, full scale. Reasoning with herself hadn't worked, so now she was trying to outshout the impulses that drove her to do stupid things.

Why did she ask him questions when she knew the answers would devastate her? If he didn't care, why should she? She wasn't clinically trained, but she'd done her time in personality theory and human sexuality classes. She knew self-defeating behavior when it bit her, and yet the impulses tugged at her like the lyrics of some incredibly sappy love song. Highly trained or not, her mind couldn't make them go away.

She hadn't even changed her clothes when she came in, just kicked off her heels and flopped down on the bed, totally winded. He'd knocked the breath out of her, and the hills had done the rest. Her thoughts were still spinning. He'd taken on his own people and said things about her she could hardly believe she was hearing, wonderful things.

And as much as he tried to downplay it, something stubborn inside her wanted to believe he felt more than obligation.

Wanted to believe he felt more . . .

Wanted to believe . . .

Wanted . . .

That was the refrain she was trying to out-shout now.

The hotel room's three air-conditioning vents had twenty slats each. The queen-size bedspread had a little over two hundred cabbage roses — she'd divided the spread into quarters, counted the roses in one of them, and multiplied the number by four — and all the dresser drawers and nightstands had thirty brass pulls combined. She was a little compulsive, okay? She counted things when she was frustrated or unhappy. It eased the tension.

What she needed to do was talk, but there wasn't anyone here, and her closest friend in San Francisco was vacationing in Europe. Jennifer had planned to drop by the University of Washington to visit her favorite professor while she was here. Bob Talb had been her adviser and mentor while she was fighting her way through the university's rigorous doctoral program. He was a good friend who knew about her situation with Russ and had helped her through it. Maybe she ought to go soon.

She rose from the bed, undid her skirt, and

left it on the chair by the desk. The room swam with rich, golden twilight. It flooded through the window, warming her as she went to look out. From the twelfth floor she could see beyond the towering skyscrapers to the majestic red cranes that unloaded the freighters, and the harbor cruisers, sun white as they glided across the navy blue waters of the sound.

Below on the street, she spotted some personal landmarks, a magazine kiosk, a Swedish bakery, and the Chinese bistro that she and Sharon had hiked to when their cravings for pot stickers became overwhelming. Jennifer felt pangs of loneliness as she remembered the food and gabfests their hurried lunches had been. They'd shared almost everything in those days, and Sharon had been her closest confidante. Later, when Jennifer began to take flak for her unorthodox interview methods, Sharon was the only one who encouraged her to develop her ideas, her only friend and supporter.

After Jennifer left Seattle, she hadn't stayed in touch with her friend the way she should have. She'd needed to put the past behind her, and Sharon had been part of that past, a painful reminder. Jennifer's relationship with Russ was the one thing they hadn't shared. All three of them had worked downtown together, and Jennifer had been concerned that Sharon would feel compromised by having to keep their secret. Ultimately, that secret was the wedge that divided them. Jennifer wondered now what her friend would have advised. She would never know.

Who had abducted and killed Sharon Myer? Why did he pick redheads, and how did he pick them? Since reading the police reports, Jennifer was perplexed by an endless string of questions, including the pattern of the strikes. So far, he'd struck twice a year and only in the warmer months. The first was in the spring of last year, the second in the summer. This spring he'd struck again, and this summer, it was Sharon.

But Sharon was different than the others. It appeared that she had been bound with duct tape, blindfolded, and abducted in a similar way. But, according to the crime scene analysis and the autopsy, which were still ongoing, the lividity on her body indicated that her hair may have been removed after she was dead, which could mean that whoever killed her was trying to make her look like a Violator victim. It could also mean the Violator's compulsion to remove her hair was so great he had to complete the ritual, even after he'd killed her.

What perplexed Jennifer more was how he'd managed to gain entry to the apartment of a homicide detective. It didn't make sense. He'd broken into the other victims' apartments through an unsecured door or a window. It wasn't clear how he'd broken into Sharon's place, but she'd had an alarm system, and Jennifer couldn't imagine that she'd left doors or windows unlocked.

She could think of a couple other possibilities. It was either a very sophisticated break-in or Sharon knew her killer. He was a relative, a friend, or a lover. He might even have had a key. Someone she knew . . .

As Jennifer stood in the amber light, wearing nothing but her jacket and slip, a dark silhouette began to form in her mind. Soon all she could see was the formless image. It blocked out the Chinese restaurant and the skyscrapers and the cranes — and was far more compelling than any of those things.

This had happened to her before when she was about to interview a witness on a particularly horrific case. It was the face of the assailant. She couldn't see the details yet, but they would come, and possibly quite rapidly. During the interview, as she and the witness chatted about other things than the crime, Jennifer would interject random comments and questions. In some cases she would refer to skin tones, asking the person to choose a number between zero and ten, zero being a translucent complexion and ten being an ebony one. Other times she would ask them to draw a facial feature, such as an eyebrow, with colored pencils, paying careful attention to the colors they chose.

It could take hours, but as the barriers protecting the witness's psyche came down, and she became involved in re-creating the face she'd seen, the formless image in Jennifer's mind took on shape and color and texture, too. That was the likeness Jennifer drew, the one that materialized in her mind as she and the witness chatted about whatever subject interested them.

Jennifer often felt as if she'd witnessed the crime, too, but she'd never thought of herself as telepathic or clairvoyant or in any other way a psychic. She didn't see visions, and she rarely had premonitions. She was an artist, trained in therapeutic intervention, and this was part of her creative process, just as other artists could see a sculpture, fully formed, in their minds, or a painting in their dreams.

She had the feeling now, as she stood in a pool of waning sunlight and stared into the darkness, that she was here for a reason, and it wasn't only because of her ability to ferret salient details out of a frightened witness's subconscious. It might even have something to do with her own subconscious. Other than the fact that she had once lived here, she had no reason to make such a connection, but Jennifer had the strangest feeling that she might know the assailant, too, or know of him, and that he might even be right there in their midst.

She rarely had premonitions, but she was having one now.

Russ spotted the man a half block away. He'd come out of the shadows, and he was heading straight for Russ. The failing light made it difficult to see him clearly, but he appeared to be wearing a jacket and slacks. Not a homeless person or a gangbanger. Still, Russ readied the Beretta. It was a reflex. His bicep nudged the shoulder holster forward.

The man broke into a jog, and Russ slid his hand into his coat. "Stop right there," he called out.

The other man kept coming.

"Stop where you are!" Russ shouted.

"Sadler? Take it easy! It's me."

Russ recognized his partner's voice, but Kent Wright was almost on top of him before his flushed face was visible. He was puffing from the climb, which made it tricky to carry off the Joe Cool image he was known for.

Wright was from a prominent family with a reputation for philanthropy and public service. They'd made their money in real estate, and there was enough of it that Wright should never have needed to work at all, much less as a lowly police detective. That should have said good things about him, except that he so clearly didn't give a shit about public service. He was in it for other reasons: power and politics. Kent wanted to be a movie hero. The real thing was too much work.

He gave Russ a skeptical look. "How goes our knight in shining armor?" he asked. "Was the fair maiden duly appreciative of being rescued?"

Russ's tone was dry, edgy. "Maybe a little less television, Kent? You're beginning to talk like a Saturday morning cartoon."

"Better to talk like one than to act like one."

Touché, Russ thought. He'd been feeling a little foolish about his grand gesture in the bar. Of course, Wright didn't need to know that.

"How's the DMV search going?" Russ asked.

"Like swimming through quicksand, thanks. We're covering King and Pierce Counties, and we've narrowed the list to BMW R1200C bikes that were purchased or leased in the year before the first strike. Once we get that done, we'll cross-check the owners against VICAP to see if they have any priors."

"Excellent," Russ said, "add the SUV to your list and cross-check that as well." He was debating whether or not to have Kent run a similar check for the trailer, but the field was still too broad. They didn't even know the make. Russ had an idea how to narrow the search, and it related to the powdery dust the victims reported feeling on their hands while they were bound in the trailer. He wasn't anxious to share his theory with Kent, however.

"I'm going to need someone to reinterview the first three victims," he said. "We still haven't figured out how he selects them."

Kent was already shaking his head. "Been there, done that. I was on this case for months before you came aboard, Russ. Between Sharon and I, we questioned the victims multiple times. There's nothing that connects them."

"There has to be, Kent. I've studied this guy's MO, and he's not selecting them randomly. Something ties the women together. Maybe it's where they get their hair done, where they shop, or what they have delivered to their homes."

"There is no connection, I'm telling you. I've talked to the women. The first one's a secretary who's heavily into metaphysics. The second is a religious nut who's heavily *not* in metaphysics, and was insulted when we mentioned it. There was no point asking the third, and Sharon wasn't into that shit. Every boat we rowed had holes, just like that one. If you want my opinion, the selection is random."

"Thanks, Kent, but what I want is your cooperation. Go and find me that connection — because there is one."

Kent sucked in a breath. He looked like he was going to refuse, and Russ almost hoped he did. Neither man spoke until Russ relented. "It's *important,* man. If we figure out how we selects his victims, we can set a trap for him, and you'll be the guy who did it."

"Yeah, right, throw me a bone." Kent's exhalation was as steamy as his face. "There's going to be a shitload of publicity when this case is closed," he said, "not to mention glory. I'm guessing you want it all for yourself? Or maybe you want your friend, Jennifer, to get some? That way maybe *you'll* get some from her?"

Russ grabbed him by the lapel and backed him up until he hit the nearest wall. Kent let out a grunt of surprise when his shoulders connected with the cement. "Jeez, Sadler, chill!"

Russ was developing a strong aversion to the word chill. "Maybe you should *chill,* Kent. Maybe you should find yourself an ice pack for the concussion I'm about to give you."

"You hit me, and your career is over. I'll go to Kate!"

"You've already been to Kate. I know all about the backstabbing." *Whiny little bastard,* Russ thought. Kent was easily Russ's height, but he was a small man in so many ways.

"You're withholding information," Kent accused, "and you're sticking me with donkey work to get me out of your way. I'm your partner, and you won't tell me what's going on."

"You know everything you need to know."

"What's that supposed to mean?"

"Pretty much what you think it means."

"I don't know anything! I don't even know if you've got a suspect yet."

Car brakes screeched, and a shiny new Volkswagen pulled to the curb about a hundred feet down the hill. Doors slammed loudly, and a small herd of teenagers tumbled out. Fortunately, they were headed the other way.

Russ eased back, releasing the other man. Kate had put him in charge of the task force and anointed him peacekeeper. A shrewd move on her part, because it forced him to take the high road, again and again.

"I'm being cautious, Kent," he said. "The press is all over this case, and I don't want it turned into a feeding frenzy. The less information out there the better. We're under enough pressure as it is."

"Now you're saying I can't be trusted with information?"

That's exactly what I'm saying, asshole. "Of course not, Kent. I don't have anything to tell you beyond what Kate announced. There are no new leads, but if anything turns up —"

"Yeah, *right,* I'll be the first to know."

Kent straightened his lapel and yanked on his sleeves, aligning his jacket at the shoulders. Russ wouldn't have called him a clothes horse, but he was particular about his look, always checking out his hair in mirrors and picking lint off himself.

Now he was studying Russ suspiciously. "You've never been a glory seeker, Sadler. You're the aw shucks type who goes out of your way to avoid it, so this is about something else, isn't it? You've got something to hide. How close *were* you and Sharon?"

"What the hell is that supposed to mean?" Russ threw the suspicion back in Kent's face. "I wasn't Sharon's partner when this happened. You were. Maybe *you* have something to hide. Like not being able to account for your whereabouts the night she died?"

Kent gave out with a mighty huff of outrage. Indignation was written all over him, but he'd also begun to sweat. Russ didn't know if it was the weather or guilt, but there was some major perspiration action going on, including the drop running down his nose. Unfortunately, there was no real reason to suspect Kent. He was probably capable of almost anything, but only if he had something to gain, and Russ had yet to see how Kent might gain from Sharon's death.

"Here." Russ pulled a handkerchief from his pocket and handed it to the other man. "Blow your nose."

Not so cool now, Joe.

With that, Russ turned and began to climb the hill. Alone.

Chapter 7

"Men are quite docile," Myrna Simone declared. "Haven't you noticed? They just want to please. Like puppies, in a way."

Actually, Jennifer hadn't noticed. Few of the men in her life had been puppylike. Wolves, maybe.

What Jennifer had noticed was that Myrna was a character. As Russ had said, she was heavily into well-loved scarves. She wore a tattered remnant knotted around the long gray hair that fell down her back in a French braid. Another floated around her neck, and a third trailed from the shopping bag she carried. The handkerchief that was looped around her wrist was big enough to qualify, too, and the dominant pattern was paisley. Purple paisley.

She was probably beautiful once, or at least that was the impression Jennifer had as she listened to Myrna carry forth on the subject of men. Her face had the slanted cheekbones and exotic features of an aging Romanian Gypsy, except that Myrna's skin wasn't tawny and her eyes weren't dark. Her features were pale, like watercolors. Her irises were a faded blue, her cheeks a powdery pink, and her hair was woven with silvery strands.

"You probably have all kinds of male admirers," Jennifer ventured. She wanted to keep the rapport going, especially since Myrna had dropped her guard when they began talking about the opposite sex.

"Oh, no," Myrna protested. "They can't be counted on, you know. Men can't be counted on. For anything."

Apparently the men in her life hadn't been all that eager to please. She'd been divorced twice and had little good to say about either husband. She had nothing at all to say about the son she'd lost touch with. When Jennifer brought him up, Myrna became pensive and changed the subject. She wanted to talk about her reign as homecoming queen of Liberty Bell High, her alma mater, and how she'd had to make her own dress because her mother "drank a little and didn't know a needle from a pin."

She warmed to certain subjects — her fragile health and the Pacific Northwest where she'd lived her whole life — but she was completely cold to others, including the most casual reference to the crime she witnessed. Jennifer's indirect questioning approach wasn't working with Myrna. She seemed tense, even evasive, and yet her confusion about the details of that night appeared to be sincere.

The police reports had described Myrna as

a highly inconsistent witness. During her initial interview with the officer who was called to the hospital, she tried to tell him she hadn't seen anything. She'd been out walking because it was hot and she couldn't sleep. Only when he confronted her with the story she'd babbled to the paramedics before losing consciousness did she admit that she'd seen a man force a woman onto a motorcycle, bind her wrists around his waist, and ride away with her. The man and woman had come out of an apartment house together, both wearing helmets that concealed their faces. Myrna didn't realize anything was wrong until the woman suddenly tried to fight the man off. That's when his visor flipped up, and Myrna got a look at him.

The Violator's first three victims had been blindfolded, but they were able to approximate his build and his clothing. They'd each sensed him as a big man, at least six feet tall. Myrna had described him as shorter, around five feet ten, but Jennifer wasn't surprised at the discrepancy. A dozen witnesses to a crime had been known to describe a dozen different crimes. And eyewitnesses were often the least credible because of the trauma of seeing the event. In Myrna's case, her memory could be protecting her by making the biker seem smaller in order to make him a less fearful adversary. It was also possible the victims had sensed him as larger because of their extreme vulnerability.

There were infinite possibilities when dealing with traumatized minds, which was why the trauma had to be neutralized. Jennifer didn't doubt that Myrna was frightened, but she also seemed to be conflicted about what she'd seen and perhaps guilty that she'd run instead of trying to help.

Fear and guilt were powerful motivators, and in this case, both were at work, which was why Jennifer had been brought in. She was here to do the impossible: re-create the image of an assailant no one had seen except a terrified senior citizen under the influence of narcotics in the dead of night, who apparently wished she hadn't. But even if Myrna hadn't seen this man with her eyes, she'd seen him with her mind.

Now it was up to Jennifer, and it was time for a breakthrough.

She and Myrna had talked about secondhand Birkenstock sandals, which Myrna was wearing, about their mutual love of black licorice, and of course, about unreliable men, but there had been no revelations. Jennifer had nothing on her sketch pad but a black helmet with the visor thrown up. There was no face inside, no human features.

"Is that a crystal pendant you're wearing?" she asked Myrna.

Myrna brightened. "My traveling charm?" She lifted the gold chain in her fingers, letting the crystal facets sparkle in the fluorescent lighting.

The pendant reminded Jennifer of its wearer, but she wasn't sure why. Because it was overlarge, rather showy, and perhaps fake? That was the thing about metaphysical objects — and women like Myrna — you didn't know what was substance and what was flash. In a case like this, with so little to go on, you couldn't dismiss anything.

"It protects you from evil spirits," Myrna explained. "They do exist, you know. Everyone has them, hovering about, ready to do harm if given a chance. You should have a charm yourself."

"Actually, I do." Jennifer had been given a crystal by the mother of a young kidnap victim who'd been rescued because of the sketch Jennifer did. She wasn't necessarily a believer, but she'd tucked the crystal in her purse anyway, just in case. That was a few years ago, and she'd had pretty good traveling karma since, except possibly for this trip.

"Where did you get yours?" Jennifer asked.

"At a street fair in Belltown. I bought myself a chunk of licorice, the real stuff that looks like tire treads, you know, and this necklace. They had pyramids and dousers and those colored candles for casting spells, but there was something about the necklace."

"I didn't know they had street fairs in

Belltown." The area had undergone a major face-lift. It was now very urban and upscale and populated mostly by middle-aged yuppies and DINKs, an acronym that popped easily into Jennifer's head, but required her to think for a minute. Double income, no kids?

Myrna's mouth tightened. "It was before they started *improving* everything. They don't make licorice like that anymore," she added, as if that were the final word on the matter.

Jennifer knew where to get some mail order, made fresh and shipped warm from the heartland farmhouse of two unmarried sisters. It looked more like thick shoestrings than tire treads, but it was yummy stuff.

She was about to tell Myrna when she noticed a subtle transformation.

The other woman's eyes had taken on the faraway look of a trance, and she had begun to reminisce. "I used to be quite a beauty," she said softly. "I had powers of attraction."

As Jennifer watched the other woman drift, she had the sense that Myrna might never have been the beauty she desperately wanted to be, and however many men she'd attracted, it wasn't enough. She seemed wistful, but not for things that were, for things that hadn't been. Looks still counted for too much, in Jennifer's opinion, but in Myrna's day they were all a woman had except her homemaking skills, and Jennifer doubted that

Myrna had spent much time in the kitchen, at least not cooking.

"I'm sure you were lovely," she said.

Myrna seemed to be smiling, but Jennifer wasn't sure she'd heard. She stroked the crystal meditatively and closed her eyes. Her lids were translucent and blue with veins. They fluttered as if she were dreaming.

"I used to know about things before they happened," the other woman said. Her voice was faint, breathless. "I used to have power, but it's gone now."

Jennifer softened her own voice. "What do you mean by power?" It didn't sound like she was talking about attracting the opposite sex. Most likely she meant psychic power, but Jennifer didn't want to lead her in any particular direction.

"Things would come to me. They were in my head, things I knew."

"Images? You could see things, like visions?"

"No, not visions." She shivered and dropped the crystal. Her eyes squeezed tight, and the blood seemed to drain from her. Even her eyelids were white. "It's not like that anymore."

"Not like what?"

"I don't see things," she whispered. "They're told to me."

Jennifer wasn't sure what she meant, unless it was that she heard voices or could read other people's thoughts, which sounded like some form of telepathy. Myrna's head was bowed, but the meditative state had vanished. Her fingers worked urgently at the handkerchief knotted around her wrist.

Jennifer's heart was pounding. She broke a rule. "Myrna, did you know what was going to happen to the woman who was abducted that night? There were four women in all, four who were abducted. Did you know what was going to happen to them?"

"No, no, I can't do that. It's not like that."

"Can you hear the thoughts of the man who did it? Can you see him?"

Myrna's eyes snapped open. They were bright with fear. "Four? Is that how many there were? He isn't going to stop, you know. He can't stop. He's an evil spirit, and I'm . . . Oh, I'm *so* afraid."

She seemed to be babbling now, and if Jennifer were to salvage any of this and discover what Myrna knew, she had to calm the woman down. She rested her hand on Myrna's arm and felt how chilled she was. It was almost as if her blood had stopped flowing. Jennifer lifted her hand, but rather than remove it, she began to glide it just above Myrna's arm.

It was a risky move, but she had to try it. She sometimes used a gentle, nonintrusive method of massage called Reiki to relax the people she worked with. You didn't actually touch the subject, rather you concentrated on letting your own energy pour through your palms as you moved your hands just above the physical plane of their body, a hair's length away.

Myrna's fingers were curled around the handkerchief, but they had fallen still. A good sign, but now Jennifer faced another crucial decision. Most investigators would have been anxious to avoid talking about Myrna's psychic abilities. That sort of thing didn't hold up in court, and it could make the witness even less credible than she already was, though it seemed impossible to make Myrna less credible. But Jennifer had an entirely different goal. She wanted access to the woman's subconscious, and this might be her way in. Some researchers claimed to have found a higher occurrence of psychic abilities in people who were more deeply in touch with their unconscious processes, which was exactly where she wanted to go with Myrna.

"Myrna, can you feel the energy from my hand? I'm not actually touching you, but it should feel warm."

Myrna glanced down at Jennifer's hand as it hovered above her forearm. "Yes, I can feel it. What are you doing?"

Jennifer explained the concept of Reiki to Myrna and then asked her to close her eyes, to breathe, and to relax. The metal chair creaked stiffly as Myrna leaned back.

As Jennifer rose from her chair, she remembered that there was a video camera recording everything that happened. There was also a two-way mirror, although Russ had promised that no one would use it to observe the sessions but him, and then only if he informed Jennifer first. At the time she'd honestly been leery about whether she could trust him to tell her, but since she would never know if he was there or not, she'd had to take him at his word.

Right now it was the camera on her mind. It was housed in the far corner of the ceiling, and she had pointed it out to Myrna before they started. Myrna seemed to have forgotten all about it, too, which Jennifer had hoped would happen. What concerned Jennifer was how her relaxation techniques would look to a department full of highly traditional law enforcement types, Russ included.

She would undoubtedly find out.

She stood alongside Myrna and closed her eyes, focusing. Warmth gathered in her hands, creating a burning sensation in the hollow of her palms. Very slowly she moved her hands up Myrna's arm, over her shoulder and around to the back of her neck, where she hesitated. There was a cool spot, which could mean blocked circulation. She knew Myrna took pain pills. Maybe this was why, a neck or shoulder injury. Concentrating, she inched down her spine as far as the chair would allow and then back up until she'd reached the top of her head. She returned to the cold spot, felt more warmth there, and repeated the process.

When Jennifer was done, Myrna was breathing as peacefully and naturally as a sleeping baby.

"You can open your eyes whenever you'd like," Jennifer said. She wanted to ease back into the conversation they were having while preserving this deeply peaceful mood.

Myrna looked almost serene as her eyes flickered open. Her pupils were large, dark pools, giving her a doe-eyed quality, and her mouth was relaxed.

She really was lovely with the calmness shining through, Jennifer realized. The stress had vanished from her features, smoothing wrinkles and lines and making it possible to see what she might have looked like when she was younger. If she wasn't a beauty, she was certainly very exotic.

Ironically, Jennifer's stress levels had risen from the moment she remembered there was a video camera running. She had no idea what Russ's reaction would be, but she couldn't worry about that now, because she was just getting started. Myrna had seen something that night, and Jennifer was going to find out what it was, no matter how non-traditional that required her to be.

"Myrna," she said as she returned to her chair. "Could you tell me about the crystal? It's very beautiful. Do you wear it all the time?"

She nodded. "It makes me feel safer."

"Is it the crystal that tells you what's going to happen?"

"Oh no, it's not like that. The crystal doesn't talk to me."

"Who does talk to you, Myrna? Where do the voices come from?"

Jennifer leaned closer. She reached out to touch her arm, but Myrna moved away. A wary look had crept into her eyes.

"You think I'm crazy, don't you?" she said. "It's not voices like you're thinking. I used to know about things before they happened. They just came to me, but I don't have that ability anymore. It was taken away from me because —"

Because what? Jennifer held herself in check, waiting for Myrna to finish. She couldn't remember feeling this much frustration with a witness. She didn't know if it was Myrna or her. It would have been easy to overreact to the pressures of this case.

Myrna picked up her shopping bag and put it in her lap, as if she were getting ready to leave. The scarf tied to the bag floated into her lap, and she began to stroke the tail. Apparently she'd gone as far as she was going to. Jennifer was pierced with disappointment.

"It would be nice to have a dress made of scarves," Myrna said wistfully. "I've never had one of those."

Jennifer was going to lose her. She could see that, but she had to stop pushing. Myrna was resisting her on every level, and if she decided to get up and walk out, no one could stop her. Witnesses couldn't be forced to answer questions or work with sketch artists unless there were issues of national security involved or they'd been subpoenaed before a grand jury, neither of which was the case here.

Desperate, Jennifer rifled through her tote and came out with a plastic bag of licorice strings. It was the rich, black chewy stuff that came through the mail. She bit off a wad and began to chew slowly, savoring. The stuff was so pungent it was almost alcoholic.

Myrna was watching her avidly, she realized. She opened the bag and shook a couple strings out, where they could be easily reached.

The other woman smiled and accepted.

Jennifer secretly cheered. It was the smartest move she'd made all day. Too bad it involved bribing a witness and it had been caught on videotape.

"Imagine that you're looking in a very still pool," Jennifer said, "but the reflection you see is a man's face. What does his mouth look like? Is it thin or full?"

"More full than thin." Myrna chewed her licorice and worked the dials of the Etch-A-Sketch on her lap. "Something sinister about it, though. Makes me think of one of those Greek statues. Cold like."

Finally, Jennifer thought. They were getting somewhere.

When Myrna had agreed to stay, Jennifer had pulled the Etch-A-Sketch from the paraphernalia in her tote bag. She'd discovered the drawing toy required a level of concentration that kept the user engrossed in the process and distracted from the fear of what was being created. It also forced them to focus on their ability to master details. She'd encouraged Myrna to draw anything that came to her mind while they chatted. The point was to get her relaxed yet involved or they'd been subpoenaed before a grand jury, neither of in what she was doing, and it was working beautifully.

"There's a shadow around his mouth," Myrna murmured, "like he didn't shave."

Jennifer shaded the area around the lips she'd just drawn with light sidestrokes of her charcoal pencil. She was going by what Myrna said, not by what she drew, and the face taking shape on Jennifer's pad was very different from Myrna's. Jennifer could easily have blamed the differences on Myrna's drawing skills or the Etch-A-Sketch, but there were already sharp contradictions in the way

Myrna described the imaginary man and the picture she was creating.

She'd just drawn a mouth caught by surprise, lips stretched tight in a scowl.

It was not the mouth she'd described.

Jennifer was beginning to suspect that Myrna's mind may have captured two separate images of the assailant, split seconds apart; the first when she saw him and the second when he saw her and realized he'd been identified. That would explain the shock superimposed upon the cold determination of a man trying to subdue a woman.

Jennifer quietly pulled another drawing pad from her tote and began a second sketch. She'd never done this before. She was going to draw both images to be sure she had the one most dominant in Myrna's mind. Jennifer didn't release a sketch until it had been approved by the witness, and she wanted the best odds possible.

"Look again at the reflection, Myrna. How would you describe his eyes? Almonds or marbles?"

"Marbles," Myrna said, "dark ones."

Jennifer filled in the irises of the eyes she'd just drawn, wondering if she dared allow herself to feel hopeful. There was always some guesswork in her field, and it was particularly hard with someone as unpredictable as Myrna. The trick was to choose the right sketch to show the witness when the interview was done. It was important to pick the image that was foremost in the witness's mind in order not to create more confusion.

At some point in the session Jennifer realized that she'd lost track of time. She'd been working feverishly, trying to keep up with both drawings, and finally they were getting close. But something was wrong. She was surprised to see that the original sketch was shaping up more strongly. The features did resemble a statue. They were cold, hard, inanimate. Jennifer couldn't seem to draw any life into them, and that was what she did best. It looked like a sketch created from composite catalogs of facial features — a set of eyes, a mouth, and a nose. There was no expression or emotion to give the features depth and context.

"Let's see what you've got," Jennifer said.

The Etch-A-Sketch face that Myrna presented made Jennifer wonder if the magnetic particles had shifted. One eye was larger than the other, a dark mass that resembled the empty socket of a Halloween skeleton, and the nose was set at a strange angle. It looked like the jumble Jennifer would have drawn if she'd tried to incorporate all Myrna's contradictions into one man.

"Would you like to see mine?" Jennifer asked.

Myrna hesitated, and Jennifer could see her apprehension. This wasn't a game anymore.

She was about to be confronted with the face that had terrified her.

"It's just the two of us in this room," Jennifer said soothingly. "No one can hurt you, and when we're done here, an officer is going to drive you back to the Hoffmann House, where you'll be safe."

The woman's shelter was named for the family who'd donated the house. Kate had decided Myrna should have a secure place to stay, mostly to ease Myrna's fears. No one really believed the Violator was going to hunt her down. She was nothing like the women he targeted, and serial assailants rarely struck outside their profile victim, even to eliminate a possible witness. The dark urges that drove them simply weren't there.

At last Myrna nodded. "I'll look at it."

Jennifer held up the sketch, watching Myrna's reaction closely.

"Who is that supposed to be?" the other woman whispered. "That's not him. It doesn't look anything like him."

Myrna seemed startled by the image on the pad, but not in the way that Jennifer had expected. She looked a little incredulous, as if she couldn't believe what she was seeing. Jennifer didn't know what to make of her reaction. Either she really had never seen this face before or she was in deep denial.

Jennifer turned the pad facedown on the table. The drawing was unusable, and it would only frustrate Myrna or block her further to pursue it. When a witness was in denial, you couldn't force them to acknowledge what their mind told them wasn't there. The question facing Jennifer now was whether to show Myrna the second picture and take the risk of alienating her further.

In other circumstances Jennifer would have ended the session and started fresh at a later time. They'd hit a wall, and there was nothing more powerful than a wall thrown up by the psyche. Pounding was useless. It was better to step back, take a breath, and look for a door. But Jennifer didn't have that luxury now.

She'd known this case would be difficult, but not that she would be faced with this kind of mounting pressure. On her other assignments, she was a paid professional, brought in by consensus. There was support for her expertise. Here she was the intruder. It wasn't even clear how much time they would allow her with Myrna. This session could be it.

The second drawing sat on the table in front of her, and Jennifer couldn't delay any longer. It was always difficult to reveal her work. A simple shake of the witness's head could dash everyone's hopes for catching a killer. But letting Myrna go without showing her the picture had its risks, too. There was no guarantee that she could be convinced to come back for another session.

Jennifer picked up the sketch pad and made her decision. There was no clear choice, so she was going with her gut. From an artist's standpoint, this was the drawing she strongly preferred. The other was a lifeless mask. These features had dimension and expression.

For everyone's sake, let this be the right choice.

She turned the pad over with that one thought on her mind. But when Myrna saw the picture, she visibly stiffened and said nothing. Jennifer's hopes dwindled as Myrna remained stubbornly silent. Her only obvious reaction was a skeptical frown.

"His eyes," she said at last, "they're wrong. They should be dark, like the ones I drew." She gave the Etch-A-Sketch a nudge, pushing it toward Jennifer as if she didn't want to touch it.

Jennifer didn't understand. She had darkened the man's eyes until there was no distinction between the irises and the pupils. They were the black marbles that Myrna had described.

"Not both eyes, only that one." Myrna stabbed her finger toward the suspect's right eye. "That one is dark," she said, "like an eclipse of the moon, black and hollow in the middle. It's the evil eye."

Eclipse of the moon. Myrna had used that reference to describe Russ's eyes when she said he frightened her. Obviously it couldn't be Russ she was describing today, which made Jennifer wonder if the eclipse was a symbol that Myrna associated with evil, like the spirits she'd talked about. If that was the case, she might associate it with any man who frightened her. Besides, Russ didn't have just one dark eye. They were both dark.

Jennifer still needed Myrna's confirmation that this was the right sketch to release. "Is this the man?" she asked. "Is he the one you saw that night?"

Myrna began to shake her head. It was barely discernible at first, but suddenly the chair made a terrible creak, and she turned away. She wouldn't look at the drawing. She averted her eyes and shook her head.

Jennifer spoke calmly. "I need an answer. It's important."

"It wasn't him," she said. "I never saw that man before."

Jennifer was stunned. *But Myrna, you described this man,* she wanted to scream. "Are you sure?"

"Can I leave now?" Myrna's eyelids were fluttering, and her fingers were tangled in one of the purple scarves. "Please, I'm very tired."

Jennifer was devastated, but she'd already pushed past the limits she usually imposed on a session. The rapport she needed with Myrna was gone, and when a witness refused to look at a drawing, there was little she could do.

"Yes, of course." Jennifer went to the door and called in the officer assigned to drive Myrna back. Within moments her witness was leaving, trailing scarves and without even a good-bye. She wasn't being rude, Jennifer realized. She'd escaped to a world of her own creation again. Somewhere it was safe.

The case was pushing Jennifer to the limits of her creative abilities. She told herself that was a good thing, but maybe it was the only way she could justify her actions. She'd never tried to draw two sketches simultaneously before, and she'd certainly never done anything like the action she was contemplating now. It would be going against protocol, and quite possibly it was unethical.

Both sketches lay side by side on the table in front of her. She'd been studying them since Myrna left, fifteen minutes ago. Jennifer actually admired Myrna's ability to evade and escape. It would have been easier to pack her tote and follow her out the door than to sit here, struggling. But for Jennifer, that would have been more questionable than what she was considering. She was certain they'd been close to a breakthrough, but Myrna's fears and conflicts wouldn't let her acknowledge it.

When Jennifer had put the drawings side by side, she'd noticed something she hadn't seen before. A different face than either of the first two she'd drawn was materializing in her mind. Her training told her to relax and let it take shape, and eventually she began to realize that she was seeing a composite of both faces. If she put certain features of the first and the second together, she might be able to create the image that her brain was already beginning to form.

That was when she decided to finish the sketch. Without the witness.

She ripped the drawing from the second pad and began to draw a third one, as fast as her mind could throw the details at her. Her hand was unsteady, and before she could get all the features down and refine what she saw, she had to stop. She was shaking too hard to complete the drawing. But suddenly she could sympathize with Myrna.

Jennifer was feeling some fear and conflict of her own.

She knew this man.

Chapter 8

Junior Gordon knew one thing that Russ Sadler didn't. As a matter of fact, he probably knew several things, but he knew one for sure. Russ was a hunk of burning love for Jennifer Nash. Or maybe, technically, he *had* a hunk of burning love for her, but the man was burning.

"*Jennnn . . . Jennnny . . . the Jenn babe . . . Jennninator.*"

Junior grinned as he molested the name the way he imagined Rob Schneider would have in one of his copy room sketches. "*Jennn, making faces . . . Jenneeeee, the face maker.*"

Schneider wasn't Junior's favorite *Saturday Night Live* player. Junior was a diehard Belushi fan and had tapes of most of the big guy's signature skits. As far as he was concerned, March 5, 1982, was a dark day for *SNL* fans, and the show hadn't been the same since. But Schneider's copy room skits were decent, and it wasn't like Junior had anything else to do on Saturday night.

A timer went off somewhere in the newly expanded lab facility, probably alerting one of the technicians that a test was done. The police department had established a small crime scene unit of its own a couple of years back, after negotiating with the Washington State Patrol to share its lab space on the second floor. Since then a bioscience unit had been added with DNA identification technologies, and Junior's domain had nearly doubled in size.

Now he was in the main lab, and it was lunchtime, so there were only a couple technicians around. He'd been waiting for this lull to perform a test of his own. He left the scanning electron microscope, where he'd been studying the remnants of two pieces of ripped duct tape for a match, and slipped on some rubber gloves.

A stainless steel refrigeration unit sat against the wall behind him. Junior opened the heavy door, retrieved a test tube of blood from a storage rack, and took it across the room to the serology section, where there was a sequential metabolic analyzer. Before he inserted the tube, he pulled the flashlight from his lab coat pocket and illuminated the incubating brew. Not that there was any need to. The analyzer would do all the work. The flashlight was force of habit. He could hardly read a comic book anymore without beaming the page. Next to his tweezers, a flashlight was a crime lab guy's most valuable tool.

Junior was a biologist with a background in medical research, and his official function was to supervise the lab operation, but he preferred the investigative side, and it wasn't unusual for him to be the first at a crime scene and the last to leave. The homicide guys were more than happy to indulge him whenever he wanted to play in their backyard because he was good, and he made their jobs easier. In fact, they encouraged him.

He'd been given credit for discovering the evidence that had cracked a difficult sex crime case earlier this year. His specialty, he thought, smiling. S-s-s-sex crimes. He'd love to have a couple more of those under his belt.

"Wouldn't it be fun to drop the Violator case in their laps?" he murmured.

He set the tube in the rotating tray and then programmed the analyzer for the test he wanted. Once he had the thing going, all he had to do was wait. It would be done in a matter of moments, he would have a printout of the results, and all the guesswork would be over.

He took a cautious sip from a triple nonfat capuccino grande, trying to determine if it was cool enough to drink. It had nearly burned the lining off his tongue when he bought it, but the short walk back from Starbucks had cooled it off. With a sigh, he licked the foam from his lips. He'd been looking at a wedge of crumb cake to go with it, but like a good little boy, he'd left it in the pastry case. He wanted to lose a couple pounds, which meant he hadn't savored the fine Doritos Extreme in awhile either. Maybe twenty-four hours. Pretty soon his hands would be shaking.

Despite the lunchtime lull, it had been a busy morning in the crime lab. Down at the far end of the counter, one of the new techs was bent under a bluish light, using what looked like an oversized makeup brush to dust a television remote for prints. Next door, DNA comparisons were being run on backlogged cases. Violent crime was up this summer. The media blamed the heat, but what else could you expect from the press? Even the crime beat flacks lacked imagination. They were followers, packs of dogs. The media wouldn't exist without criminals, Junior realized. But then neither would he. Long live criminals.

"Jennnerama," he warbled softly. *"Jenn, the sketch maker, Jenn, the crime breaker."*

Or should that be heartbreaker?

Junior couldn't figure out how smart people like Russ and Jennifer could think that their secret was actually safe. When a man and woman had that kind of chemistry, they created their own energy field, one that could suck up enough power to cause rolling blackouts. He'd seen them on the back stairs once without their realizing he was there, and the sound effects alone had been enough to piss him off. Nobody should be having that much fun when he wasn't having any.

As far as he could tell, they were fully clothed and technically, nobody was having sex. Actually they probably weren't doing much more than kissing, but the only word for it was *hot.* He'd heard moans, sighs, and low growls of appreciation. He'd heard hunger. And feared for the sprinkler system.

He should have been worrying about Russ. Poor guy was never quite the same afterward. His transformation might have passed unnoticed by the security guards who manned the metal detector on the first floor, but those who knew him could see it. You couldn't miss it. It was reported that he had actually smiled and said good morning to an intern in the hallway the next day. Junior had thought the sun would go out before something like that ever happened. Few people even dared to speak to him before lunch. Russ wasn't a morning person. He wasn't much of an afternoon or evening person, either.

The analyzer was still whirring. *Almost there,* Junior thought.

He cracked his knuckles because he could.

What he didn't understand was why Jennifer had disappeared like that. She was so clearly gone on Russ. Just once he wanted a woman to look at him that way. Her eyes were dilated, and she couldn't catch her breath. Her damn panties were probably damp. She glided around like there was air under her feet instead of linoleum. She was happy.

Junior didn't get it. Why did women bail if they were happy? That was the question of the millennium. Back in those days, the mere sight of Jennifer had made him writhe in envy. He and Russ were competitive about everything, and Jennifer had been no exception. But Junior had clearly never had a chance. She obviously went for the strong, silent, *surly* type, as so many women did.

Junior picked up his coffee too quickly, and cappuccino slopped out the blowhole. Frustration burned through him. Stupid bitches. Why did they always go for guys who made their lives miserable? He slurped up the spillage and checked the analyzer again. He hadn't set it to buzz when it was done because he didn't want to attract attention. There was no such thing as privacy in this lab unless you stayed after hours.

The printout was already there, he realized, whisking it out of the tray. He quickly skimmed the results. He'd run a Beta Subunit, the most sensitive of blood tests for the condition, and the results were well within the normal range. A whistle slipped through his teeth. "Thank you, God!"

"For what?"

Junior swung around to the skeptical countenance of Russ Sadler. He was standing not three feet away, arms folded.

"She's not pregnant," Junior said, grinning.

"Who's not pregnant?"

"That's my little secret."

Russ frowned. "You actually got a woman to go to bed with you?"

"Jealous?" Junior's grin had the stretch of a rubber band. He was truly exultant, and that alone probably gave too much away. Whether Russ believed it or not, there were women in this world who did not find Junior Gordon repulsive. At least there'd been one. The pregnancy test story was true, but Junior had said all he was going to about it to Russ or to anybody else. There would be no details, no who, when, where, or how the hell. This was — and always would be — Junior's little secret.

Jennifer left her rental car in a space in C-8, the lot nearest the psychology complex, and hurried toward Guthrie Hall, where she'd once worked. She was intimately familiar with most of the huge University of Washington campus. It felt as if she'd spent half her life there, studying for her doctorate in eyewitness psychology. From the corner of her eye, she noticed a former fellow teaching assistant, parking his car in the same lot.

She started to call out his name, but he'd seen her, too, and he quickly looked away. Jennifer would have been hurt had it been anyone but Rick Morehouse. Apparently he still suffered from social anxiety disorder, a condition that made him ill at ease around most people, and in his case, especially women.

It wasn't easy to recoil like a turtle when you were six feet tall and built like a loading crane, but Rick had always looked as if he were trying, even with Jennifer. It had taken ages for him to relax when they were TAs together, and now apparently she, too, was outside his comfort zone. He may not have recognized her, but he'd looked straight at her with those heavy black-rimmed glasses of his.

Jennifer walked on, leaving him in peace to park his battered old VW. It was the same car he'd had when they worked together, and honestly, it surprised her that he — and the car — were still around. They had both TA'd for Bob Talb, the professor she was on her way to see, and Rick should have finished his doctorate shortly after she did. If the university had become part of his comfort zone, he was probably having a hard time leaving. It was also possible he was on staff now.

Rick had been a brilliant researcher, but he was generally thought of as remote and a bit eccentric. Jennifer had seen him as rather sweet and very shy, a victim of his own overactive nervous system, and she'd made a special effort to reach out to him. They'd actually progressed beyond hallway nods and were having real conversations before she left.

Her concerns about Morehouse faded as she entered the ivy-shrouded building where she'd toiled so long and hard. The place represented years of effort and angst and joy. It was the repository of her greatest hopes and some of her greatest heartbreaks. Jennifer's mother was gone, and she had long been estranged from her father, so school had filled the gaps. It had become everything — home, work, and a social outlet — and if there'd been one person at the center of it all, it was Bob Talb.

Her relationship with Talb wasn't the most complicated one in her adult life — that honor fell to Russ Sadler — but it was close. She'd had little contact with Bob since she left the area, but they'd been unusually close for academia. When Jennifer lost her mother to cancer, Bob was the first person she told. He'd lost his mother to a tragic accident when he was a child and wasn't able to talk about it without emotion. The lovely silver-framed picture on his wall had always reminded Jennifer of Patricia, her own mother. She wasn't aware that Bob had any other family alive, and Jennifer might as well not have, given the painful estrangement from her own father. Her bond with Bob had been an important one, but even it had been strained during the events that led up to her leaving Seattle.

His office was on one of the lower floors, so Jennifer chose the stairs over the elevator. As she ascended, her linen jacket caught and twisted in the straps of her tote. She pulled it free, ironing the fabric with her hand. Bob had always been meticulous about his work and about himself, and because he was her adviser and mentor, she'd strived to live up to his standards. At the time it had forced her to do her best work, and for that she was grateful. Today it just made her nervous.

Apparently she still wanted her mentor to be proud of her.

Perspiration beaded her hairline and traced a chain across the back of her neck. The linen jacket matched her cranberry red sundress, and as light as the summer outfit was, it was still too warm. By the time she reached his office, she was damp all over, and there he was, cool and Perma-Prest and totally focused. Professor Pristine, she'd once called him. He was bent over some papers and making comments in the margins.

Jennifer knew all about those comments and how stinging they could be when the work wasn't up to par. She hadn't been spared his scathing pen.

"Which poor schlub is getting the Talb treatment today?" she asked, using the irreverent tone that had often crept into their bantering.

He looked up and silently took her in, the

expensive linen suit, the expertly cut dark hair, and subtle summer makeup. "Too bad it didn't work on you, Nash. You might have made something of yourself."

They locked gazes for a moment, neither moving. Perhaps they didn't dare to. At last Bob threw down his pen. He rose with a push of the chair.

"Christ, Jennifer," he said. "It's been too long."

He came around the desk, and Jennifer's tote bag hit the floor as they caught hands. He tugged her into his arms, and she hugged him back, fighting tears. This was the homecoming she hadn't dared to hope for.

"I saw you on TV," he said as he released her. "The Violator case. That has to be hell on earth for you, given your history with the department."

"I've had better times."

"Yeah, walking on hot coals?" He held her back for another look, but seemed to sense her self-consciousness and gracefully backed off. She took the chair behind her, one she'd sat in many times, and he sat on the edge of his desk.

She'd always kidded that he looked like an Ivy League MBA instead of an ivory tower psychologist. His shirt was pale blue silk, his pants a finely tailored lightweight wool, and his hair was neatly layered to control the heavy waves of abundance, which were graying now, at the temples, of course. His glasses were the darkly tinted wire rims he wore at all times, even inside.

"Looking good," she said, wondering exactly how old he was. Maybe forty-seven, forty-eight?

His shrug was self-deprecating. "I guess you might be needing reinforcements about now? Or is this strictly a friendly visit?"

"I wish it were," she said. "We have some catching up to do, I know, and I apologize for taking so long to make this visit. I wish it were under different circumstances, but you're right about the Violator case. That's what brought me back to Seattle . . . and it's why I'm here today."

"Something's wrong? You need my help? Just ask, anything."

She thanked him and took a moment to catch a breath and get her bearings. There were so many things she needed to say to him, but she'd come for another, much more urgent reason. It wasn't personal, and it couldn't wait.

"If you're watching television, then you know the case isn't going well," she said. "In fact, it's going nowhere. The only thing they have so far is an eyewitness, and she's highly unreliable. Nevertheless, I'm working with her now, and we've come up with some sketches, none of which she's satisfied with, so, of course, I won't be releasing any of them."

"Do you need help with the witness?" he asked. "Is she blocked or frightened?"

"Both, apparently. What bothers me most is the way she changes her story and contradicts herself. And now there's a bizarre twist that I can't explain."

Jennifer searched through her tote bag and pulled out an envelope large enough to carry X rays. Inside were the three sketches. She took them out and handed all three to Talb.

"I've numbered them," she said. "Take a look and tell me what you think."

He looked at the first sketch, studying it for a moment before he went to the second. He had no visible reaction to either, but when he got to the third sketch, he murmured something unintelligible. He turned to Jennifer immediately. His face had gone pale, and he was holding the drawing up for her to see.

"Is this some kind of a joke?" he asked. "Your suspect looks like me."

Chapter 9

"I wish I could explain it," Jennifer said.

Bob Talb seemed thoroughly bewildered, and she wondered if she should have prepared him for what he was about to see. It felt as if she'd been trying to catch him off guard, and she wasn't absolutely certain that she hadn't been. Investigative instincts ran deep. They couldn't always be suppressed, even when a dear friend was involved.

"You have to admit," she said, "there aren't too many people walking around with one permanently dilated eye."

Bob looked up from the sketch he was holding. "Your witness said the suspect had one permanently dilated eye? She used those words?"

"She said he had a dark eye. 'Like an eclipse of the moon' was how she put it. She was a pretty dramatic character, into things like crystals and telepathy, and when I showed her the drawing, she insisted that I black out the suspect's right eye."

"Weird," was all Bob managed. He peered at the sketch through the metallic blue lenses of his glasses. He'd worn them for as long as Jennifer had known him, even indoors. He said it caused him great pain to take them off, and Jennifer had only seen him without them once, briefly. She knew his right eye was dilated from an injury, but he'd never explained how it happened, and she'd never asked.

She joined him at the desk, concerned about his silence.

"Bob, please don't think I'm accusing you of anything. I'm just trying to understand this uncanny resemblance. The witness contradicted herself so often, I had to guess at what she really meant, and neither of the first two sketches looked like you at all. I couldn't see the resemblance until I started putting the features of the first two together. That's how I ended up with this sketch."

She wasn't sure he'd heard her attempt to explain. He'd taken the other two sketches out of the envelope and placed all three on his desk.

"Don't these Violator things usually take place at night?" he asked. "How close a look did the witness get at him?"

"Not close enough to see the color of his eyes, and yes, it was night, so his eyes would have been dilated anyway. Now that I think about it, several things could have created that eclipse effect: his helmet, the shadows, her own imagination. She has a pretty vivid mind."

She positioned the third sketch so that she

could examine it, too. "It occurred to me that I might have created the resemblance," she said. "Do you think there's any possibility the image could have come from my subconscious rather than Myrna's?"

Bob turned to look at her. "Myrna? That's her name?"

Technically, Jennifer shouldn't have revealed a witness's name, but she hadn't been doing much of anything right lately, so why start now. She nodded, anxious to get on with her point.

"I keep wondering whether this sketch really represents what Myrn— the witness — was trying to describe. What if it was triggered by her reference to the dark eye? Do you remember my 'one salient feature' theory?"

"Yes, it was part of your thesis. You argued that one very noticeable feature could alter a witness's recall, especially if the witness had any negative associations with that feature."

"Right, for example, if the suspect had a scar, and the witness was frightened as a child by someone with a scar — even a movie villain — those images could become confused. The subconscious can bury powerful emotions so deeply that we can't remember them, but it remembers them as if they happened yesterday. It isn't hampered by logic or time constraints, and it doesn't differentiate between reality and fantasy."

"So, in this case, the witness mentioned dark eyes and an eclipse of the moon, and your subconscious conjured up an image of me. Why would it do that?"

Bringing up their past was more difficult than Jennifer would have expected. "Because of what happened before I left?"

Bob didn't seem to know what to say, and Jennifer realized it was going to be one of those supremely awkward moments. She took refuge in the sketches.

"If you consider them individually, there are features in these first two drawings that resemble yours." She arranged them so that she could show him what she meant. The suspect was wearing a helmet in both sketches, but the faces were more narrow than wide. That was evident by the angles and contours.

With her finger she traced the outlines. "You can see that the general shape of the face is the same — lean and angular. But there are discrepancies, too. In both sketches his mouth is wrong. It doesn't look like yours at all. It's wider, and flatter against his teeth. That's the way he frowns — and probably smiles."

Jennifer hesitated, wondering where she'd seen a smile like that before. It was familiar, and it wasn't Bob Talb's, of that much she was certain.

She'd watched the videotape of the interview afterward, trying to figure out how she'd come up with the last sketch, and she'd congratulated herself for being able to produce one sketch, much less three. She'd actually done a reasonable job of tracking Myrna's hairpin turns during the first two drawings, but it was impossible to know what might or might not have triggered Jennifer to create the third one. If it wasn't her one salient feature theory, then it was possible she was being guided by some subtext in Myrna's ramblings.

"And he doesn't have bags under his eyes."

There was a wry note in Bob's voice, and Jennifer was glad to hear it. "Who wouldn't have a few bags with ex-students like me showing up," she quipped.

"You can show up any time you want." He gave her a stern look and returned to his chair. "Just quit drawing mug shots of me, hear?"

"I could autograph this one." Jennifer gathered up all three sketches and put them back in the envelope. "You might want to frame it."

She could see herself wink in the highly polished surface of Bob's old oak desk. She'd always thought of his office as a perfectly organized rat hole, and that a scholar of his stature deserved better. But academia frowned on worldly trappings, and except for Bob's quest for neatness, he was a true academic. The last time she'd been in his office, she'd counted over 200 precisely hung diplomas and commendations on his Honors Wall. Now it looked as if he had one more. There was a large framed certificate of some kind, and horrors, it was crooked!

His office was tucked away in a corner of the building with windows too high to see much of anything but overcast skies. Back in the days when Jennifer was his TA, the gloom had made it necessary to burn lights constantly. But today sunlight streamed in sheets as bright as the ones on Jennifer's hotel bed. She was starting to get used to hot, sunny weather in Seattle. She'd never imagined that was possible, either.

"Jennifer, you didn't finish your thought."

"What thought?"

"Why you felt a subliminal need to draw me instead of whoever the witness was describing."

Oh, *that* thought. Irony burned through her smile and made it sad. "Conflict, confusion, guilt, loss of control? Take your pick."

"You're still conflicted about what happened?" He settled back in his chair. "I'm sorry to hear that. All I wanted was to help, not to make your life more complicated."

"Oh, I know that, Bob." She stuffed the envelope back into her tote and sat down, relieved to have her questions answered. "You did what you could to help me understand what was going on with Russ, but ultimately it was something only I could do. And as it turned out, the deeper conflicts probably weren't about Russ at all. They were rooted in my childhood and my relationship with my father. I was ten and very impressionable when my illusions about him were shattered, and that was only the first time."

"I didn't know. We never talked about your father."

"I know. I couldn't then." And she didn't want to now. It was still too raw a discovery. "That's what I meant about having to get it figured out on my own."

"And did you?"

"Get it figured out? I think so. . . . I hope so."

"But you can't share it, even with me?"

If Jennifer could have shared it with anyone, it would have been him, she realized. He had been her teacher, adviser, and in many ways her closest friend for years. She'd taken everything to him eventually, even her problems with Russ, and she'd admitted things to Bob that she hadn't admitted to herself.

How quickly it had happened with Russ, for instance. She'd been drawn to him almost on sight, and even though something about him had made her apprehensive, she hadn't been able to talk herself out of it. Things only got worse when Russ made it clear the attraction was mutual. Jennifer's defenses should have taken up their posts, readying for the siege. Instead, they promptly began to crumble.

Russ's command of situations and his steely presence of mind were legend in law enforcement circles. As was his unpredictability. But those traits played havoc with intimacy. Jennifer never knew what to expect. He was constantly surprising her and catching her off guard. There was also a tremendous sexual charge between them, and he seemed to know that, and play off it.

She'd never felt more alive. Her skin was gooseflesh, every hair pricked and waiting. But what had thrilled her silly at first became more and more threatening as she realized she was falling in love with him. She never seemed to be able to catch her balance. It felt as if he had all the power.

Was it safe to love a man like Russ Sadler?

By the time she confided in Bob Talb, she was feeling seriously out of control. She didn't understand the nature of her attraction to Russ and feared it was fueled by some kind of dark fantasy rather than by reality. Was it a fatal attraction? Or was it love? And if it was love, why couldn't she let herself go with it?

Bob had gently suggested that she might not be in love with Russ at all. Their obsessive attraction might actually be a way to avoid intimacy, a flight from responsible love he called it. He was involved in a new study on the elements of surprise in arousal, and he offered to let her participate in order to help her understand. She wasn't open to the idea at first, but eventually, the conflict she felt brought her back.

The study had subjects watch videotaped material while being monitored, and Jennifer responded to the elements of surprise with high levels of arousal, but despite Bob's efforts to make her see the connection, she found it difficult to relate the experience to her situation with Russ. She'd since realized that she was deeply in denial and that Bob was determined to make her see what she was doing. That probably explained what happened next.

Unknown to her, he'd devised a new protocol to better test his theory, and he'd actually had Jennifer in mind when he'd come up with a role-playing scenario. But he intentionally kept that information from her because the experimental results would have been meaningless if she'd been informed. The idea was to surprise her and monitor her responses. Still, Jennifer felt shocked and betrayed by what he'd done.

She received an E-mail at school from someone who called himself a secret admirer and claimed to appreciate her work as much as her physical beauty. He revealed that he would be at the arts reception on campus that evening and hoped they could meet. The E-mail said she would find an evening bag in her desk that she was to carry if she wished him to approach.

Jennifer hadn't actually thought of it as dangerous at the time. It was a campus function and a public event, where there would be several people she knew and lots more that she wanted to meet. She was certainly curious and secretly flattered, but it wasn't like her to do things impulsively. She couldn't have explained at the time why she went along with the E-mail invitation, and that was part of her alarm afterward.

All evening she held the small jeweled bag and wondered who her admirer might be. A server whispered that a gentleman was waiting for her on the veranda, but Jennifer found no one there. Disappointed, she left through the gardens — and was surprised by a man who stepped out of the shadows. Darkness concealed his identity, but Jennifer could see the hand he extended.

Her heart went crazy. She ought to have screamed or run, and it terrified her that she didn't do either. Was she so cut off from her feelings that it took this to make her feel alive? Was she drawn to danger?

She was shaking, and when her fingers touched his, she gasped.

It felt as if someone else clasped the outstretched hand and was led into the heart of the gardens. He stopped beneath ivy-drenched bowers, and by that time, Jennifer was reeling. She could feel his breath on the back of her hand. He brought it to his lips and brushed a kiss over her fingertips. Her pulse soared with emotions she couldn't begin to understand: fear, anticipation, excitement, wild disbelief — all of it so powerful she felt dizzy.

Her bag fell to the ground, and he bent to pick it up. That's when she realized the man was Bob Talb. This was the new experiment, he explained, and the bag was wired to monitor her vital signs.

He apologized for frightening her, but Jennifer was deeply disturbed, and when he suggested that she might be in denial, she denied that. She felt betrayed, even after he explained that the experimental results would have been negated if she'd known what to expect. She asked if he'd had the experiment approved by the Ethics Committee. Subjects were routinely kept ignorant of the study's goal, but not that they were involved in an experiment of some kind. That was part of informed consent.

Finally he admitted that he'd come up with the idea to shock her into seeing what she was doing. There hadn't been, and wouldn't be, any other subjects. It was his "Jennifer experiment," and he had only done it because he was worried about her, worried that she was unwilling to look at what she was doing. He assured her that her responses were normal, but she found that impossible to accept. She'd never thought of herself as reckless, but then, she was hopelessly drawn to Russ, which was exactly Bob's point.

She was flooded with questions that were even more disturbing than the experiment. Was she taking risks and seeking to be caught and punished? Did this have something to do with her past, her father? She couldn't talk to Bob. Whether he'd meant to or not, he'd violated her trust, and there was no one else. Ultimately, she'd left the area in order to clear her head and get the distance she needed to understand.

A ringing phone brought Jennifer out of her thoughts.

Apparently Bob had been watching her as she mused. He continued to, letting the phone ring.

"I'm glad you're here," he said. He made no further reference to what might have preoccupied her, or to her father, or to anything other than his pleasure at seeing her.

Jennifer appreciated that. "I am, too."

"I think you might be right about the sketch," he said. "You probably do have some unresolved conflict about what happened. If you remember, your vital signs showed all the signs of an adrenaline spike. Racing pulse, wet palms, trembling, shallow breathing. That's more than excitement, Jennifer, that's fear. You were terrified, probably of yourself."

"But it's been two years."

He smiled. "To quote Jennifer Nash, the psyche doesn't make that kind of distinction. It could be two days as far as your mind is concerned. When a memory surfaces, your subconscious knows it's being rocked by powerful responses, and that's all it knows. It registers them as a real and present danger."

The window light changed from bright to hazy. Jennifer felt the drop in temperature immediately and wondered if the weather was breaking. Something needed to break.

"Bob, I don't blame you. You know that, don't you?"

"Yes, but I think it's still hard for you to feel comfortable with the way you responded."

That was true. She'd been embarrassed at her lack of judgment and control, but she had also come to realize that he hadn't meant her any harm. He really had been trying to help. And she'd realized later that her intuition had been right. The source of her confusion about men and sex had more to do with her father than it did with Russ or Bob or psychology experiments. At a much too tender age, she'd discovered some terrible truths about Philip Nash — a man she worshiped because of who she believed he was and what he stood for — and it had left her unable to trust easily, especially men and especially with her most vulnerable feelings.

"Just as long as you know that I don't blame you for anything."

She came forward in the chair, and he waved away her concerns. "Hey, it's better than being blamed for the demise of moral standards on today's college campuses. I get that all the time. We psych professors have bull's-eyes on our backs."

His humor eased them past the difficult moment, and Jennifer felt a sense of relief as she reached down for her tote. She thanked him again for his sensitivity to her concerns and made promises to drop in again before she left Seattle.

One last thought stopped her at his door. "Bob, the pressure is on to find the Violator. They really want this guy, and so do I, but the witness has me stymied. If anything comes to you that might be helpful, anything at all, give me a call, okay? I'm staying at the Madison Renaissance."

"Happy to," he said, and then added, "sounds like what you really need is another witness."

"No kidding. Unfortunately, no one else in the neighborhood saw anything, which is hard to believe, considering where Sharon lives. Capitol Hill isn't exactly a quiet area."

The incongruity of that struck Jennifer as she stood there. When she'd gone through the police reports, she hadn't noticed who canvassed the neighborhood or how thorough a job they'd done. Russ had just taken over the case with Sharon's death. If it was him, maybe she could relax. Maybe.

"Remember, you can call me, too," he said. "If you need anything, I'm always here, me and my bull's-eye."

He got up and came around the desk, but only that far. There seemed to be an invisible barrier between them since their discussion of the past, and she had put it there. He was respecting her need for distance.

"You're not the only one who feels like a target these days," she assured him. With that, she gave him a nod, intending to be on her way.

"Jennifer?"

She hesitated, but very reluctantly. She wanted to go, wanted to avoid the question she feared was coming next.

"I have no right to ask, and you have every right not to answer," he said, "but I was wondering how things are going with your ex-fiancé? That must be tough, everything considered."

When she didn't respond, he began to apologize. "Look at me, acting like an overprotective father."

She tried to smile. "Overprotective big

brother. You're not that old, Bob. And it's worse than tough. Things with my ex-fiancé are unmitigated hell."

"I was afraid of that." He released a sigh. "Listen, I don't want you to take this wrong. There's nobody out there who can nail a sketch like you can, and I have total faith in your ability, but when it comes to this case . . . Jennifer, have you thought about whether or not you're the right person?"

She nodded, mostly because her throat was tight with emotion. She had hardly thought about anything else.

Jennifer took a little detour on her trip back to the Public Safety Building. She drove around Lake Union. The clouds had thinned enough to let the sun rip through, and it was hot again. Steaming. She'd opened the car windows to cool off, but no heat wave could slow the frenetic pace of this busy working lake. It was abuzz with activity.

Gleaming pontoon planes glided across the water's choppy surface to deposit passengers at destinations of their choice. Skiers sliced through the waves of their towboats, and parasailors dotted the blue sky like clouds. On rotting dry docks, craftsmen built seaworthy vessels entirely of teakwood.

It was breathtaking, and Jennifer felt like a tourist as she craned to catch everything. But this was more than a sightseeing trip. It was another blast from the past. Russ Sadler had lived on Lake Union during the time they were involved. She wondered if he still did.

Gas Works Park was an old oil refinery that had been cleverly converted into a brightly painted park and recreation area. Children played happily on a huge jungle gym of multicolored storage tanks, pipes, and valves. As Jennifer drove past the sprawling greenbelt, she looked across the lake at the houseboats dotting the opposite shore. She spotted his immediately and felt sharp pangs of nostalgia. The quaint three-story barge had a natural shake exterior and shutters that gave it the effect of a floating cottage. Cantaloupe-colored begonias hung from the exposed beams, and pots of red geraniums dotted the deck.

Somehow she'd expected to see it looking run-down and neglected. Apparently he hadn't sunk into depression the way she had, and ceased to care about anything. She ought to be grateful for that, but frankly, she wasn't feeling all that noble these days. The thought that he'd not only survived, but done well without her, was not a gratifying one. In fact, she might have some trouble forgiving him for that.

Still, she was glad to see the houseboat doing so well. It was prime rental real estate, and he'd had an option to buy, which they'd decided to do. They were going to live there once they were married. Russ had been left money in trust by his paternal grandparents, and he'd built a substantial portfolio through careful investing. They'd talked about using that money to buy and renovate the boat, and Jennifer had loved the idea. It was just one of the things she'd loved about him, and about them. At moments like this when all she could remember were the good parts, she had difficulty fathoming how it could have gone so wrong.

She switched on the radio to distract herself, but it did no good. Toni Braxton was not the singer to listen to when you were in a blue mood. Jennifer even missed Russ's unpredictability. Not all of his surprises had made her feel like she was on a carnival ride. Some of them had been achingly tender. They had a favorite waterfront restaurant on the opposite side of the lake, aptly called The Cove because of the secluded inlet it occupied. They met there after work, but always with the concern that they might be discovered together, which made their rendezvous seem imperiled and that much more precious.

One particular night he'd had to cancel because of a case, and Jennifer was bereft at the thought of not seeing him. One night. It was only a few hours, but it didn't seem possible to get through them alone, and that realization had frightened her. She went to the restaurant and sat in the bar, thinking she would be closer to him there than anywhere else.

The Cove had live music on weekends, an old-fashioned piano bar with a throaty, big-breasted songbird named Delia, who sipped Manhattans through every set. By the last one, Delia was plucking roses from her hair and nestling them in her ample cleavage. Russ may have enjoyed that, but Jennifer liked the weeknights better when a gaudy old jukebox played. They'd danced in the dark to Top 40 hits, just the two of them. The bar was rarely crowded, but it wouldn't have mattered if it had been. There was no one else in the world.

Jennifer had had a glass of wine that night and decided to leave. She'd made a side trip to the ladies' room, and as she came out, she saw Russ standing in the foyer. He was searching the bar area for her, and he looked almost as desolate as she did. She'd never seen Russ Sadler look desolate. Never even considered it a possibility, and the sight rocked her. But not nearly as much as he was about to.

When he saw her, he told her he'd been looking for her everywhere. In a rush of words, he admitted that he found it hard to spend one night away from her. Right there in the foyer, he told her that, and then he said he didn't want to spend another one. Not one night. He didn't ever want to have to search for her again. And he didn't want to listen to that damn voice mail of hers, either. He needed to know where she was, all the time, every minute. Or if not that, at least he needed to know that she was his. All the time. Every minute.

His declaration of love shocked her, and when she found the composure to ask him if he'd been drinking, he lifted her off her feet with a kiss and told her that he was cold sober. Unlike her, he didn't want to be *emotionally safe*. He wanted to risk it all on love. It was quite an admission for a man who kept everyone at bay with his tough guy act. Jennifer's doubts melted away, although it did confound her that this proud, stubborn, self-reliant man could change. For *her.*

He didn't propose to her that night, although she kept expecting him to. He saved it for the stairway where they met. Step 153. She said yes on 154, when he lifted her into his arms.

They made plans to elope but had to postpone them when Russ was called away on a case that turned into a high-profile kidnapping of a politician's daughter. The case dragged out, requiring Russ to travel frequently, and Jennifer wondered if it was a sign. She'd been running on nerves ever since saying yes. She couldn't eat or sleep. Finally, she had to talk to someone, and Bob Talb was the one person in her life who knew about Russ.

When Bob asked her what was wrong, she told him about the elopement — and knew immediately that she couldn't go through with it. Something was wrong.

Bob advised her to listen to her instincts. She was afraid, and the fear was trying to tell her something. Jennifer's turmoil eased for the first time. Russ was away again, but she was supposed to meet him in Vegas that weekend, and they were going to be married. That night she left him a voice mail, trying to explain. She followed it up the next day with another message, asking him to call her, but she never got an answer. She tried once more after that and finally decided that his lack of a response *was* a response. He had come out of hiding for her, risked something that a man like him might well fear more than death: intimacy. It had cost him too much.

A honking horn made Jennifer realize she'd been drifting again. It was a miracle she hadn't had a car accident. Small wonder she wasn't getting anywhere on the case. Her mind was permanently stuck in the past. Bob Talb had asked her how things were with Russ Sadler, and she'd told him the truth. But not all of it. She loved the man then, and she loved him now. But timing was everything, and she had waited too long. Russ didn't want to hear her epiphany, no matter how badly she needed to tell him.

Chapter 10

"Detective Sadler! Is it true that you've lost control of the Violator case? We were told that Jennifer Nash is taking over. Do you have a problem with that?"

"I would have a problem with that if it were true," Russ said.

An aggressive young newspaper reporter had spotted Russ as he tried to make a stealth exit from the Fourth Street employees' entrance. Now the reporter was running alongside him, plaguing him with questions about the case, and of course, about Jennifer.

Russ had spent a grueling day in the field trying to track Sharon's movements in the days preceding her death. He'd stopped at the office to pick up the video of Jennifer's interview with Myrna, and now he was headed to his houseboat, probably to put in several more hours on the case. He was in no mood to play games with an overeager reporter, but he didn't like what he'd just heard. It sounded like there'd been a leak, perhaps from Russ's own unit. Nothing would surprise him, considering all the animosity toward Jennifer.

"Is she taking over the case?"

Russ quelled him with a sidelong look. "Ms. Nash is doing exactly what she came here to do — a sketch of the suspect. When it's ready, we'll release it. Until then, I'm not prepared to talk about it."

Russ took off toward his car, which he'd parked on the street. The reporter dogged his heels. "Have you seen the sketch?" he asked. "Can you tell us what the Violator looks like?"

"I have nothing else to say," Russ growled. Out of the corner of his eye, he saw a small cluster of guys from the fifth floor. They seemed to be watching his plight with interest, and among them were two of Russ's *closest* friends: the new hotshot criminalist and Kent Wright.

Russ began to smell a setup even before Wright gave him a wave and a vaudevillian wink. Wright wasn't flirting. He was gloating. He'd pulled off a good one, or so he thought.

"Detective Sadler, did you once have a personal relationship with Ms. Nash?" the reporter asked. "Did she jilt you, Detective? And if she did, how can you ever work with her again? How can you possibly trust her?"

Russ stopped in his tracks, and the reporter nearly crashed into him. Russ turned on the man like a lion on a yapping hyena, ready to take his head off. He didn't, of course. He spoke in the calmest voice imaginable. "Who told you that?"

The other man shook his head and had the sense to look nervous. "I can't reveal my sources."

He didn't have to. Russ knew the source of the leak. He shot Kent Wright an angry glare, but his voice remained calm.

"Ms. Nash and I have an excellent *working* relationship. She's one of a team of specialists, who was chosen because of her unique expertise, and I support her totally in her efforts. That's all I have to say, and if you hit me with one more question like that, I may have to hit back."

Russ left the startled young man standing on the steps of the Memorial Plaza. His only thought as he strode to his car was of the Chinese stir-fry he'd picked up for dinner — and the six-pack. Well, maybe there was one other thought. He'd always liked the maxim that it was smarter to get even than to get angry, and in this case, getting even meant only one thing: taking back control of his case. As soon as fucking possible.

The woman has to be out of her mind.

Russ hit the power button on the remote and turned off the VCR. He set the remote on the countertop, but other than that, he didn't move. The screen had gone dark, but his mind was on fast-forward. He was standing by the wet bar in his media room, and he'd just watched the videotape of Jennifer's session with Myrna Simone. His plan had been to eat some stir-fry and drink a beer while he watched the interview. But once the tape started, the food was forgotten.

Bribes of licorice and mystery massages? The investigation had been brought to a virtual halt while Jennifer pissed away the better part of the day with the state's only witness. She had nothing to show for it except three sketches, two of which the witness had rejected and one she hadn't seen — and oh, yes, some mumbo jumbo from Myrna about hearing voices.

Privately, Russ didn't believe that Jennifer would ever break through this particular witness's barriers, because Myrna's barriers were intentional. She wasn't confused, she was holding back, and Russ had some thoughts of his own about what she was trying to conceal. He also had his own reasons for wanting to be the one to question her — and his own way of interviewing. No one would have called it kinder and gentler, but it got the job done.

He hit the Rewind button and let the tape spin. He hoped no one had leaked *it* to the press. The department's credibility would be shot to hell, if it wasn't already. And now apparently the media wasn't satisfied with second-guessing every step of the investigation and scaring the public witless with "expert" predictions of future strikes. They were delving into Russ's personal past and opening up old wounds for their own amusement. He reported directly to Kate on this case, but there was little point in going to her. She was the one holding the investigation hostage in order to accommodate a sketch artist who was acting more like a 900 number psychic than the forensic scientist she claimed to be.

Russ picked up his food and crossed the room to the refrigerator. He needed to move, to release some bad energy, and he was glad now that he'd had the houseboat made larger and less claustrophobic. He'd added a media room on the second deck, along with a kitchen area and a master bedroom. The upper deck had been made into a guest bedroom, and the lower into a great room with a living, dining, and kitchen area.

After his breakup with Jennifer, the renovations had absorbed him, and the boat had become his substitute for a personal life. She was his woman, his pride and joy. The former owners had called her *The Cradle*, and he hadn't bothered to change it. The name seemed appropriate somehow.

He put the food away, opened himself a cold beer, and went outside to the balcony above the bow. The view was spectacular. The sun had just set behind the Queen Anne Hills, and the lights of downtown Seattle were beginning to twinkle. As the sky darkened, you could see a reflection of the entire city stretching across the surface of the lake. No postcard could have done it justice.

He heard laughter somewhere, a woman's laughter. God, what a lonely sound that was. The beer tasted bitter, and he set the bottle down. Nothing helped, he thought. Nothing ever really helped when he felt like this.

The houseboat was on its own water bed, and the rhythms of the lake usually lulled him into a state of relaxation, especially in the evening. But there wouldn't be any relaxation tonight. And no way to escape her. There wasn't anything else that could be done until he figured out how to handle this situation with Ms. Nash, and he could not imagine that it was going to be resolved easily.

She wouldn't back down without a fight, he knew. She was passionately committed to the method she'd devised, and she also had a reputation to uphold. She needed credibility, visibility and, most of all, another victory. He'd heard she was putting together a book on her technique. But she also had a personal stake in this case. Sharon Myer was her friend. And Russ Sadler wasn't.

Meanwhile, there was a serial assailant at large and a statewide task force to run. Russ had people working around the clock, trying to come up with one solid lead. They were mired down in questions that defied logic, even criminal logic. They didn't yet know how the Violator picked his victims or why his strikes were seasonal. It wasn't clear why he used a motorcycle to abduct the women, but may have used an SUV to drop them in parks, unconscious and dressed only in paper examining gowns. Or dead, in Sharon's case.

Russ was pursuing some leads of his own, and they would remain *his* leads for now. The game was turning cutthroat, and he'd never been a particularly trusting soul anyway. But beyond his hunches, there was only one window of opportunity that was actually open, and that was Myrna. After seeing the tape, Russ knew he had to talk to her again, but he couldn't get near her until Jennifer was done with her.

The French doors closed behind him with a bang as he returned to the media room. He went straight to the telephone at the end of the bar, picked it up, and tapped out the number of the Madison Renaissance. Instead of Jennifer, he got a voice mail message that she wasn't taking calls.

The message he left wasted no words. "We need to talk, and we need to talk tonight. Otherwise, you're going to hear what I have to say tomorrow, in Kate's office."

His next call was to the chief. She wouldn't be there, but when she arrived in the morning, there would be a message waiting for her.

"I'll be in your office first thing tomorrow," he said. "I have some words for you regarding our consulting sketch artist."

Silence was Jennifer's friend tonight. Sitting cross-legged on the hotel bed, surrounded by manila folders and untouched Thai takeout, she read through the details of Sharon Myer's abduction and murder, report by report. She'd only had a chance to skim them before her session with Myrna. Tonight, she'd started at the beginning, and she was going through them in chronological order, forcing herself to concentrate on reams of crime scene data and fanfold computer printouts of BMW sales and repair shops.

Forcing herself to concentrate when her mind was a million miles away. Or possibly ten, in a beautifully renovated houseboat.

Jennifer sighed and tilted her head, stretching the muscles of her neck.

She pushed back the flaps of the nearest take-out container and stirred the aromatic drunken noodles with her chopsticks, tempting herself. She hadn't eaten since that morning, and her stomach might be ready for food, but her mind wasn't. *Maybe later,* she thought.

If the inside was as nice as the outside, he must have lavished time and work on the project. Maybe before she left, he would give her a tour. She wondered how painful that would be. More evidence that he'd left her behind, in the dust of a remodeled houseboat.

She glanced over at the phone on the nightstand and found herself wishing it would ring. No chance of that, however. There'd been a half-dozen hang-ups when she checked her voice mail, one right after the other and just minutes apart. Figuring that someone had the wrong room number, she'd asked the hotel operator to hold her calls, and she'd turned off her cell phone as well.

She'd known the reports were going to be difficult, and she didn't want to be distracted. She was lucky to have the convenience of her hotel room to work in. They were short of office space downtown, and Kate's assistant had made copies of the reports so Jennifer could bring them back.

The envelope that contained her three sketches lay on the desk by the window, abandoned there as soon as she entered the room. She'd already made the decision not to show them to anyone, and they were essentially useless since she couldn't release them. Nor would she have wanted to, given whose face she'd drawn. She certainly didn't want to implicate Bob in any way, especially since she'd checked — that investigative instinct again — and learned that he'd been out of town the night Sharon was killed. The psychology department's secretary had told her that Bob was the keynote speaker at a behavioral neuroscience association meeting with five hundred attendees.

She set the drunken noodles aside and went back to the paperwork. She was going to need another session with Myrna, but she'd chosen to put off that discussion until tomorrow. It would be a bloody battle, she feared. Better to wait until she'd had some rest. Meanwhile, she had to get through the rest of the reports. There was a lot to be accomplished still. Bob Talb had given her an idea when he'd joked that she needed a new witness. He might have been kidding, but Jennifer wasn't.

She found it hard to believe that no one else had seen a man in head-to-toe black leather trying to force a woman onto a motorcycle. Capitol Hill was an all-night-long kind of place, and there were always people about, even at midnight. Maybe the neighborhood was so hip they didn't pay any attention to serial abductions, but Jennifer doubted that. The police reports couldn't tell her everything she wanted to know about that night, but they would reveal how thorough a canvassing had been done and how many interviews had been conducted.

It was easy enough to overlook potential witnesses among the people who had actually been interviewed. Jennifer was also curious about those who *hadn't* been interviewed —

the teenager sneaking out of the house at midnight, the snoopy neighbor going through trash cans. Not everyone was tucked in his bed by midnight, and Jennifer wanted to know what the insomniacs were doing that night. Of course, there was only one way to satisfy her curiosity on that score.

She tilted her head to one side and then the other, letting out a little groan of pain. *As if she didn't have enough battles to fight.*

"You see my point?" Russ clicked off the VCR and turned to Kate, who was sitting at her desk, still focused on the TV monitor that sat on her file cabinet. Her executive chair was tipped back so steeply, she could have been watching a Sunday football game in her recliner.

"How could I miss it?" She rolled her head toward Russ. Her tone was dry.

But Russ's was drier and laced with plenty of weary sarcasm. "I want my case back," he said. "I want my *witness* back. Myrna Simone is hiding something. The woman pops painkillers, and I think she's lying through her teeth."

Kate's chair came up. "Russ, please understand that what Jennifer does takes some time."

Russ took the cassette from the VCR and returned it to his briefcase. "I understand that she and Myrna just spent hours in an interview room, and we have nothing to show for it. No, we have *less* than we had before. We've lost time, credibility, and our witness is playing us for idiots. Myrna Simone doesn't need coddling. She needs to be motivated. Let me have her for a couple hours, and I'll find out what she's hiding."

Russ hesitated, catching a whiff of something he recognized. It was a light floral fragrance . . . lilies of the valley? Something like that. *Shit.*

He turned into the laser sights of Jennifer Nash. She was standing in Kate's doorway, and Russ had no idea how long she'd been there, but it was long enough. He liked her navy jacket and capris ensemble. He didn't like the expression on her face. She was flushed with annoyance, anger, agitation. One of those *A* words. It wasn't always easy to tell when the female of the species was involved, but he'd learned from experience if you got it wrong, they usually got more agitated.

"You need to stop sneaking up behind people," Russ told her.

Jennifer's voice was as taut as her body. "You need to stop talking about people *behind* their backs."

Kate came out of her recliner state and beckoned Jennifer into the room. "Come on in. We were just discussing the Violator case, and we need your input."

Jennifer created quite a breeze as she marched past Russ to Kate's desk.

"I hope you don't believe that nothing was accomplished in my interview with Myrna," she told Kate. "You can't always get the sketch you want in one session. Trust has to be established and a bond formed with the witness. That's what I was doing with Myrna, regardless of what Russ might think."

Russ started to speak, and Jennifer gave him a look.

He shrugged his shoulders as if to say, *Okay, okay.*

Kate took on a soothing tone. "I know you're doing your best, Jennifer, but the public pressure is mounting, and we have to give them something."

"That's not a problem," Jennifer assured her, "but I'll need another session with her, possibly two. Give me that much time, and I'll have your sketch."

Russ had been quiet for as long as he could. "We don't have that kind of time, nor should we bank on getting a sketch out of Myrna Simone. She's hiding something. *Let me find out what it is.*"

Jennifer's dark hair danced as her head swung around. Not her body, which was still as rigid as a flagpole, just her head. "Myrna may be hiding something," she informed Russ, "but the subconscious doesn't lie. Once I get past the blocks, she'll tell me what she saw that night. I'll have his face, feature for feature, and the entire country will mobilize to help us find him, just like they did with the Polly Klaus case."

"Too bad we don't happen to have a missing child," Russ intoned. As near as he could figure it, Jennifer had probably mentioned the famous child abduction case because it was broken by a sketch done by Jeanne Boylan, a forensic artist who'd devised the interview method that had inspired Jennifer's. Boylan's sketches had been responsible for the apprehension of some of the biggest names in modern criminal history. She'd also written a book and gone on to the fame and fortune that Jennifer seemed to covet.

"It's worth every minute of the wait," Jennifer was telling Kate, "even with a traumatized witness."

Russ had been hanging back, giving Jennifer her due. Now he approached Kate's desk. "Myrna isn't a traumatized witness. She's a dangerous witness. Her testimony could do us more harm than good."

"She doesn't have to testify. Once the Violator's face is on TV screens across the country, our odds go up exponentially."

Russ wasn't sure about her math, but he could argue that later. "Only if we've got the right picture and if someone sees him. We'd have to be damn lucky to have both of those things happen before he strikes again."

"I don't need luck," Jennifer countered, "I need *you* to back off. Either you don't believe anyone else is competent to break this case, or you're afraid someone else will. Giving me a couple more sessions with Myrna isn't the real problem, is it, Sadler?"

"That's ridiculous." Russ's voice took on a warning edge, but nothing seemed to faze Jennifer.

"Then back down gracefully," she insisted, "and if you really want to be useful, go back out there and find some more witnesses. Sharon lived in a busy downtown neighborhood. I can't believe there weren't any other people on the street."

"Well, start believing. We've been over that area multiple times."

"When? The night it happened? I've read the police reports from cover to cover, and the Capitol Hill area *hasn't* been canvassed for witnesses since the day after Sharon was abducted. Someone should be out there every night."

"Maybe you'd like to coordinate the search detail while you're at it? And find me the manpower to do it?"

The questions came out under Russ's breath, but Jennifer's expression said hell, yes, she could do a better job of it than he was doing.

Kate was moving now. She rushed around

both of them to shut the door, and as she did it, Russ realized they were drawing a crowd. Several people were hovering by the bulletin board in the hallway, pretending to read various announcements.

"Enough of this," Kate huffed as she returned to her desk. She was a big woman, but she got around very efficiently for her size. And she was clearly annoyed, angry, agitated. One of those *A* words.

She leaned precariously over the top of her desk, supported only by her knuckles, which were digging into a calendar blotter. "An honest difference of opinion is fine," she said, "but you two are starting to squabble like kids, and I won't have that."

Only the chief's breathing could be heard for the next few seconds, and Russ realized she was deciding their fate. Next to him, Jennifer had curled her fingers into her palms, not quite fists, but at the ready.

"Jennifer, you want two more sessions with Myrna? I'll give you one, and that's all you get. If you don't have a sketch ready by quitting time tomorrow, we'll go forward with the sketch our own artist made."

Russ glanced at Jennifer's hands, pleased to see that they were now fists. She wasn't happy, and that made it easier, because he wasn't, either.

"Russ, I want you to do everything you can to cooperate with Jennifer. Is that clear? Give her whatever information and support she needs to get the job done. And her point about canvassing Sharon's neighborhood for other witnesses is a good one. Put someone on that."

Jennifer raised her hand, and Russ's instant impression was that she looked like a high school kid going for brownie points from the teacher. She looked a little smug, too. Clearly she thought she'd bested him. He hated that.

"I'd like to accompany whoever Detective Sadler assigns to the search detail," Jennifer said. "I think it would help me enormously to see the neighborhood at night and to get a feel for what happened there and what Myrna might have experienced."

"No way," Russ said softly. "No fucking way."

Kate pursed her lips, torn. While she considered Jennifer's request, Russ considered how heavy her desk was and how much force it would take to upend it. That was how angry, agitated, and annoyed *he* was.

"I'm sorry." Kate was firm as she addressed herself to Jennifer. "I agree with Russ. That area can be unpredictable, and we have a serial assailant at large. The department can't be responsible for your safety. Besides, it's not what you're trained for, and you could actually impede the search."

Jennifer nodded, but Russ could hear her disappointed sigh, and he didn't take quite as much satisfaction in his victory as he expected to.

Kate was smiling now, apparently pleased she'd pulled things together, or maybe she was just role-modeling the kind of camaraderie and esprit de corps she expected from them. Russ was used to that kind of rallying-the-troops behavior, and he pointedly ignored it. Hopefully, Jennifer would, too, because he wasn't about to shake hands and be friends at the moment.

"Jennifer, go forth and sketch," Kate said. "Were you able to schedule an interview with Myrna this morning?"

"I'm due there now," Jennifer said.

Her tone was pleasant enough, but she gave Russ a haughty look as she brushed past him and disappeared out the door. He couldn't tell if it was a warning or if she was being a good sport and making an effort to acknowledge him. But he could feel the cool breeze she created. And he could smell the perfume. It *was* lilies of the valley. How could he have forgotten that?

Chapter 11

"Sick? She *can't* be sick. Can you put her on the phone?"

"Sorry, Ms. Nash. Myrna says the light stabs her eyes, and she's afraid it's going to blind her. She won't come out of her room. Personally, I think it's a migraine."

Jennifer stared out the conference room window, fighting the desperate feeling in her gut. She had the shelter director on the phone, and she was trying to find out what had happened to her witness. Myrna was a no-show again. Jennifer hated to think that Russ was right, but it was becoming difficult to defend the woman. She must have been a celebrity in another life. It was that difficult to get an interview with her.

Jennifer tapped the windowpane, summoning help from the brilliant blue sky outside. Maybe there was a patron saint for sketch artists.

"You have my cell phone number," she told the director. "Would you call me if she changes her mind? It's crucial that I see her as soon as possible. Please —"

"I will, Ms. Nash. Maybe she'll be better tomorrow."

"I could come there and talk to her," Jennifer suggested — and not for the first time. It had been her theme song throughout the conversation. She'd been given until tomorrow at quitting time to complete a sketch, and the morning was already gone. Now it seemed she was going to lose the entire day. This woman was her only connection to Myrna. She didn't want to let her go.

"Good-bye, Ms. Nash."

"Call me," Jennifer implored as the director hung up.

Jennifer snapped the mouth of her cell phone shut. The question of what to do next loomed. She debated going to Kate with the news and asking for more time, but she didn't want Russ to know what had happened. He would somehow use this latest disaster to his advantage, she was sure. The sound of her tapping fingers pushed her to make a decision. She would not tell either of them immediately. She would wait to see if she got a call from Myrna.

Right. Julia Roberts would be calling her before that happened.

Jennifer blew some cool air across her face. The air conditioner was spluttering as always, and she was reduced to being her own fan. She'd worn the lightest outfit she had with her, but even that was too warm. Naked would have been too warm.

Now she had to figure out how to leave

the building without being seen. She would have her cell phone with her, and the temptation to go out and do a little investigating on her own was strong. It would be in direct violation of Kate's orders, but Jennifer had the rest of the afternoon and evening ahead of her, and given the situation, it seemed criminal to waste the time.

She'd never been one to flagrantly break rules. Her law enforcement background had taught her a healthy respect, and she'd seen firsthand the consequences of breaking them. But there were times when rules became arbitrary. Their purpose was to provide structure and security, not to bind you like a straitjacket.

She had a small window of opportunity that would soon be closed, and if she did nothing, she would have to live with the knowledge that she hadn't even tried. On the other hand, there was a component of risk to what she had in mind. Even if she found the witness she was looking for, she would be putting her relationship with Kate and the department on the line.

She gazed out the window at the bright sky above and the busy street below, where reporters and all manner of strange predators might be lying in wait. Apparently, no patron saint was coming to her rescue today. There were two vans from competing television stations parked on the street. Lately they seemed to be there around the clock. But Jennifer was far more concerned about the other kind of predator, specifically the one whose image was locked up in a woman's mind. And possibly in her own. If anything drove her to act, it would be that.

Delayed gratification. He didn't let himself turn on the light immediately. He knew what was coming, and he wanted to prolong the anticipation. It was both pleasurable and unbearable, like a rubber band being stretched until it snapped. His eyes were open, but the room was so dark they could have been closed. He liked it this way. The darkness was his home. It fed, protected, and sheltered him.

When he had delayed all he could, he flipped a series of switches on the wall panel to his left. Sharp beams of light from an overhead track system illuminated the unframed photos tacked to the walls.

They were black-and-white snapshots of crime victims. Stark and ugly to most eyes. Beautiful to his. The pale, denuded bodies represented his best work, but it was their faces that thrilled his soul. Their shiny skulls were as devoid of hair as newly cast porcelain. Even their eyebrows and nose hair had been removed. And their eyelashes. Singed right off the lids with chemicals. The four women would never bat those eyelashes again.

They barely looked like women now, and he wondered if they were grateful for what he'd done. He'd gone to enormous efforts to make them see the error of their ways. If not for him, they would have ended up like trailer trash. Cheap, flashy whores who lured with their painted faces and long, red hair. Bargained with their flesh.

But he had educated them and transformed them into this — his gallery of good little girls all in a row, minding their manners, watching their step, properly humbled, properly subdued. They were his projects, and he had given the best that he had.

He wondered if they knew.

Each of the victims had her own section of the wall, her own personal montage of anatomical shots and crime scene photos. But when he felt the need to be alone with them, like now, he preferred the poster-size blowups of their faces.

Victim One wasn't looking at the camera. She'd averted her eyes the way he'd taught her. Obedience, humility, and respect were the lessons she'd needed to learn, and he doubted she would soon forget them.

I remember you well, he thought, gazing at her lovely, downcast face. *Those body piercings, that lime-green fingernail polish, and that short red-striped top. You dressed like that to get attention, didn't you? Well, you certainly got my attention. Happy now?*

And you. His gaze drifted to the second woman, whose features were drawn and defeated. *Church three times a week and a silver crucifix dangling around your neck for show. You had me fooled for a minute with your plain-Jane clothes and your innocent ways. I wasn't going to give you a second glance, until you gave me one. A sly look, a coy smile. You actually fluttered your lashes, and I knew instantly that you weren't just a Jezebel, you were a hypocrite as well. Pretending to be pure, when what you really wanted was boys panting after you like dogs after a bitch in heat.*

The woman to his right was staring back at him with blank, unfocused eyes. But that wasn't the way she'd looked the night he'd first seen her.

Remember? You were sitting on a bar stool, wearing a short skirt, your legs crossed, teasing me. Teasing every poor sucker there. Flipping your curly red hair, smiling, and then looking away flirtatiously. If ever a brazen temptress lived, she was you. I had to teach you a lesson. And I did, too.

I humbled every one of you. But are you grateful? Any of you? Do you realize the time it took to plan your abductions, the mental effort?

I couldn't let you know I was there, although women like you are rarely aware of the dangerous men surrounding you. You get into your cars and buzz around town, go shopping and visiting friends, never realizing Fate may very well be only a few yards behind you.

I remember the preparations I made before entering your homes. One precisely torn strip of duct tape to be used over your mouth. A longer strip to quickly bind your wrists. That was done before I entered so the noise of the fabric ripping wouldn't awaken you. The tape was stuck to the front of my leather jacket for easy access, and there was an extra roll in the back pocket of my jeans. I also had a blindfold for your eyes, and the helmet that would conceal it was the one I wore. There was another one waiting for me right outside your door.

When the clock struck midnight, I entered.

One tape was pressed to your lips and the second wrapped around your wrists to immobilize you. If you fought me, I bound your ankles, too, but only temporarily. I took my time with the blindfold. My identity was concealed by the helmet, but the image you saw through the black Plexiglas shield must have looked terrifyingly distorted.

That was the point.

We took that hushed walk to my bike, you in front, blinded and guided by my hands, and I felt you shivering. I heard you cry. Music. My music.

Once I had you on the bike, I brought your bound hands over my head and looped them around my waist. The ignition threw hot sparks. The engine rolled over, fouling the air with gasoline fumes, and we were gone.

Into the night. Into the darkness. My night. My darkness.

And into my lair.

"Keep your eyes closed or I'll kill you. Do you understand?"

I removed the helmet and blindfold, then ripped off the tape. I ordered you to strip, but I could hardly look at your pale, ugly body as you did. This was not the pleasure for me. This was torture, and that was why you had to be tortured. Forced into the corner, forced to humiliate yourself the way you humiliated me.

"Turn away so I don't have to look at you! Get down on your knees in the corner and pray that I don't destroy you right here and now, because that's what you deserve. I'm here to save you, slut. To save you from yourself and to rid the world of your sickness. But before you can be made pure, the impurities must be exposed. You can't be allowed to hide."

Touch yourself, seduce yourself, seduce me. Try. Try, bitch.

This is the part that sickens me the most. Your pathetic attempts to be alluring to me. You can't even do that right. But soon it will be over, and we will both be at peace. I will send you back into the world, shorn and harmless, a lesson to any woman with the intelligence to acknowledge it. Cheapen yourself, and it will cost you. Sell yourself, and you will pay the price.

I recall the soft cry you made when I turned on the electric shears and began cutting the hair from your head. It fell like crimson rain all around you, pooling on the floor in red puddles. Then came the spray or the gel, whichever I was in the mood for, and finally the warm water, shaving cream, and straight razor. Every whorish inch of your body slowly and carefully denuded of hair. Every inch.

By then you were quite insane with fear, weren't you?

I imagine you were, but it no longer mattered to me how you felt. Once I had removed all signs of your power, I had no further need of you.

No further need. A calming wave enveloped him as he let himself imagine that state of mind. Having no need of them. That was his quest. Their subjugation and his freedom. His perfect calm. This room took him there for moments at a time. The abductions took him there for hours, days. But it was all gone too quickly. It slipped away from him too quickly.

Why? Why did nothing work to end this craziness he felt? Why couldn't he stop them for good? God, how he hated the bitches. Why wouldn't they let him rest?

A pulsing red light burst painfully in his head, and he had to tear his gaze from the wall. His breathing had become ragged, and sweat filmed his temples but it did nothing to cool him. Slowly, he willed his fingers to relax. Willed his mind to relax. His nails had dug red slashes in the palms of his hands.

There was just one section of the wall left, and it was time to deal with that now — the stark evidence of his own failure.

There was no victory in looking at Sharon Myer's lifeless body. She'd forced him to kill her, and in that sense, she had won. It had not made him feel powerful to end her life. It had weakened him. She wouldn't be humbled. She'd struggled after he got her to the trailer, and he'd had to subdue her with his bare, ungloved hands. She'd contaminated him. But that wasn't why he'd killed her. She had died because she opened her eyes and looked at him without fear.

And now the time had come. He would find another lost soul to save, and then he could take Sharon off his wall and throw her away, replace her with an image that would bring him peace forever. And there was only one woman who could do that.

Soft red hair, the color of an autumn sunset. Delicate white skin with a scattering of freckles. Sleek, elegant neck. Morally degraded. Wanton and lustful. Sexual and provocative.

Yes, he thought. *Only one.*

Gratification delayed, but not too long.

Blame it on Sharon.

The street was dark, and the woman was confused about where she was. Not lost, exactly. Just confused. She had a sense of purpose but no real sense of direction. The area was familiar to her, though. She'd been here before; perhaps she had even lived somewhere nearby and was trying to find her way back home. If she had a home. It wasn't clear. Nothing was clear except the vague feeling of urgency that spurred her to walk faster and to search the shadows.

She could hear water dripping. It sounded like a bathroom tap or a leaky shower. A television blared from an open window, and somewhere nearby cats were circling each other with howls of outrage.

Odd that she wasn't afraid when there was so much to be afraid of.

She was looking for something out here in the dark. In the same way that children peek under the bed for monsters, she was looking. But everyone knew that monsters weren't there until you turned your back, and then it was too late. Your only warning was an icy draft.

The glare of a streetlight enclosed her. As she moved out of its halo, she saw someone just ahead. It was hard to tell at first if the man was coming toward her or walking away. He was as tall as a tree and dressed in glittering black leather. A motorcycle helmet hid his identity.

The darkness swallowed him, and she realized that he was walking away.

"Wait," she called after him. She was afraid to raise her voice above a whisper. Something was desperately wrong. It was too quiet. The cats had stopped howling, and the TV had gone still.

She hurried to catch up with him, praying he hadn't disappeared. It was imperative that she find him, and yet terribly dangerous. It was dark everywhere. Night everywhere. All her eyes could see was blackness.

All her eyes could see was him.

He turned, and a tiny scream whistled in her ears. Her own startled reflection bounced from his opaque visor. The helmet looked like one great dark all-seeing eye.

"Who are you?" she asked.

His voice came from somewhere else. It rumbled like big engines, like horses and thunder. "I'm here to teach you a lesson."

She wasn't supposed to know his identity, not now, not ever. That would be breaking the rules, and the consequences would be swift and terrible. This was Judgment Day. It was certain death, but she was Eve in the garden, and it was impossible to live in ignorance, even if the truth could destroy you.

She reached up and opened his visor. The dark visage she revealed made her stumble backward. "You?" she whispered.

You . . . you . . . you . . . you . . .

It echoed in her head like the thunder of his voice.

She dropped to her knees in shock.

Jennifer couldn't breathe. She sprang up in bed, covered in sweat and shivering. The air in the room felt wet and hot. She could hardly draw it into her lungs, and yet she was racked with cold.

She had recognized him. She'd seen the killer's face and recognized him on sight. It was a dream, but her subconscious was trying to tell her that he was someone she knew. She pulled the covers around her, shivering painfully, and a sense of frustration swept her. That knowledge wasn't of any use to her now. The screen had gone blank. The image was gone.

His face was gone.

She closed her eyes and willed it back. She had to get it back.

Images flashed through her mind, but none of them brought any reaction, and how would she know the right one if she saw it? The shock of seeing him had brought her back to consciousness so abruptly that her memory had been wiped out.

Trauma, she realized. She was dealing with the same thing that her witnesses struggled with when they tried to remember what their mind was determined to protect them from. The mind could not be trusted. Jennifer had learned that incontrovertible fact in her years of working with victims. It altered events in order to protect its host. Sometimes it lied outright. It kept you in the dark when you were frightened, and the more you struggled, the worse it got. The psyche acted like an eraser wiping chalk from a blackboard.

And that's where she was now. There was nothing but blackness.

It was the same kind of streetlight she'd seen in her dream. Jennifer pulled over and parked her rental car under the glowing beacon, wondering if she had the nerve to go through with her plan. She'd already driven around the neighborhood with the intention of scoping it out. From the police reports she knew what territory had been canvassed and what evidence had been collected. Someone had even drawn a map of the area, but with every corner Jennifer turned, she had to remind herself that she was there in violation of orders.

She was virtually certain the street she'd seen in the dream was here in the neighborhood where Sharon lived. But she wasn't doing this for the investigation. She had already assured herself of that. It wasn't even for Sharon. She was doing it to satisfy her own curiosity. She had to know if being here would bring it back — his face — and if she happened to come across some pertinent information while she was having a look around, all the better.

She slipped a denim jacket on over her tank top and let herself out of the car. She had on jeans and sneakers because those were the only casual clothes she'd brought, and her hair was in a ponytail because it was close to eighty degrees in the city at midnight, and she didn't want to stick out like a sore thumb. She'd thought the outfit might help her blend, but in a scruffy neighborhood like this, it probably made her look like Sally Sociology on a field trip.

Scruffy was right, she thought, checking out her surroundings.

She was a couple blocks south and east of Sharon's apartment complex in an area dotted with all-night convenience stores, restaurants, bars, and other such places. There was a twenty-four-hour tattoo parlor just up the street from Jennifer where a small pack of guys in baggy pants, tight shirts, and knit caps were engaged in some clandestine activity that looked like it might be a street game. She hoped so.

Jennifer wandered past them and into a convenience store, where she bought some tire treads, red this time. When she came back out, the guys were kneeling in a circle, and they appeared to be throwing dice. Jennifer didn't recognize the game. She barely recognized the language they were speaking.

"Eyeballs!" one of them crowed as a pair of dice hit the wall and rolled back onto the sidewalk.

"Aiiiyiiyiiyiiyiiballs," somebody whooped. "Throw me dem bones, Homey. Hard Six! We talkin' Viagra!"

Either they hadn't noticed Jennifer or it wasn't the cool thing to do.

She bit off a chunk of licorice. "Hey," she barked, giving her best imitation of a street-wise chick, "I'm looking for my old man. He wears black leather and a motorcycle helmet. Seen anybody like that around here?"

One of the guys glanced up at her, his gold teeth twinkling. "Why ain't he home witchooo, babeee? Thas where m'ass ud be."

"Lotta guys look like that," another growled. He thrust out his arm and stabbed his finger in a northerly direction. "There's a biker hangout over on Hudson. Go check it out, bitch, and leave the *men* alone."

Jennifer thought that was the best idea she'd heard. She was on her way up the street when one of them bellowed at her. "Yo, mama, where you be gone with dat lickrich?"

Jennifer pulled out a handful of treads and tossed them into the circle, leaving the *men* to scramble like kids.

Two streets over, she spotted Big Dog, the biker place. It had been covered in the original report, but Jennifer wanted to check it out for herself. It actually looked like a reasonably nice restaurant with a patio for outdoor dining and a combined bar and grill inside. The motorcycles lined up at the curb were mostly expensive makes with lots of chrome and extras, but the crowd inside looked authentically rough and ready.

Rock music boomed from the open doors, forcing people to shout over it to be heard. Jennifer eased her way through the throng in the entry and headed for the bar, which was end-to-end men. Big men. Big, hairy men with mean eyes and small, sharp teeth, who could with one look make the dice players wet their baggy pants.

Jennifer wished she hadn't worn her hair in a ponytail. The only other woman she could see was the bartender, and she was sporting a Mohawk that made her look freakier than some of the guys.

Jennifer ordered a beer. "Whatever you've got on tap," she said.

She did not say please, and she did not ask for lite, although both words burned in her throat. The bartender was probably going to be Jennifer's best source of information, but whatever she did, it needed to be quick. She was already drawing unwanted attention. A big, shaggy mastadon of a biker at the end of the bar had just pointed her out to his friends.

A mug of beer slid Jennifer's way. She thanked the bartender and pointedly laid out two tens, as if to say, *More where that came from,* and then she eased around to check out the room. There was plenty of black leather, but none of it on anyone who looked familiar. There were plenty of dark eyes, too, but nobody with just one.

Jennifer was careful to avoid eye contact as she scanned the packed room. To really check the place out, she would have to get up and move through the crowd, but that was too dangerous. When the bartender came by again, Jennifer asked if she'd seen anyone who matched Myrna's description, a biker with one eye that might have been permanently dilated. "Dark," Jennifer said, using Myrna's exact words, "like an eclipse of the moon."

The bartender stared at her as if she were measuring her for a padded cell, which Jennifer took as a sign that it was time to think about leaving. Her only potential ally had already turned on her. Another beer came sliding Jennifer's way. The biker at the end of the bar winked. Apparently he was measuring her for something other than a padded cell. Maybe his lap. She slipped off the stool and hoped no one would mind that she didn't say good-bye.

Perspiration cooled Jennifer's face as she crossed the street and headed down the block in the direction of her car. Her tank top stuck to a damp spot between her shoulder blades, but she kept her jacket on. Other than the canister of pepper spray she'd slipped in the pocket, it was the only protection she had.

The Capitol Hill area took on the surreal quality of her dream as she rushed through the night. A bead of sweat blurred the lights from the streetlamps, and noises assailed her. Finally her car came into sight. Was that it the next block down? She was straining to see when she heard someone behind her.

A quick glance over her shoulder confirmed that a man was following her. It was too dark to see him clearly, but he was big enough to be terrifying, and not even fifty feet away. Her first thought was that he was one of the bikers from the Big Dog, maybe even the one who'd sent her the beer. There wasn't enough light to make out the features of his face, but he had on jeans and a sleeveless T-shirt. And boots. She could hear the heels hit the pavement with each long stride.

She quickened her pace. And soon she was running. She'd had self-defense training. It seemed suicidal to whirl and confront him, but she would never outrun him. Her mind churned frantically. A honking horn drew her attention. She was half a block from the corner — an intersection with stoplights and traffic. She had to get there.

Jennifer never saw the other man, the one who was hidden in the doorway.

It all happened so fast that none of it seemed real. For several seconds she couldn't believe what was happening to her. That must have been why she didn't scream when a disembodied hand snaked out as she dashed by. It grasped her upper arm like a vise, catching strands of her ponytail in its punishing grip. Her head twisted around as she was pulled into the darkness.

Jennifer's mind was screaming, but she couldn't. *Help! Help me!*

A hand clamped her mouth and an arm came up against her stomach, forcing the breath out of her. She caught a glimpse of the man who'd been following her. He slinked past the doorway, no longer interested. She was someone else's prey.

Now Jennifer screamed. She screamed and struggled, lashing out with her elbows and kicking with her feet. She couldn't see who had grabbed her, but her terrified mind filled in the blanks. It could only be the monster who'd killed Sharon. And Jennifer was next. It was kill or be killed. She went for his groin, and he shouldered her up against the wall to block her.

Stunned, she gasped out his name. "S-Sadler?" It was hard to see his face, but she had felt the scar on his forearm.

He was breathing heavily from the struggle to keep her under control. That seemed to be all he could do, that and glare at her. "What the hell are you doing out here?"

"I had a dream." She didn't have the energy to lie, or the presence of mind.

"You had a *dream?*"

"Well, yes —" She got the rest of it out between breaths. "I know it sounds crazy, but I saw his face, and then I woke up."

"Whose face?"

"I think it was the Violator's. I was looking right at him. I knew who he was, but it's gone now. I thought coming here would jog my memory."

His expression made her wish she'd said anything else. "Okay, it wasn't *just* a dream. You and I both know the case is in desperate need of credible witnesses, and we both know this neighborhood. You can't tell me someone in Capitol Hill didn't see something happen. This area had to be canvassed again."

He released his hold on her, but he didn't let down his guard. He clearly thought she was losing it, and it wasn't the first time someone had looked at her that way tonight.

"Do you know how close you came to being assaulted? Raped? Murdered? Take your pick."

Jennifer could see that he was furious with her, but she wasn't all that happy with him, either. She didn't like being dragged into doorways by her hair.

"What are *you* doing here?" she asked.

"Following the chief's orders, which is exactly the opposite of what you're doing. Kate wanted the area searched again, and I don't have the manpower. It was either pull someone else off an assignment or do it myself."

"Did you find anything?" she asked.

"Yeah, *you.*" His glare lit the darkness. "I found you. There wasn't much time for anything else."

Jennifer realized something. He might be yelling at her, but he'd obviously gone out of his way to rescue her from someone he thought was going to hurt her. He could have left her to her fate, and his life would have been far less complicated. But he hadn't. One other thing became immediately apparent. One crucial thing. Russ Sadler was shaking.

She hadn't put up that big a fight. It couldn't be fatigue. "Is something wrong?"

"No. . . . What? I'm fine."

And elephants can fly, she thought. She couldn't stop herself from scrutinizing him. His hands, his breathing. It was all highly suspect — and suddenly it was imperative that she know what was wrong.

"I am," he insisted. *"Fine."*

"No, you're not. Look at you."

The hand she pointed to immediately became a fist. He was trying to hide it, but something had affected him. Could it be her? It was difficult even to let herself think that.

"I lost my partner this way, okay?" he told her, almost belligerently. "I'm not going to lose you, too."

Jennifer went as still as the stone wall behind her. She had no idea how to respond to that. She'd been scrutinizing his every breath, and now she couldn't bring herself to look at him. *He didn't want to lose her, too?* She was afraid to think what that meant, mostly because of what she wanted it to mean.

God, this was confusing. A few words from him, and she was in turmoil.

"Are *you* all right?"

"I'm fine." She started to insist that she was, but then she saw the irony in his expression. They were both in denial. And had been for so long.

"Russ, we have to talk," she pressed, "if only to clear the air so that we can work together. Don't you think?"

Apparently she'd given up on pacing her rejections.

"I think the air is fine. This is Seattle."

"Russ, please."

A pressured sigh said he was deeply reluctant. Still, he nodded. "Okay, let's get out of here."

She pointed out her car, and he actually took her hand as they began to walk toward it. It was probably just to help steady her, but for a moment, Jennifer wondered if she was still dreaming. Maybe she'd never awakened at all.

Chapter 12

Somehow they ended up in a waterfront bar that was dark and secluded — and should have been relaxing but wasn't. A guitarist strummed softly in the corner, his eyes closed as he murmured the lyrics to moody, melancholy ballads that seemed to expose everything that was locked up inside Jennifer.

She and Russ shared a small bistro table, which under other circumstances might have been romantic. But it was cramped, and their knees brushed continually, and no one said anything. *Can you spell awkward?* Jennifer thought. She glanced around, but there was nothing to count in a place like this except the number of times the guitarist repeated the word *lonely*.

Russ picked up his shot glass of Scotch and drained it. He let out a ragged sigh. "You scared the holy hell out of me," he declared softly.

Jennifer could hear the emotion that roughened his voice, and it made her the most sensitive of barometers, attuned to the slightest vibration. She wanted to tell him the fear was mutual. He had terrified her, lurking in that doorway, but that wasn't what he was talking about, she realized. Right now, he was afraid *of* her, not for her.

"You . . ." She nodded her head. "You scared me pretty good, too."

Her glass of wine sat untouched. If she'd picked it up at that moment, he would have seen what was happening inside her. She was emotional, too. Regret ran through her mind like a refrain, so poignant the guitarist should have been singing the words: *How could I have run out on this man? What was I thinking?*

"I guess . . ." He moved and bumped her knee. "Oh, sorry."

"It's okay. You guess what?"

"Nothing."

They both shifted at the same time, bumped again, and Jennifer froze in place. If she breathed, they touched, so she wouldn't breathe. Finally, in her search for something to say, she noticed the scar on his forearm. She'd grazed it in the doorway. That was how she'd known who he was.

"How did that happen?" She pointed to the *X* just above his wrist.

"I got in the way of a frightened kid's knife," he said, shrugging it off. "It looks worse than it actually was."

He fingered the empty shot glass. "I thought we were . . . Aren't we here to talk?"

He was prompting her. Now, there was a switch.

"Yes, of course, I —" Something seemed to be caught in her throat. "I've been wanting to tell you why . . . well, to explain and to apologize."

Tell him the truth, she thought. *He deserves that much, and so do you.*

"I *had* to leave, Russ. I know that now. I couldn't have done anything else at the time. I can't apologize for what I did, but I can apologize for the way I did it. That was cowardly, and I'm so sorry."

His nod was almost expressionless. Jennifer doubted that anyone else would ever have noticed the tiny flinch in his facial muscles. Even her apologies seemed to inflict pain.

"Do you understand?" she asked.

This was impossible. She'd waited all this time for the chance to talk, and she couldn't get anything out. Her voice was a raspy mess.

"I wasn't running from you," she said. "I was running from me. There were things I had to figure out about myself that I hadn't allowed myself to see. It goes way back, family stuff that I won't burden you with . . ."

There was more, but this was all she could risk right now. He might hate her if she told him the rest of it, about her mother, her father.

She bowed her head. "There are times, like tonight, when I can hardly believe what I did to you, and I regret it, Russ. I *regret* leaving. Do you understand?"

Russ understood that she was distressed and that he was in big trouble. The impulse to take her in his arms was powerful. God, yes. He also understood that whenever he was with her he ended up gasping like a hooked fish. It hurt to breathe.

"Jennifer . . ."

He couldn't hold on to what he was going to say. When she looked up at him, their gazes connected, and something fatal happened. Maybe he shifted toward her, or possibly they reached out at the same time, because suddenly they were kissing. Their lips brushed with just the lightest of contact, a feather caress, but it was lethal. All of his walls came tumbling down.

She bent in, deepening the kiss. Their mouths melted.

Russ couldn't catch his breath. He ripped himself away dizzily. This time their eyes connected with bewilderment. Suddenly he was up out of the chair, moving around, searching the bar. This looked exactly like the place where he'd impulsively told her he loved her and wanted to spend his life with her. She'd been too stunned to answer, and quite honestly, he'd stunned himself, but he'd seen the look on her face, the answer in her eyes, and he'd known that this was exactly what he wanted. Her. Forever.

Was this the place? He had to know.

"What's wrong?" she asked.

"Have we been here before?"

Jennifer watched him turn in a circle, searching their surroundings, and finally she understood. He had this place confused with their restaurant, The Cove. She would never have suggested that place for tonight. It was too fraught with memories.

"Not here," she told him. "That was two years ago. Please, come back and sit down. Russ . . ."

He did finally, but his heart was still working too hard. "What are we doing here, Jennifer? What do you want?"

"I don't know, Russ. Stupid things, I guess. I thought we might talk it out, or maybe just talk a little. I thought we might even dance."

Dance? The guitarist was playing "*Fools Rush In*," an old Sinatra song that made Russ wish he could carry a tune. And this woman made him want to say and do things that only a blithering idiot would say and do. He didn't know whether to love or hate her for that. But he could not dance with her. That would not be safe.

"There was something silver poking from his back pocket," Myrna said. "I saw it when he was struggling with the woman."

Jennifer tried not to show her surprise. The witness's remark was totally unexpected, and in actual fact, a thunderbolt. She and Myrna had been talking about any number of things since they'd closeted themselves in the interview room earlier that morning. The Mariners' lousy season, the record-breaking humidity, and Myrna's heat rash were all topics of discussion. Jennifer hadn't even slipped in a question about the crime yet, but apparently that's what Myrna wanted to talk about now.

"Silver?" Jennifer proceeded cautiously. Tracking Myrna was like trying to keep your eye on a winged insect, and today she was a dragonfly. Her scarves were variations of navy and iridescent cobalt with golden threads woven through them. They weren't expensive accessories. They were the kind you picked up at the Dollar Store or the Goodwill, but she wore them well.

"It looked silver against all that black," Myrna was saying.

"Black leather?"

"Yes, and it was on the left-hand side," she announced.

"The silver object?"

Myrna nodded. Her lids drooped, fluttering as if she were coming out of a trance. It was impossible for Jennifer not to wonder how much of what she did was real and how much was for effect. Russ had insisted Myrna was playing her, and even though Jennifer didn't want to accept that possibility, there were signs.

She was almost certainly playing for the

camera. It was mounted high in the far corner of the room, as unobtrusively as possible, but Myrna was clearly aware of it, and she was well over the self-conscious phase. She'd taken to primping in the way that she smoothed her hair and adjusted her scarves, and she loved to announce things in a dramatic tone. It put everything she said into question, but this was something Jennifer had to follow up on.

"A silver object could be anything . . . a comb?" Jennifer suggested, hoping Myrna would correct her and reveal what it was. Myrna knew. Her true eye had seen it.

"No, not a comb." Myrna worked the silky fabric draped around her neck between her thumb and forefinger. The scarf sparkled, and her lids fluttered. "But it was in the left-hand pocket. I know that because he's left-handed, like me."

Where did that one come from? Jennifer scooted her chair closer to Myrna's. "How do you know he's left-handed?"

Myrna was silent, her lids fluttering. Her hands were frozen now, and she appeared not to hear Jennifer.

For the first time it occurred to Jennifer that her witness might know the man she saw. "Myrna, do you know him? Have you ever known him?"

Myrna gave what looked like a slight nod, but her eyes were still closed. The water cooler jug behind them made gurgling noises that sounded like a tidal wave in the quiet, and the air conditioner suddenly kicked in.

Jennifer prayed all the noise would not break the mood. She moved closer. "Is he someone in your life now?" A drug dealer, perhaps?

Myrna didn't respond in any way. She was utterly still, and Jennifer feared she'd lost her. She was trying not to sound urgent, but wasn't succeeding terribly well. Unable to let it go, she touched Myrna's arm. This was not the way Jennifer worked. She never pressured a witness, but it couldn't be helped.

"Can you tell me, Myrna? Do you know this man? Have you ever known him?"

"*Ever* known him?" Myrna echoed. She'd begun to nod again, and finally her eyes opened. But she did not have the dazed look of someone coming out of a trance. She looked fearful and evasive as she reached for the Styrofoam cup of tea that Jennifer had brewed for her.

Jennifer was immediately wary. She had to take into account the possibility that Myrna might not be telling her the truth.

In a soft, faraway voice, Myrna said, "Do you mean have I known him in another life?" She cupped the tea in both hands. "Yes, I think so. It's like that."

A screeching sound made Jennifer start. Apparently Myrna had run her thumbnail down the side of the Styrofoam. Perhaps it was an accident, but Jennifer's nerves were on edge. She came out of the chair and went to the window. There were at least ten cars stopped at the intersection below. Eleven, twelve, thirteen — Jennifer stopped counting abruptly and turned to her witness.

"Myrna, I want a straight answer. Do you *know* the man you saw?"

Jennifer's tone startled both of them. Myrna's scarf fell away, but her thumb and forefinger kept working as if the material were there. Her eyes were bright, first with alarm and then recognition. She shook her head.

"No, I don't know him!" Her voice rose until she was almost shouting. "I'd never seen him before that night."

"Then how did you know he was left-handed?"

A bewildered shrug. "Because the silver thing was in his left-hand pocket, I suppose."

"The silver thing? The comb?"

"No, it wasn't a comb. It was a . . . chain? I think it was a chain."

Jennifer believed her now. Fortunately, Jennifer's intuition seemed to be working again, and she would have bet any amount of money that Myrna was telling her the truth. What was more, Myrna had said something very significant — that she'd never seen the man before. That meant that she did see him that night — and clearly enough to know that she didn't know him. Jennifer had to explore that. But how?

Myrna's flashes of memory were as fascinating to Jennifer as they were frustrating. They might well prove helpful to the case, but they weren't what Jennifer needed now. She needed to talk about a killer's face, and she couldn't tell whether Myrna had been specifically avoiding going there, or if she'd already revealed everything she knew.

Avoiding, Jennifer told herself. Nearly all witnesses avoided to some extent. It was their only defense mechanism against the horror. Russ's theory that Myrna was hiding something was correct. But it wasn't a sinister plot to conceal evidence as he seemed to believe. It was self-protection. His negativity was throwing Jennifer off, fouling her instincts. She rarely ran into this kind of interference, but that was because she was brought in as a paid consultant. They didn't want her here, or at least Russ didn't.

Jennifer walked to the water cooler, aware of the camera and the two-way mirror. She should never have agreed to either of them. It was a weak moment, and she wished to God she could take it back. It was a violation of the client's and the interviewer's right to privacy, and worse, Jennifer's work was being watched, judged, and dismissed — by Russ.

Twenty-two slots in the drain beneath the

bottled water spigots. Maybe twenty-three. Jennifer was counting again.

She wanted to try something different, a technique called sandbox therapy. This was the only shot she would get, but she knew it would open her to more criticism, and if she didn't get results, it could damage her work in a larger way. Her credibility. They would never stop talking about how Jennifer Nash had blown the Violator case with her playground games. Screw them.

"Myrna, how do you feel about playing in the sand?"

"At the beach?"

"No, in a sandbox."

She considered the idea with a frown. "Has anybody peed in this sandbox?"

"No one, I guarantee it," Jennifer said, chuckling. "No one's ever *been* in this sandbox."

"Might as well then, as long as I can take off my shoes."

Myrna kicked off her Birkenstocks, and Jennifer went to get her tote. Her heart was pounding too hard, but Russ and his negativity be damned. Kate and her rules be damned. They couldn't fire her. She'd never been hired. They would have to ride her out of town on a rail, and let them try. This really was her only shot. Her time was up tonight, and it was unlikely she would get Myrna in for another session. Jennifer had been surprised — and grateful — to see her here this morning, bright and early, and showing no signs of the migraine she'd complained of yesterday.

Jennifer didn't understand the change in attitude, but she wasn't going to question it either.

Playing me, Jennifer thought indignantly. The woman was terrified. This interview room might be the only place she felt safe.

"Myrna, could I borrow one of your scarves?"

The other woman clutched her neck as if Jennifer had suggested she disrobe entirely. "I never take off my scarves. I don't feel safe without them."

"Just this once, Myrna, please? You'll see why in a minute."

Unsteadily, Myrna untied the scarf that hung around her neck and handed it to Jennifer, who went immediately to the video camera and wound the silk around the barrel of the camera in a way that covered the lens.

She turned back to Myrna and gave her a conspiratorial wink. Myrna grinned as if to say, *Let the games begin.*

Moments later, as Jennifer poured a small sack of white sand into a plastic tray with high sides, she felt a cold prickle of foreboding. It actually raised the hairs on her arm, and she glanced over her shoulder at the two-way mirror. No scarf was big enough to cover that. She would have to hope that no one was watching. But even if they were, it was a risk that had to be taken. She was convinced now that Myrna had the information she needed locked up in her memory stores. But more than that, Jennifer was coming to believe that she herself might know the killer, and that her mind was struggling to supply her with the face that Myrna couldn't quite describe.

Interesting that she'd looked right at the window. Russ had forgotten for a moment that she couldn't see him watching her. He'd resisted the impulse to flinch, but it had been there, deep in his gut. That was the impact she had on him. Still. Her and those big, beautifully alarmed eyes.

She had reason to be alarmed now. At least he could wring some small satisfaction from that. This was capital offense number two for Jennifer Nash. Russ could have had her banished in disgrace for what she'd done last night alone. She'd violated direct orders. And just now she'd disabled surveillance equipment.

What did they do to women as defiant as that?

He resisted the impulse to answer that question. He was always resisting impulses where she was concerned — except when he didn't.

Once again, her fate was in his hands, and life was giving him the perfect opportunity for a little payback. This was a chance to even an old score, and something in him still wanted badly to do that. Maybe he even needed to do it, just for the karmic balance, but this was the wrong way. It would have given him no satisfaction to damage her career.

He took a swallow of iced coffee. The weather was too hot for the black crank case oil he used to drink, and even though this stuff was practically water, he wasn't wasting a drop. As long as he'd fallen off the wagon, he might as well make the most of it. Hit the ground and roll for awhile.

No, he wasn't thinking about payback as he watched Jennifer work with Myrna Simone. The two of them were playing in the sand like a couple of kids, drawing boogeymen with their fingers. But as much as he might have wanted to bring her to her knees, even symbolically, he was thinking about courage under fire. Her courage. He was thinking about dedication and duty and defiance. And mostly he was thinking that she made him look like a piker when it came to those things.

How many people would have come after him the way she had? If he was supposed to be the lion — and people had called him much worse — then she had repeatedly braved him in his den. *Fearlessly braved him*. Hell, he was the one who was frightened. One green-eyed woman had the incredible ability to make him quiver like a kid. All he'd been doing was trying to find some goddam way to defend himself. But everything that he had been calling emotional self-defense was beginning to feel like excuses to him now. She wasn't the coward; he was.

Russ turned away from the window. He'd seen enough to know that where he needed to be right now was back in his office or out in the field or anywhere other than here. They weren't finished, he and Jennifer Nash. They had more to say, more to do, and he couldn't run from it forever. He just wished he had her resilience.

It looked like wolverines had been mating on his desk.

Russ stood on the threshold of his office door, staring at the mess. Mile-high stacks of file folders had given way and crashed to the floor, scattering their contents. Wads of notebook paper and empty Doritos bags littered the area around the wastebasket.

He didn't even want to go in there.

He hoped the wolverines had enjoyed themselves. Somebody ought to be having a good time. As he passed his overflowing wastebasket, he emptied what was left of the watery coffee, crushed the cup, and let it fall.

No one would ever notice.

"This is no way to conduct an investigation, Sadler."

The indictment came out under his breath as he began to organize the chaos on his desk, most of which had landed on the floor. There were accordion foldouts of the results of his DMV search for the trailer and scribbled notes of his attempts to trace Sharon's whereabouts. Plus, there were the files from all his other open cases, most of which were being completely ignored. His productivity wasn't worth shit these days.

If he had a right to be angry at Jennifer Nash about anything, it was that, he decided, the way she distracted him. Now *there* was a reason to back her up against a wall and —

Another aborted impulse. What he should have been thinking about was wringing her skinny little neck, right? That's what he must have wanted to do, no matter how primitive the impulse. But instead he was caressing her throat, bending to kiss her. It was criminal how he wanted that woman. *Still.*

Whatever had pulled tight in the depths of Russ's stomach would not let go. He would go to his grave with that fist clutching at his insides. He exhaled a breath and let his mind go quiet, listening to the muted commotion that was the fifth floor, absorbing the familiar in an effort to block everything else out.

He could hear the harsh jangle of a fax

machine, the soft clicks of a computer keyboard, two women talking, a man's bark of laughter. The ever-present asthmatic air-conditioning system. But it was another sound that captured his attention as he stood there, legs braced against the floor, arms folded across his chest. It came from behind him. A sigh.

It took him a moment to figure that one out. And once he had, he wanted to sigh, too. In utter defeat. Another leaf had dropped from the ficus.

He turned to the plant, wondering if there was room in his wastebasket for it. *Get it over with now,* he told himself. *If you can't save something, let it go.*

But as he picked up the drooping, dried-out houseplant, he noticed something barely discernible in the midst of all the yellowing death and destruction. One tiny bright green bud. As green as her eyes. *Life,* he thought. *Hope*. The plant didn't know how to quit. Just like her.

How was he supposed to throw the damn thing out now?

Chapter 13

The tenth floor of the Public Safety Building was dark. Everyone had long ago gone home, but Jennifer couldn't make herself leave. Myrna had made her exit hours ago, scarves fluttering. The sketch was finished. It had been submitted to Kate, and it would probably be on this evening's news.

Jennifer's work was done. She could pack and go home, reclaim her life and her professional identity . . . presuming that she could get out of the chair.

Presuming she could do anything.

It wasn't him. She knew it and Myrna knew it. The face she'd sketched was not the Violator. There was a feeling that came over you when the features were right and the monster came alive before your eyes. For Jennifer it was a rush beyond any other intoxicant. It made her dizzy. She felt as if she'd connected with the assailant's soul, however dark it might be, and the witness was a part of that rush. All three — artist, assailant, and witness — were bonded in an instant of awareness and understanding. Fearful understanding. *This was him.*

But that had never happened with this sketch. Despite their promising start, Myrna had become confused and contradictory again before it was over. Jennifer didn't understand where her method had failed. She'd worked on hundreds of cases since she started developing and perfecting the technique, and this was the first time she'd been unable to establish a bond of trust. That had to be the reason. Even though Myrna had seen the man — Jennifer felt certain of that much — she'd become ambivalent when Jennifer showed her the sketch, as if she was no longer certain that what she'd seen and recounted to Jennifer was true.

It was bizarre. She didn't seem to recognize the face that she herself had described. And the session was doubly disappointing because Jennifer had hoped that working with Myrna might help her access the image in her own mind, the one that had vanished when she woke up from the dream.

Now she was beginning to question whether she'd seen anything. And how could she fault Myrna when she was struggling with the same kind of block? It was as if they were both afraid to identify the killer. Their minds refused to let them know who he was.

To make matters worse, Jennifer had been ready to toss the sketch when Myrna suddenly changed her mind.

"That's him," she insisted. "That is the man I saw."

Jennifer tried to talk her out of it, but Myrna couldn't be dissuaded, and finally Jennifer agreed to submit the sketch to Kate. Witnesses could be wrong, and often were, but when they positively identified an individual, whether in a sketch or in a lineup, that was the suspect until proven otherwise.

Besides, how could Jennifer say it wasn't? Was she going to argue that it wasn't the face she dreamed? The face she couldn't remember herself?

The air conditioner roared to life. Jennifer felt a cold blast of air and scrubbed her bare arms for warmth. Her wraparound silk jersey dress had a matching jacket that was hanging on the coat rack not ten feet away, but it seemed like ten miles. She hated to think that Myrna was hiding something and Jennifer couldn't see it because of her own struggle. What a tragedy if she were identifying too closely with the witness.

She might be too close to this case in every way. The victim was her friend and the lead detective was her ex-fiancé. It was impossible to separate the personal from the professional, and even without that, the crimes themselves were bewildering. She had no idea what leads Russ was following, but for all the complex questions the case raised, there was only one plaguing Jennifer at the moment, and it was simple. She wanted to know who the killer was.

A sudden shiver forced her out of the chair. Perfect air-conditioning system, she thought. It only worked at night.

The two-way mirror caught her attention as she was putting on her jacket. There wouldn't be anybody out there now, but the sight of it still made her uneasy. And moments later, as she left the building through the fourth-floor employees' exit, her uneasiness increased. There were motorcycles everywhere. The street was jammed with them. It appeared to be some kind of parade, though there were no floats or marching bands, and the bikers looked remarkably authentic. It could have been a casting call for a remake of *The Wild Bunch*.

A crowd had collected on the corner of Fourth and Madison. Jennifer was about to ask one of them when she saw a banner that read: The Love Ride, a Bikeathon for Muscular Dystrophy. A worthy cause, but it was also perfect cover for the Violator.

Not my problem, she thought.

Wahoo's across the way was jammed. There was a line of hungry people out the door and down the street. Normally, Jennifer would have been counting them by now. Fortunately, that was a fleeting notion tonight, and she had no taste for fish tacos anyway. Since it was impossible to cross the intersection with all the bikes, she headed down to the next block, hoping to bypass them. She wasn't quite sure where she was going. Her empty hotel room held no appeal, even with all the hang-ups on her voice mail for entertainment. On the other hand, maybe it was time to pack and go home.

Jennifer was wrong about there being no one else on the tenth floor. The cleaning crew was quietly going about their business, and she also had unseen company in the form of one Junior Gordon. He'd come up to do a little photocopying of a personal nature, noticed her alone in the interview room, and stopped out of curiosity.

Jennifer Nash did not appear to be in top form. In fact, she looked bad. Even the freckles on her nose seemed to have disappeared, washed out by the pale cast of her skin. She was also clutching herself as if cold, but Junior didn't find that too odd. It *was* cold. Maybe she ought to be grateful, considering the sweatbox of a summer they were having. He was.

The papers he carried rustled as he rolled them up for safety's sake. He hadn't expected to run into anyone from the department, which was why he'd come up at this hour, and he didn't want her, of all people, to see what he was carrying. If she didn't already think of him as a pervert, that would clinch it.

She shivered, looking as forlorn as he'd ever seen her. Obviously something was wrong, but Junior wasn't about to try to guess what it might be. Call him insensitive, but he found it hard to dredge up sympathy for a woman who had a lot more of everything than he did, including looks, national recognition, and probably money. She'd also chosen Russ over him, although that was no contest. They all did.

Junior stepped back as Jennifer rose and came to the coat rack by the window. She looked resigned, even sad, as she slipped on her jacket and picked up her bag. Maybe he did feel some sympathy. Something made him stand there as she pulled herself together and came out of the room. He didn't know what he was going to say or do if she turned his way, and his hands had begun to stick to the posters he was carrying. Fortunately, she was going the other direction, toward the elevators. She never saw him at all.

There was a photography section in the lab where Junior could have done anything from video stills to crime scene processing, but he wanted some privacy. The tenth floor had a copy room with a Kodak machine that made poster-size blowups, and Junior had a vital mission. He'd come to enlarge some porno comic book covers. He'd had the brilliant idea of papering the bathroom walls of his apartment so he wouldn't have to bother holding the magazine. But as he was keying in the instructions on the machine's panel, he noticed there were photographs already lying in the tray.

Junior sucked in a breath as he saw what they were. He'd taken several of the ghoulish pictures himself. They were shots of a bedroom and varying angles of a woman's shaved head and body. The woman was the first victim in the Violator case, the one who looked just like Jennifer. At least she did to Junior.

They had all looked like Jennifer to him.

He fished a rubber glove from the pocket of his jeans, tugged it on, and carefully took the blowups from the tray, wondering if he could lift any prints from them. Apparently someone else in the department was into posters of sick and disgusting crime scene violence. Wouldn't it be fun to find out who? Meanwhile, though, he needed to crank out some artwork of his own and get his bad self out of here. The night was young, and Junior Gordon had some plans.

He pulled the bike around the back of the coffee shop and left it in the alley, parked behind a Dumpster. There was less chance of the law finding it there, although he wasn't too concerned about that tonight. A charity bikeathon was being held this weekend, and the city was overrun with motorcycles. He was one of a very large, very noisy crowd. He made it a point to know things like that — and to stay one step ahead. It was his one inexorable rule of survival. The only way to evade them was to think the way they did — think with your gut instead of your head.

Danger had its own astringent scent. It was sharp, cleansing. *Piercing.* Animals could sense it on every level. They could hear it coming and feel its vibrations in their nerve endings. Gut instinct kept them alive — that and the cover of night. His one foray in the daylight had been reckless, the bravado of a victorious hunter. That wouldn't happen again. He worked better at night. And they didn't. They had to see him to shoot him, those blundering men with guns.

The back door of the coffee shop was open. He knew it would be on a hot night like this, and he hesitated on the threshold to get the lay of things.

She was at the counter, dutifully changing the condiments at each stool.

He watched as she emptied the contents of the salt shaker, filling it with fresh salt and adding some rice to absorb the moisture. Watched and felt his throat go hot. She was the one, he thought, pure and gentle, incapable of cruelty and deceit. He'd seen her do this before. He'd seen her do many things, and he'd known from the very first time.

His stomach felt tight and unsettled. He

was almost queasy. But it was all good, he told himself. All good because he wouldn't have to feel this way much longer. This one would go with him willingly. She would trust him because it was her nature. She knew nothing about the world of predator and prey, this pretty little coffee shop waitress with the long, shiny hair and the freckled nose and the tidal pool eyes. She was lonely and unfulfilled, waiting for Lady Luck to wink at her or better yet, a kiss from the prince.

The restaurant smelled of hamburger grease and grilled onions, along with the heady scent of strong black coffee. To his left as he entered was a row of eight or nine booths with stiff wooden backs, the kind that actually offered some privacy. Plank tables that had never seen a tablecloth separated the bench seats. To his right was the long counter with chrome stools, topped with dark green vinyl. The place wasn't crowded tonight, which suited his purposes.

He slid into a booth, his back to the door.

Normally, he didn't like sitting with his back to the door. Made him too vulnerable. But he'd noticed that when she wasn't busy with orders, she stationed herself at the end of the counter, presumably so she could keep an eye on things. So, if he wanted to continue to watch this lovely creature without being too noticeable — and he *did* want to continue to watch this lovely creature without being too noticeable — he'd just have to sit with his back to the door.

As if she had radar tuned to his frequency, she appeared from the kitchen, smiled directly at him, and even gave him a little wave. "Be right with you," she said in a voice that could have only been harmonized in heaven. He tried to swallow, but it felt like there was a rusty bottle cap lodged in his throat. She took an order pad from the corner of the counter and headed his way.

In his mind, she glided more than walked. When she smiled, she beamed. Her eyes sparkled like stardust. There was no part of her that he could not embellish with romantic modifiers. He was truly and madly enchanted by her, and he knew it.

"You're getting to be a regular regular around here," she said, smiling.

"Right," he managed to reply. His lips twisted into a grin that he prayed looked normal and friendly.

"What'll you have tonight? The usual?"

His usual was a cup of black coffee and a slice of whatever the pie was that day. He never ate the pie. But how would she know that was his order unless she was aware of him, too? He gave her a quick nod. "Yeah, sure."

She offered another smile, and he could feel something happening. Either the booth was getting hot or he was. It was so warm and steamy he wanted to peel off his leather jacket. God, she was too much. She didn't smile that way at everybody. This was different and she knew it, too. He wouldn't have been surprised if she could read his mind and knew his intentions. What amazed and pleased him most was her lack of fear.

This one wouldn't run, he thought. *This one would go willingly. Stay willingly.*

As she jotted his order on the pad, she glanced up and arched her eyebrows. Then she turned and was gone.

He exhaled long and hard. The thing to do now was to move slowly and easily. He wanted to whisk her out of here tonight and never bring her back. She deserved better than this dump. But maybe he would do things the socially accepted way: introduce himself and ask her out to a movie or dinner.

He was rehearsing his lines when she appeared from the kitchen.

"Smoke break, Karen?" she said to the other waitress.

"Sure," Karen replied, "take five."

He watched in confusion as she grabbed a pack of cigarettes and a cheap lighter from the back counter and started for the door that led out back. She hadn't brought him his order. She couldn't have forgotten. It was just moments ago they were talking.

The disappointment he felt was swift and

sharp. She might as well have cut him with a knife. She didn't give a shit. What had made him think she did? His own pathetic fantasies? He could feel anger flaring inside him, embers that if allowed, could ignite into something deadly.

But that wasn't going to happen because as she reached the door, she turned and threw him a glance that was so inviting it sent an icy tremor up his spine. He sat up straighter. Did she want him to follow her? He didn't know what else it could have meant.

She disappeared from his sight, and he struggled with indecision. Should he go out and see what this was about? Or should he play it safe and stay here until she returned? If she was waiting for him out back, and he didn't show up, she'd think him a coward. He couldn't have that.

He waited until the other waitress, Karen, was busy taking an order, and then he slipped out of the booth and made his way to the back door. He didn't want to be seen leaving. It would be his luck that she'd given up on him already and changed her mind. Women could change that quickly. They wanted you one minute and the next you didn't exist.

The alley was dark and filled with the stench of old garbage. A few overhead lights weakly illuminated cracked, buckling pavement. But it was still night, his battleground.

And there was still plenty of cover. His animal instincts were deeply aroused.

Up ahead, hidden within the darkest shadows, he heard a woman moan . . . or groan. Followed by a frantic whisper. "No, don't!"

He moved in the direction of her cries. She was in trouble. He couldn't see clearly, but he knew it was her calling out for help. As he crept toward the sounds, he pulled the knife from his boot and the blade zinged open.

He found them not five yards from the café's back door. She was bent forward over a pile of cardboard boxes, her blue uniform dress pushed up to her hips, her panties down to her slim ankles. A thin, muscular man stood behind her, his hands gripping her hips as he had his way with her.

A flood of pure rage propelled him. He ran full on into the man, knocking him off the woman. "Motherfucker," he said in a voice so quietly malevolent it frightened even him.

The man glared up from the pavement. "What's your problem?" He saw the knife, and his eyes narrowed. "Hey, put that away."

The woman looked dazed, as if she couldn't fathom what was going on. But when she saw the knife, her eyes widened in degrees until they rivaled the size of the tidal pools he'd imagined. "What's wrong with you?" she gasped. "That's my boyfriend. Get the hell out of here and leave us alone!"

His confusion vanished, replaced by the one question that had plagued him for most of his adult life. How could he have been this stupid? He should have learned the lessons of deceit and betrayal by now. The humiliation of being so wrong about her was bad enough. It felt as if he'd been violated, as if something essential were being ripped out of him again and again. Trust. Belief.

All of it. Illusions. Her, too.

He watched in disbelief and growing disgust as she kicked away her soiled panties, smoothed her dress, and rushed into the coffee shop with her back-alley lover.

He would never be able to detail the complexity of emotions he felt as the two of them vanished from his sight. But one thought linked itself to another and another, forming a chain that finally seared through the chaos. He wanted to go back inside and drag both of them out here into the howling night. Into the jungle. His jungle. They deserved to know what it was like to have their trust violated and their illusions so carelessly shattered. The only question in his mind was which one to use the knife on first. The man? Or the woman?

It was easily answered. The man. So the woman could watch and live through her own grisly death twice.

Chapter 14

The bartender told Jennifer that Sex on the Beach was good for fighting the blues, so she had two of them and ordered a third, determined to give the drink a fighting chance. It was hard to imagine anything except liquid Prozac lifting her mood tonight, but if she had the choice of sitting in a lonely bar or in a lonely hotel room, listening to ominous clicks on her voice mail, she would take the bar.

There'd been another hang-up waiting for her when she picked up her messages tonight, and for the first time, it had frightened more than annoyed her. The abrupt *cahh-lunk* was a sound as hollow as her stomach. She'd come up with a short list of who might be doing it, but none of her suspects seemed very probable.

The hotel operator had assured her it wasn't someone calling the wrong room. Callers were asked to give the last name of the occupant they wanted, as well as the room number, to avoid mistakes. Reporters had been known to call incessantly and hang up rather than leave a message because they didn't want to lose the element of surprise. It could always be random pranksters, of course, or someone at the office, trying to scare her off.

She could have lived with any one of those answers, but she had the feeling it *wasn't* any of those answers — or something she could live with.

The operator had apologized but said there was nothing they could do unless Jennifer was being harassed by a caller. If that happened, they would report it immediately to the authorities. Jennifer had felt plenty harassed, but she hadn't wanted to deal with the Seattle Police Department tonight. She'd just wanted to step away from it all for awhile.

That's how she'd ended up at Danny's Dock, nursing her wounds with mood-elevating drinks. She'd tried the hotel bar first, but between the bikers and businessmen, she'd felt like a corn-fed cow at auction. She'd come to Danny's because it was the last place she expected to see Russ after what had happened here the night before.

Another asinine assumption, as it turned out.

Bottled courage, Jennifer thought as she stared into the shallow depths of her drink. Sounded great in theory, but it didn't work. Even her confidence that she'd chosen the right place to drown her sorrows was fading. Her shoulder blades felt hot, as if some energy were being concentrated there. It was the same feeling you got when someone was watching you, but that had been happening so often lately, it was beginning to feel like a paranoid fantasy.

Nevertheless, she glanced over her shoulder at the entry.

No one there. See?

She told herself to ditch the drink and go. It wasn't solving any problems, and it was probably making her morose and self-pitying.

She didn't, of course. And a moment later, she turned the other way, to the windows overlooking the water.

And there he sat. Hair like a dark river. His gaze cast moodily downward as he stared at the empty chair across the table from him. Only the furrowed brow and the hints of asymmetry in the bridge of his nose kept him from the ranks of the classically handsome. He was even wearing his signature color, black. He was at the table where they'd lived out their past, present, and future, all in one night. Her first thought was that she had no idea what he was doing there. Her second was that she had a million of them.

He was there because he still loved her, and he wanted to apologize for how difficult and insensitive he'd been. He wanted her forgiveness. It was the only thing in life that mattered to him. He was sorry if he'd hurt her. She was the last person in the world he wanted to hurt, but the pain he felt had made him lash out. Yes, he was sorry. Inexpressibly. He would spend the rest of his life making it up to her, if only she could find it in her heart to forgive him. Nothing else in life could make him happy and complete but her. *"Jennifer, I love you. You are everything to me, my life —"*

"Jennifer —"

"What?"

A blink brought the voice into focus. It was the bartender. Jennifer didn't remember telling him her name, but if someone had asked her what planet she was on, she would have had to think. He jerked his thumb toward the windows. "Do you know that guy?" he asked.

Russ was up. He was coming across the room.

Jennifer was vaguely aware that he was carrying something, a piece of paper, and when he reached the bar, he presented it to her.

"This is all over the news," he said. "It doesn't even look like your work. What's the deal?"

Her sketch! The last thing in the world she wanted to see tonight. Her only thought had been to escape the dejection she felt for a few hours, and now she was being confronted with her two greatest failures: him and that drawing. She wasn't going to discuss the sketch with him under any circumstances, but once she'd collected herself, she did manage to ask a question.

"Is that why you came over, to show me this?"

He didn't answer, but his expression said, *What other reason would there be?*

Jennifer knocked back the rest of her drink like a pro and fished some tens from her purse. She had no idea how much Sex on the Beach cost, but here she was paying for it when most people got it for free. She left three bills on the counter and slid off the stool with a vengeance.

Think I disappeared two years ago? Watch this, she thought as she headed for the door. *I really am gone this time.*

He caught up with her just as she reached her car and was trying to find her keys. It was dark, and worse, she was dizzy. The three drinks had decided to hit her all at once. *Now.*

"I thought it was a mistake, and they'd released the wrong sketch," Russ said. He seemed determined to explain, whether she wanted him to or not. "It doesn't have your strokes or your detail. You're better than that, Jennifer."

"I didn't know you were such a fan of my work," she snapped.

"We used to work *together.* I know what you can do."

She didn't want to believe that he was being intentionally cruel, but how could he not see that she was already down? There was no need to kick her. Silence swelled inside her until it felt like it would burst.

"I guess there was no mistake," he said.

She'd given up trying to get into the car, but she didn't turn around. "Yes, there *was* a mistake. That sketch was a mistake. It shouldn't have been released. I never got through to Myrna. I never got the face right."

"So, it's close. We don't need photo identity."

Now he was being condescending? "It's not close enough, and now, because I have some supposed credibility, they'll be looking for the wrong man."

"Jennifer —"

She spun too quickly. "You were right. I should never have come back to this city. All I did was slow up the investigation. A monkey with a composite catalog could have put together a better drawing than that."

"That's BS. Your worst sketch is better than —"

"Don't, Russ," she said. "Don't say anything else." He couldn't make her feel better. Nothing could. This was a deeply personal defeat, and she would have to work it out on her own terms.

Her silence swelled to encompass him, too. Somewhere in the darkness there was a soft crack and a splash. It could have been a distant gunshot and a body dropping into the water. Jennifer preferred to think it was a fish, slapping against the surface of the lake.

"What do you want to talk about?" he asked.

The moonlight silvering his dark hair made her think of surface ripples.

"I want to go, Russ. I need to go." It sounded as if she was pleading with somebody now, maybe herself.

"Go where?"

"Back to the hotel. And then, home. This was a mistake in every possible way. Everything I came here to do has backfired."

"Does that include talking to me?"

She wouldn't look at him. He knew it did.

"Because I thought you handled that pretty well," he said.

"Don't make jokes."

"I'm not."

"Then don't humor me!"

"I'm not doing that, either."

Jennifer's emotions were at the breaking point. The drinks must have lowered her inhibitions, but she wasn't in any shape to play games with him. There was no way to win, and she'd already lost so much. "I thought things would be different," she said.

"And because they're not, you're going to run again?"

"I'm not running. But what's the point in

staying if nothing's going to change? Apparently the whole concept of forgiveness is foreign to you. You can't even talk about it. Why would I stay here and torture myself . . . or you?"

"Who said you were torturing me?"

"I'm not?"

He seemed to be struggling with something, and Jennifer was reasonably certain it wasn't the question she'd just asked. It wasn't that hard. His arms were folded and his brow taut, but she got the distinct feeling that whatever he was going to do, it was not going to be classic Russ Sadler.

After what seemed like an interminable space of time, he announced, "I'm not an easy man to like, much less to love. I know that, and I don't blame you for running. I would have run, too."

Nerves had compressed Jennifer's lips into a taut line. Now they were soft with surprise.

"I did plenty of things to frighten you and make your heart race," he admitted. "Maybe I even got a kick out of it. Nobody can gasp as sexy as you can. But I never wanted to hurt you, ever."

Russ had edged closer, probably not with the intent of backing her against the car, but that was what happened. He was doing it again, making her heart rip out of control.

"I didn't know I could feel this way about anyone," he said. "I didn't know it was in me."

Jennifer's voice dropped to a whisper. "Love scares the shit out of you, doesn't it?"

He nodded.

"Me, too," she admitted.

"I'm such a jackass," he said.

"Me, too." Jennifer found herself wanting to laugh, trying to laugh. But her eyes stung with tears, and the sound of it was all warm breathlessness and sweet despair.

"God, Russ," she whispered.

She was hopelessly woozy even before he touched her. The drinks, she told herself, but she knew that was only part of it.

He grasped her by the arms, as if to steady her, and his strength felt wonderful. His strength. His warmth. Gentle. Wonderful. Jennifer swayed, her head lolling back a little. There was a sense of things happening in slow motion, and she went with it. She could have managed on her own, but why, when this was so nice? And maybe she was expecting something to happen . . . something as electric as a meeting of gazes, followed by a space of smoldering silence, all of it leading to the moment that he bent over her to . . . what?

What was he doing? He seemed more interested in searching her features than anything else, but he *was* bending, and she did feel some electricity.

"Jennifer, how many of those drinks did you have?"

So much for smoldering. He was checking

her out the way a patrol officer would a DUI suspect. "Three," she informed him. "And it was your fault I finished the last one."

"That settles it," he said. "You're not driving."

She put up no argument, but moments later, as they were heading out of the parking lot in Russ's unmarked company car, she insisted that she could have driven herself just fine.

"If I had any doubts that you were under the influence, they're gone," he said. "Your judgment is as bad as your balance. And you smell like a distillery. Not that I mind that smell."

"Ever the charmer." She let out one of those little gasps he'd talked about. "Hey, you just took a wrong turn. Where are we going?"

"To the houseboat."

"The one where you live?"

"That one, yes."

His tone was beautifully dry, and Jennifer couldn't get herself past the sound of it for a moment. Apparently he thought she wasn't capable of driving or anything else, and it was his job to sober her up. Or . . . he was taking her to his place for some other reason. She smiled. Her Sex on the Beach–enhanced imagination could just run wild with that one.

"Oh," was all she said.

* * *

Jennifer couldn't have counted the steps if she'd wanted to. There were three short flights down to Russ's houseboat from his street-level garage, but she lost track at the first landing. *Was that five or six?*

She tried to look back and nearly took a tumble.

"Alley-oop," Russ said as he hooked an arm under her knees and lifted her into his arms. "Let's get you down in one piece."

She wasn't drunk, not even a little, but if he wanted to persist in thinking that, well, let him. She didn't have a problem with being carried down some stairs in the middle of the night and into a man's houseboat. Russ Sadler's houseboat.

Say what?

She *was* drunk. If she didn't have a problem, she ought to. Nothing about this made sense. Up until this moment, he'd dodged talking to her at every turn, unless it had something to do with the case. Her mere presence had made him uncomfortable. Why, suddenly, was he bringing her to his holy of holies, the houseboat? What could he want with her? Without too much effort, she could think of several things, each more shocking than the next. Sex? Revenge? Both? At once?

She didn't mention her concerns until they were inside and the lights were glowing in the cabin. The decor was mostly nautical with blue and gold accents, and the walls and built-ins were paneled in teak. They'd talked about how to decorate the boat when he bought it, and she'd suggested some softer tones, but he'd been determined that he wanted it to look like a boat, not a house. Still, he'd gone with the carriage lamps she picked out, and the window curtains were the lush blue velvetlike brocade she loved.

She was pleased and touched.

His home was beautiful, and she told him so from the cushy sectional couch where he'd left her. He'd already gone to the kitchen and was making some coffee. She was wildly curious about the rest of the house, but the boat didn't feel very steady, so she decided to stay put.

"Am I here for the tour?" she asked. This wasn't anything like the tour she'd imagined in her hotel room.

Russ looked up from the countertop, where he was measuring heaps of a jet-black drip grind into a snow-white filter. He wasn't leveling the scoop precisely, just dipping and dumping. That was Russ. Get the job done, and the details will take care of themselves. He could be infuriatingly precise, but only when it counted.

"You're here because I didn't think you should be left alone."

"I would have been fine. I can handle myself." *How many times had she said that?*

"Maybe, but I wanted to be sure you

didn't drink any more."

"You make it sound like I'm a lush. I rarely ever drink."

"I know." He lowered the lid on the coffeemaker, pressed the On button, and almost immediately the cabin was filled with the pungent aroma of brewing coffee. "That's the problem," he said. "I've never seen you in this mood, if that's the word for it."

"Mood? Am I a little down? Yes. Could things be going better? *Yes.*"

She shrugged as if to say, *What do you want from me?* His answering shrug told her that her point had been taken. End of lush discussion. Fortunately, he wasn't so far away that body language couldn't be read.

The kitchen was part of the great room that ran the entire length of the cabin, and a polished Corian countertop with a built-in range top and grill separated it from the dining and living areas in the otherwise open space. Brushed chrome appliances gleamed from the kitchen where Russ worked, and copper cookware dangled from a rack hanging over a freestanding chopping block.

Russ was getting a tray together, and she could smell food cooking, which meant he had another project going besides the coffee. She settled back into the pillows of the couch, thinking that all this attention was rather nice, even if she was a bit suspicious. The fact that she didn't know what to expect was classic Sadler, too. The man could surprise God.

Sleepiness was overtaking her, and her eyelids had begun to droop by the time Russ arrived with the tray. It was loaded with plates of eggs that were scrambled with ricotta cheese and mushrooms and chives. There were buttery stacks of golden sourdough toast, little silver pots of jam, and the largest thermos of coffee she'd ever seen.

His tastes were pretty refined for a tough guy. The first birthday of hers they'd celebrated together, he'd taken her on a picnic in a rowboat on the lake, and the wicker basket he'd brought had been packed with goodies. Lump caviar and champagne to start, followed by pocket sandwiches stuffed with smoked salmon, goat cheese, and fresh scallions. And for dessert, an old-fashioned chocolate layer cake, afire with candles. The picnic concept had been surprise enough. When she found out he'd selected and prepared most of the food, she'd been amazed.

"Have some coffee," he directed, pouring her a cup.

She refrained from saluting, although it was an effort. The food looked delicious, but her stomach wasn't ready for any of it, and the gentle roll of the boat didn't help. She bravely tried the toast, waited a minute for it to settle, and then finished off an entire slice. She was hungry. It had been a long time since she'd last eaten. Possibly breakfast.

"Not eating?" she asked as she tucked into the eggs. It didn't look as if he'd touched anything. He appeared to be watching her instead, and there was a tinge of sadness in his expression. Regret looked good on him, she thought. It pulled at his mouth and accentuated the way his eyes fell at the corners, like a suffering artist's or a puppy dog's. It exposed him.

"I was just thinking that this was how it should have been," he said.

Jennifer's food was forgotten. "With us?" Her voice had lost its strength. It was all she could do to sit up.

He nodded, and Jennifer's blood began to race. She told herself to play it cool, but she couldn't do it. "What do you mean?" she asked. "Tell me what you mean."

He reached for his tray of food, as if he were going to take it back to the kitchen. "Never mind," he said. "It was one of those weak moments."

"Russ, I don't want to never mind. I like those weak moments, especially when you're having them!"

"No big deal," was all he would say.

But to Jennifer it was a monumental deal. Desperately pent up, she said, "Why? Why can't we talk about us? There are some things I need to tell you, things I *have* to tell you. I'm not asking you to love me again —"

"Jennifer, hush, you're drunk."

"Well, thank God," she exclaimed. "If I wasn't, I might let you shut me up again, but I'm drunk, so I won't. I won't, Russ!"

"Not now, Jennifer." His laser-edged glare told her to back off. And before she could respond, he whisked up his tray and went back to the kitchen.

Winning through intimidation. More classic Sadler. He should put out an all-time best hits album. Jennifer set down her plate of food, fighting off dizziness as she rose from the couch and marched up behind him.

She gave him a good sharp tap on the shoulder. "Why not now?"

She could see him counting to ten, but he could count to ten thousand. She wasn't going anywhere. The time had come. This was why God had made drinks called Sex on the Beach.

Finally he turned, and to her shock, he fired off the only reason that could possibly have stopped her. "Because I don't feel emotionally safe with you," he said.

"Well . . . I guess I had that coming."

He wasn't finished. Those long-suffering eyes of his were ablaze with smoldering male pride and frustration. "You're going to explain why you left. You're going to tell me everything, right? I can't let you do that."

"Why not?"

"Because your explanation might make sense,

and if it did, I might have to forgive you."

"And you don't want to forgive me?"

"God no — and open myself to those feelings again?"

"Oh," she said softly, and with little if any condemnation, "the dreaded feelings."

"Yes, the *dreaded* feelings. The same ones that brought me back to life, and then made me wish I were dead."

After several moments of deliberation, she nodded, wondering if she should leave. This was an impasse beyond anything she could have imagined. He was back where she'd been when she picked up stakes and ran away. "I guess this means we're not going to talk. Ever?"

He stared directly into her eyes for one brief, electrifying second. "We'll talk when you're sober."

"Promise?"

"I promise. In fact, that's the reason I brought you here. If you still want to talk, we'll talk."

"In that case . . . maybe I'll stay . . . awhile."

The boat moved, or at least she thought it was the boat. She grabbed his arm to keep from toppling over. Quick to react, he scooped her up again and headed toward the stairway. "I'm taking you upstairs to bed, in case you're wondering."

"Yes, I was . . . wondering."

"It's the quickest way to get sober."

"Sex?"

"No! Sleep, although I like the way you think."

As he carried her up the narrow spiral stairway, she tucked her face into his blue denim shirt so he couldn't see her and smiled. This was the kind of stairway that she'd wanted. She'd argued that it could connect all the decks, yet look graceful and take up less space than the wooden steps he had in mind.

"You can have the master bedroom," he said. "I'll take the hammock out on the deck . . . in case you were wondering."

"Who, me, wondering?"

The lake's rhythmic ebb and flow quickly lulled Jennifer to sleep. But it didn't keep her there. She had no idea what time it was when she awoke, but the moon was high and as round as a Gypsy's crystal ball, and the frogs and crickets were in full song.

She threw off the covers and realized that she was fully clothed. No wonder she was perspiring. The wraparound dress she wore acted like insulation, holding in her body heat. She untied the belt, undid some snaps, and let the dress drop to the floor. By the time she had her panties off, she was left with only a champagne silk bra-slip, but at least she would be cool. Maybe she could find a robe around here somewhere, and if not, well . . . at least she would be cool.

There was a good-sized head in the bow area, where she washed her face and throat with cool water, rinsed her mouth, and finger-combed her hair. When she was done, she went on a search for other human life, following sprinklings of pale light to the French doors that led to the upper deck.

Russ was lying in a hammock, wide awake, and swaying with the waves that rocked the boat. His arms were folded behind his head, creating a remarkably powerful cascade of fluid muscle and long, relaxed limbs. The image was impaired only by the fact that he was wearing soft cotton workout trunks.

He looked as if he could have been floating in water the way the moonlight accentuated his chest, his biceps, and his abdomen. That was how gently the light and shadow flowed over him. But it was the contrast of gentleness and raw masculinity that made Jennifer stare.

"You're up?" he said.

"Yes," she said, "and that isn't all. I'm sober."

Chapter 15

How could I have run out on this man? What was I thinking?

Jennifer wondered if she would ask those questions to her dying day. Her remorse was sharp, but the answers hadn't changed. They were a part of her survival manual, the one her nervous system had written specifically for dealing with Russ Sadler.

She'd known he would hurt her when she first laid eyes on him. She didn't know the reason then, at least not the real one, but she had known it would happen — and she'd fallen in love with him immediately. That was why she'd had to run. He was either her destiny or a fatal attraction — and both had frightened her. It was also what had brought her back.

Her problems were rooted in childhood, and Russ was more a symbol than a cause, but she was still a trauma victim where he was concerned. The way some people were afraid of heights, she was afraid of Russ Sadler. He was her personal and private phobia, and it was time to deal with the fear. And with him. No matter how much he overwhelmed her, *like now.*

He didn't even have to speak. It was the way he looked in the flickering moonlight, gazing up at her as if she were the very thing he'd been lying there thinking about. All night long, thinking about her. Sleepless and intent upon the woman who lay warm in his bed. Sleepless and intent. On Jennifer Nash.

God, how she wished that were true. If she'd thought it could be done, she would have tried to gain entry into his mind the way she did a witness's. Breaking and entering, perhaps. But she would gladly have taken the consequences. And she might have been surprised at what she found there.

He had been thinking about her. All night he'd been thinking. Russ's imagination had run the gamut from the sweetly obscene to the pure and innocent. He'd thought about hot, sweaty sex in a hammock and about proposing to her on the back stairway of the Public Safety Building. He wanted Jennifer Nash in all those ways and as badly as he'd ever wanted anything. It was like nails being pounded into his palms. But as he saw her enter the doorway and hesitate, hovering there in her slip, his mind took an unexpected turn. She looked breakable, like a Christmas angel. Anything could do it, even a callous look. *He* could do it. God, so easily. She was as vulnerable to him as he was to her. Now, there was some power.

He didn't know what was going to happen

tonight. This could be another hit and run. And either one of them might be the driver. He did know they were two people terrified of each other, of what they needed from each other and of the pain they could cause each other. They knew because they'd already caused it. Indelible pain.

"Excuse me?" Her voice was softly inquiring. "I said I was sober."

"Congratulations."

"You *promised*."

"And *I* keep my promises."

She looked wounded, and it gave him a pang. But what was a little power, if you couldn't wield it. He told himself it would be the last time tonight.

"So let's talk," he said.

She moved closer to the hammock. "Should I join you?"

He didn't answer immediately, and she rushed to assure him that she only meant it would be easier to talk if they weren't so far apart. She could sit on the floor by the hammock. She didn't need to be inside with him.

Russ smiled. She sounded like a sea siren, trying to assure a boat captain that she wouldn't wreck him if he came a little closer to the rocks.

"Come on in," he said. "I'm already on the rocks."

More sniper fire. He couldn't seem to resist, could he? He wanted her near, but not too near. Too bad a man couldn't have it both ways.

There was no way to sit on the edge of a hammock. Jennifer discovered that as she sank into the soft mesh cording and rolled back over Russ's legs.

"Sorry," she said, but no amount of sifting and sorting could save her from direct contact with his naked shins. And what shins they were. Layered with long, lean muscles and finished with skin as golden as pecan wood. They were long and strong, and the rest of him looked pretty interesting from that angle as well. His cotton knit shorts defined the very things they were supposed to be hiding. Of course, she already knew he was well built. She could remember the intimate details, although she was trying hard not to.

"Are you comfortable?" Russ asked.

Her nod was quick and unconvincing. Russ decided not to make her more uncomfortable by pointing out that her slip was no longer doing its job, if its job was to cover her up. It had crept to the top of her thighs, but she wasn't tugging on it. Probably hadn't even noticed it yet, he decided. She wasn't being provocative. It was the weather. When it was as warm and sticky as this, if you didn't strip down to nothing, your clothes turned into shrink-wrap. In her case, it looked good.

Legs. The way she'd landed in the hammock, she was nothing but legs. They were silvery and smooth and seemingly endless, although he knew exactly where they ended. He'd been there, and it was strawberry fields forever. Maybe he was a leg man, but her arms were nice, too. Softly hugging her breasts as she lifted and squirmed, trying to achieve some stability.

Damn. No such thing as stability in a hammock, Russ thought sardonically.

He rolled a bit, thwarting her struggle for equilibrium. God, he was a bastard. He wanted to play with her a little. He wanted her off balance so he could feel in control.

"Hold still," she chided.

"Sorry." And he almost was. But then her flesh shivered like liquid, and he felt an echoing response in his belly. Deep in his belly. The dark pit of sensation where the beast was sleeping. She was as mouthwatering as the icy cold milk you quaffed with warm chocolate cake. God, he must be hungry. He was imagining strawberry gelatin molds made of sweet, jiggling mounds. His jaw was taut and his belly felt pleasantly empty.

"Are *you* comfortable?" she inquired.

"Couldn't be better," he said, husky-voiced. He sounded as aroused as the prowling creature inside him, and he wondered whether she could hear it. In some primitive part of his brain, the hunter was already on the move, and Jennifer was starting to look like a five-course meal. It was a dangerously powerful instinct, but he told himself to tread carefully. She was dangerous, too. If he went there, it wouldn't be on impulse. And it wouldn't be unarmed.

Jennifer had not only heard the huskiness, it had raised gooseflesh on her skin. This man could startle her without even trying. When he'd made love to her for the first time, she'd actually found herself trying not to respond. It was the only way she could keep her balance in their relationship, the only way to maintain any control. But he'd sensed that she was holding back, and he stopped making love to her.

"I want you, not your body," he'd said. "I can't be inside you until you want me there."

He wouldn't accept anything halfway, not from her, and he was more than willing to wait. She was all he wanted, but he wanted all of her, and by rejecting her halfhearted offer, he had made her feel wholly accepted.

"Look at me," he'd whispered when they did make love.

And she had. Wet from his kisses, she'd looked into his eyes and seen everything she wanted there. It was the last time she was able to hold anything back from Russ Sadler.

The experience had been so intense she'd nearly fainted. Such a simple thing, and yet so powerful when the right man was doing it.

That was the night she discovered that sexual love could shatter you with its sweetness. It was also the night she started running. And she had never been more clear on the reason why than at this very moment. That part was so good it had terrified her. If she'd allowed herself that much pleasure, she would never have been able to survive without it.

Jennifer rocked forward as the giant swing moved. Either her hammock-mate was restless or she was. She tried to adjust and couldn't. Every time she shifted, she nearly tipped them over.

"Quit rocking the boat," Russ said, chuckling.

"I'll get a chair from inside and sit on the deck," she suggested.

"No . . . don't."

Something in the tone of his voice stopped her. Two words, but when the right man said them . . .

"We're going to tip over." She pretended to be preoccupied with balancing the hammock, but she was really trying to balance herself. She didn't dare look at him, not right at that moment. There was so much tension in the air she could breathe it.

The frame of the hammock creaked, and the sound made Jennifer think about what it would be like to have a man deeply inside her while they swayed in the breezes. *Entwined with him in heated bliss.*

“I should get a chair,” she protested softly, but she didn’t move.

Jennifer wasn’t fooling anyone, least of all Russ. She was as still as a mouse, and as much as he appreciated her efforts not to sink them, he wasn’t buying the reason. She was as sweetly agitated as he was. He could see it in the way she breathed. Or barely breathed. The air seemed to get caught in her throat and quiver there for a moment before she released it.

Suddenly he had just one goal. To help her release that air. Whatever it took, he would sacrifice himself, because he had to know how it would feel to stroke her quivering throat until it surrendered and expelled all of its warmth into his mouth. He wanted to be the man kissing her while she gasped and let go. And while she struggled not to. *What a choice battle that would be.*

The hammock tilted precariously, and Jennifer got out. She’d just dashed his dreams. He wondered if she knew that. Her only concern at the moment seemed to be with making herself presentable. For who? Him? He didn’t care if her slip was lying correctly. Toss it overboard.

“Come here,” Russ coaxed as he rocked in the cradle, demonstrating its wonders. “It works fine when you stretch out. You don’t have to fight the momentum. You just go with it. Swing, know what I mean?”

"Swing and talk? Next to you?"

"Sure," he lied. "Sure, we'll talk. Come here, Jennifer."

It surprised the hell out of Russ when she did it. Of course, she tried to arrange herself on the part where he wasn't. She even gripped the side to glue herself there, but the minute she let go, she rolled into the bucket with him. He thought everyone knew that about hammocks. It was the first rule of physics. There wasn't anywhere to go but the middle.

That first rush of contact was incredible. She was all soft arms and bare legs and body heat. And she bumped up against him so breathlessly that he was ready before he could even think about it. More than ready. He could have competed with the teakwood deck for hardness. Maybe the iron hull.

This could complicate things.

Russ had barely registered the thought before a squeal came out of her that told him it already had. He couldn't remember hearing a sound quite like that. It was a squeak. It was a popped balloon. It was a baby mouse who'd just been pounced on by a drooling cat.

"You're . . . you know," she informed him.

"No. What am I?" He didn't want to be perverse. She kept supplying him with weapons.

"You're physically excited, Russ."

That Kinsey guy had nothing on her. "And

what would you like me to do about that, Jennifer?"

"Fight the urge?"

Russ was fighting a million different urges, all of them strong, most of them wicked, but the Eagle Scout in him finally won out. He carefully helped her find a position where she wasn't oozing all over him like pancake syrup, and she stayed that way for all of thirty seconds. As soon as the boat began to undulate and the hammock began to sway, she was right back in his lap.

"Help me," she said.

He pushed her away, and she rolled back again. It was a beautiful thing. Their overheated bodies were magnetized. Her breasts pillowed his chest, and her thigh brushed up against his aching dick repeatedly. He had to believe it was accidental, but every time she touched him, it sent a shaft of white fire through him.

He wanted her. There was a no-brainer. Right here in the hammock. On top of him, underneath him. He didn't care which way it went. He just wanted to feel her trembling against his naked body, all of her.

He told himself that was crazy, but in the next breath, he was arguing that it was fine. Perfect. Exactly what he wanted to do. It was obviously some kind of revenge motive on his part. Shake her up, make her vulnerable. Let her know how it felt. As long as *he* wasn't vulnerable. Hell, no. He was fine. Just a little hungry, that's all. Hungry for what only she could give him. Starving.

Fortunately, she didn't seem at all aware of the internecine warfare going on inside him. She snuggled up and draped her arm across his chest. And even though he held himself back, the battle was over when she rested her head in the hollow of his shoulder. Someone had won, and he had no idea who.

They lay that way for some amount of time. Swayed that way. He lost track in the wild beat of his heart. How was it possible for a body to be so still and yet so damn busy at the same time? He was beginning to wonder if sex could kill a man. He knew love could.

Just as he was getting used to the idea of her lying beside him, it all changed. She began to move, and suddenly she was on top of him, or close to it, gazing directly into his eyes. "Aren't we supposed to be talking?"

"I thought we were talking. Isn't this talking?"

"You know what I mean."

She caressed his open mouth with her fingers, perhaps as a tactile aid, but it sent skyrockets of desire through him. Her knee was nudging his overheated groin. She wanted him to talk while she was molesting him?

"Okay . . . so, J-Jennifer . . . tell me why you jilted me."

"Oh, hell," she whispered against his open mouth. "Kiss me, Russ. Kiss me hard."

Chapter 16

It was one of those giddy woman-on-top moments that are over all too quickly. Jennifer was peering into Russ's eyes one second, and the next, she was flat on her back, and he was peering into hers. She wasn't quite sure how he'd managed it so effortlessly, but he had a willing accomplice in their rolling bed. The hammock had struck again.

"Kiss you . . . hard?" He murmured the words as he studied the lips they came from. There was a vibration in the hollow of his throat, and even though Jennifer couldn't hear it, she could feel it with her fingertips. In her experience, only men made sounds like that, deep in the well of their throats. Sounds of sensual appreciation, of wonder and lust.

"Maybe I will," he said.

He sounded a little too nonchalant, as if he could take the kiss or leave it. But Jennifer wasn't fooled. She was learning to pay attention to the burr in his voice and the banked fires in his gaze. He wasn't nonchalant. If anything, he was imagining all the other ways he could kiss her.

In fact, Russ was awash in the options. He

was reveling in them, especially now that he had her below him and effectively pinned down. The quiver no longer fascinated him. Now it was the dew point. Her face was flushed, and her breath was damp. Everything about her seemed moist and ready. Even her eyes were sweetly brimming, and when she wet her lips and he saw the rosy tip of her tongue, he imagined how warm that shy little creature would be, how wet and warm her open mouth would be . . . and he wanted to be inside. Deep inside.

The vibration in his throat became a low hiss of desire.

Jennifer's response was quick and involuntary. Answering desire flared through her loins so hotly it made her ache. He might as well have opened her legs and touched her there. Her back arched, and the impulse she felt was startlingly wanton. Wonderfully wanton. God, if only she could. She wanted to strain toward him, to offer her breasts. She wanted to be touched.

"Either kiss me or talk to me," she said breathlessly. "On the count of three. It's your choice. One, two —"

Number three never had a chance. His hands looked large enough to encircle her arms twice, and Jennifer felt their strength as he lifted her up and brought her to his mouth. He didn't kiss her immediately. He dared her to count. The one thing she couldn't do. Her head was filled with the secret knowledge of what was going to happen next, and it was crowding out everything else. She already knew what this man was capable of. She'd already felt him moving inside her. She knew the power.

"Three," she whispered.

His breath burned her lips. It was the only thing that separated them, that rush of steam and sweet frustration. He was going to kiss her so hard she would shudder and melt to nothing. Her silk slip would be the only proof of her existence.

"Talk," he threatened softly.

"What about?"

"Anything you want. Tell me why you're moving that way."

"Moving?"

"Squirming," he said. "You haven't stopped."

"I'm not —" She glanced down and saw that her slip had done quite a lot of moving, even if she hadn't. It had crept up to her hips, revealing the auburn curls that were her natural color. She wore no panties, and to be so unexpectedly exposed startled a sound out of her. A clutch of excitement made her tighten all the way to the soles of her feet.

"I *can't* stop," she whispered.

She rose, needing to kiss him, and her breasts bumped his arm. It was a tender collision, an accident, but he sounded as if he'd been shot. More heat bathed her face. Another fiery hiss.

Their eyes met and held. Sparks flew. Internal sparks.

"Kiss me," she said. "Make me soft and wet."

"Your mouth?" His gaze darkened. "Make it soft and wet?"

"Yes, my mouth . . . first."

The touch of his lips was hot. It was like drops of water on a griddle, dancing and bubbling. She could feel him moving over her. A leg dropped between hers, but her only real awareness was of the powerful hand that supported the back of her head and the powerful mouth that caressed hers.

"Soft enough?" he asked.

"Mmmm."

"Want it hard now?"

"Oh, God, *yes*."

Her neck arched with the pressure. His hands were on her throat and in her hair, and his tongue stole into her mouth in a way that promised bliss. *Physical bliss*. He drove her head back, and all she could think was that if he was taking possession, he had better hurry, because soon there would be nothing left to take possession of.

"Hard enough?"

"Oh, *God*, yes."

She was as limp as the silky slip that he peeled off her. Her arms fell open, and her head rolled back. His gaze burned over her nakedness, and she couldn't move. The sensations were so strong she couldn't do anything, not even squirm, and he seemed content to let her lie there. Lie there and bathe in her own pool of wonderment.

His fingers wandered, caressing her belly and thighs.

With his thumb, he traced the deep flush that tightened her aureole, traced it as lightly as a breath, and then ran his nail across its softness. She gasped at the contrast. Light and sharper. *Lighter and sharper.* Suddenly she was doing what she dreamed of earlier: arching her back and offering her breasts.

Touch me.

Heavy cream, sweetened and whisked into a billowing cloud. It was made for savoring, and so was she. He cradled the sweetness in his hand, tasting her with his lips and nuzzling her with his cheek, his nose, and his beautiful dark eyelashes. He supped on her languidly, as if she were a treat that would take him all day.

Jennifer's skin blushed and tingled, achingly sensitive. But it was the way his lips drew and pulled on her that made her want to cry out with pleasure. The sensations flowed through her in rivulets, nearly paralyzing her. She couldn't summon the energy to do anything but moan breathlessly as he slipped his other hand between her legs, and his fingers began to stroke her to a kind of completion she'd never experienced.

She was limp and yet vibrantly alive.

His fingers were wet with her moisture, and he murmured something about "dew point." With surprising grace for someone of his size, he shifted his body and moved down to the lily pond he'd discovered. Something deep in Jennifer's belly contracted as he replaced his hands with his mouth. His lips were velvety and warm. How could a tough guy be so outrageously tender? How did he know about those places where she couldn't bear to be touched . . . and couldn't bear not to?

Her heart was running too fast to count the beats. One beat became a string of them, but somewhere in the midst of the thrumming flight, she gave herself over to the experience. A cry of joy was caught inside her, and as it slipped out, she dissolved in helpless bliss. But as her body began to tremble, her mind carried her back to another night when she'd felt frighteningly helpless in much the same way.

She'd had a bad dream and become entangled in the bed sheets. It had felt like bondage, but when she'd asked Russ to help her, he'd hesitated. He'd said that she looked like the *Venus de Milo* with her arms caught behind her in the white sheets, and that he'd never seen anything so seductively beautiful.

She'd known right then that he wasn't going to free her, and she'd begun to moan and writhe. She'd watched him become aroused before her eyes, as gleaming hard as marble.

He'd taken her that way, without ever freeing her, and Jennifer had thought she would go mad with excitement. It was primal, thrilling beyond comprehension. But the loss of control was terrifying, and ultimately, too much for their fragile relationship to bear. It was the last time they made love with anything close to that kind of abandon, the beginning of the end.

Jennifer couldn't. He'd asked her continually what was wrong, but she hadn't been able to explain what she didn't understand. She'd left without being able to tell him that she was running from the very thing that had brought her back here tonight: the joy of surrendering to what you want most.

For Russ, the joy came in watching what was happening to her. She responded to his touch and his kiss with sensations that swept her body. A kind of madness overtook her, and it was beautiful to watch. He was mesmerized by the sexual flush that blotched her breasts and fanned out over her throat and face, the budding tightness of her nipples, the breathing that changed and nearly disappeared as she was close to climaxing. It was like the silence before the storm.

He had no fear of getting close to her now.

That was the force that drove him. He wanted to be as close as it was possible to be. He wanted to be part of her, one with her, merged. Maybe that should have sent up red flags, but it was beyond rationalizing. He wasn't even going to try. Feelings he thought were dead and buried wouldn't stay dead. She had resurrected them, and now they would both have to deal with the ghosts.

She reached out for him, murmuring something unintelligible. At first he thought she'd read his mind. It sounded like she was saying "ghosts," but as she tugged on his hand, he realized it was his name on her lips. She was calling to him, wanting him inside her, and it was time. *God, it was time.*

The hammock swayed as he moved over her.

The lake shimmered with moonlight, and the boat rocked gently.

She opened her legs to him, and he almost couldn't breathe for a moment. She was incandescent. Her body glowed. It was coming down from the frenzy and crying out for completion. And his was crying out for the same. In his mind, he was already immersed in the sweet pulsations of her sex, and he hadn't even entered her.

Her fingernails dug into his flanks, urging him to plunge deeply. But when he tried to enter her, he found the walls clenched so tightly, they had to be coaxed to receive him.

She was feverishly sweet and welcoming, and he wanted to be there as much as she wanted him to, but her body wouldn't accept him until he'd cajoled and sweet-talked and loved it into submission.

When at last he drove into her depths, it was with a savage groan of pleasure. With one shuddering thrust, he was enveloped in bliss. Steam-heat and utter bliss. Her legs curled around him, and he flexed into her deeply.

He took possession, and from the moment he did, it began to happen to him — all those changes he'd witnessed in her body. He could feel a sexual flush creeping up his chest, burning his skin. His face was warm, and his nipples were taut. And finally, his respiration began to change. Just like hers, it began to deepen and slow, to cease altogether.

He closed his eyes, lost in breathing silence as he was about to come.

Was this revenge or was it a miracle?

"Talk to me now," he said. "For Christ's sake, Jennifer. Talk to me now."

"I love you," she whispered.

He heard the words and felt himself release inside her, *explode inside her,* and the sheer beauty of it confounded him. He had rarely let himself trust another human being until her, and she'd taught him he was right. They couldn't be trusted. To be human was to lie, cheat, and betray. But she had just given him more than her body, she'd given herself. That was trust. And it was enough to make him believe he might have been wrong.

The Cradle rocked them into the night. Exhausted from their intimate battles, they slept deeply and peacefully, and without a thought to the possibility that any harm could come to them. They were immune, protected by the spirits of the lake, who guarded all those floating on its waters, even lovers reckless enough to try it again.

But in the middle of the night, something remarkable happened. The heat wave broke. Jennifer woke to droplets splashing on her face. She wasn't going to wake Russ at first. They were naked anyway. The air was still warm, and they would dry as they rocked. But then lightning painted the sky silver, and a cloudburst pounded the lake, drenching everything in its path.

They scrambled from the hammock and raced into the house, where Russ got them bath sheets to towel off. As they helped each other with the inaccessible areas, Jennifer saw what had happened to them both. Their naked backsides were crisscrossed with the hammock's mesh pattern. She could see her own derriere in the mirror, and she wondered if it would look a waffle iron for the rest of her life.

Their laughter broke through the noise of the storm.

"They could serve me for breakfast at IHOP," Jennifer said, trying to cover herself.

"They could serve us both." He showed her his hip, which was even more deeply indented, perhaps because of his weight or the fact that she was mostly lying on top of him.

"Scarred for life," she said, touching the welts on his leg.

"Yup, both of us."

She met his gaze almost shyly. It seemed their roles were reversed now, and she was the one always taking chances, always pushing for something more. But there lived inside her that stubborn little whisper of hope that he was ready to take some risks, too, and perhaps already had. She was here, after all.

"Maybe we should work on healing the scars?" she suggested.

Russ said nothing, but he did pull her into his arms and begin to gently massage her checkered backside, and the murmurs of appreciation in his throat as he kissed her shoulder was its own kind of answer.

The room was illuminated by flashes of lighting and buffeted by the sound of rolling thunder. Rain pelted the windows, but all Russ could think about was the last time they were together before she left. If he'd known then that it would be the last time they would make love, he would have kissed her better, held her tighter, loved her longer, opened his heart more.

Maybe if he had, she would have stayed. And now that he was with her again, he was going to make love to her as if every time were the last. He would remember everything, just the way he was taking it in now: the natural perfume of her damp hair, the silky warmth of her skin, and the pattering rain of her heart. He would remember it all because he couldn't face another last time.

Jennifer felt his arms tighten around her, and she hugged him back.

She was struggling with the ability to express herself, too. She had told him she loved him, and she had no idea how he felt about that. Should she try to explain that it was the heat of the moment so he wouldn't feel obligated in any way? She'd meant every word of it, but she was always pushing too hard.

"Russ, we can take this slowly if you want. I don't need to hear any earthshaking commitments."

"I do," he said, kissing the top of her head.

She laughed, cried, shook her head — and wondered what he meant.

It seemed to her that he had whispered the words "talk to me" all through the night as they lay in the hammock, but there had never been that possibility until this moment. They were either making love or drugged by the effects of it. There was so much to make up for, so much hurt to heal, and that was the way they'd chosen to communicate their needs. Maybe there weren't words that could match their body language for eloquence.

Like the way he was hugging her now.

Jennifer awoke to the scent of a fresh-washed world. Her chest lifted and fell, drawing in a breath just for the pure pleasure of it. The air was clean and clarifying to the senses, but her empty belly instantly made her aware of another irresistible aroma. Coffee and rolls.

She threw off a light down comforter that was almost better than a man for the cuddly warmth it provided. *Big crusty rolls,* she hoped, *with icy pats of hard yellow butter and tart berry jam. Or marmalade. Or honey. Oh, yes, honey!*

She was already falling in love with this place, and that feeling was confirmed as she found a huge terry robe at the bottom of the bed and wrapped it around herself. It was his. Wasn't that wonderful? His robe. In her mind she could picture him out on the deck. It would be the lower deck where there was a table and chairs. He had to be there, she thought as she picked her way down the exceedingly narrow circular stairway. She wasn't sure what would happen if he wasn't. Some things just had to be.

He wasn't to be found in either the great room or the kitchen, and she couldn't quite resist taking advantage of his absence.

Perhaps she felt a little guilt, but it *was* the perfect opportunity to have a quick look around on her way out to the deck — and she found several things of interest. She was secretly pleased that he'd kept the motorcycle magazines from a subscription she'd given him for a birthday. She also came across a small pewter box she'd found in an antique store. It seemed he hadn't been able to erase all traces of her from his life. Was that by choice?

A floor-to-ceiling curio cabinet with leaded glass doors stood against the wall in the great room. It was the most beautiful piece of furniture in the room, and Jennifer glanced around, making sure she wouldn't be discovered as she went to investigate. She spotted the photograph even before she opened the doors. Framed in filigreed silver, it lay facedown.

She didn't have to turn it over to know that it was a picture taken the day Russ bought the houseboat. The real estate agent had offered to take a picture of them, and Russ had pulled the For Sale sign from the ground and held it in the air. Jennifer was next to him, laughing as he hugged her close.

She left the picture where it was, afraid it would break the spell of the morning. She didn't want to be sad, not today.

The lake was already abuzz with activity as she stepped out on the deck. Across the water on Queen Ann Hill, the radio towers glinted in the sunshine and kites of every color were flying in the breezes. Russ was sitting under the umbrella in one of the deck chairs, watching a plane come down and drinking a mug of coffee. The rolls on the table next to him looked like croissants, flaky rather than crusty, but who cared.

He was barefoot and very casually dressed in khaki shorts and a Hawaiian shirt that hung open, revealing the burnished chest where she'd rested her cheek while they slept in his bed. Bathed in sunlight, he looked as relaxed and unguarded as she'd ever seen him.

Maybe it was the slightly giddy mood she was in — a state of mind she rarely allowed herself — but she wondered what that might mean. That Jennifer Nash and Russ Sadler were good for each other? Never in her wildest dreams would she have imagined herself thinking that just twenty-four hours ago.

He glanced over his shoulder and saw her, and his face seemed to light up with pleasure. She hadn't thought she'd made a noise, but wooden decks creaked. Or maybe he was that tuned into her. She could almost imagine an electric arc connecting them, the same one that had connected them last night.

"Good morning." She hurried over to him, but the anticipation she felt wavered a little as he rose from the chair. There was clearly something on his mind, and her first thought was that he was having doubts about what they'd done. He didn't look as if he was ready to throw her over the side, but the smile she'd seen had become more measured and reflective.

Philosophical looked good on him.

"Is something wrong?" she asked.

He took her hands in his, possibly to reassure her. "I don't know," he said, "and I think you're the only one who can tell me."

His eyes were paradoxical. They seemed to absorb light. The brighter it was, the darker they got.

"What is it?"

"Maybe nothing, but I need you to answer my question."

"Which question?"

"The one I asked before we committed original sin in that hammock. Why *did* you jilt me?"

Oh, *that* question. She was almost relieved. "I told you, I was afraid, but of myself more than anything."

"I know that's what you told me, Jennifer. But I want the *real* reason. The one you've kept locked up inside you all these years."

They released hands, and she watched his drop to his sides. Hers went to her waist, where she held herself. Now she understood his unyielding tone. She'd explained that she had to leave, that it was the only thing she could have done at the time, but she hadn't told him all of it, and being the sleuth that he was, he'd figured that out on his own. He must have sensed the demons that drove her away — and would continue to drive her if she didn't confront them.

He wanted her to open the door to the basement where all the dead bodies were hidden. She'd come back with every intention of opening that door herself, but now that she was faced with the reality of it, she wondered if was safe to enter the burial ground of her past. After all these years, the things she'd done still seemed unforgivable, almost unimaginable. She wondered if he could ever understand, and if he couldn't, there was so much to lose.

Chapter 17

Russ could see that he'd startled her. He'd done it intentionally. It was the most basic of interview techniques — catching your subject off guard. Not fair, maybe, but he'd had a sudden change of heart about her reasons for leaving. He wanted to know what they were as badly as he'd wanted not to know.

And he wanted them to make sense.

She came over to the table, but she was visibly uneasy as she pulled out the redwood deck chair and sat down. She tilted on the edge of the seat, looking lost in his white terry robe. She looked lost anyway, and he hated to think that he'd frightened her.

"It wasn't you, Russ," she said. "When I had some time to think, I realized that it was never really about you. It was about my father."

He hadn't expected that. "You've never said much about your father, except that it wasn't a good relationship."

"He did something terrible, and I should have stopped him. But I never did. I lied for him and protected him."

Her voice was full of revulsion, and the warm tones of her skin changed before Russ's eyes. His thoughts went to his own relationship with his father and the way his father had brutalized his mother. He'd stood up for her, but at least he had a fighting chance against the man. He didn't want to think that Jennifer had had to go through something like that. If her father had even come close to that kind of abuse, he would find the bastard and —

"Did he hurt you?" Russ's voice was calm, but he wasn't. "Is that what happened? Your father hurt you?"

A fly buzzed the tray of croissants and landed near his arm. As it crawled toward the pastry, Russ felt an impulse that was sudden and explosive. A second later, the insect was a spot on the table, and Russ was using a napkin on his fist. The pest was gone, but the desire to lash out was not. For reasons that only he understood, Russ wanted blood.

Jennifer looked at him as if she was expecting an explanation, and Russ didn't have one ready. He knew all about brutal fathers, but that was the past, his past. They were talking about hers.

"What happened?" he asked. "Can you tell me?"

"Are you all right?"

She had set her coffee cup down wrong, and it was wobbling on the saucer. Russ reached over to steady it. This time he hadn't intended to frighten her. Mixed up somewhere in the violent impulse was a powerful need to protect her. It had been with him since his first encounter with her startled green eyes, and maybe what had attracted him most was the fact that she didn't frighten easily. That much was obvious to anyone who knew her, and it was why he'd begun to think there was something deeper going on with her — and always had been.

"I'm fine," he said. "I don't like flies."

"No kidding."

A speedboat roared by, and they both fell silent, watching it. The sun glinted blindingly off the water, and Jennifer wondered if it was going to get hot again. She tucked the robe around her. The breeze was actually a little chilly this morning, but its scent was lovely. A pale pink rosebush sat among the potted geraniums, its fragrance almost too delicate to detect.

"My father had an affair." She announced the news abruptly, her gaze still fixed on the water. A canoe glided by, quickly overtaken by a college sculling crew. Across the lake a cluster of sailing skiffs was engaged in a fierce race.

"There must be a dozen boats out there this morning," she said. "Is that a lot for a weekend?"

"Jennifer, don't count. Talk to me."

Always the detective, she thought ruefully. Somehow he'd ferreted out her most annoying quirk. She was reasonably certain she'd never told him about it, but he was forever analyzing, evaluating, and probing the inner workings of the mind, just as she was. Normally he went after criminal minds, and perhaps for him she had once fallen into that category. She'd stolen his heart, but he could never have probed deeply enough to discover the real reason. For that he would have to have known the whole sordid tale of her childhood.

Huddled in the robe, Jennifer began to speak with painstaking care and precision. It was important that she get this exactly right, that she not leave out any vital detail of her confession, or there would be no absolution.

"My mother had ALS," she explained, "a devastating disease of the nervous system that cripples and eventually kills. In my mother's case, it took several years, and toward the end, my father got involved with her closest friend, a single woman who lived next door. My mother had no idea, even though it was happening right under her nose. I came home sick from school one day and discovered the two of them in our garage. My father tried to tell me the neighbor wanted to borrow some gardening equipment, but I saw them . . ."

In each other's arms.

"And I heard him . . ."

Tell her he loved her and promise they would be together when my mother was gone.

Jennifer tore off a chunk of croissant and began to chew on it. She was queasy. It felt as if she'd been queasy since the day she walked in on them, and that was nearly twenty years ago. She was ten years old, and up until that moment, she had held her father in awe. He was everything she thought a man could or should be: fearfully strong and competent, brutally honest. She feared him, but she revered him, too, so much so that she had never noticed a flaw or a weakness. She hadn't realized that was possible, especially not such an unthinkable flaw.

"I tried to sneak away," she said, "but I must have made a noise because he saw me. He turned and looked right at me."

"And what did he do?"

"Nothing. I ran to my room and waited for something terrible to happen. It felt as if I waited for days, but he never mentioned it, and neither did I . . . to anyone."

"Maybe your mother didn't want to know. People often deny things that are right under their noses."

The bread wouldn't go down. Jennifer helped herself to a tumbler of juice and drank some if it. It felt as if she were going to choke. "My mother didn't know because I made sure she didn't. I lied for my father. He continued to see the neighbor woman, and I covered for him. He didn't ask me to. I just did it."

"You never told your mother?"

"She was already dying. Why add to her pain? Why break her heart?" The choking sensation was terrible, and she couldn't wash it away.

Russ studied his coffee cup. His thumb worked the edge of the handle. "Then you did what you had to."

"Maybe, but in a way, I also conspired with him to betray her — a dying woman who believed that she could love and trust us. She did trust us!"

"Jennifer, you did what you *had* to. It was the right decision."

It wasn't that easy to absolve herself, but he didn't understand, and how could she expect him to? For years she'd tried to bury it, but on some level, she'd felt like the worst kind of traitor, disgusting and despicable. Her father was a formidable man, and simple fear kept her from confronting him, but by protecting him, she'd probably made it possible for him to continue the affair. After her mother died, Jennifer went to live with an aunt, her mother's sister, and never saw her father again, but it was herself she couldn't forgive.

Russ rose from the table. He walked to the railing and dumped the remainder of his cold coffee over the side. When he turned back, he had the look of a man who'd thought the situation through. His arms were folded the way he did when he wanted to be sure he was going to be heard, and his focus was on Jennifer.

"Your father betrayed you, too," he said. "He not only broke faith with his wife and the mother of his child, he broke faith with that child."

And she's never trusted a man since, not with her heart.

The thought brought Jennifer great sadness. Still, she was grateful that he could so easily see the truth of it. That had taken her years.

"I knew I had problems with commitment," she said, "but ending our relationship forced me to face what I'd been doing all my life."

"Running from love?"

She bowed her head. It was a good guess. "I thought loving a man meant opening yourself to pain and betrayal. My father was my role model for your gender. I trusted him completely. If he wasn't capable of commitment, who was?"

She sounded calm and logical. Even Russ, who'd been on the receiving end of her conflicts, probably saw her as over the crisis and ready to go forward, but the hardest part was still ahead of her. It was one thing to talk about trust, and another to do it. The wounds went deep. As a kid she'd found ways to avoid the ugliness — her drawing and probably her compulsion to count things — and as much as she wanted to stop avoiding now and to trust with her whole heart, she wondered if any man could ever make her feel safe enough to risk it. Sometimes it felt as if she were permanently scarred. Permanently scared.

"So it *wasn't* me who frightened you away?"

She glanced up at Russ's skeptical smile and tried to smile back. "You don't get off scot-free," she was quick to inform him. "I suspect you've frightened off your share of females, but I'll give you credit for being braver than I was. You were ready to open up to someone."

"I was ready to open up to *you.*"

She actually shivered inside the robe. He had made her remember how wonderful it was to have a man's voice give you the chills. He hadn't lost the gift.

"I knew that. I saw it happening, and it frightened me to death," she said. "I was falling in love with you, and you reminded me so much of my father."

"Good God," he breathed.

"No, I don't mean that you'd had affairs or were some kind of romantic gunslinger. It was a style thing. He was tough like you, and emotionally guarded. He acted as if he didn't need anyone or anything."

"The ones who pretend they need nothing are the ones who need the most."

"You know this for a fact?"

"I live it," he said.

If she'd had a sketch pad handy, Jennifer would have tried to capture the fleeting emotion that shadowed his face. The bleakness had reminded her of black-and-white photographs of prisoners of war. But she didn't have a pad, and the moment was past.

"What your father did was wrong," he said. "It was reprehensible, and I'm not defending him, but is it possible that he needed the very thing your dying mother couldn't give him?"

"Sex?" Jennifer shuddered. "Couldn't he have waited until she was gone? And why didn't I confront him?"

"Not sex, intimacy. And you didn't confront him because you were ten years old and he was an adult, a terrifying adult. My father had a violent temper, and when I tried to stop him from hitting my mother, he bounced me off a wall and knocked me unconscious. When I came to, she was locked in the basement with the rats to teach her a lesson. My lesson was half a dozen cracked ribs and a broken nose."

Jennifer stared at him. "You told me your nose was broken in a motorcycle accident."

"Accidents are easier to explain," he said, dismissing it.

She barely knew how to deal with what he was saying. She'd had victims describe assaults that were much more gruesome. But this was Russ. Proud, surly, bulletproof Russ.

The thought of him being thrown against walls, a defenseless child, was hard to conceive of. It made her feel sick and confused — and yet it explained everything.

Everything except why he'd let *her* into his heart when he wouldn't let anyone else. Jennifer Nash, the worst bet on the planet if you were looking for a woman to fall in love with. She wondered if he understood how sorry she was.

"Was your mother all right?" she asked, encouraging him to talk.

"She survived, if that's what you mean. Eventually I convinced her that she had to run away — and leave me behind. I knew he'd hunt her down and kill her if she took me. If I stayed, she might get away . . . and she did."

He was not a man who had ever allowed himself to suffer, so he had little practice at hiding it. Jennifer could see the turmoil in the raised veins of his forehead. Sadness, too. He was burning up with sadness.

"At least you were able to save her," she said.

"And so were you. You saved your mother a great deal of pain."

Perhaps, she thought, but there were too many lies, and worse, there were times when she feared that her mother knew the truth, no matter how hard Jennifer had tried to conceal it.

"Where's your father now?" she asked Russ.

"Alive and well in the family home on Whidbey Island, probably torturing the latest in an endless string of female companions. He always seems to have one, and they always leave. The only reason my mother stayed was because of me. Fathers are supposed to teach sons how to be men. Mine taught me how not to trust men and how to drive women away."

He'd already turned back to the water before Jennifer could protest. The forbidding set of his shoulders was telling her that he fought his battles alone, and he would fight this one that way, too. Except that he wasn't alone. She was there.

"You're nothing like him," she insisted. "You don't hurt people, you protect them. You put your life on the line every day. And you didn't *drive* me away."

A flock of seagulls swooped overhead, crying out in alarm. One dived for a morsel of food floating on the water, and the others followed.

Jennifer crossed the deck, her footsteps hidden by the clamoring birds. She knew intuitively that he wouldn't want her to intrude on his dark mood, but she had decided not to give him the chance to object.

"Russ, did you hear what I said? *You're nothing like him.*"

Maybe he could hear the regret in her voice, because his head dropped forward, and his shoulders slumped. She touched his arm, not knowing what to expect. "Is this okay?" she asked.

The silence was pierced with the cries of seagulls.

Jennifer could hear the noise of her own heart as she waited for him to respond. At last he reached around and clasped her hand. He simply held it, not moving — and neither did she. It was enough for that moment. It was more than she expected. This was a connection beyond the intense sex of the night before, perhaps beyond anything they'd had.

"There's the car." Jennifer pointed out the little red Datsun rental as Russ pulled into the parking lot of Danny's Dock. The car was virtually surrounded by parked motorcycles, as if they'd escorted it into the lot like a squadron of fighter jets. Unfortunately, the restaurant looked as if it were packed to the rafters with the bikes' owners.

"Must be the Love Riders," Jennifer said. "The city was overrun with them yesterday. They've taken over the entire town."

Russ pulled his unmarked company car as close as he could to her rental. They'd planned to have a late lunch, after which she would drive her car back to the hotel, where there was overnight parking for guests. They had no plans beyond that, and Jennifer didn't know whether this was the beginning or the end of their reconciliation. The man played his cards too close to the vest. He didn't talk enough, damn it. A girl needed to know where she stood.

Suddenly Jennifer was riddled with doubts. She shouldn't have said what she did. She'd told him she loved him. Talk about showing her hand! And why did it seem that the more anxious she became, the more subdued he was? He'd been pensive since their talk on the boat this morning, and Jennifer didn't know what that meant. When she asked him, he'd said the word women hate to hear: "Nothing."

Nothing.

Nothing meant everything when it was uttered by the man who had just had carnal knowledge of your trembling body. The man who held your heart in the palm of his hand. Maybe this was karma. She'd broken his heart, and now he was going for some payback.

"We could have lunch at the hotel," she suggested. Room service, perhaps.

"Is that what you want?"

Something in his tone made Jennifer look at him. He seemed to be waiting for her answer, but it was with an intensity that left her wondering how to respond. Finally, the only thing that made sense was the truth.

"No, I don't want to go back to the hotel — not for any other reason than to drop off the car, pick up some clothes, and go back to your place."

"Done. Go get your car."

"What's done?"

"We're going back to my place."

"Russ, I'm not charity," she huffed. "You don't have to take me in like some stray. If you want me to stay with you, fine. If you don't, just say so."

"Jennifer, I want you to stay with me."

"You do?"

"I want that more than I can express to you in words."

You do? She was now, officially, breathless and stupid. "Well . . . all right, then."

She was more than a little off balance as she let herself out of the car. Things were changing between them so rapidly, she could hardly make herself believe it was real. All she'd hoped for was to talk with him and explain herself. She hadn't expected there to be any chance of reviving their relationship and certainly not that they would so swiftly be lovers again.

Her most fervent hope at the moment was that she could drive herself back to the hotel. She prayed to the traffic gods that she didn't have an accident and die on the way, because apparently this reconciliation wasn't over yet — and she wanted to be around to see how it ended.

"By the way, I strongly prefer your natural color."

Russ rose up over her supine body and kissed her lightly on the mouth.

"My natural color is auburn," she said, as dizzy from the taste of him as she was from the pleasure that sparkled and streamed through her senses. There were hints of honey and musk on her lips.

A tiny red corkscrew curl was entwined in his fingers. He showed it to her and bent to her ear. "Duh," he whispered.

Jennifer could feel herself coloring, although it was hard to imagine that she could still blush after the things they'd been doing this afternoon. He was lucky he didn't have little red corkscrews in his teeth. On the way back from her hotel, they'd stopped at a new take-out grill for steak tacos, warm corn tortillas, and salsa to go. The weather was breezy and beautiful, but instead of eating lunch on the deck of the houseboat, they'd had a very private little picnic in bed and spent the rest of the afternoon having dessert.

Russ kissed her belly a fond good-bye and stretched out next to her. She couldn't help but notice that he rivaled the length of the bed as he unfurled his six-foot frame. A good-sized man. She also couldn't help but notice that.

Her blush deepened, and he smiled. Wrenching her gaze from his more muscular regions, she concentrated on his eyes and the nose that would have been aquiline except for the ridge where it was broken. Jennifer felt closer to him knowing the truth about the injury. In the past they'd shared their work and a maddeningly irresistible physical attraction, but not much else. Now they were linked by the agony their fathers had caused, and Jennifer had to believe it was a defining part of who they were.

He studied her dark tresses from the pillows he'd stacked behind him. "Were you washing me out of your hair? Is that why you changed the color?"

She stacked her pillows, too, then gave the sheet a tweak so that it floated over them. "Exactly — and do you read minds? Is that how you know what I'm thinking?"

"If I did, what would I be reading now?"

"Me," she said, "counting."

"Your money?"

"My blessings."

He reached under the sheet and found her hand. Their fingers entwined so quickly and tightly that Jennifer felt a tug on her heart. This was just astonishing. Every new connection was electric, no matter how innocent.

"No second thoughts about being here?" he asked. "No guilt or fears?"

"Did you miss the smile on my face?" She was probably beaming. "I have half a mind to go downstairs and put right that picture of us in your curio cabinet."

He looked a little startled by her declaration. Apparently he had tried to put some things firmly out of his mind, thinking they could be rendered harmless. But buried feelings had a half-life of their own that time couldn't touch, Jennifer had discovered. Quite possibly he had just discovered that, too.

"We were fully clothed in that picture, as I remember." He gave her hand a pull, as if to bring her closer. "I think we could come up with a pose that has much more potential."

She laughed and pulled back. "I don't want to end up on the Internet, thank you."

"No? We could name the site Undercover Cops. Make a fortune."

"Clever beast."

The next pull on her hand turned into a sweet, drowning kiss, and Jennifer was glad she hadn't resisted. She fell into his arms with a sharp little cry, and he kissed her so deeply it felt as if they were making love already. A terrible knot of longing swelled in her throat, and when he scooped her up and brought all of her close, it was only with a supreme effort of will that she was able to draw back.

"One thing, Russ," she said.

"*Anything,* baby," he murmured, continuing to kiss and nuzzle and nibble as she tried to speak.

"No, there's one thing I am feeling guilty about."

"I won't put us on the Internet," he promised huskily.

"Hey, I'm serious here."

"Okay, okay." He let her go with a groan that was only slightly appeased by her promise that it wouldn't take long.

"It's the case," she said. "I've already disrupted things enough, and now, here I am, luring the lead detective into bed. I know it's the weekend, but normally you'd be working around the clock on a case like this, wouldn't you? I'm sure the rest of the task force is working."

"That's their problem. They haven't got you, naked in their hammock." He bent to kiss her, groaning as she stopped him again. "You *are* serious."

She was. There'd been something on her mind all morning, but it hadn't made any sense until now. "I think I know why my method failed with Myrna. What if she was trying to describe two different men? That would explain the contradictions in her recall."

"Myrna told you that Sharon was abducted by two men?"

"She never said there was more than one man at the scene, but each time I finished a sketch and showed her the suspect's face, she insisted that she'd described the features differently. But she hadn't. We have her on tape. By the time it was over, I had the feeling she'd seen two men, maybe without realizing it.

"Don't ask me how," she said defensively. Russ was sitting cross-legged, his fingertips were pressed together like a judge's, and she was already feeling uncertain in the face of his skepticism.

"Myrna was pretty schizo, Jennifer. None of her testimony made much sense, and why would it? She was under the influence of drugs that night, and she was knocked unconscious. She could have been seeing double — two of the Violator — for all we know. Remember that none of the victims reported there being more than one man."

Jennifer nodded. She'd gone over the police reports several times, and all they'd done was raise questions. "What about the possibility that Sharon's killing was a copycat?"

"How does that jibe with your theory that Myrna saw two men?"

"It doesn't," she admitted, "but it might explain why Sharon wasn't shaved until *after* she was dead, as well as why she was killed and the others weren't. It might also explain the fact that she'd had sex and none of the other victims had."

"And it would complicate the hell out of things," he pointed out. "It's harder to catch two suspects than one — and much harder to build a strong case."

The last thing Jennifer wanted was to make

things tougher, but trying to understand what had gone wrong with her sketch had brought her in touch with some of the discrepancies in the case.

"Actually, it doesn't have to be two men *or* a copycat," she said, thinking aloud. "It could be an image of anyone's face that's confusing Myrna — one of the men who rescued her or an orderly who was there when she came to in the hospital. She could even have had a dream. But what about the fact that two different vehicles were used — a motorcycle to kidnap the victims and an SUV to dump them in the parks?"

"We can only connect the SUV treads to one of the cases, and lots of us have two cars, Jenn, even men with criminal records. VICAP came up with several in this area who own both motorcycles and SUVs, but none of them have checked out. We're searching DMV records, of course, and rental agencies in the counties where the strikes have taken place. What we need is to narrow the suspect field, not widen it, so . . ."

He touched her nose. "I'm hoping to hell you're wrong. Sorry."

Jennifer felt faintly patronized, but she wasn't prepared to defend a hunch. The case had plenty of other elements that didn't seem to connect.

"Why wasn't there a condom found at the scene?" she asked. "A *condom*," she repeated as his frown deepened. "If Sharon had sex with a lover, and there was no sperm detected, why didn't they find a condom?"

"I don't know. The sex was interrupted, or her lover used a sex toy for penetration? Maybe Junior's theory is right, and the Violator is a woman."

He let out a quick sigh of frustration. "Do you have anything pertinent to offer on where the Violator's trailer might be located? Or why all three victims reported feeling a powdery substance on their hands while they were tied up in that trailer? Because that would be helpful, Jennifer."

"Powdery substance? I didn't see that in the lab reports."

"There was nothing to analyze. There was no hair on their body to catch any particles, and according to the victims, he put them in a hot shower and scrubbed them with antibacterial soap before he left them in the parks."

"Bath powder? Dusting powder? Isn't there a powder that people use to brush their teeth with?" Jennifer was trying, but it seemed that she didn't have anything pertinent to offer.

"Russ, I want to help," she told him. "I really do."

He nodded against his steepled fingers. "I know you do, and that's a good thing, because the lead detective could use plenty of it. Help, that is."

"What kind of help?" she asked, not entirely sure where he was going.

"Following a new lead." His gaze was very intent as he looked up at her. Silently, he began to trace a path from the curve of her lips to a point near her earlobe, and eventually Jennifer realized what he was doing. He was connecting the dots of her freckles.

"The lead detective is conducting his own private investigation on what makes a woman so criminally tantalizing that a man has to abduct her and keep her captive on a houseboat."

"Or go *criminally* insane? And what has his investigation shown so far?"

"It all seems to start with the fact that her name is Jennifer and that she has freckles on her thighs."

"On her thighs? Really?"

"Mmmm . . . yes, freckles like tiny copper pennies . . . Pick one up, and all day long, you have good luck."

Jennifer was already aware of the feelings he could evoke in her. It all seemed to start with a deep ache in her belly, she thought ironically. And it was spreading like fingers toward the tender nest that crowned her thighs. His fingers. He touched her so beautifully.

"And that her natural color is red, of course."

"Of course." A sound slipped out of her as he began to touch the coppery pennies. It was a casual exploration, but eventually their path took his fingers on a journey from the inside of her knee to the matching curls between her legs, and the sound became whimpering need. The deep ache began to melt and run, and at the same time, the cords of her back tightened into an arch. She gasped softly. It wasn't fair that he could do this to her. It was criminal. She barely cared that he kept putting her off when she wanted to talk about the case. She barely cared about the case.

Chapter 18

Jennifer didn't know what had roused her, but she couldn't even lift her head off the pillow. The events of the day — and the night — had exhausted her. All she wanted to do was go back to sleep. But the house-boat was rocking as if a boat had chugged by, and it was the middle of the night. That was her best guess, anyway. It was so dark she couldn't see the clock radio, or Russ, who was lying next to her.

She rolled over with the thought of snuggling close and discovered that his side of the bed was empty. She murmured his name, wondering if that was why the boat felt unsteady. It was him, moving around. He'd gone to the bathroom or downstairs to check something. He would be back any minute.

A soft rustling sound told her it was raining again.

Yawning, she inched over to his side to wait for him. The bottom sheet was chilly against her skin, and it made her wonder how long he'd been gone, but her mind wasn't on anything but his return.

Come back, she thought. *I didn't get a chance to tell you what it meant to have your support this morning when I told you about my father. And I want you to be proud of the way you tried to protect your mother. She owes you her life.*

The rustling sound brought her back from the edge of sleep. Through a misty veil, she thought she saw someone standing in the shadows by the dresser.

"Russ?"

For some reason he didn't respond, and she didn't have the energy to get up. "Come to bed," she said, wondering if she was dreaming.

She reached out a hand to him, but he was too far away. Was it the rain, the shadows, or was someone actually in the room with her? She was asleep before she ever got an answer to her question.

Lake Union was a sea of broken mirrors, each of them reflecting the brilliant morning sun. All that remained of the overnight rainstorm was a cooling breeze that created a slight chop on the surface of the slate blue water. The heat wave had run its course, and Seattle was back to normal. Or so it appeared.

It was midmorning, but the lake was unusually quiet. A rustic old tug that had been converted into a tour boat chugged its way back to a loading dock, to deposit its sightseers and pick up more. Overhead, a flock of swallows flew in military wing formation, heading for a grove of trees in Gas Works Park. And stretched along the east shore, a row of vintage houseboats sat placidly, their decks washed clean by the midnight shower.

Inside the very last houseboat in the row, Jennifer was just opening her eyes to the brightness. Silver motes sparkled in the sunlight that streamed through the windows and pooled in large circles on the bed. One of those circles was warming her feet, but her legs were tangled up so tightly, she couldn't move them. It was a moment before she realized that she'd been taken captive again by the sheets. *Ironic how that kept happening to her.* She must have tried to kick them off in the night.

By the time she was free, she had seen the note on Russ's pillow. It was handwritten on lined tablet paper, and next to it lay a long, knobby door key that looked old enough to be an antique. Alongside that was one pale pink rose from the bush on the deck.

She sat up to read the note, greedy for any contact with him.

You gave me an idea, you and the rain. I may be gone a couple days. I left word with the duty desk, but no one else. I don't want any interference from the department, but don't feel you have to cover for me. It would be better if no one knew we were together. And meanwhile, please don't go anywhere. I need to know you're going to be there when I get back. I need that, Jennifer.

His last words brought an aching lump to her throat. Years of grief mingled with the sharpness of newfound joy. "I'll be here," she said.

That was her promise, and after she whispered it, she buried her face in the pillow and let out the sobs she'd been holding back. She had to stop hurting people. She had to. The people you loved deserved better than that. She'd broken all ties when she left Seattle. It was Russ she regretted most deeply, but she'd cut herself off from others, too: Bob and Sharon. There would never be another chance with Sharon. Her friend was gone.

There would never be another chance with her mother, either, and Jennifer would carry that burden with her always. Just before her mother died, she had asked about the liaisons in the garage, and Jennifer had lied. Now she believed that her mother had known and probably thought Jennifer was lying to protect him when it was her mother she was trying to protect. Jennifer hadn't known what to do, and it had ripped her apart.

It took a little time, but eventually Jennifer collected herself and read the note again.

There was still a tender lump in her throat, and it was all she could do to get her emotions under control as she realized what it meant. This was his handwriting. It was tangible proof that she was forgiven.

God, she was sad. She was *happy.* She had to tell someone.

Jennifer saw the jogger drop to the ground, and she began to walk faster. Within seconds, she was running toward him. Her first thought was that he'd tripped, but she was too far away to see exactly what had happened. He might have been ill. He was down on all fours, and he appeared to be crawling around in the grass. It was only as she got closer that she recognized who it was.

"Are you all right?" she called to him.

Bob Talb glanced up in surprise and sat back on his haunches. He was wearing running shorts and a tank top, and the sweat band around his forehead was soaked. When Jennifer had worked with him, he'd run every day at this time on this campus jogging path, which was why she'd come looking for him here. He'd never missed, even when he was sick.

It looked as if he'd dropped something, but the way he was staring at her struck her as odd, too. His glasses appeared to be off kilter, but as she neared him, she saw that there was a lens missing.

"Can I help you?" she said.

Tears streamed from his right eye as he covered the open eyehole with his hand. "One of the lenses fell out of my glasses, and the grass ate it. I can't see well enough to find the damn thing."

Jennifer got down on her knees with him and began to search. If she gave a thought to getting grass stains on her white capris and lime green blouse, it was fleeting. The lens was nowhere to be found on the lawn, but she quickly spotted the dark blue sphere about three feet behind him on the jogging path. It was in plain sight, and it surprised her that he hadn't been able to see it there.

"Thanks," he said as she handed him the piece of plastic. "I probably couldn't find my way back to Guthrie Hall without this thing."

"Are you really that light-sensitive?"

"No, I'm really a vampire. Didn't I tell you?"

"Too bad you didn't lose your sense of humor," she tossed back as he deserted her for the shade of a large, leafy maple tree.

She hung back as he took off his glasses and positioned the lens to pop it back in the frame. She didn't want him to feel any more self-conscious than he already did. He was a bit of a fussbudget about his appearance. It was part of the Professor Pristine thing she kidded him about.

She soaked up the bright sunshine and the

warmth as she waited. This was one of her favorite parts of the campus because of the huge old trees and rolling greenbelts. It had been taken over by the joggers and power walkers, but if she'd been one of them, she would have been out here every day, too.

Finally Bob had the glasses back on, and she went to join him.

"If you really wanted to help, you'd wipe my brow," he said, pulling a towel from around his neck and doing it himself.

She made an anemic attempt to blow air on him. "Better?"

He pointedly ignored her and continued blotting, but when the towel was gone, she saw a huge tear rolling down his cheek. It could have been sweat, but she knew it wasn't.

She couldn't think what to say, and then a group of students saved the day. They jogged by, yelling for him to join them. He flipped them the bird, ensuring his reputation as a tough SOB, but Jennifer could see that he was pleased by their attention.

She bent down and picked a daisy from the flower patch that bordered the tree. Absently she plucked at the petals and congratulated herself on having something to do besides count. *He loves me, he loves not, he* . . .

When she looked up, Bob had finished toweling off, and he was staring at her. "Maybe I should ask if you're all right?"

If she had any doubts about telling him, they were lost in the uncontrollable suddenness of her laughter. "I'm great," she said. "I think I may be losing my mind, but I'm great."

"Women who are losing their mind are only great when —" His powers of deduction made him grimace. "Tell me it's not true."

She dropped the daisy and moved closer to him, speaking in whispers. "Bob, I'm scared to death. I don't know if I'm doing the right thing. It just happened. Russ and I have been together for the last couple days. I'm staying at his houseboat."

Bob didn't seem to share her giddiness. He looked gravely worried. "You're not losing your mind. It's gone."

"No, it feels right. It does." Jennifer could feel herself panicking. She needed someone to share this with, someone to be happy for her and reassure her. Bob had taken on an avuncular role in her life, and she counted on him for that, especially with her mother gone, but she wasn't going to get that kind of support today.

"Bob, you're not seriously worried, are you? He's a good guy. I'm the one who ran out on him."

Now he was moving closer, whispering to her, and Jennifer was startled.

"Apparently you don't remember the anguish you went through, trying to understand your feelings for him," he said. "You were in torment, Jennifer. You may not choose to remember it, but I do, and I don't want to see you go through that again."

"It wasn't about him, Bob. It was about my father. I've had time to think and sort things out."

"Time to rationalize it."

She could see that he wanted to say more, but he was holding himself back. His features were ashen against the dark glasses. Normally he did look much younger than his age, but not today.

"Bob, do you know something you're not telling me? Because if it's me you're worried about, don't be. I can handle this."

She made her voice sound strong, but it didn't seem to have any impact on him, and she didn't know what to do. "Bob, I need to do this. You understand that, don't you? There are things that people have to go through in their lives. You can't protect them, even if you love them."

He had the towel in his hands, and he was twisting it into a fat terrycloth rope. Each twist bound the thing tighter, and finally it would go no further.

Jennifer didn't realize how shaken she was until she touched his arm. Her hand was unsteady, and when he saw that, he released the towel. As it unfurled, his features seemed to relax, too.

"Of course, you're right," he said.

"Thank you."

Her relief was so evident that he reluctantly looked up. Jennifer just barely managed a smile, and his voice broke. "Be careful," he said. "You be careful, dammit."

Jennifer's car wouldn't start. Stranded in a university parking lot, she sat perched on the Datsun's totally inadequate back fender, waiting for the rental agency to show with a replacement. It was too hot to wait inside the car, and she couldn't leave it long enough to find some shade or get something to drink.

Thirty-eight minutes. Thirty-nine. They'd told her it would be fifteen. Apparently someone in that agency couldn't count as well as she could.

She and Russ had left the Datsun in the hotel parking lot last night, so they could drive back to the houseboat in his car. Obviously neither of them had realized that he would be getting up in the middle of the night to go investigating and that she would be stranded without a car. Then again, maybe he'd planned it that way. It would be one way of making sure she couldn't leave.

She smiled at that possibility. She'd ended up taking a taxi to the hotel this morning to pick up the rental. She hoped no one had tampered with it. Batteries didn't go dead after just one night.

"You waiting for somebody?"

The brightness forced Jennifer to squint as she looked up. She couldn't see the face of the man silhouetted against the sunlight, but she knew by the halting sound of his voice that it was Rick Morehouse, her former fellow teaching assistant.

Jennifer was already up and angling herself around, trying to get the sun out of her eyes. "Hi, Rick," she said, aware that she was overly anxious around him and always had been. It was the unspoken obligation she felt to put him at ease. Who had put that in her job description, she wondered. Make the uncomfortable comfortable or fail miserably at your obligation as a member of the human race."My car won't start," she said. "The rental agency's supposed to be bringing me another one."

"I could take a look," he mumbled.

"Oh, would you? Thanks."

Before Jennifer could say anything else, Rick had virtually disappeared inside her open hood. She hovered next to him, sporadically trying to make conversation that he totally ignored. Finally she stifled the urge and went back to watching the road.

When Rick emerged, moments later, smudged with grease, he took off his glasses to wipe his face, and Jennifer experienced a jolt of recognition. She'd never seen him without the glasses, and her first thought was that he reminded her of someone, but she had no idea who. She couldn't make the connection.

"Try it now," he said. "I think it's fixed."

Jennifer hurried to do as he said. She keyed the ignition, and the motor turned over immediately. She goosed it to be sure it wasn't going to die, and then did it again, just for the pure joy of hearing the engine rev and roar. It couldn't have taken more than a few seconds, but by the time she got out of the car to thank Rick, he was already heading across the parking lot.

Jennifer watched with a sense of helplessness as he walked away. Either he didn't understand the rules of polite social interaction, or he wasn't capable of them. She was half tempted to go after him and illuminate him. It was time someone did, but that wasn't her job, she reminded herself.

As she turned back to her idling car, her attention was riveted by a flash of silver. It could have been someone sending her signals from a mirror. She looked around, expecting to see another car pulling in or the tow truck she'd called. But the flashes were coming from Rick's direction.

He was wearing jeans, she realized, and there was a chain hooked to his belt loop and clipped to the wallet in his back left pocket. A silver chain. The kind bikers used.

Chapter 19

Bent over her college yearbook, Jennifer flipped through the pages, searching for the photograph that might help explain the urgency she felt. A raspy-voiced librarian of uncertain gender had sent her to this alcove on the fourth floor, where the yearbooks were shelved. Jennifer had found her graduating class immediately, and hidden herself away in a carrel for privacy, but she wasn't looking for her picture. It was also the year Rick Morehouse had graduated.

Another lifetime ago, she thought. Six years that felt like a lifetime.

They'd both been psych majors, but she hadn't known Rick when they were undergrads, which was why she'd decided to see what he'd looked like back then. Maybe it would help explain her reaction when he'd pulled off his glasses, and she'd had a good look at his grease-stained face. She'd found herself staring at him almost rudely. He'd reminded her of someone else, but she hadn't been able to pinpoint who it was.

The seniors were listed alphabetically, which put Morehouse about two-thirds of the way through the maze of pictures. Jennifer let out a defeated sigh when she found him. He was down at the bottom right-hand corner of the page, and in six years he hadn't changed at all. The heavy, black-framed glasses dominated his features, probably the exact pair he had on today. His hair was dark and spiky, and his face had the same lean, long-jawed angles.

Even looking directly into the camera, he seemed withdrawn. Jennifer studied the shot anyway. She'd never really seen him straight on, she realized. He didn't deal with people that way, when he dealt with them at all. It was always from the side. You got half of him, never all. Posing for the standard graduation mug shot had forced him to face the all-seeing eye.

It was still as a graveyard in Jennifer's alcove, and the quiet should have helped her focus. But there was no sense of recognition as she searched Rick's features this time, even as she lightly traced them with her finger. Her disappointment was sharp as she closed the yearbook, but she couldn't let go of the feeling that she was missing something.

She left the library, still grappling with the possibility that Rick Morehouse might have some connection to the Violator case. Jennifer was certain that Rick had problems with women. She had no proof that they went beyond his inability to get a date, but his pathological shyness sometimes bordered on the sinister. The Violator was obviously deeply disturbed by the opposite sex, based on the nature of his serial crimes. Rick was highly intelligent and well educated, and there was every reason to believe the Violator was, too.

It could be pure coincidence that Myrna had seen something silver protruding from the Violator's back left pocket and that Rick Morehouse wore a silver wallet chain in the same back pocket, but Jennifer had the disturbing feeling that it wasn't. She'd worked from hunches, and this was the strongest one she could remember.

On the other hand, Jennifer had never seen Rick on a motorcycle, and there was no reason to think that he owned one or that he could drive one expertly enough to make off with a captive woman. The odds were that he couldn't afford the kind of bike the Violator used. BMWs were expensive machines. Also, Rick had never shown any signs of the aggressiveness it would take to break into women's homes and abduct them. Still, serial assailants often had violent tendencies bottled up, and when their inner conflicts became too great, they acted out in dangerous and sometimes deadly ways.

There was no compelling reason to think he could be the man responsible for a series of abductions that had escalated to the murder of a female homicide detective, but there wasn't any compelling reason to think he wasn't, either. And for the moment, Jennifer could not get that notion out of her head.

Jennifer was on her cell phone all the way back to the houseboat. She was trying to call Russ, and for some reason, he wasn't answering. His phone rang forever, which meant it must have been turned on. Otherwise, it would only have rung once and gone straight to voice mail. She'd already left him three messages. Of all times! She wanted to tell him about her suspicions, and she couldn't go to anyone else in the department. It wasn't substantial enough to involve Kate, especially since Jennifer was going on what Myrna had told her about the silver chain, and Myrna wasn't considered credible. With Russ she had a chance.

A storm front seemed to be chasing her as she crossed the University Bridge. The clouds looked like thunderheads, and they were coming up fast. Within moments a shadow had blanketed the road, and raindrops had begun to pelt the roof of her car. They hit as fast and furiously as bullets, and even though it wasn't unusual for a storm to blow in quickly around here, Jennifer was uneasy. The weather was more volatile than she could ever remember, sun and storms in the same breath, as if no one was in control, not even Mother Nature. There was a strange smell in the air, too, like steam heat from old radiator pipes. It felt like an omen, and not a good one.

By the time she reached the houseboat, the wind had whipped the rain into sheets of steel, and the baby willows that bordered Russ's property were bent nearly in half. There was nothing Jennifer could do about that, but a door was banging so loudly, she could hear it from inside the car. As she looked around, she realized it was the metal storage shed next to the garage.

She wasn't dressed for rain. Her capris and top were lightweight cotton, and her boat shoes were canvas, but she was going to get drenched anyway, and the racket was terrible. Might as well get it over with. She let herself out of the car and made a dash across the driveway.

The padlock was broken. The way it hung from the hasp made Jennifer think that someone might have smashed it. Her first impression was a break-in, but nothing seemed to be disturbed inside the shed, including the massive motorcycle that took up most of the space. Jennifer had once had mixed feelings about the bike, but seeing it now brought her pangs of nostalgia. It had been Russ's favorite mode of transportation, and if he'd had his way, they would have gone everywhere on it. She wondered if he used it anymore. Perhaps he'd put it in storage for the same reason she'd changed her hair, as a way to move on.

She found an iron bar in the shed that would hold the door until Russ could get the lock fixed. But as she let herself out, she noticed a smudge of dirt on her capris. Her tennis shoes were mud-splashed from the rain, but this was darker, grainy, and slightly moist. It had come from the fender of the bike, she realized. There was dirt on the wheels, too, and it looked fairly fresh.

Apparently the bike had been used recently. Jennifer didn't quite know what to make of that, so she let it go. There was a much larger problem to deal with in Rick Morehouse, and she was anxious to get herself down the stairs, into the houseboat, and out of the storm. Once she was inside and her head had cleared, she could decide what to do.

Drenched wasn't the word. The wooden steps were slippery, and she had to hang onto the railing and make her way down with extreme care, which allowed plenty of time for the rain to soak her through to the skin. There was water pooling in her pockets and her bra cups. The word was drowned.

She shook herself like an indignant cat the minute she got inside.

"Russ?" She called his name, not expecting him to respond. If he'd been there, he would have answered his phone.

Jennifer noticed the photograph while she was stripping off her wet shoes and socks. He'd put it right. The sight of it made her lightheaded with surprise, and she almost took a tumble. Both of her hands were involved in peeling off a sock, and she was teetering on one foot. Fortunately, the door was right behind her.

It was the snapshot taken by the real estate agent, and Jennifer had remembered the pose almost exactly. Russ had hoisted the For Sale sign in the air and drawn Jennifer close. What she'd forgotten was the kiss. He'd bent down and whispered that he loved her just as the button was clicked. Jennifer had been smiling as their lips touched.

Puddles formed on the tile around Jennifer's feet as she thought about the meaning of a picture set right. She'd kidded him about it last night, but it hadn't occurred to her that he would feel compelled to do anything like this. It was exactly what she would have wished him to do to show her that he wanted her back in his life.

I was just thinking that this was how it should have been.

Jennifer sat down on the floor to finish pulling off her socks. Otherwise she was going to hurt herself. It took a deep breath to contain the emotion that had welled up inside her. For the first time in a long while, the future looked bright. She could see the pink of a sunrise coming up behind those dark hills, but she was almost too superstitious to allow herself to think of it in any other terms than those very guarded ones.

Sitting in a puddle of rainwater, she struggled with a smile that would not be suppressed. God, she was happy. Maybe that shouldn't have alarmed her so much, but it did. Search as she would, she could find within her no reason to believe it would last — and every reason to believe it wouldn't. When you were a child who'd had your happiness snatched away by forces beyond your control, you grew up waiting for it to happen again, expecting that it would.

It would. Of course, it would. Something terrible happened to you, so you must have done something terrible to deserve that, right?

But she wasn't a child anymore. And maybe this was different. Maybe it was her turn, her time. When it came to reading and predicting the emotional lives of others, she was a seer, but she'd never been able to predict her own, and so much was out of one's control anyway. But as she peeled off the soggy socks and wrung them out, she told herself that no matter how tough it got to believe that Jennifer Nash might have some happiness coming, too, she would hold in her mind an image of the picture he'd put right. That would get her through it.

* * *

By nine-thirty that night it was dark, and Jennifer wasn't so sure that a picture would be enough. She still hadn't heard from Russ, and she'd tried his cell several more times. She was reduced to reassuring herself that everything was going to be fine. He was fine. *They* were fine. When he got her messages, he would call her back and they would figure out what to do about Morehouse, if anything. The silver chain was beginning to feel like a fluke to her now. There must be millions of them out there, and maybe Myrna hadn't seen a chain. Maybe she'd seen a silver comb sticking out of his pocket. Or a weapon.

As she lapped the kitchen, Jennifer pulled her hands from the pockets of her robe and retrieved the glass of red wine she'd left on the countertop. Well, technically, his robe. She'd slipped it on after throwing her wet clothes in the dryer. The wine was a merlot that she and Russ had picked up on the way back from the hotel yesterday. They were supposed to have had it with dinner tonight. So far, the wine *was* her dinner. She could barely taste it, but she kept hoping it would quiet her nerves. Nothing could quiet the questions that kept surfacing.

Russ's note said the rain had given him an idea. That had to mean he was following up on a lead. What frightened her was the thought that he might actually locate the Violator, and there would be a deadly confrontation. Serial assailants were the most cunning of adversaries. She'd never known Russ not to be able to handle himself, but there was always a first time, and what a tragic coincidence if that first time was now, just when they'd found their way back to each other.

Jennifer finished her wine and wondered how many miles she'd walked. She'd already checked with the duty desk and was told that Russ had not called in. He'd asked her not to say anything, and she hadn't, but she was wondering if it was time to break her silence. She had Kate's home number, and she trusted the chief more than anyone else in the department. All she had to do was tap out a few numbers, but a towering sense of obligation stopped her. Russ was counting on her, and she wanted to prove her good faith this time. She owed it to herself as much as to him.

Good faith, she thought, was an act of enormous courage.

As the night ticked away, her investigative instincts took over. She hadn't looked around the house to see if there was anything that would tell her where he'd gone — a scribbled note, a phone message. He'd said he had an office on the boat. Maybe she could find his case notes. There should be clues there.

It wasn't snooping, she told herself. It was concern.

She went through the kitchen first and found nothing that helped, but when she played back the messages on his digital phone machine, she was astounded to hear the one from two years ago where she broke off their engagement. It startled her that he would keep that one. Why, when it must have given him so much pain?

Her mind wanted to grapple with his reasons and try to explain them, but she wouldn't let herself. She had to let go of it just as she had the shed. These were questions that could only be answered by him, and before that could happen, she had to find him. It did concern her that he hadn't told her where he was going or what he was doing, but she knew he worked on hunches, as she did, and sometimes a hunch couldn't be communicated until you'd checked it out.

She continued her search of the house, but the only other thing she found that night was a locked door. She had thought there was just the one great room on the lower deck, but at the end of the entry hall, she found another room that she couldn't get into. The door didn't budge when she tried the handle, and although she probably could have forced the lock she chose not to. He clearly didn't want anyone in the room, and that included her.

The boat seemed to be as constantly in motion as she was, and it was making her dizzy. She had to stop, she told herself. Everything she did created more anxiety. It was late, but there was no point in trying to go to bed. The empty pillow would be a constant reminder of Russ. She could lie on the couch and watch TV, maybe fall asleep and escape all this uncertainty for awhile.

Two in the morning? A frantic buzzing sound awakened Jennifer, and the first thing she did was look at her watch. She'd fallen asleep on Russ's couch with all the lights and the television on. The persistent buzzing confused her until she realized it was her cell phone. She kept it on vibrate during her interview sessions, and she'd neglected to reset it.

She fished the tiny phone from her bathrobe pocket and fumbled to find the Talk button. "Russ?"

"Is this Jennifer?"

It was a woman's voice, and Jennifer's heart sank. "Yes, who's this?"

"Jennifer, it's Kate. We need your help. There's been another strike. This time he tried to snatch a woman from a motel in the Madrona area, but she got away from him."

"He?" Jennifer sat up and closed her eyes. Her forehead was splitting. Too much wine. Way too much. "The Violator?"

"We think so. The victim was taken to

Providence Hospital for treatment and observation. Her shoulder was dislocated, and she sustained a head wound, but she claims she got a good look at him. Says she could draw the picture herself. It sounds like a slam dunk. I could put our artist on it, but I'd rather have you, Jennifer."

A second chance. Kate didn't seem to realize she was doing Jennifer a favor. "You want me to interview her at the hospital? When and where?"

"Now, at Providence, the trauma unit on the first floor. The patrol officer who answered the 911 call is with her, and I'm on my way over there now. Can you get there in say twenty minutes?"

Jennifer was surprised to hear that Kate was putting in an appearance. With Russ gone, it should have been Kent Wright or one of the other detectives on the case. She said nothing, though. Hers was not to question why at this point, especially when there was so much cloak-and-daggering going on. Everybody involved seemed to have their own theory, and that probably included the new chief of police.

"I'll be there," Jennifer promised. "But Kate, no composite books or mug shots, okay? Give me a clear field this time?"

By the time Kate agreed, Jennifer was already on her feet and heading for the closet, where her tote bag was stored.

* * *

"She's waiting for you in her hospital room, but there's something you should know," Kate told Jennifer as the two of them slipped like ghosts through the dimly lit hallways of Providence Hospital's ground floor.

"What is it?" Jennifer asked. Kate had been mysterious from the moment Jennifer arrived, and it was beginning to make her uneasy.

"The victim's name is Nell Adams," Kate said, "and she escaped while her attacker was trying to force her out of her motel room. He never had the chance to restrain her or remove her hair, or any of the other things the Violator does to his victims. She has all her hair, and she wears it long and styled very much like yours. Her eyes are green."

Jennifer listened with growing disbelief as Kate described the woman's other features. She had fair skin and freckles. She was twenty-nine years old, five seven, and weighed 120 pounds. The latter were almost exactly Jennifer's dimensions.

"If she weren't a redhead," Kate said, "she'd be a dead ringer for you."

If Jennifer had been uneasy before, she was positively spooked now. It was her job to visualize faces, but she couldn't visualize her own, not in this circumstance. She just couldn't see it, and none of Kate's efforts to prepare her worked as she opened the door of Nell Adams's hospital room.

Jennifer and the victim weren't identical twins by any means, but Nell's wide, startled gaze could easily have been mistaken for Jennifer's. Especially now, when it was searching Jennifer's features in mounting confusion. Apparently she'd noticed the resemblance, too.

Nell was resting in a hospital bed, and Jennifer walked right over to introduce herself. It was her job to comfort victims and reassure them that they were in safe hands — and now, a career first — to play down any likeness there might be between the victim and the sketch artist.

What the hell is going on? This case gets creepier by the minute.

"How are you feeling?" she asked Nell. "That looks like a nasty bump on your forehead. Did they give you anything for the pain?"

The other woman touched the bandage that covered her temple. "I think it happened when I hit my head against the edge of the footboard. He was trying to put some duct tape over my mouth, and I kicked him as hard as I could in the knee. We both went down."

"That's okay," Jennifer said soothingly. "We don't need to talk about what happened quite yet. Let's make sure you're comfortable first. I'm going to get you another pillow for your head and find someone to bring us some hot water for tea. Do you like herbal tea?"

"I usually drink raspberry leaf," Nell said. "It's very relaxing."

"I think I might have some of that in my tote." Jennifer turned to Kate to see if she was joining them, but the chief shook her head. She was buttoning up her Burberry raincoat as if she intended to leave.

"I'm going back to my office and call an emergency meeting of the task force," Kate said. "You can join us as soon as you're done here. By that time, we should have something from the crime scene people."

Jennifer walked Kate out to the hallway. Neither of them mentioned Russ's absence, and Jennifer decided that discretion was still the better part of valor. Kate had to be aware by now that Russ was gone, although she wouldn't necessarily assume that Jennifer knew, which could explain her silence.

"No pressure," Kate muttered under her breath, "but get it done fast."

"I'll have something for you soon," Jennifer promised. "And thanks for giving me some time alone with Nell. I'll make good use of it."

Jennifer returned to the hospital room determined to do that, and fortunately, it didn't take long to make a connection with Nell Adams. She and the victim shared an avid interest in nutrition, and once Jennifer had brewed some tea from hot water provided by one of the orderlies, the two women were comparing notes on herbal supplements and antioxidants.

"I don't know how long I'm going to be in this place," Nell said, lowering her voice, "but maybe you could score some B for me? Ever had a niacin flush? It's a real rush. Makes your earlobes itch."

Jennifer laughed. "Maybe I'll score some for both of us."

Nell's grin made her wince. She was clearly feeling some discomfort from the head wound. Jennifer had swiped an extra pillow from an empty bed across the hall and used it to give her some additional support for her neck and head. If Nell had a concussion, it was important that she stay awake. But she seemed alert enough at the moment, and very talkative.

"Fresh blueberries are the bomb," Nell said. "Loaded to the gills with antioxidants, if you don't mind a blue tongue."

Jennifer was about to comment that she preferred blue tongues when Nell began to stare at her oddly. She cocked her head, scrutinizing Jennifer.

"I keep thinking you look like someone I know," she said.

Jennifer waited for the punch line. Nell had to be kidding, but the other woman just pursed her lips and looked perplexed.

"Maybe it'll come to me," she said.

She seemed so earnest that Jennifer tried not to smile. Apparently the resemblance wasn't as striking as Jennifer and Kate had thought, but it was definitely there. They hadn't both imagined it. In a truly paranoid moment, Jennifer wondered if the other victims resembled her, too. She'd seen crime photos of them, but they'd been completely denuded and under terrible stress. It was impossible to know what they looked like under normal circumstances.

Jennifer pushed aside her concerns and got on to the business of the interview. Nell explained that she'd moved down to the Seattle area from Bellingham, and she was staying in a motel while she looked for a job. She and Jennifer chatted about that and the crazy weather, but Jennifer noticed that Nell wasn't at all hesitant to talk about the attack when Jennifer interjected a question. She seemed to have a need to talk about it, and Jennifer saw no reason to discourage her. Some victims dealt with the emotional trauma that way.

"How did you happen to see his face?" Jennifer asked, as she hurried to capture the features that Nell was describing.

Nell rested her head on the pillows and touched the bandage on her head. Her eyelids flickered as if the light pressure had hurt. She was still showing signs of physical discomfort, but they wouldn't give her pain medication if there were any chance of a concussion. Jennifer debated calling a nurse, knowing that an interruption could jeopardize finishing the sketch, especially if the nurse decided that Nell needed to rest and asked Jennifer to leave.

"I sleep with pepper spray in the pocket of my flannel nightshirt," Nell explained. "I didn't think I'd hit him, but somehow the spray got inside the visor of his helmet, and he ripped it off. That's when I saw him."

Her lids drifted closed, and Jennifer rose from the chair.

"Are you feeling all right?" she asked. "Should I call someone?"

Nell's eyes popped open. "God, no," she protested. "They'll drag me back down to X ray and take more pictures of me, although I don't know what's left to X-ray. I'm a little sleepy, but don't leave, okay? I could almost draw the guy myself, I swear."

Jennifer called the nurse anyway, who shined a light in Nell's eyes and took her pulse. Before the nurse left, she assured them both that Nell was not suffering from a concussion. More likely she was coming down from the adrenaline rush of the attack. Jennifer was relieved, and Nell insisted that she could continue, despite her fatigue. She wanted very much to go on with the session, and since Jennifer desperately needed to finish the sketch, they began again. Within moments, they were proceeding as if they'd never been interrupted.

"You know, he had really dark eyebrows," Nell said at one point. "Like 'it was a dark and stormy night' eyebrows?"

"Perfect," Jennifer said, reaching for her charcoal pencil.

She'd never drawn so fast in her life, nor had she ever worked with a victim this strangely eloquent. It wasn't clear whether she'd infected Nell with her own urgency or if it was coming from Nell herself. At times she appeared to be fighting to stay awake, but the details came tumbling out anyway. She seemed to fear falling asleep before she'd described her attacker, as if this might be her only chance.

It might be Jennifer's, too. Still, Jennifer could hardly keep up with her, and it was a very different experience from working with Myrna. Nell wasn't contradictory or conflicted about what she saw, and that should have been reassuring, yet somehow it wasn't. In Jennifer's experience, victims who were dead sure of a face in a lineup were often dead wrong. Something else was at work. They were trying to alleviate their own fears and loss of control, which drove them to identify a suspect just to have someone taken off the streets. Their certainty gave them a sense of security, so they clung to it, even if it meant they'd identified the wrong man.

That could be the case with Nell, but Jennifer didn't have time to stop and question it now. She had to sketch furiously just to keep up, and there was another concern weighing even more heavily on her mind. The closer she came to completing the sketch, the more anxiety she felt. And finally she had to admit the truth, but only to herself.

There was *one* similarity to the session with Myrna.

Jennifer knew the suspect.

When it came time to show Nell the sketch, she held back. She asked how Nell felt and queried her about her job search. Meanwhile, Jennifer turned the tablet facedown on her lap. She couldn't believe what was happening, that it could be happening again. Her own inner conflicts must be filtering into the interview process. They were contaminating her sketches. She'd drawn the one man who couldn't have done what this woman was saying he did. That was impossible.

Jennifer had never shown a rendering to a victim hoping the victim would say it was the wrong face. Her stomach churned, but she fought back the nausea and turned the sketch pad over. Finally, she held it up.

"Is this the man who tried to abduct you?" she asked. "Please, Nell, be very sure before you answer."

Fear lit Nell's eyes for the first time. Her head pressed into the pillows, as if she were trying to escape the image Jennifer had shown her.

Jennifer knew that reaction well. It meant she'd done her job. This was the moment every forensic sketch artist lived for — when the features were right and the monster came to life before your eyes. She'd been there before, and it was a rush beyond any other intoxicant; *it felt as if she'd connected with the assailant's soul, however dark it might be, and the witness was a part of that rush. All three — artist, assailant, and witness — were bonded in an instant of awareness and understanding. Fearful understanding. This was him.*

It was the moment a forensic sketch artist lived for . . . unless you were Jennifer Nash, and then it was filled with dread.

Chapter 20

Jennifer hesitated at the conference room door. She took a moment to brace herself for what was to come. Kate and several task force members were inside. She'd managed to assemble two-thirds of the fifteen-member group — everyone from their own Junior Gordon to a representative from the prosecuting attorney's office and detectives from the other counties involved. While Jennifer had been working with Nell Adams, they were dissecting this new attack and strategizing their next moves. It was now nearly five a.m., and she was supposed to have a sketch ready to show them, the sketch that would break this case.

Jennifer heard a snap and a mournful creak. It came from somewhere down the hall behind her, but she didn't turn. It was wood expanding and contracting, the changing moisture in the air. The building had always had a haunted sound about it. It carried on conversations with itself, but you could only hear them when it was quiet, like now.

Get it over with, she told herself. *Stalling will only make it worse.*

She opened the door, and every head turned toward her.

Kate, who had been speaking to the group, hesitated. "Jennifer, come in. We've been waiting for you."

Jennifer had what they wanted, but she couldn't give it to them. Her sketch might break the case, but the repercussions would be unthinkable. They could break the department's back. No matter what kind of pressure the task force put on her, she'd resigned herself. She wouldn't show them what she'd drawn until she knew what it meant. Given her track record with sketches lately, it would be irresponsible to do anything else.

"I'm going to need more time with the victim," she said. "The sketch isn't —"

"Isn't ready?" Kate broke in. "How can that be? She told the patrol officer that she was close enough to spit in his face."

The door clicked shut behind Jennifer, but she didn't sit down.

"Nell Adams is in intensive care," Jennifer explained. "They think she may have had a seizure. They're running tests, but it could be hours before they know what's going on. Meanwhile, she can't have visitors."

That part was true. Nell's temperature had spiked dangerously high, and she'd briefly lost consciousness. It had happened just before Jennifer left, and she'd been concerned that the interview was too stressful, but the doctor who'd treated Nell assured Jennifer that wasn't the cause. He'd told her Nell might have died if Jennifer hadn't been with her and sought immediate help.

It was also true that Jennifer needed more time, although not to finish the sketch. It was already done and approved by Nell. But only Jennifer knew that, and she had to determine what had gone wrong before anyone else found out. The method she'd worked for years to perfect was failing her. She was supposed to tap the victim's subconscious, but she couldn't seem to suppress her own.

Revisiting the past could be dangerous, especially Jennifer's past. She was already on emotional overload when she came into the case. She'd had a personal relationship with the deceased, plus she was facing a hostile department and an emotional confrontation with the lead detective. Her work was intuitive, and a highly charged situation was as distracting as radio static. It took very little to alter the signal. But whatever the cause, Jennifer had to know whether she'd drawn the man Nell described or whether she was supplying her own details again, as she had with Talb.

Kent Wright was on his feet. "No visitors? What the hell does that mean? We don't even have a preliminary report! No one's been allowed near her."

Jennifer stepped forward. Playing victim's

advocate had always been part of her job, and it came naturally. "It means you'll get your report and whatever else you need when Nell Adams is out of danger."

"Chief —" He turned to Kate in frustration. "The victim swears she *saw* the Violator. She knows what he looks like. Get me some time with her — fifteen, twenty minutes — I'll get a description, and we'll nail this guy."

"Sorry, Jennifer gets first crack, and you know the reasons why."

"Jennifer *had* her crack." He snorted through his nostrils, furious. "At least let me talk to Adams. I won't push for a description. I'll question her about the attack itself. You can do that much, right? Speak with her doctors?"

"Pressure will be brought to bear," Kate assured him. "However, we're supposed to be in the business of saving the women of this city, not killing them. Try to remember that, Kent."

She turned to Jennifer. "I'll have the hospital notify you as soon as the victim's able to continue, so eat, drink, and sleep with your cell phone. As soon as you have a sketch, we'll bring Myrna in. If she agrees it's our boy, we'll replace the sketch that's circulating with the new one. Now, the rest of you, let's hear what you've got. Junior, give me a report on the crime scene."

Relief washed over Jennifer. She was uncertain what her next step would be, but at least she'd been given a reprieve. First she had to find some way to make an exit without attracting any more attention, and then she would go over the sketch again, and compare it to the others. She couldn't let go of the idea that her psyche was trying to tell her something, and possibly through the sketches.

"The security cameras weren't working that night," Junior was telling the group. "The desk clerk said they'd shorted out weeks before, and no one had bothered to fix them. . . ."

Jennifer found herself drawn to Junior's report, not because it was riveting, but because it wasn't Junior. Somehow he'd been transformed into a shuffling regurgitator of forensic facts. He'd shoved his hands in the pockets of his jeans, and he was moving listlessly and speaking in a monotone that made her wonder if he was depressed in general or if it had something to do with the Violator case.

Normally, he could unnerve even hardened detectives with the gruesome accounts of his findings. He was a fiend for the details. He never carried a notebook as most investigators did. It was all in his head, casebooks of glorious blood and gore. He could have written his own trivia game for crime buffs. Tonight it sounded as if he was talking to himself, but perhaps it was Jennifer's state of mind. She was distracted, too, and very little of his monologue struck a chord until he brought up the discrepancy in the tire treads.

"Looks like we could have two different motorcycles," he said. "If that's true, then either this guy has his own dealership, or —"

"Or we consider the possibility of a copycat killer." The lawyer from the DA's office broke in with that bombshell. She was blond and fortyish, a veteran prosecutor with killer instincts. Jennifer remembered her as highly regarded and widely feared.

Kate frowned, and everyone else looked startled. The copycat scenario had already occurred to Jennifer. She'd even mentioned it to Russ, but it was the last thing she wanted to hear tonight.

Jennifer changed the subject, speaking to Junior. "How do you know the tire treads are different?"

"The weather," he said. "It rained last night, and it rained the nights he snatched the first two victims. We have tire prints from all three abductions. He was driving a BMW R1200C during the first two strikes. This time he wasn't. We don't know the make yet."

"Our boy changed bikes? Maybe he just changed tires." Kate asked the question.

"Or it's a different boy." The prosecutor persisted with her theory. "Remember that he also used a different MO with Sharon, and based on what we know so far, there are more discrepancies with Nell Adams. He didn't strike at midnight, and he didn't wait until the victim was sleeping, which was probably why she was able to escape. We could be dealing with someone who wants us to think he's the Violator."

Jennifer had to find a way to leave. The woman's assertions were making her feel ill, and she couldn't let herself think about the reasons why, if she even understood them. She was being bombarded with conflicting information, and she knew things the task force didn't know, *couldn't* know. Where the hell was Russ? She needed to talk to him and tell him what was going on. He was the only one who could explain all this to her.

Someone had to know how frightened she was.

Kate was shaking her head. "I'm not buying this copycat thing. I think our boy is nervous. We're getting closer, and he's getting sloppy. He gave her a good look at his face, and then he lost her."

She nodded. "It's the Violator, but he wants to get caught, ladies and gentlemen. Let's oblige him."

Junior had stopped walking and talking. He was listening to Kate.

Kent Wright was peering at the chief, too. "Where the hell is Russ?" he asked, echoing Jennifer's thoughts.

Kate sat back in her chair. She actually

fidgeted, tapping her fingers against her lips. At last she said, "He's in Okanogan County, and that information is not to leave this room. If the press gets wind of anything I'm about to say, I'll hold every one of you responsible, and you'd better have your résumés ready."

She hesitated for effect. "Russ has reason to think that's where the Violator has been taking his victims. He's checking out trailers in the area."

Jennifer was stunned. Stunned and relieved, but mostly stunned. Why hadn't Russ called her? If he'd managed to get a call through to Kate, he could have called her as well. He must know that she was worried.

Wright's voice was harsh. "What the hell is his reason? And why all the secrecy? I'm his partner. Whatever he's doing, I should be in on it. I should be there."

Kate bristled at him. "That's all I'm prepared to say, Kent. Someone's been leaking information to the press, and if this gets out, it could tip our boy. We wouldn't want that now, would we?"

The tension in the room had escalated, but Kate's news had actually taken the pressure off Jennifer. She knew where Russ was. He was safe and apparently following a very strong lead, which relieved some of her concern about him, as well as her urgency to produce a sketch. But she still didn't understand why she hadn't heard from him.

"Excuse me." All eyes veered to Jennifer as she walked to the door. She was leaving, and no one was going to stop her.

"Jennifer?" Kate asked, "is something wrong?"

Lie, she told herself. *Lie through your teeth.* "I just realized that I left my tote somewhere, and my unfinished sketch is in it. It may be at the hospital. I'll check on Nell Adams's condition while I'm there."

Jennifer expected protests, but there were none. An ominous quiet had fallen over the room. She closed the door on it.

Jennifer's tote was actually in the front seat of her car. Kate had assigned her a temporary parking spot in the basement of the Public Safety Building, and Jennifer had left the bag here when she'd gone up to the task force meeting. The unfinished sketch was inside, and she couldn't take a chance of anyone seeing it. She also had all the rest of the sketches, her earlier renderings, and a copy of the sketch that the department's artist had made.

The sketch was where she'd put it, separate from the others in its own envelope glove. She glanced around to make sure she was alone in the neon-bright parking area. Satisfied there was no one around, she laid the sketch out on the passenger seat.

Thank God, she was still numb inside. She didn't want to feel anything as she forced herself to acknowledge the uncanny likeness. She only wanted to think. Think and bring every brain cell to bear on making rational sense of what she saw. It was Russ's face. There was no mistaking the famous furrowed brow, the broken nose. The mouth that could burn you with words or kisses.

It was Russ, but she knew now that it couldn't be him.

He was in another county.

Thank God.

She was too close to the case. That was the only thing that made sense. She had no other way to explain why this face was Russ Sadler's, and why he was the first person she thought of when she stepped back from the completed sketch and really looked at it. She'd seen it instantly.

More proof for her theory. One feature had tipped the scales again, and in this case it was probably Nell's description of the suspect's nose. "The bridge was uneven," she'd said, "like it had been broken and healed wrong."

One salient feature. It had to be that. Everyone knew Russ had a broken nose. He'd just told Jennifer how it really happened. His father had done it. It couldn't be that Jennifer was looking for reasons to sabotage her reconciliation with Russ. Her same fears of intimacy at work? How could she be in love with a killer? How could any woman be in love with a killer?

No, that was ridiculous.

She was beginning to see the value of videotape. She would have given anything to have one now. But none of that mattered, really. Nell Adams had okayed the sketch without any ambivalence at all. She was certain this was the man who'd tried to abduct her.

Jennifer glanced in the rearview mirror. She thought she'd heard a door shut, but she couldn't see anything by the stairway exit. It could have been a car door — or the building was talking again. Still, she knew the task force would be breaking at some point, and she didn't want to explain why she was still sitting in her car.

She returned the sketch to its glove and slid it back into her tote. She needed a safe place to go over all the sketches. She was looking for any common thread among them, but she couldn't do it here. Time was running out, and she had to get this resolved. If she was contaminating the work, then she would have no choice but to excuse herself from the case and turn everything over to the department's artist.

Should she go back to the houseboat or to the hotel? She needed to be somewhere that she could block all extraneous thoughts and concentrate only on the faces in front of her.

Her hotel room was a more neutral setting, but she needed to go back to the houseboat for another reason. There was one more thing she had to do there, just to be totally sure that none of this had anything to do with Russ.

Junior was the next person to excuse himself from the task force meeting, and he did it almost as abruptly as Jennifer.

"Nature calls," he said, pushing back his chair.

No one seemed to notice when the toe of his sneaker caught on a loose tile and nearly lifted it off the floor. They didn't notice his furtive, apologetic exit, either, and Junior was grateful. He didn't give a shit about a bunch of self-important, by-the-book hacks. There was about as much imagination and brainpower in that room as in one burned-out lightbulb.

As soon as the door closed behind him, he headed for the elevators.

Nash might be the exception, he allowed. As far as he could tell, she was the only one who had the intuitive — and possibly even the deductive — skills to figure out what was going on. But, fortunately, she was so messed up in the head over Russ that she didn't know right from left. Or right from wrong? Jennifer, the miracle worker, had lost her gift, and Junior couldn't be happier. She was his secret weapon now. By slowing down the investigation, she was playing right into his hands.

"Jennerahhhhma," he murmured.

When he reached the second floor, he entered the darkened, windowless lab and immediately locked the door behind him. Except for the digital display lights on the monitors, it was as black as a cave, but that was his intention. He had an affinity for the dark and was good at finding his way around. He made his way back to his office without having to touch anything, and once he was safely inside, he closed the door, leaving that room dark, too.

Now he would need a little help from his friends.

The narrow beam of his flashlight led him to a black lacquered cabinet that housed a CD player and was arguably the only piece of furniture in the room. It was unlocked, which also distinguished it from all the other files and equipment.

Junior kept a flashlight in his lab coat pocket, one hooked to a loop on his belt, and one in the glove compartment of his car. Virtually every place it was conceivable to stash a flashlight, he had one. He shined the blue beam on the cabinet's brass pulls and groaned as he knelt down. He'd landed on the wrong knee, the one he'd hurt recently in a fender bender.

He laid the flashlight on the floor in order to lift the CD player out of the cabinet. When he had the player set so the flashlight illuminated the instrument panel, he made some adjustments, ostensibly to balance the sound. A drawer slid open. It was empty, but he'd expected that. With a little pressure in the right places, he removed the bottom, revealing another compartment.

He felt around in the shallow depths, but found nothing.

This one was empty, too. Empty? Junior had *not* expected that.

"No way," he whispered, grabbing the flashlight. The beam exposed what he couldn't believe. Couldn't fucking believe. Someone had found his hiding place. They'd taken the journal and his notes.

An icy sweat filmed his forehead. His stomach began to churn, and he felt as if he were going to be sick. He was going to destroy them. All along he was going to. He'd never meant to keep them. *Why the hell hadn't he destroyed them?*

He reached up to wipe the sweat from his forehead, but his hands were shaking, and he rubbed some of it into his eyes. It burned like acid. He dropped to all fours, blinded and certain he was going to be sick. *A crime scene! This is a freaking crime scene, you idiot, and you're an investigator. Stop shaking and dust the cabinet for fingerprints. Check the rug for fibers.*

But he wasn't going to find anything, and he knew it. Whoever did this worked for the department.

Chapter 21

Jennifer stood frozen at the open shed door. The bike was gone.

If her spine hadn't been so rigid, she might have collapsed. It was the only thing holding her up. *He wasn't the Violator.* She would never believe that. It was absurd to think that Russ was abducting and torturing women. He wasn't a copycat killer, either. He had no reason to want Sharon or anyone else dead. There was no motive.

Jennifer's racing mind began to slow as she realized the logic of her thoughts. It was true. There *was* no motive. If she'd been thinking rationally, she would have seen that before. She hadn't slept since Kate woke her up, and the stress and confusion of dealing with Nell Adams had left her emotionally exhausted. But she couldn't argue with simple logic. She didn't even have to debate whether or not Russ was capable of abduction, torture, or wanton killing. It was moot. Without motive you had nothing.

As she stared into the gray belly of the storage shed, she thought of several more things that helped to settle her mind. She hadn't locked the shed securely. She'd put the bar on the outside to keep the door from banging. Anyone could have opened it and helped himself to a very expensive bike. *The bike had been stolen.* Russ might not be happy about that eventuality, but it relieved Jennifer's mind considerably.

She found the iron bar lying in the grass by the nearest willow tree. Because her instincts were trained, she searched through her tote for the plastic bags she always carried and found a small garbage sack. Taking care not to smudge any fingerprints that might be there, she slid the bar into the sack, carried it back to her car, and left it in her trunk. From there her thoughts turned to what lay ahead.

The plan was to take a quick shower and change. She had no idea when a call from Kate might come in, sending her back to the hospital, and she wanted some time to study her sketches and make a decision about whether or not to bring in another artist. She also wanted to talk to Russ. She'd tried his cell on the way over, but she kept getting the same message, that he was out of range.

She let herself in with the key he'd left her, shivering as she dropped it in the zip pocket of her tote. The weather had cooled so swiftly, it had given her a case of the chills, and she had no idea how to get any heat going. There wasn't time to start a fire, but a hot shower should help.

Something clinked against the hardwood floor. She knew it was the door key even before she looked down. Apparently, she'd missed the pocket. As she bent and picked it up, she fingered its old-fashioned contours and wondered if it was original to the houseboat. It had a large notched head and a spindly blade that reminded her of the kind of key that Benjamin Franklin attached to a kite in a lightning storm. If it was original, it might fit some of the interior doors as well.

The locked door to Russ's office was at the opposite end of the hall.

Jennifer drew in a breath and made a difficult decision. She needed answers. This wasn't about invading anyone's privacy — it was about life and death. Nell Adams had described Russ, and that made him a suspect, whether Jennifer believed he was or not. The room was probably just an office, but she had to see for herself.

The key fit. She inserted the head and turned it forcefully. Tumblers clicked, and she felt the lock release. The door groaned open with a touch, but Jennifer could see nothing. There was no hint of light inside the room. If there were windows, the shades were drawn. She felt along the wall for a light switch and found a panel of switches. When she touched the first one, a spotlight came on. It took a moment for her eyes to focus, and then she realized she was looking at a woman's naked body.

Jennifer stepped back. Something dug into the curve between her shoulder blades. It was the sharp edge of the open door.

A photograph. She was looking at a snapshot, blown up to small poster size and tacked to the wall. The woman was standing against a black backdrop and staring at the camera with a look of frozen horror. Every follicle of her hair had been removed from her body. She was the first of the Violator's victims. Jennifer had seen pictures of the early victims, and she would not quickly forget the contrast of their pale, hairless skin and dark, wounded eyes. They'd looked like living corpses. Clustered around the blowup of this victim were other pictures, smaller in size. They were poses from different angles, as well as shots of her bedroom, the abduction scene.

Jennifer touched the next switch, and another light came on. Another blowup. Another shorn body. They were all there, she realized as she flipped more switches and flooded the room with light. The last light illuminated Sharon, dead and lying on the park grounds in a paper examining gown, where the Violator had left her to be found. There were morgue shots of Sharon, too, and pictures of her apartment.

Jennifer stared in ringing disbelief, unable

to reconcile what she was looking at. Beyond the shock of discovering the photographs, she felt as if she, too, were violating these women by gaping at them this way. But then how must he have felt? And why had he done it? Her heart wasn't pounding now. She couldn't even be sure it was beating.

Detectives did this, she told herself. They carried murder books with them with pages of crime scene photos. Sometimes they blew those photos up or had them scanned into a computer to see more detail. Some of them went to extremes to get into the mind of the UNSUB and discover how he thought. They did it in order to predict and trap him. They immersed themselves in the minutiae of the case, profiled the killer, stalked the killer, thought like the killer, became the killer.

Russ was one of those detectives. He never did anything halfway. He might do this, too. Blow up crime scene photos. Study them. Immerse himself.

Jennifer's back was to the door, and she was nodding at her own analysis. This was logical, too, wasn't it? It was possible. It certainly wasn't proof that there was anything wrong. These were legitimate photos. She could see the markings, the department's date stamp.

It was logical, wasn't it?

She bowed her head and let out a shaking breath. This couldn't be as devastating as it felt. Nothing could be that devastating. She was almost too stunned to react, and that might be the only thing on her side, because if she did react, it would be horrible. She was sure she could hold it together, and that was the one thing she *had* to do right now. Hold it together.

She felt along the wall to turn off the switches. She wanted to turn off the switch in her mind as well and leave this room totally dark. It was a house of horrors, and she couldn't let herself get trapped in here. She couldn't let herself obsess. In time she would understand what it meant and why he'd done it. She would understand it all, but for now she had to finish what she'd started, take the exact steps she'd laid out, and do whatever she could to help with the investigation. There were other things more important than this room to deal with. When Russ arrived, she would tell him what she'd found and give him a chance to explain. That was what she had to do. Take the steps, put one foot in front of the other, and start by leaving this room.

Leave the room, Jennifer.

She turned off the switches, hesitating on the last one that was focused on Sharon. Something told her to look at it again, and as she was turning, she saw the book. It wasn't in the crime scene photo. It was lying open on a worktable that was piled high with what seemed to be research: criminology books and magazines, newspaper clippings, and photocopies of police records. There were plastic bags of evidence that he apparently had never turned in.

He worked in here, she told herself. He did research. He immersed himself like other detectives did — the good ones, the ones who understood that when you constantly walked a tightrope between good and evil, you risked falling off.

Had Russ fallen off?

Jennifer left the light on. She walked over to the table, and as she picked up the book, she saw that there were dated, handwritten entries. It was a woman's handwriting, a woman's diary. She skimmed the open pages and realized that she was reading about someone's love life. It was a relationship the diarist feared was dangerous.

I have to tell him it's over. It's not safe for me to keep seeing him. Someone in the department will find out, and it will ruin my chances for promotion. I'm not going to be a junior homicide detective forever, running DMV records and doing grunt work. I want to run the place. I want Kate's job.

It was Sharon's diary, Jennifer realized. She recognized the handwriting — and the ambition. Sharon had never hidden the fact that she wanted to succeed in what was essentially a man's world, and Kate was living proof that it could be done. These pages were her last entries, and this one was dated the day before she was murdered.

Jennifer leafed through the earlier entries but couldn't find any mention of the man's name — or anyone's name, except the one reference to Kate. That might have been a slip, because Sharon was obviously concerned about someone finding the diary. She hadn't even identified herself, but the details confirmed that it was hers. She and Sharon had been friends long enough for Jennifer to have known some of the intimate details of her life.

There was one last entry on the morning of her death.

I'm going to tell him tonight. The thought of it scares me, but I have to go through with it this time. I can't believe he'd hurt me. That would be crazy. He doesn't love me. It's all about sex, and that's what's scaring me, the sex. He has a sinister side.

The sex scared her. Jennifer turned away from the pictures, the diary in her hand. She reached to turn off the light, and the hardbound book clattered to the floor. She glanced down at the book and back up at the panel. For a moment, she didn't know what to do. She had just realized there was one last spotlight, which must mean one last black area of wall. She was afraid to turn that switch. She was afraid to turn at all. Instead, she picked up the diary and fled the houseboat.

The lobby of the Madison Renaissance would have been empty except for the man waiting by the escalators. The solitary figure was the first thing Jennifer saw when she walked through the front doors, and he brought her to a halt.

Russ, she thought.

She knew almost immediately that she was wrong, but the powerful first impression left her staring at him in surprise. Her disappointment was sharp as she realized the man she wanted to be Russ was actually Kent Wright. That surprised her, too, because the two detectives didn't bear any strong resemblance in her mind, except that they both dressed well.

"Well, well," Wright said as he approached her, "if it isn't the sketch *artiste,* and she's all alone. Where's lover boy?"

He slipped his hands into the pockets of his suit pants, and his jacket gaped open, revealing an expensive monogrammed shirt. It was all very *GQ*, but Jennifer wasn't impressed. She pretended to have no idea what he was talking about, but he wasn't having any of it.

"I want to know what Russ Sadler's up to," Wright said. "And don't tell me you don't know."

"I *don't* know. Why do you think I would?"

"Because you spent the night at his houseboat?"

"What?" Jennifer flared at him. "You're spying on me? I was ill, and Russ has a spare room. He was concerned about me spending the night alone in a hotel room."

His grin said, *Whatever you say, lady.* "I'm not going to say anything about this. Just tell me where he is and what he's up to. How hard could that be?"

"It could be impossible since I don't *know.*"

An elevator binged and the doors slid open. The women who exited gave Jennifer a curious glance, which made Jennifer wonder if she looked as crazy and disheveled as she felt. Her cotton jersey twinset and pants had held up reasonably well, but her head still felt as if it might crack open from tension, and her skin felt pinched and tight.

Kent waited until the woman was out of earshot before speaking.

"You want to play hard to get?" he said, *sotto voce,* "I'm going to have your boyfriend's ass kicked off this case. I'll make damn sure they know who was taking poor, sick Jennifer Nash's temperature all night long."

"No wonder Sharon hated you."

Jennifer said it with all the bottled fury she felt, and suddenly Wright was no longer looking quite so *GQ*. The pocketed hands had curled into fists, and the lumps were ruining the line of his perfectly tailored slacks.

"Who the fuck told you that?"

No one had told Jennifer that, but if Sharon hadn't hated working with Kent Wright, she should have. Without a word or a glance, she brushed past him and stepped on the escalator to the second floor. She would take the elevator up to her room from there. Let the arrogant bastard tell whoever he wanted whatever he wanted. If Wright had caught her at any other time, she might have tried to bluff her way through the encounter, mostly to protect Russ from any hint of scandal. But she didn't know whom to protect anymore. She didn't know anything, except that she wanted to find out who had tortured the women in the photographs she'd just seen. *And who had killed Sharon.*

The red message light was flashing on the hotel phone. Jennifer saw it the minute she walked in the room, and a cord pulled at the base of her throat. She dropped her tote on the floor and went over to the nightstand next to the bed. It was probably Kate, calling her back, but it could be Russ, too. If he'd been trying to reach her here, then it must mean that he hadn't taken her cell number with him. His only option had been to call the hotel.

Hope and dread assailed her.

Please, let it be him, she thought as she sat down on the bed and picked up the receiver. A button connected her to the hotel voice mail. There were nine messages waiting. Nine? At least one of those had to be Russ.

They came up in succession, and although the wait between messages was only seconds, the anticipation of hearing a familiar voice was terrible, especially since the first two were messages she'd forgotten to delete, and one of them was from Russ. His voice made her heart jump painfully, and then she realized it was an old call.

The next six were all hang-ups. Who the hell was playing these games? There was nothing from Kate or anyone at the department. Nothing from Russ. Jennifer wanted to bang down the receiver she was so frustrated, but there was one call left. Taking it felt like Russian roulette, but she waited.

There was a short space of silence, and Jennifer was almost certain she was going to hear another click that would end everything, her last chance to restore some sanity to her life. But suddenly there was a woman on the line, and she was crying and pleading.

"I'm his mother," she rasped, "and I would do anything to protect him, but I can't stop him. He loves you, and I know you love him.

Please stop him from hurting people!"

The woman's urgency was raw and disturbing, but Jennifer didn't recognize the voice and wondered if the message was meant for her. She played it again, aware that there was little chance for messages to go astray in this hotel because the operators asked the caller to give the guest's name, as well as the room. There could have been a mistake, but Jennifer doubted it.

"He loves you, and I know you love him."

Jennifer had no idea what she could be talking about. There was only one man in her life like that, and she couldn't have meant him. It had to be the worst kind of coincidence that she and Russ had talked about his mother on the houseboat. Jennifer didn't even want to think about that night at a time like this. They'd shared themselves, and it had brought them closer. Despite everything, she didn't want that tainted.

"Please stop him from hurting people!"

A woman's voice broke into Jennifer's thoughts, but this time it was a recording, telling her to hang up and dial again. She was still holding onto the receiver. Involved as she was in the Violator case, Jennifer naturally thought it must be related, but the message could have been about anyone. The caller gave no clue as to who she was or why she was calling, other than the anguished message.

Jennifer quickly rang the hotel desk to see

if there was some way to identify the caller or get her number. She used the excuse that the message was garbled, and she couldn't hear clearly. "I need your help," she told the clerk. "It was urgent, but I can't return the call."

The clerk apologized and suggested Jennifer check with the local phone company, but Jennifer knew what it took to get access to those records, so she didn't bother. She glanced at her watch and left the bed. It was close to noon, and she didn't know where the time had gone. How long had she been in that room, staring at the pictures on Russ's wall? It had only felt like moments.

She needed to clean up, change her clothes, and get on with what she had to do, but there was too much turmoil inside her. She went to the window and opened the curtains. It didn't look like noon. It looked like midnight. The sky was ominously dark, and massive storm clouds were gathering over the waters of the sound. They were going to have another thunderstorm, and considering her current state of mind, Jennifer wondered if she'd caused it.

Russ, she thought. *What's happened to Russ?*

Her mind was flooded with all the things that had occurred since he left.

She'd discovered his motorcycle before the most recent attack, and the dirty tires told her it had been driven at some point in the last few weeks. When she went back after leaving the task force, the bike was gone. She sketched his face, and the victim positively identified him as her attacker. She found the room, the blowups, the bags of evidence. She read the diary that gave him a motive. His ex-partner's diary. What was he doing with Sharon's diary? And why had he discounted all of Jennifer's concerns when they talked in the houseboat about the Violator case?

His past disturbed her, too. He was raised by a man who brutalized women. And now this phone call. All the hang-ups, and then this message from a distraught mother. Jennifer didn't understand. She didn't want to understand. If she could have given this case to the department's sketch artist, she would have. It might have been better for all concerned, but that wasn't possible, either. No one knew about any of this but her. They didn't know about Rick Morehouse. They didn't know about Russ. Either she had to go to Kate and tell her what was going on, or she had to *do* something.

Chapter 22

Watching the storm made Jennifer feel caught and helpless. She turned away, certain that there was something missing, a piece or several pieces that would make all the fragments come together in a cohesive image. There was some reason for all these coincidences, and she was convinced that's what they were, coincidences. She still could not make herself believe that Russ had done anything wrong. And she wouldn't believe it unless she heard the words from his mouth, although if it went that far, they would probably accuse her of being in denial, or possibly even protecting him.

The families of serial killers were often stunned and disbelieving when the heinous crimes were exposed. Some refused to believe in the face of conclusive DNA evidence. And it wasn't mere denial. Children who endured ongoing abuse often had to split off from themselves to survive. It wasn't unusual for them to develop coping personas that were textbook normal. To the world around them, they were great guys, schoolteachers, scout leaders, and churchgoers. But the deeply buried shame and rage did not dissipate.

Locked off from any hope of expression, it fed on its own sick energy. It grew until it had to find release somehow, and the only real release was to hurt the way they'd been hurt.

In the worst cases, where their abusers had stripped them of their identity and psychologically annihilated them, they were driven to destroy the abuser in order to find themselves. To exist they had to kill the godlike figure, but buried along with their rage was an abject terror of the abuser that forced them to destroy symbols rather than the all-powerful god himself. It was ultimately unsatisfying — and maddening — because to find relief, the symbols had to be destroyed again and again.

Jennifer wasn't aware that the Violator had ever been profiled, but it was obvious from his signature behavior that he needed to control and humiliate his victims. More revealing was his need to teach them a lesson and to punish them, apparently for their sexuality and their perceived moral lapses. In the Violator's case, it seemed he was holding women responsible for being abused and punishing them rather than the abuser. It was like blaming the victim for being raped.

That wasn't Russ. She knew that wasn't him.

What she had to do was find out who it was.

In her tote were copies of all the sketches.

She pulled them out, arranged them on the hotel bed, and drew up a chair to study them. She needed to clear her mind and relax. And most important, she had to trust herself this time. Her instincts had never failed her before, and maybe it was possible that they weren't failing her now. What if she'd been right all along? What if Myrna Simone had seen Bob Talb that night or someone who looked like him? And what if the most recent victim had seen Russ? *Or someone who looked like him.*

Jennifer sat there, stunned. She didn't quite know what to make of her thoughts. It felt like an epiphany of some kind, but all she had was a powerful feeling and nothing to support it. Another hunch, but still, the possibility intrigued her. Was it possible that she hadn't contaminated the sketches? And if she took that idea one step further, was it possible that the witnesses themselves had been contaminated — that someone had tampered with their experience of the crime in some way, maybe through the use of tricks or illusions?

Was the Violator that good? If he was, they were dealing with someone who was light-years ahead of them all, including her.

She'd hit on something, but she had no idea where to go with it, and she was still haunted by the feeling that the sketches had something to tell her. For now she needed to stay with that rather than let herself be distracted.

She tried letting her mind go blank as she gazed at the sketches, not looking for anything, not expecting anything, just taking them in as if she were seeing them for the first time. As her concentration deepened, she let herself imagine that she was a victim, faced with a lineup of suspects, and that one of these men had assaulted her. Which one had done it?

Of all the sketches she'd drawn, it was the very first one that kept pulling her back. It wasn't Russ's face, she noted with relief. There were similarities in the narrow lines and angles, but she doubted that anyone would have identified this man as Russ. The sketch was also the clearest example of Jennifer's method at work. She'd drawn it before Myrna had begun to inundate her with contradictions and before she'd mentioned the eclipsed eye. And probably before Jennifer herself had begun to skew the drawings with her own perceptions.

This man's eyes were dark, unusually dark, but they were equal in size, intensity, and focus. And Jennifer had seen them before. The image seemed to soften and blur as she realized that this could be the thread, the connection she had been trying to make for days, but it was still beyond her.

She rose and turned out the lights in the

room. She wanted to be alone in the gloom, alone with those eyes. She didn't need to look at the sketches anymore. She would gaze into his eyes and let him gaze back. If this man were really known to her, he would reveal himself. The challenge would be to surrender her control enough to let it happen.

She had no idea how much time had gone by when everything began to change, including her own vital signs. It wasn't a gradual thing, as she'd expected. It was swift and sudden. Her breath was coming short, her heart fast, and her inner focus was transforming. The field was widening like a spotlight, and where his eyes had dominated, it was now filled with the image of a man.

There was no fog to lift, no shadows to burn away. She saw immediately who it was. He was looking at her with the same intensity as he had the day he'd fixed her car.

He'd taken off his glasses to wipe his face, and Jennifer had noticed his eyes for the first time. The darkest orbs she could imagine, as if they'd been artificially dilated. It was a bright day, as she remembered, and he'd had his head under the hood of her car. Did the dark eyes explain her sense of recognition? Or was it because without his glasses, he resembled someone else? Russ, perhaps? The two men were similar enough in build to create confusion. She'd never seen Rick on a motorcycle, but she had seen the chain.

Jennifer turned on the night table lamp and picked up the phone. Myrna had insisted it was one dark eye, not two. Still, Jennifer wanted to talk with her. If Rick was the man she saw that night, she might be able to ID him now. Jennifer could sketch his face and see if Myrna recognized him. There wouldn't have to be any mug shots or lineups involved.

Jennifer got the shelter's director on her first try, but she was dumbfounded to hear that they hadn't seen Myrna since the day Jennifer last interviewed her. She'd signed out around noon, left no word where she was going, and didn't return.

"Why wasn't someone told?" Jennifer asked.

"I called Mr. Sadler, the lead detective, and he assured me they would track her down. I assumed he'd decided to have her stay somewhere else."

Jennifer said no more. She didn't ask for details because she didn't want to alert the shelter director to a problem or inadvertently reveal something sensitive about the case. She thanked the woman and hung up the phone with the sick feeling in her stomach that was becoming familiar. Questions were flooding her, and she couldn't answer them. But she couldn't let them swamp her into inaction, either.

Nell Adams was in intensive care, and their only witness had disappeared. Normally,

Jennifer would have called for police support, but if she couldn't answer her own questions, how could she answer theirs? As she turned to the pictures again, she was immediately and painfully aware of her options. There was no time to search for Myrna, and Jennifer would have to go through Kate to get to Nell. That left her with only one choice that made sense right now. The sketches had told her everything they were going to. She had the face that had been eluding her. She would have to follow up on her suspicions herself.

Thirty minutes later she was in the bathroom, stripping off her clothes. She had gone to a nearby drugstore and bought an auburn hair rinse. She finger-combed the lotion through her hair and while it processed, she turned on the shower and let it run until the water was hot. Once inside the steaming canopy, she worked the shampoo into a lather and hoped for the best.

By the time she was done with the shower and toweling herself off in front of the mirror, she'd formulated her plan. Another bath towel was wrapped around her head, and when she pulled it free, her hair tumbled to her shoulders. Even though it was wet, she could see that she had the effect she wanted.

There, she thought, turning to catch the deep red highlights. Soon she would be ready for Rick Morehouse.

* * *

Jennifer's Datsun crept slowly through the narrow aisles of C-8, the psychology parking lot. She was looking for Rick's VW, and the odds were good that she would find it. The lot was large, and it was full, but unless things had changed, Rick would be there. He practically lived on campus.

As she turned up the next aisle, she saw a faded blue beetle at the other end on the right-hand side. She didn't know his license plate number, but the rusting bumpers and dented fenders were familiar enough to convince her that it was Rick's. She pulled up behind the car, left her rental running, and let herself out. His windows were rolled up, and the doors were locked. The trunk was locked, too.

She discovered all that in a matter of seconds, jiggling handles while she kept an eye out for the campus security patrol. She wasn't going to take a chance on breaking into the car and getting caught, but if she couldn't get his home address this way, from his car registration, she would have to find some way to get the information from him, and that was risky. She'd already looked in the phone book but hadn't expected to find him listed. Registration hadn't been willing to give out any information when she stopped by there, but that hadn't surprised her, either.

His car was her only real shot at getting what she needed without a confrontation. Now she would have to deal with him, but she'd prepared for that. They would be in a public place in broad daylight. The trick was to get him alone long enough to accomplish what she needed. She'd dressed for the part in snug jeans and a cardigan with several buttons undone, but the red hair was her coup de grace. She wanted to catch him by surprise in the hope that he might reveal something, not necessarily by what he said but by what he didn't say, his body language. It wasn't evidence that would hold up in court, but it would tell her whether she was on the right track. The difficult part would be distracting him long enough to get her hands on his driver's license.

She didn't find him in his cubicle, but one of the other TAs directed her to a classroom where Rick was correcting papers. That was a stroke of good luck. She had no chance unless he was alone.

A sense of unusual calm prevailed as she opened the classroom door. She didn't know if she believed in a higher self or alter egos, but some latent aspect of her personality seemed to have taken over. This had to be done, and there was no one else to do it. If Rick Morehouse was the Violator, then she had to find a way to stop him. It wasn't an option. She was out of options. If there was a risk, she would have to take it. If there were consequences, she would have to take them. She was ready for the worst.

She suspected that someone had it out for Russ, and possibly for her, too. He was being framed, and she was the only one who knew it. Even Russ didn't know, and she wasn't certain she would have told him if she had the opportunity. This wasn't just about proving him innocent. She had to prove it to herself.

Rick was sitting at a table at the front of the room. He barely looked up as she entered the room.

"I have something for you." Her voice was full of softness and breathy resonance as she approached him. She held up her tote, where she'd put the package.

He looked baffled and frightened, as if he wanted to run. But he sat very still as she set her tote on his table and pretended to be searching for a gift.

"I wanted to thank you for helping me with my car," she explained. "I never really got the chance."

"It's okay," he mumbled. "You don't have to —"

"No, but I do!"

He looked so startled she couldn't imagine him hurting anyone. Was she wrong? His eyes were huge and dark behind the thick lenses of his glasses, but maybe that was an effect of the prescription. Why wouldn't Myrna have mentioned the glasses if he was the Violator? Jennifer doubted Rick could drive without them.

"Sorry, I can't seem to find the gift," she said, "but I know you're going to love it."

She bent over deeply, letting her unbuttoned cardigan fall away from her breasts to reveal her black lace demi-bra. She'd worn the sweater purposely, betting on the effect it would have on Rick. His discomfort was palpable. He was blushing and fidgeting, unaware that the red pencil in his hand was making slash marks on the paper he was grading. Jennifer knew she was embarrassing him, and that made it all the more difficult. He'd always been nice to her, distant, but gentle and nice. She wasn't picking up hostility or rage. It was pure fear. But fear, she knew, could be twisted into rage under the right conditions.

Get this over with, Jennifer. She found the package and set it in front of him. The table that separated them was not more than three feet wide, and he had papers stacked to his right and left. He could have surrounded himself and made a fortress out of it. Maybe that was the idea.

"Open it," she coaxed. "You already have one of these, but this was special. It had your name on it."

He unwrapped the package with the wariness of a bomb squad specialist. Inside the jewelry box was a sterling silver wallet chain with his initials engraved in the latch. Jennifer had bribed the jeweler to do it while she waited.

He managed a thank-you, although he didn't seem to want to touch the chain. He wasn't being ungracious. He didn't know how to receive gifts from women, perhaps from anyone.

"Do you like it?" she said. "Why don't you put it on and see if it works."

He shook his head, and Jennifer knew this was not going to be easy. She picked it out of the box, trying to entice him.

"Take off the one you have," she said. "Here, I'll help."

She started to come around the table, but he sprang from the chair.

"I'll do it," he said.

Jennifer watched him fumble with the chain he wore. He was clearly left-handed. "Don't be silly," she said. "Let me help. You saved my life with the car. It's the least I can do."

He'd backed up as far as he could go. He was pressed against the desk next to the table, and he thrust out an arm as she neared him. Jennifer was actually a little frightened. She was invading his boundaries, and there was no telling what he might do if she became too threatening.

"You're missing the latch," she said,

handing him the chain. “Hold this, and turn away from me so I can do it.”

He took the chain, but when she touched his arm to turn him, he froze. This was what Jennifer had been counting on. With a little pressure from her, he moved around, and she quickly drew the wallet from his pocket, pretending to be unhooking it from the chain. His driver’s license was in the first slot, but the plastic casing was cloudy, and the print was too small to read. She pressed it out with her fingers and slipped it into the pocket of her jeans. That wasn’t the plan, but she would have to take the chance.

“Done,” she said. “Trade chains with me, and I’ll put the new one on.”

Jennifer pried the chain loose from his rigid fingers and set to work. She got it hooked to his belt, but before she had the bolt ring fastened to the wallet, Rick had come to life again. He’d fished his cell phone from his shirt pocket and he was tapping out numbers.

“Rick? What are you doing?”

Jennifer thought he was calling security. She rushed to get done, but the bolt didn’t want to engage. As the lecture room door opened, she thought she felt it slide in, and she stuffed both the chain and the wallet into his pocket.

To Jennifer’s great relief, the man who entered the room was Bob Talb. She’d had visions of being carted off for identity theft.

Talb's expression was quizzical. "My two gifted former students," he said. "Are you here for my class? Can't resist my rapier wit?"

Jennifer laughed. "Rick helped me with my car the other day. I came by to thank him."

Rick still seemed fairly immobilized, which would work to her favor. She had to make an exit before he discovered what she'd done.

She sailed over to Bob and linked her arm in his. "Have you got a minute to walk me out to my car? It may be the last time I'll get to see you before I go."

"I'll be right back," he told Rick as they left. "The class starts in fifteen. Maybe you could have those essays finished so I can pass them out?"

Rick barely glanced up. A white line streaked his jaw. Jennifer didn't know if it was tension or anger, but there was no time to dwell on that now.

By the time she and Bob reached the parking lot, she'd decided to tell him her suspicions. It concerned her that he might want to contact the police, but that was another chance she would have to take. Without Myrna or Nell to identify Rick, Jennifer needed evidence, and Bob worked with Rick. He might know things that could help the case.

"Does Rick Morehouse own a motorcycle?" she asked.

They had stopped by her rental car to say good-bye. Above them the sky was dark with roiling clouds, and Jennifer wondered why it hadn't begun to pour. It looked like it might at any minute.

"Not on a TA's salary," Bob quipped. "He could maybe swing a pair of in-line skates. Why do you ask?"

"Because . . ." It was going to sound crazy, but she didn't have time to walk him through all the steps she'd already taken. "I think it's his face that I've been trying to draw."

"What does that mean?"

"I think he could be the Violator."

Bob's smile vanished. "*Rick?* Don't be absurd. He's afraid of his own shadow."

"The witness said the man who abducted Sharon Myer was left-handed. She saw something silver in his back left pocket, and Rick wears that wallet chain. She talked about his eyes, too, remember? She said one of them was black, like an eclipse of the moon. Have you ever noticed Rick's eyes? He covers them up with those glasses, but they're pitch black, Bob. You can't tell the pupils from the irises."

He shook his head, adamant. "I don't know which one of those outlandish ideas to address, Jennifer. Lots of men wear wallet chains, and Rick has two eyes, if I remember correctly. Not one."

She glanced around to make sure they

weren't being overheard. "Yes, but it was night, and he was wearing a helmet with the visor open. It could have shadowed his face. If all she saw was one dark eye that's how she would have described him."

"And that's all you have to hang your suspicions on? A wallet chain and eye coloring?"

Jennifer was surprised at his tone. Instead of the support she was hoping for, she was getting heavy skepticism, but maybe that was to be expected. Rick had been with him a long time. It was almost impossible for Jennifer to believe he could have done such horrific things, and she'd only known him casually.

"He's the face in my sketch, Bob, the one I did before Myrna got flaky on me. It's not a lock. I can't say that, but the resemblance is strong, and I need to follow up on it."

"You saw me in your sketches, too, remember? You all but accused *me*."

She had not done that. She had gone out of her way not to accuse him, but apparently that was making him question her abilities.

It wasn't raining yet, but the wind was cold and wet and fiercely penetrating. Jennifer buttoned up her sweater, wishing she'd brought something warmer. She'd seen a rain slicker in the trunk, courtesy of the rental company, but she couldn't try to find it now.

Bob was shifting from one foot to another, probably to ward off the cold. He was wearing only shirtsleeves, and his fair skin was splotchy from the stinging wind. The tint of his dark glasses made it impossible to see his eyes, and Jennifer fought an impulse to ask him to take them off.

"Rick isn't capable of hurting a woman. He can't even talk to one." With a tone of finality, Bob added, "You're on the wrong track, Jennifer."

"We'll see about that." Disappointment pierced her. He didn't know what kind of a risk she was taking, but she'd hoped their friendship would be reason enough for him to back her up. His belief in her instincts was important, especially now when there was so much reason to doubt them.

The wind gusted. They both shivered, and he looked up at the turbulent skies. "Maybe you'd better get going before the storm breaks. It looks biblical, like the seas are about to part."

She nodded and found herself in his arms. He hugged her hard, shooed her away from him, and then set out on a lope in the direction of Guthrie Hall.

Jennifer watched him go, and as she stood there, hunched and hugging herself, the clouds split, and the parking lot turned dark as night. She was drenched in seconds, but she made no attempt to escape the downpour. She couldn't remember ever feeling so alone.

* * *

Rick Morehouse lived on the outskirts of Woodenville in one of the few areas that was still undeveloped and heavily wooded. Jennifer found his place only by repeatedly stopping at gas stations and knocking on doors for directions, and when she saw how isolated the small concrete block house was, she had second thoughts about her plan. She'd left Rick back at the university, grading papers, but he might already have discovered that his license was gone and that only she could have taken it. Worse, the storm hadn't blown itself out yet, and she was concerned about getting lost or trapped by the weather.

That was the debate playing out as she pulled into the house's gravel driveway and saw the storage shed. It was right next to the three-sided carport that was adjacent to the house itself. *Russ kept his bike in a shed.*

She parked the rental, pulled on the yellow rain slicker she'd stashed in the console, and let herself out of the car. The slicker slapped wetly against her jeans as she crunched through the gravel. Her sneakers had turned into wading pools, but she was so wet she probably couldn't get any wetter. That was some consolation.

The shed was double padlocked. Jennifer couldn't hope to get in that way, but a little sleuthing yielded one boarded-up window and a rusty shovel in the carport. Awkwardly she swung and hit the wooden slats several times, hammering them, but getting nowhere. Finally she turned the shovel sideways and sliced edge-on. One of the boards splintered, and she went after it mercilessly, battering until she'd broken off a piece.

She dropped the shovel and went to look. It was dark inside the shed. The only rays of light came from the opening she'd created, but she could see handlebars and a windshield. It was a bike! Rick Morehouse had a motorcycle. How had she known that? She strained to see more detail — what color it was, what make. If she could chop out a bigger opening, she could crawl through and get inside.

She moved her head, trying to let more light in, but suddenly, everything went dark. The light streaming into the shed was blocked by something behind her. The storm. The clouds, she thought. She hoped.

She was afraid to turn, but finally she had to. And when she did, she saw an image more terrifying than her mind could ever have conjured up. His black helmet had a visor that eclipsed his entire face. The leather that covered his body was black, too, but the silver knife in his gloved hand was blood-stained and gleaming.

Chapter 23

Jennifer couldn't hear his voice above the wind, but there was no mistaking what he wanted. He made a circular motion with the knife, and her mind screamed, *Turn!* She did it instantly, making no attempt to fight. There was no way to win against a deadly weapon, and no one to hear her shouts.

She should have been watching her back every second, but even that might not have helped. He'd come out of nowhere. There hadn't been a sound, just that swooping shadow, and when she'd turned, the glare had nearly blinded her. All she could see was a pale aura surrounding a towering black form.

Maybe this wasn't real. Was she seeing things, imagining him? She'd had no sleep, no food. The last twenty-four hours had been a nightmare.

Something tapped her back between her shoulder blades. She straightened, thinking it was his hand, but she was wrong. The knife blade pierced her slicker with a horrible ripping sound. Plastic material clung to her shoulders for a second, then slithered to the ground in two sodden heaps. He had sliced open the back of her coat, top to bottom.

Rain pelted her shoulders, soaking her sweater. This was real.

He restrained her with a swiftness that would have been paralyzing, even if he hadn't used force. Her mouth was stuffed with a wad of cotton and gagged. Her wrists were duct-taped, her eyes blindfolded, and her head was encased in a helmet with a full-length black visor. He'd done this before. He was sure of himself, even in broad daylight.

The Violator didn't strike in broad daylight.

The realization staggered Jennifer. This could be the copycat. It could be anyone. She had no idea who she was dealing with, but before this was over, she would. He could kill her, if it came to that, but not before she knew who he was. She had to live that long. Her last act would be unmasking him.

He pushed her to walk, but she stumbled in the wet gravel. The blindfold and helmet created a suffocating black void. She couldn't see where she was going, and it was terrifying. The raspy noises she heard were her own frantic attempts to breathe. There wasn't enough air, and she felt as if she were smothering inside the helmet, but there was no way to tell him. The gag was too tight.

This is the way Sharon died.

He shoved her again, forcing her down the road, probably to wherever he'd left his bike. The storm whipped at her clothing, confusing her. Wind and rain rapped noisily at the helmet, but the bound wrists made her feel even more vulnerable and disoriented. She had no hands to balance herself. Somehow she had to convince him to remove the helmet and her blindfold, but that would have to wait. She was weak from shock, shaking. The acid bath surging through her veins must be adrenaline.

With no warning, she was lifted off the ground. Muscled arms pinned her waist and swung her up, setting her on the seat of the bike. She swayed to the side and nearly toppled off. A hard tug brought her back, and before she realized what he was doing, he'd raised her taped hands and looped them over his head.

She'd missed her chance. If she'd been able to see, she could have pulled back and crushed his Adam's apple, but it had happened too fast. One miscalculation, and he probably would have killed her. She could never have escaped him.

An engine roared to life, and Jennifer heard the bike's wheels grind against loose gravel, spitting it everywhere. She pressed herself against his back, afraid she would be thrown from the bike and dragged. The big machine lurched forward, and a moment later, it was digging up the road, screaming back at the storm.

Where was he taking her? To the trailer? She

couldn't let that happen. She had to stop him before they got that far.

Rain stung wherever it hit, but Jennifer forced herself to stay alert for any clues to his identity. There was little to go on, and through it all, her brain flashed frightening images of the sketches she'd drawn. There was a familiarity in the way he held himself, in the way he drove the bike, in everything he did — and not being able to see him only made her intuition stronger. *She knew this man.* Her mind wouldn't let go of that thought. It was the one thing that sustained her, a thread of recognition that could not be broken.

The motorcycle lurched over deep ruts in the road, jolting Jennifer so hard, she thought they were going to crash. An idea came to her that she rejected immediately as too dangerous, but she couldn't let go of it. There was a long stretch of old paved road before they got to the main highway. They might even be on it now, except that she could still hear rocks crunching beneath the wheels. What she had in mind had to be done after they left the gravel and before they reached the arterial that had brought her here. She didn't want any other cars around.

She hoped he was taking the same route she had.

Jennifer's heart tightened. It felt as if she'd committed herself to this plan, and it wasn't just dangerous, it was crazy. Daredevil stuff, and she didn't have a thrill-seeker bone in her body, despite the results of Bob Talb's test. But if he was the Violator, then her life was at stake anyway. It was only fair that his life be at stake, too.

They slowed and went over a large bump. Jennifer braced herself as they made a turn, but suddenly the road smoothed out beneath them. Moments later, he hit the brakes going into a curve, and she felt the back wheels skidding. This was what she needed: wet, slick pavement that would make the motorcycle hard to control. And no traffic. She didn't hear any other cars.

He had tried to render each of his victims totally helpless.

If Jennifer were lucky, that would work against him this time.

If she wasn't, they could both die.

The next curve he rounded, she pushed up forcefully from the footrests. Her taped hands broke his grip on the handlebars, and the bike spun out of control. They began to fishtail wildly, and Jennifer purposely went limp as they careened into a spin. The bike struck something that clattered and clanged like metal. It was a deafening sound, and instantly they were airborne.

As they shot upward, everything slowed down for Jennifer, slowed to a crawl. Her thoughts, her heart rate, her reactions. It felt as if they would never land, and she couldn't do anything but hang on. But when the screaming machine crashed to the ground, they were launched into the air. They were thrown over it, thrown high and hard. Locked together like skydivers.

She could not escape him. Now he could not escape her.

The impact knocked Jennifer out cold. When she came to, her nostrils were filled with the stench of spilled gasoline and burning creosote, and her thoughts were of fiery death. But the explosion she imagined never happened, and when she tried to get up, she realized she was sprawled on an unmoving body.

The man beneath her was either unconscious or dead. She tried to roll off him, but her arms were trapped, and it took all the strength she had to pull him with her onto their sides. She heaved and tugged, using her feet, until finally she had him in a position where she could work her taped hands over his head. The effort left her shaking and drained, but once she was free of him, she struggled out of her helmet and yanked down the blindfold.

That was when she saw the metal traffic sign that had snapped off at its base and impaled him. He was unconscious but still breathing, and that in itself was a miracle. If the spike had gone any deeper, it would have pierced her, too.

Jennifer let out a raw, aching breath as she lifted his visor and saw the blood pooling in his mouth. Her abductor was Rick Morehouse, and he was dying.

"Eighty-seven, eighty-eight, eighty-nine . . ."

Head down and focused on her feet, Jennifer systematically counted each step of the stairs as she climbed them. She'd wondered for all the years she worked for the department how many steps there were on the back stairs of the Public Safety Building, but she'd never managed to make it to the top without losing count. Something or someone had always distracted her.

These stairs were her Everest, and today she was going to reach the peak.

There were some rules. Each landing counted as one step, and you were not allowed to count by any artificial means. No fancy tabulators. No slide rules or abaci.

To keep her tote from getting too heavy, she switched arms every other flight, and occasionally threw it over her shoulder for variety.

"One hundred and ten, one hundred and eleven, one hundred and twelve . . ."

It was easy to lose track, so she rarely paused, which meant she was usually out of breath about halfway up. But today was different. Either she'd built up strength from her other tries, or some special force was at work. Her body felt light and fluid, and the climb effortless. She watched her feet rise and fall. She could barely feel the con-

crete, and when she passed the halfway mark going strong, she began to think that she would make it this time.

"One hundred and fifty-two, one hundred and fifty-three — What's that?"

Her foot stopped in midair. The step she was about to take had a pair of feet already on it. Men's feet, encased in black leather loafers, and blocking her way.

She knew those shoes. "One hundred fifty-three." Breathless, she looked up. "Don't let me forget that number!"

Russ Sadler crooked a brow, which for him was the equivalent of smiling. "I don't think you're going to forget the number," he assured her.

One step above her, he bent down, tipped up her face with his fingers, and dropped a kiss on her surprised mouth.

"What are you doing?" she asked.

"Proposing."

"Proposing what?"

"That we run away and do something crazy."

"Crazier than naked sex in a hammock during a thunderstorm?"

"Yes, crazier than that." His voice got husky and bone dry. "I want you to marry me, Jenn."

"M-marry?" The clatter she heard was her tote bag, banging down the stairway to the landing.

"I'm supposed to be the one stumbling over that word." His hands closed over her shoulders,

and he held her fast. "Will you?"

His eyes were dark with emotion. Fear and exhilaration fought for dominance. Passion vied with tenderness. It was all inside him, and the turmoil was beautiful.

"You can say no," he whispered. "You can still save yourself."

She cocked her head, wise to his ways. "You're not getting off that easy."

A sound burned through him, one part laughter, several parts passion. He lifted her up to the next step, balancing the tips of her toes between his.

"One hundred and fifty-four," she gasped softly. "Yes, yes, I will."

It felt as if something were scratching Jennifer's fingertips. It wasn't an unpleasant sensation, a little abrasive maybe, like being tickled with sandpaper. She tried to speak, but her mouth didn't seem to be working right, so she concentrated on opening her eyes instead. They were strangely heavy and obviously not working right, either.

"Jennifer? Are you awake?"

His voice brought her floating back to consciousness. "Russ?"

Weighted lids came open to the fuzzy image of a man's face. It was Russ, and he was gazing down at her. She had no idea where she was, but she vaguely recollected that the last time he'd looked at her this way, they were on the stairs of the Public Safety Building.

The fog in her head started to clear a little. Yes, she remembered now.

"Russ, is it you?" she asked. "Am I dead? Is this heaven? Did we ever get married?"

She heard low laughter. It seemed to be coming from him, but she wasn't sure. Her ears weren't working quite right, either. Nothing seemed to be.

"Yes, no, no, and no," he said, "but we could change that last one."

She blinked, trying to bring him into focus. The perpetual scowl seemed to be missing, but his dark eyes were very much in evidence. Liquid night, those eyes.

"Are you sure it's you? I'm not dreaming?"

Something nipped at her forearm, bringing her eyes wide open.

"Hey, that hurt," she cried out.

He'd pinched her! His off-center grin was incontrovertible proof — and now he was ducking as if she were going to swat him.

"The doctors don't want you to overexert," he warned.

The smart-ass sense of humor was very much in evidence, too. It was Russ, and she definitely wasn't dreaming. "Where am I?"

She would have lifted her head to look around, but something hurt in the vicinity of her neck and shoulders. Lots of things hurt. "This looks like a hospital."

Russ was standing right next to her bed, wearing a dark shirt and slacks and looking elegantly disheveled and sexy. The sandpaper that had been tickling her fingertips was his five o'clock shadow. He had her right hand cupped in his, and apparently he'd been pressing her fingers to his lips.

As far as Jennifer could tell, she was garbed in a hospital gown, and the obstruction around her neck felt like a surgical collar. Lovely. There were some flowers, too, along with a clear plastic pitcher and matching water glass on a stainless steel table. The flowers actually *were* lovely. Pale pink roses, hand-picked no doubt.

Odd that she could hear a baby crying, too.

"It's a hospital," he said, confirming her suspicions, "and you're in it. You took quite a spill, but you're okay. You have cuts and bruises and a case of whiplash that's going to smart if you don't take it easy, but nothing broken, nothing permanently damaged."

The grin faded, and his hand closed around hers. "Rick Morehouse wasn't as lucky, Jennifer."

"Oh, my God," she whispered as it all came flooding back to her. "He tried to kidnap me, Russ."

"And you brought him down." Russ's eyes reflected his emotion, his grudging admiration. "Sharon would have been proud of you," he admitted. "But *I'm* not," he said in the very next breath. "Don't *ever* take another risk like that."

Jennifer was actually touched by his harsh tone. It gave him away, the softie.

"How long have I been here?" she asked.

"Since yesterday afternoon. A UPS driver witnessed the accident. He saw you break Rick's hold on the handlebars, and he told the 911 dispatcher that the motorcycle hit a guardrail and became airborne —"

Jennifer had to stop him. "Is Rick dead? I saw the blood."

"He died in the crash, but we have plenty of evidence that he was the one we're after, the Violator. There were rolls of duct tape and the polyester scarves he was using for blindfolds in the bike's saddlebags. It's not clear why he chose scarves rather than duct tape for their eyes, but he may have used the helmet you were wearing on the other victims. Our ID guys found skin samples and strands of hair caught in the helmet. Red hair, but not your color. It was copper, like Sharon's."

"Sharon's color?" Apparently Jennifer had been right about Rick, but it saddened her to think that he'd been so desperately ill, and she hadn't realized it.

She went quiet, and for the first time, she was able to contemplate the gravity of what he was telling her, the enormity. The Violator had been caught. He was dead, and she was alive. More important, no one else had been hurt or killed. No one else would ever be hurt by him.

The relief that washed over her left her shaky and weak, but it was a good feeling. The best feeling she could imagine right now. She met Russ's sober gaze and took strength from it. She wasn't sure she'd ever been happier to see anyone in her life. Maybe that was the best feeling she could imagine.

"How long have you been here?" she asked, aware of the deep lines of fatigue around his eyes.

"Since yesterday. I've been waiting for you to wake up."

Since yesterday? Now there was a romantic notion that had great appeal. *Sitting by her sickbed, holding vigil while she slept? Possibly even bargaining with the heavens for her recovery?* Unfortunately, it conflicted with another romantic notion that held equal appeal.

"I guess that means you didn't propose to me on the steps of the Public Safety Building?" she asked him.

"Not recently."

He seemed confused, which was understandable, since she hadn't told him about her dream — and now she knew that's what it must have been — an incredibly real and vivid dream. It was almost exactly how he'd proposed to her two years ago. Right down to the one hundred fifty-fourth step. Or perhaps she should say up.

"I was on my way back to the city," he explained, "when Kate called and told me what happened. I came straight here."

He brushed her fingertips against his chin, and the sandy sensations were delicious, but his reference to the phone call had reminded her of something.

"You never returned my calls," she accused. She'd tried to reach him all day and night.

"I didn't know you *had* called. I wasn't able to retrieve your messages until I got back. I'm sorry," he said. Contrition burned in his dark eyes. He *was* sorry, and not a man who admitted to that easily.

"My cell phone was out of range. I called Kate from a pay phone in Okanogan County," he explained. "I didn't have your cell number with me, so I tried your hotel, but it was late, and the operator wouldn't put me through to your room. She gave me such a hassle that I ran out of change and got disconnected. I even told her I was a cop."

"Oh!" She'd just figured it out. "I know what must have happened. The hotel probably red-flagged my calls because I'd been complaining about being harassed. I guess that wasn't you who was calling and hanging up?"

"Hanging up? I was trying to get *through*."

"I wonder who then . . ." She hesitated, thinking, but her throat was too dry to finish the question anyway, and by the time Russ had poured some water from the pitcher and helped her sit up and drink it, she didn't care about a few hang-ups on a hotel phone. He actually kissed the remaining water droplets from her lips. This was so *not* the Russ she knew, and she was wildly attracted to the kinder, gentler version.

"I love it when you're nurturing," she teased. Her laughter was as throaty as it was sensual.

"And I'm in love with a lunatic," he retorted, "who had better promise me here and now that she'll never take another risk like that again. Or I may have to use my handcuffs."

"Handcuff me to this hospital bed? The nurses might not like that."

"If the nurses liked it, I'd be worried. On the other hand, *I* might like it. I might like it a lot."

"In that case, *I'm* worried."

Their gazes connected, and Jennifer felt a bolt of sensation in the pit of her stomach that nearly lifted her off the bed. Russ looked like he wanted to climb in the bed with her, a possibility that sent pleasure spiraling to her toes. Instead, he gallantly suggested that he should leave and let her get some rest.

"*No,* you can't go." Jennifer was adamant.

"Sweetness, I think the department might frown on our having biblical knowledge of each other right here in Providence Hospital, but if you insist . . ."

She was afraid it might hurt to laugh. "I want you to stay and answer my questions, Russ. There's so much about the Violator case that I don't understand. Rick, for one. What made him do it? And why did he steal your bike?"

"It looks like he was trying to frame me. We found my Harley in the shed by his house."

"Why would he want to do that?"

"You, that's why. He had Jennifer Nash memorabilia stashed all over his house, going back several years. He was obsessed with you and probably stalking you. When he found out about us, he became pathologically jealous and tried to get me out of the way by framing me. At least that's my theory. He would have been absolving himself, too."

Jennifer was thinking about her sketches. "Is it possible that he made himself up to look like you? It was your face that his last victim described, broken nose and all."

"Exactly," Russ said. "They found theatrical makeup in his house, including the putty he may have used to create the break."

"But why the punishment theme? What compelled him to teach his victims a lesson?"

Something was still missing for Jennifer. It just didn't make sense.

"Think about it this way," Russ said. "He was abducting redheaded women who resembled you, probably as a way to communicate something to you that he couldn't say — that you were a temptress, and if he couldn't have you, he was going to find a way to indirectly punish you."

Russ's shrug said he was speculating, which was all anyone could do, since Rick was dead. "We don't have all the answers yet," he told her, "but if that was Sharon's hair in the helmet, and if Nell or Myrna can ID him, we'll be able to connect him with three of the crimes, including yours."

"Nell Adams is all right?" Jennifer asked.

"She's fine, but Myrna's missing. She disappeared from the shelter the day you last interviewed her. Nobody saw her leave, and she never came back. I thought you'd had enough bad news that day, so I didn't say anything."

As if he could hear the odd thump in Jennifer's heart, he added, "We have the whole damn department looking for her. We'll find her."

Or her body, Jennifer thought. Myrna was terrified that the Violator would hunt her down, and perhaps Rick had. The possibility disturbed Jennifer deeply. She felt a sense of failure where Myrna was concerned, and this only added to it. She'd let the woman down.

"You have to find her," she told Russ.

"We *will*," he promised.

Jennifer fell silent again, aware that the case wasn't over for her — and wouldn't be until she knew what had happened to Myrna.

Finally, Russ broke the gloomy mood. "I didn't tell you the good news," he said. "We found the trailer. It's up in the northern part of the state in the Methow Valley."

"How did you find it way up there?"

"Remember the night we made love in the hammock and the rain woke us? I never got back to sleep, and I didn't want to disturb you — well, actually I did, but I restrained myself by thinking about the case. I couldn't explain the gritty powder that every one of the victims had mentioned feeling on her hands, and I kept thinking it might be road dust, which meant he had to be taking them somewhere where it was dry."

"It's been dry here," Jennifer pointed out. "Hot *and* dry."

"True, but two of the strikes took place last year, on nights when it was raining, and those victims described a powdery substance, too. After I left here that night, I went by the office to verify that I was right about the rain and the dates of the strikes. I also verified the distance to the Methow Valley, and it all checked out. The victims estimated the trip at about an hour, plus or minus fifteen minutes."

"How did you find it so quickly?"

"I limited the DMV search to trailers that hadn't had their license fees paid in the last two years."

"Of course!" Jennifer was struck by his brilliance. "The Violator wouldn't want a paper trail linking him to the trailer."

"Which meant that he stole it or let the license lapse. Either way, the fee wouldn't have been paid. Once I had the list, I recruited a couple of deputy sheriffs, and we checked the trailers out, one by one. As it turns out, we were lucky. It was in the first half-dozen — an old silver Airstream, sitting on a small plot of land in the hills. No one would ever have believed what was inside it."

Jennifer was reluctant to ask. She'd worked in law enforcement long enough to know more than she wanted to about the lairs of serial criminals.

"It was as sterile as a laboratory," Russ said. "He kept all his souvenirs in plastic bags, labeled and sorted by name and date. I found the victims' hair, their clothing, and whatever jewelry they'd been wearing. I also found the spray cans, chemicals, razors, and other paraphernalia that he used to remove their hair. I didn't turn up any specific link to Rick, but the crime lab guys are up there now, going over the scene."

Jennifer was impressed, and she told him so. He'd done some crack detective work, using clues that would never have occurred to her, and she'd gone through the same reports he had, although her focus had been different. She'd been trying to explain the discrepancies in the sketches she was drawing, and she still wasn't completely clear on that, except now she knew why Nell Adams had described Russ's face.

She was also impressed that Russ had spent the night by her side, and even though she had more questions about the case, they would have to wait their turn.

"What if I didn't wake up?" she asked him. "What would you have done?"

"I would have been right here beside you until you did," he said.

If Jennifer was surprised, she was also skeptical. She found it hard to imagine that kind of devotion. No, impossible to imagine. That a man could be that faithful and true to one woman was outside her experience. That the woman could be *her* was unfathomable. She wanted it explained, in detail, because she didn't believe he could.

A faint noise interrupted her thoughts. It sounded like a sigh, but Russ shook his head as if to say it wasn't him. A quick scan of the room turned up something Jennifer hadn't noticed before. Two things. A metal file cabinet standing on the wall opposite her bed, and the wilting, half-dead plant that sat on top of it.

A *Ficus benjamina.* Several yellow leaves had dropped to the floor, where a small pile was accumulating. But there was stubborn new growth popping out everywhere.

"It was Sharon's," Russ said. "I thought it might inspire you to get better."

Jennifer was touched. She hardly knew what to say, but the poor plant was so forlorn and pathetic, she finally had to laugh. "You mean if that ficus could get better, anything could?"

"Pretty much." He laughed, too.

Jennifer's maternal instincts were instantly aroused. She couldn't stand to see anything suffer, even a plant. She begged Russ to give it a drink of water from the pitcher, but as he went about that task, she remembered something else of Sharon's that was in his possession, and her heart sank. She could feel herself wilting like the plant.

"Russ, I was in your room — the one in the back that you keep locked." *This she would have given anything not to have remembered.*

He returned the pitcher to the stainless steel table, and she could see by the grave concern in his expression that he knew what she was talking about.

"You found the pictures and Sharon's diary, right?" he said. "It isn't what you're thinking, Jennifer. Believe me, I wish I could explain."

"You *have* to explain. We can't have secrets between us now."

"This isn't my secret, Jennifer. It's someone else's, and I'm not free to tell it — yet." He brought her fingers to his mouth as if to kiss them, but this time the sandpaper burned, and she pulled her hand away.

"Russ, please."

"I would if I could," he told her. "Honest to God, Jenn. But there's something I have to do first. It's unfinished business, and this case won't be over until I finish it. It won't take long. They're releasing you right after lunch, and I'll be back to pick you up."

There was a clock on the wall by the door. If by lunch, he meant noon, that was two hours away, an endless amount of time.

"Jennifer, I'll be *fine*." Apparently the worried expression on her face had finally registered, because he gently grasped her shoulders and pressed himself close. It was clearly a trade-off between wanting to hug her and not wanting to hurt her.

"I'll be back," he promised in low whispers against her cheek. "From now on, no matter where either one of us goes, we always come back. Agreed?"

Somehow she got the word *agreed* past the constriction in her throat. She wasn't happy that he couldn't tell her what he was doing, but she also understood that his work was like that. Her work was like that.

He was on his way out the door before she gave in to an impulse.

"Russ, do you love me?"

He stopped and laughed without turning around. Jennifer recognized it as a hopeless attempt to suppress emotion. With a long, sweet, burning glance over his shoulder, he said, "Let me *count* the ways . . . and when I get back, I will."

Chapter 24

"Have a Dorito. Help yourself, dude. Have *two*."

Junior's sardonic tone alerted Russ that his wait was over. Junior wasn't around when Russ arrived, so he'd made himself at home in the cubicle, resting his feet on the desk and helping himself to the bag of chips, which he'd found pinned to the dartboard on the wall across from Junior's desk.

Junior hunkered in the doorway, clearly not thrilled with his visitor. That was okay. Russ wasn't thrilled with his host. He could see Junior's face over the top of his Italian loafers, and for once, the Goremeister wasn't grinning.

Junior shuffled into the office, sipping from a steaming cup of coffee that smelled so damn good, Russ could have cried. He hadn't slept for going on three days straight, and he'd been living on nothing but caffeine. As of right now, he was off the stuff again, and he could feel the crash coming.

Junior pulled a dart from the board and stuck it in the innermost black circle. "Bull's-eye," he said under his breath. "You look like hell, Sadler. Jennifer beating you up again?"

"You mean my beard and the luggage under my eyes?" Russ rubbed the growth on his chin. "It's probably the Doritos. They don't seem to be doing you much good, either."

Junior ignored the jibe. "Go home and get some sleep, dude. The Violator case is closed, and you're the department's MVP. Take a rest."

"The case isn't closed, Junior."

"What do you mean?"

Russ lifted the bag of Doritos and revealed what else he had in his lap. He swung his feet off the desk and dropped Sharon's diary square in the center of the blotter, watching Junior's reaction. His friend had gone wary and silent, which brought Russ no pleasure. He hated having to back a colleague to the wall, hated it more than what the colleague might have done to deserve it. Crime fighters were supposed to be honorable men and women, although maybe that notion had gone out with covered wagons.

"What's that supposed to be?" Junior asked.

"Maybe you could tell me. I found it hidden in the false bottom of your CD player."

Junior said nothing, so Russ went on. "Someone had sex with Sharon the night she was killed. Rough sex. She writes about the guy in that diary. He was someone from this office."

Junior's retreat to silence was far more telling than anything he could have said. Russ couldn't remember his friend not having a snappy comeback.

"She was planning to break it off with him that night," he said. "She didn't mention his name, but I'll bet you could fill in that blank for me."

Junior ripped a handful of darts from the board, backed up, and started throwing them with a vengeance. His aim was amazingly good, but there was a harsh, desperate tone to his voice.

"Will it go *easier* for me if I play along?" he asked Russ. "You going to give me a *break*, good buddy?"

"Junior, don't do this. Get it over with, for Christ's sake. Tell me what happened."

Russ's voice had a desperate tone, too. That may have been what made Junior stop and wheel around. His cherubic face was pale and contorted.

"Okay, so I was having an affair with Sharon," he admitted. "We got a little experimental, but it was consensual. Nobody got hurt, and I sure as hell didn't kill her. You're not accusing me of that, are you?"

"I'm accusing you of tampering with evidence. The diary was lying on the nightstand next to the bed. The officer who responded to the 911 call saw it, but it was gone by the time Sharon's partner got there. You and your crime lab guys were already on the scene."

"Sharon's partner? You mean Kent Wright? How do you know he wasn't her lover? Maybe he removed the damn diary."

"As much as I would love to pin Wright with evidence tampering, he didn't do it. He isn't even a serious suspect. He wasn't dragging his feet on the case the way you were or trying to confuse things by claiming the Violator was a woman. And he wasn't doing pregnancy tests in the lab. That was Sharon's blood you were testing. If you'd disposed of the tube in the normal way, I never would have found it, but you stashed it right here in your snacks drawer, you idiot."

Russ grabbed a bag of chips from the open desk drawer and shook it. The loud rattle was definitely not foodstuffs. He had the hard evidence, but there had been plenty of other reasons to suspect Junior in his mind. He'd begun to have questions as soon as he learned that Sharon was with someone the night she died *and* that the diary was missing. Russ had even stalled and withheld information because of his fears that Junior might be the copycat. He hadn't wanted to reveal what he knew until he'd had a chance to check it out himself.

Junior flopped down in a chair facing the desk, resigned to his fate. "So, I tampered. So what now?"

"I have to report it, you know that, but in this case, it could be seen as an attempt to protect Sharon's reputation, not as an attempt to cover up a crime. You have no priors — I hope — so I'm guessing they'll go easy."

"How easy?"

"A short suspension and a long probation? In the inimitable words of someone we both know: 'Everybody's entitled to one screwup.' "

Junior was chewing on his lower lip, and Russ read it as deep concern. "It was just that *one* screwup, right?"

Junior nodded, but the moment he glanced up, Russ knew there was something else going on. Guilt riddled his friend's hangdog expression.

"What the hell did you do?" Russ asked.

Junior rubbed hard at his mouth, scrubbing the color from his lips. He sat forward in the chair, but he couldn't seem to get anything out. Finally, he mumbled into his bent knuckles, "I left the door open, man. Like an idiot, I left the door open."

"What door? Sharon's?"

He nodded, his eyes closed. "I was pissed. She said it was over, it was going to be our last night together. I couldn't sleep, and it pissed me off even more that she could, so I got up and walked out. I slammed the door, but I didn't lock it. I didn't even think about it."

Russ realized what he was saying. That unlocked door was the way the Violator had gained entrance. Sharon might be still alive if Junior had locked the door, but the odds were that she wouldn't be. Nothing as insignificant as that would have stood in the Violator's way.

"Somebody ought to try me for her murder."

Survivor guilt. It was all too prevalent in law enforcement, in Russ's opinion, and if allowed to run amok, it could be as crippling as fear.

"You didn't know Sharon was a target when you walked out of her place," he reminded Junior. "What you did was stupid, but it wasn't a criminal act."

"Real stupid. Unfriggingbelievably real stupid."

"Snap out of it, man. The only thing you're guilty of is self-pity, and Sharon would not have enjoyed seeing you blubber like this. She would have told you the same thing I'm telling you, and then she would have stuck a finger in your eye."

Junior nodded, but he didn't respond.

"Here, you want to be extreme? Have a Dorito." Russ tossed him the bag of chips, but Junior let it fall to the floor. This was bad, Russ realized. The kid was going to need shock treatment.

"All right, we'll charge you as an accessory," Russ said. "Will that ease the guilt a little? You'll hit the news as the Violator's advance man, and you can wear black leather on the stand."

"Don't do me any favors," Junior mumbled. He was still gnawing at his lip and probably wallowing in remorse, but when he glanced up this time, there was a hint of something brewing . . . possibly even something perverse.

This was looking more like the Junior that Russ knew — and did not love.

"An accessory?" Junior mused. "That would get me a pretty big trial, right? I mean this *is* the Violator case."

"You'd be the next Richard Speck," Russ said.

Within mere seconds, Junior's dark eyes were dancing. "A big case like that means lawyers would be all over me, wanting to defend me for the publicity. I could take my pick, and naturally I'd pick a gorgeous female mouthpiece, who wouldn't be able to save my sorry ass, which would make her deeply indebted to me."

Junior's grin and his guilt could have been mapped on a graph as an inverse relationship: the wider the grin the less the guilt.

"You had me worried for a minute there," Russ said. "I thought you actually had a conscience."

"Wait, it gets better." Junior let out a

sudden snort of glee. “While I’m wasting away in my cell, I’ll be writing the definitive crime novel, okay? Meanwhile, the lawyer chick visits me, like all the time, because she’s working madly on an appeal, pro bono, of course . . .”

Junior was still plotting his glorious future when Russ got up and left the office. He’d taken the Doritos with him, and he crunched down a handful as he headed back upstairs to his own office. His friend had it all figured out, and Russ wouldn’t have been one bit surprised if it had happened exactly the way Junior predicted. What really pissed him off was that Junior had got him hooked on these infernal chips.

“Russ, what are you doing?”

Russ set down the photograph he’d been studying. He didn’t turn around immediately. The concern in Jennifer’s voice was evident, but there wasn’t anything he could say to her that would help. He knew that for a certainty. It was the only thing he did know right now.

“It wasn’t Rick Morehouse.” He spoke softly, more to himself than to her. “It couldn’t have been him.”

“What are you talking about?”

Maybe he just needed to say out loud what had been on his mind since the case was closed, two weeks ago. And maybe he needed to say it to her.

"It wasn't him, Jennifer. Rick Morehouse wasn't the Violator."

"How could he not be? Russ?"

He turned, knowing what to expect. She hated this room. She hated him coming here, staying up nights instead of going to bed with her. She wanted him to let go of the case the way everyone else had. They now had conclusive DNA evidence linking Morehouse to half the crimes, including Sharon's murder, and the comparisons were still being run. They were satisfied they had their man, and Russ hadn't been able to convince them otherwise.

He couldn't convince Jennifer, either, and it was starting to affect their relationship.

She stood on the threshold, barefooted and wearing his terry robe. She was obviously reluctant to come into the room, and as she gathered the robe snugly around her, he was briefly distracted by what she might be wearing underneath.

Not the time, Sadler.

She was trying hard not to look at the crime scene photos plastered all over the walls, but they were pretty difficult to avoid in the glare of the spotlights. The room was a gallery for the sick and twisted. Junior would have been in ecstasy here. But Junior didn't know the room existed. No one did but Jennifer, and she didn't understand.

"I don't like this pit, either," he told her,

hoping she could hear the revulsion in his voice. “But I have to know what’s important to these freaks, what drives them, what they can’t live without. Once I have that, I have them.”

Even in the dim light, the freckles on her nose stood out against her fair skin. Maybe he would grab her by the hand and take her upstairs, start counting those adorable freckles. She had a lot of them. It might take him the rest of his life. *That’s it, Sadler. Take her hand, and on your way out, slam the door behind you and never darken this dungeon again.*

“I understand that you have to immerse yourself,” she said. “It’s the way you work, and you’re a brilliant detective. That’s not the problem.”

“Then what is?”

“You won’t let go. You refuse to, despite all the evidence that Rick was the Violator. You’re clinging to this case, and I don’t understand why.”

“What about all the evidence that he *wasn’t* the Violator?”

“What evidence is that?”

Russ almost wished she hadn’t asked. He had nothing to say that she was going to want to hear.

“Talk to me, *please*. Don’t shut me out this way.”

She teetered on the doorstep, not knowing what she was asking.

"All right," he said reluctantly. "First of all, it wasn't Rick's trailer *or* his land. A man named Frank Nathan owned both, and he's been dead twenty years. It looks like Nathan's son paid the license fees up until a couple years ago, but we haven't been able to locate him."

She dismissed him with a quick shake of her head. "The fact that Rick didn't own the trailer doesn't prove he wasn't the one using it," she argued. "Maybe it was abandoned, or he was renting it under the table."

Russ stood his ground. "That's possible, but the trailer was surgically neat and tidy, remember? Rick's house off campus is a pigsty. He wasn't neat or methodical, and the Violator was both."

"Two different and diametrical facets of his personality. Ego states in rebellion," she pronounced. "It happens all the time, even in normal people. The fanatically neat parent ego state despises the messy child ego state and vice versa. In Rick's case, the tension would have fueled his conflicts and made him more aggressive in the parent state, which is what the Violator was. Yes?"

She pushed up the sleeves of the robe and folded her arms. "I could go on and on," she said. "You forget I have a doctorate in psychology."

What the hell *was* under that robe? Her diplomas?

"You can psychologize all you want, Doc, but you'd have a hard time selling that one in court. Most of us aren't neat freaks *and* slobs."

"Is that *all* you've got?" she asked, challenging him.

In fact, it wasn't. And her freckles were looking less adorable to him all the time. "Rick didn't act like a serial criminal. We found nothing in his apartment or the trailer that explained how he selected his victims or how he planned the crimes. *Nothing.* That isn't normal for a psycho who uses a motorcycle to abduct redheaded women at midnight and then relieves them of all their hair. Most serial assailants have elaborate selection criteria. His walls should have been papered with plans and machinations."

She looked perplexed, but only for a moment. "He didn't keep the plans at his apartment. He didn't want them discovered. He had a locked room somewhere, like this one. If you were to find that room, you'd find everything. Not that I'm suggesting you look for it."

"Then why did he keep *your* pictures and clippings in his apartment — you and only you? It was like the other victims didn't exist. There wasn't a hint of them there, but you were all over the place, everything from national newspaper headlines to your published journal articles."

She shuddered, and he was almost sorry he'd told her. He'd been shielding her from what he'd discovered because he knew how badly she wanted to let go of the past and move on. She wanted to talk about the future, not Rick Morehouse. She'd been spending her days at the houseboat, working on a proposal for the book she planned to write, and she obviously expected to spend her nights with him. But he'd been holed up in here, the one place she avoided above all others.

"I don't know why it was just me," she said. "I don't want to know."

It sounded as if she'd conceded, but that gave him no pleasure. All he had were discrepancies, no proof. Most of it could be explained away as she'd just done.

"Russ, you're using this case to avoid me, to avoid *us*."

He started to deny it, he wanted to deny it, but he wasn't sure he could. *When in doubt, conduct an investigation. It was the way guys like him got through life, even when terrible things happened to people they cared about. They never stopped investigating, and if they were lucky, the pain had eased enough to be bearable by the time they had some answers.*

That was the way he got through Sharon's death. It was the way he got through life. But was he doing it now? Avoiding Jennifer? Avoiding any possible pain of losing her again?

"You said if either one of us left, we would always come back. I want you to come back, Russ."

The soft anguish in her voice was like knives, and he didn't know how to duck them. She had perfect aim. It was entirely possible that he was trying to avoid her. She was the source of all *his* anguish. No one could hurt him more. Or open him more to life, to joy. He could not possibly love anyone more than he did her, which was why he was terrified. And running. Now *he* was running.

He walked to the wall panel next to the door, flipped off the track lighting, and turned on the overhead light. With one last look around the room that had been both hideaway and hell, he pulled the wastebasket out from under the table and put it in the middle of the room. He then proceeded to pull the photographs off the wall one by one and deposit them in the basket as he went.

"What are you doing? Russ?"

"I'm closing this case," he said.

When he had the wall clean and the basket full, he turned to find her watching him in astonishment.

"Russ, are you sure?"

Tears were streaming down her face, and the sight came perilously close to choking him up. She was in his arms before he could open them, and as he held her close, it hit him how much he loved the warmth of her arms, of her heart. How much he loved her . . . and how much he hated this room.

"I'm sure," he said.

"Jennifer, what are you doing?"

All Russ could see was the white terry robe at first, and then he realized it was her, bent over the wastebasket, pulling out the crime scene photographs. She was hurriedly sorting through them, as if looking for something specific. She'd already arranged a couple of them on the table.

"Come here," she said, beckoning for him to join her. "Quick."

Maybe *he* was dreaming. Was this the same woman who earlier this evening had stood in the doorway of this room, begging him to vacate it? The doorway where he was now standing?

"Jennifer? It's four in the morning."

"I couldn't sleep," she said. "I kept thinking about what you said about victim selection criteria, and I wanted to have another look at these pictures. I think there might be something here, Russ. Something that tells us what these women had in common besides their red hair."

"I've gone over and over them. There's nothing. I thought we agreed that this case is closed."

"Couldn't we agree to open it again, just for a couple minutes?"

She glanced over her shoulder imploringly, and Russ tried to imagine saying no to that puss. If she'd wanted help in planning her next serial killing, he would have agreed.

He joined her at the table, where she'd arranged shots of the first three victims' bedrooms on the table, side by side.

"What about Sharon's bedroom?" he asked.

"Okay, listen to my logic now," she said. "I'm not including Sharon because I don't think she was a true target. She was a threat, a police detective who was getting too close. The fact that she was a redhead made it convenient, because she could be made to look like a Violator victim. I would also classify myself as a threat, and Nell Adams was probably selected in order to frame you."

That was his theory, too. "The first three women were chosen because the Violator was obsessed with them and wanted to teach them a lesson."

"Exactly, and what does that mean? Anything they have in common could be a clue to his selection criteria."

She looked so pleased with herself Russ wanted to whip that robe right off her. *Right now.*

"Russ, the photographs? Pay attention?"

He had the damn photographs memorized he'd studied them so thoroughly. One of the bedrooms was decorated with an angel motif, another was piled high with stuffed animals, and the third was as plain as a dormitory, except for a large, gold, space-age object on the dresser that seemed to have caught the light from the flashbulb.

Jennifer spotted the gold object immediately. "It's a pyramid," she said, pointing out the triangularity. "They're sold at metaphysical shops and street fairs. They collect positive energy, something like that."

Russ had reason to think otherwise. "This is the third victim's bedroom," he told her. "Nothing in her interview indicated an interest in this stuff, and the crime scene report described the triangle as an award, a bowling trophy or something."

She gave him a look. "You haven't heard of pyramid power?"

"Jennifer, this could be important," he cautioned. "You need to be sure." He pointed to the next photograph, a room with stuffed animals heaped on the bed and chairs. "What about this one? Are you going to tell me teddy bears have positive energy?"

"No, but crystals do. See the chains hanging from the dresser mirror? They attract good luck and provide protection to the wearer." Jennifer had one in her purse, a traveling crystal, and Myrna Simone had worn a crystal pendant around her neck, hidden in all those scarves.

Jennifer picked up the picture to examine it more closely. "It looks like she has a collection of candles, too. I see red for passion, green for prosperity."

"This is the first victim's room," Russ said. "She's heavily into the New Age scene, but I wouldn't have known those chains were anything other than ordinary jewelry. What about angels?"

He indicated the third photograph, a room with angel figurines, mirror magnets, and mobiles.

"Same thing as the crystals, but heavier on the protection angle. You know, like guardian angels?"

"I thought angels were religious symbols."

"Not necessarily. They're very much a part of New Age spirituality now. Everybody believes in angels."

Russ wasn't so sure he believed in angels, but Jennifer was looking more like one every minute. She may have found the commonality, except that there was still one major problem.

"This one isn't into New Age anything," he informed her. "According to the file, she's devoutly religious and very much against that kind of thing."

"Okay, but she collects angels, and what better source of angel paraphernalia than a New Age store? She might frequent them to find the pieces she doesn't have to fill out her collection."

"So all these women could be patrons of New Age stores?"

"Right, but how does that jibe with the Violator's MO?"

"I don't know, but it's not red hair."

She picked up the first photograph and studied it. "If Rick Morehouse was into metaphysics, I wasn't aware of it. But Myrna was heavily into that stuff. She had a crystal that was supposed to ward off bad luck."

Russ found that interesting, but he didn't see how it could have anything to do with the victims. Myrna was a witness, not a target. A missing witness.

"For her sake, I hope the crystal works," he said. "I don't know how much longer Kate can be persuaded to keep the search going for Myrna."

"There are no breaks?"

"Nothing so far, and even though it would be handy to have her identify Morehouse as the guy, it's not necessary."

Jennifer sighed, and Russ took her hand. He rubbed it against the sandpaper that shadowed his jaw, and she grimaced, but it was really a smile. It was getting harder and harder to make her do that these days, smile.

"Do you know what's hotter than a woman in a man's robe?" he asked rhetorically.

"A man in a woman's robe?"

Now she was fighting a smile back. "Why don't you go up," he said. "I'll turn out the dungeon lights and be right behind you."

Apparently she intended to make sure of

that, because she pulled the rubber band from her old-fashioned ponytail and let her luscious auburn locks tumble around her face. Her next move was to undo the robe and flash him before she ducked out the doorway.

He now had no doubt about what she was wearing under the robe.

Russ could hear her squealing as she darted up the stairs.

He didn't bother turning out the lights.

"One guess who Frank Nathan is."

Jennifer looked up from the laptop screen, startled to see Russ looming above her, blocking the morning sun. He'd left for work two hours ago, and she hadn't heard him return. The deck hadn't even creaked. That's how stealthy he was. Probably trying to make her squeal. He seemed to enjoy that.

There'd been no breaks in his singular pursuit of the Violator case, but there had been a few breaks in their relationship — good ones. This wasn't the first time he'd come home unannounced in the last week, and it was interesting that she was thinking of the houseboat as home.

"Frank Nathan," she mused. "Elvis's real father? Elvis himself?"

Russ pushed his sunglasses up into his hair, revealing the dark displeasure that only he was capable of. Clearly he didn't appreciate her attempt to provoke him, but that was just tough. She loved his scowl the way he loved her squeal.

"Jennifer? Paying attention?"

"Bated breath," she assured him, stealing a glance at the thriving ficus plant, which was sitting next to her on the patio table, enjoying the shade of the umbrella.

"Frank Nathan was Myrna Simone's first husband," he said. "Our missing witness owned the trailer where the Violator tortured his victims."

Jennifer shot out of the deck chair. She nearly tipped over the table, her laptop, and the plant. "My God," she whispered. "What does that mean?"

"I don't know, but I'm going to find out. The search for Myrna is back on."

"Can I help in any way? Russ, let me help."

"You want to assist the lead detective?" He leaned over to kiss her, and his mouth melted against hers. *"Mmmmmm."*

"Did that help?" she asked.

"Yeah," he grinned. "Now let me tell you the plan."

"The plan?" That sounded slightly ominous. Jennifer's sigh was part frustration, part anticipation. She wanted them to find Myrna. She did want that, but this was beginning to feel like the case that wouldn't die. And right now, she didn't know if that was good or bad. However, it seemed to have worked for the ficus.

Chapter 25

Jennifer rushed toward the lecture hall, flushed and breathless. Her face and the nape of her neck were hot. Even her thighs were growing warm from the friction of her Lycra cocktail dress, but she didn't want to attract attention by coming in late to the ceremony. Fortunately, the black sheath she'd chosen for this evening was extremely fluid with her movements. It clung like Saran Wrap, but it permitted her to run, and she appreciated that in a dress.

People were still filing into the hall when she got there, but the auditorium was nearly full, and she quietly slipped into an aisle seat near the back. The black tie event was being held to honor several professors for their distinguished contributions to their field. Bob Talb was among them, and he was being cited for his groundbreaking work in behavioral neuroscience.

Once the lights went down, Jennifer lifted her skirt and fanned it to cool herself off. The hot weather had turned muggy, but that was only part of the reason she was on edge. Her thoughts were racing as fast as her blood. Tonight was when it all came together, and not just for Bob Talb.

She felt twinges of nostalgia as the dean of the school of psychology took the podium to describe the awards and to introduce the honorees. The first recipient was a professor of clinical psychology, who received polite applause as he thanked the dean and the regents for his award. Bob was next, and a group of his graduate students began clapping and whistling even before he'd reached the podium.

He was loved and feared, and Jennifer felt a mix of emotions as he spoke, one of which was great sadness. So much had changed since she last sat in an auditorium like this, a rapt student, listening to her hero speak. She had gone on to accomplish some worthwhile work, and hopefully there was more ahead of her, but it was the tragedy behind her that haunted her now. Two people were dead, one of them a victim and one a victimizer, one good and one bad. But it wasn't nearly as simple as that, Jennifer had come to realize. Everyone was capable of good and bad. We were all potential victimizers, and the seeds of our darkest impulses were sown in childhood.

"Thank you all," Bob said as he wrapped up his acceptance speech. He held the gleaming plaque in the air. "I would have happily taken cash, and no engraving would have been necessary, but this is great."

He was exceptional as always, witty and ingratiating, but Jennifer had already stayed too long. She slipped out of her seat and left the auditorium. Her next destination was only a short distance away, next to the architecture building. She knew this campus well, even at night.

The office she wanted was dark. She could see the windows as she approached the building, which was also dark, except for a few isolated rooms, where diehard academics were probably sweating out research projects or preparing for the new fall quarter. She took the stairs too fast and was panting by the time she reached the office, but the instant she turned on the light switch, she was struck by the room's military precision. It wasn't just neat. The rubber bands were sorted by color and size.

She could only recall once that she'd noticed anything out of place, and that was the last time she visited. Her gaze went to the wall of plaques behind his desk. The framed certificate in the center was still askew. The average eye wouldn't have caught it, but Jennifer was an artist, trained to be aware of balance and perspective.

Her suspicions were confirmed as soon as she lifted it off the wall. There was a combination safe hidden behind it. She didn't know the sequence of numbers, but she had the tools and the expertise to quickly gain entry. Her teacher was an expert on locking mechanisms and other such things: Russ Sadler.

To open the safe, she had to hope that some random-looking numbers she'd found jotted on a Post-it note were not really random. But that wasn't as much of a stretch as it seemed because she'd found the numbers taped to the back of Rick Morehouse's driver's license when she'd taken it out of his wallet, and her first thought was that they had been some kind of combination.

Russ had taught her how to distinguish between the sounds of moving gears and the click of releasing bolts, and she could hear all of those sounds now, as she carefully moved the dial back and forth. When she reached the last number, there was one final click, and the door moved beneath her fingers.

She held off for a moment before opening it, thinking she might need the time to prepare herself. But she was wrong. A lifetime wouldn't have been enough. There was no way to prepare for the ghoulish paraphernalia she found inside. The safe was filled with souvenirs: shreds of women's lingerie and pieces of their jewelry. There was a tiny crystal in a locket, a nose ring, and gold angel earrings — and, of course, tendrils of red hair in plastic bags. She also found packets containing eyebrows, eyelashes, and pubic hair, and there were tissues blotted with lipstick and makeup.

Sickening. It sickened her to think that he had hoarded the proof of his cruelty like trophies and gloried in them. Jennifer wasn't sad anymore. She was outraged at the lies and depravity. She would never understand this kind of inhumanity.

She took one of the bags from the safe, closed the door, and replaced the picture. Her watch told her that time was short. Defiantly, she sat in his chair to wait for him, knowing that he would soon be there. She had left a message on his cell, asking him to meet her in his office after the ceremony, and saying it was important.

"Jennifer? What brings you here?"

Jennifer had been watching the doorway, waiting for Bob Talb to appear for the last several minutes, and there he was, hesitating on his own threshold.

She didn't even wait for him to enter. "This," she said, picking up the bag of red hair.

He was carrying his award, and Jennifer could see his fingers go white against the wood and brass plaque. But he never registered any more than mild surprise. "What's that?" he asked.

"Take a closer look," she suggested. "I found it in the wall safe behind the certificate."

He laid his award on the desk and picked up the bag. "Looks like hair," he said.

"Red hair, to be precise. And what would you like to bet that it came from the Violator's victims? I found it in your safe, Bob, along with the women's lingerie, their jewelry, their *eyelashes*."

Jennifer stood to confront her mentor. She had looked up to him once. Now he could look at her and see what he'd become in her eyes, the horror and revulsion.

He shrugged as if to say, *No big deal.* But he seemed to barely be breathing, as if every ounce of his energy was involved in self-control.

"You found some things in my safe," he said. "It proves nothing. Rick Morehouse had the combination to the safe. He was using it to store personal items."

Jennifer couldn't believe what she was hearing. "You let him keep the souvenirs from his crimes in your safe?"

"Of course not. I never bothered to check what was in there. I'm a busy man."

If Jennifer had expected him to be terrified or remorseful, she'd guessed wrong. He seemed confident, even smug, as he asked her if she'd told anyone else about her ridiculous theory.

"Were you expecting someone, Bob?" She nodded toward his doorway. "You seem to have another visitor."

An elderly woman stood in the shadow of the hallway, wrapped in scarves, the kind that could be used for blindfolds.

Jennifer beckoned her into the room. "Come in, Myrna. There's someone I want you to meet. Actually, I think you two already know each other. Bob, you know Myrna Simone, don't you?"

Myrna hesitated, cowering, as Bob gaped at her. She was clearly terrified, and he was clearly stunned. His breath hissed through his teeth.

"What are you doing here?" He didn't give her time to answer before he'd assaulted her again. "What the *hell* are you doing here?"

"I'm sorry, baby boy," Myrna whispered. "I had to tell them the truth. But they know it was all my fault."

"You didn't tell them anything," he ground out, "and they wouldn't believe you anyway. You're delusional."

He started toward her, and Jennifer leaped to her feet. She wasn't two steps around the desk before Russ Sadler appeared in the doorway.

Talb halted in his tracks.

Myrna had begun to cry. "Baby boy, you shouldn't have told me about all those women. What was I supposed to do? I knew it was my fault. That's why I had to stop you. That night you kidnapped the policewoman, I went there to stop you. I saw you drive away with her on the motorcycle, only it didn't look like you."

"It wasn't me!" Talb snarled.

"It had to be, baby boy."

"Don't call me that!"

Myrna's eyes were red and flooding with tears. "You told me you were going to get rid of her. You told me about all of them, how you kept them in the trailer where we used to live, how you shaved off all their hair because red hair made women act like whores."

She twisted and tugged on her own long gray hair. "I made mistakes, I know that now. I expected too much of you, but you were such a smart one, smarter than me. I kept forgetting you were just a little boy."

Her eyelids fluttered, all but closing as she began to choke out a confession, much of it incomprehensible. She blamed her negligence on medical problems that had caused an addiction to pain pills, and she apologized repeatedly for bringing male friends to their small trailer and exposing him to things he should not have seen.

"I told you not to look, but you did it anyway," she whispered. "It was my fault that you put out your eye."

Bob turned away from her, his mouth a dry white crack. "Somebody shut her up," he said under his breath. "She's fucking crazy."

Myrna turned to Jennifer with a plea for understanding. "He hated it when I had men over. He was like a jealous suitor, banging around the trailer. He'd get into terrible black moods, and I didn't know what else to do, so I let him be with me while I was shaving my legs and doing my personal things. It seemed to calm him when nothing else would."

"Shut her up! Shut her *up!*"

Jennifer observed Bob closely. She had been betting that he would crack when he came face-to-face with his mother, and she was right. He swept a letter opener off the desk and waved it wildly.

"He won't hurt me," Myrna said, a hint of pride in her voice. "He can't. I'm his mother."

She was right, Jennifer realized. Bob had tortured her emotionally with the details of his crimes, but he couldn't inflict physical damage. No matter what she'd done to him, he couldn't hurt his mother that way, and there was no one else to hurt but himself. He would be his own victim, the last one.

He gripped the letter opener in both hands, and Jennifer realized he was going to use it.

"Stop him," Myrna cried. "He'll put out his other eye! He'll kill himself!"

Russ made a lunge for him, and the two men fell to the floor. As they wrestled for the letter opener, Bob began to curse and rant. He was outmatched by Russ, who was larger and trained. Bob's flailing was childlike and ineffectual. His blows and kicks were blocked, and it drove him crazy with rage. He grabbed the leg of a chair and tried to topple it on Russ.

Jennifer felt helpless. She reached for the desk lamp to hit him, but Russ shouted at her to stay away.

Myrna began to wail. She pleaded with Russ not to hurt Bob, but the damage had already been done, years ago. The chair fell against a set of bookcases, and by the time Russ had Bob pinned and helpless, he'd regressed to an infantile state. He was sobbing and writhing.

Myrna dropped to her knees and crawled to her son. Russ allowed her to soothe Bob's brow and whisper to him. It was a calculated risk. Her presence could have set him off, Jennifer knew, and they would never be able to question him. But Bob began to calm down. The very woman who had made him insane was the only one who could reach him now.

Jennifer watched, disbelieving. Under his mother's gentle coaxing, Bob Talb confessed to everything, including using an accomplice for his crimes. He admitted that Rick Morehouse had kidnapped the women and delivered them to the trailer, where he left them for Bob, who arrived later that night, after having established an airtight alibi. He and Rick never discussed in detail what Bob did with the hostages, but they did discuss the police investigation of the Violator, whom they both had come to think of as an entity separate from themselves.

"Rick would clip the newspaper articles," Bob said, "and gloat over the muddle the police were making of the investigation. He loved to talk about the Violator's next move and how we kept everyone spinning in circles, even the media. Of course, he never did anything but abduct them. I did all the work."

Jennifer wasn't surprised at his attitude. It wasn't unusual for successful serial criminals to develop God complexes and begin to think they were too smart to be caught, which is exactly why they were caught. As Bob went into more detail, Jennifer finally understood why her method had failed. It was Rick who abducted Sharon, and it was Rick's face that Myrna saw when the visor flew up. But Myrna had expected to see her son, and her mind told her that she *had* seen him, despite the discrepancies. She'd been trying to describe two men, the one she saw, and the one she thought she saw, which explained her vague recall of Rick's features, and her denial of them when she saw the sketch. It also explained why she insisted that Jennifer darken the suspect's right eye. The orb that she called an eclipse was her son's own permanently dilated eye.

At least now Jennifer understood that her own struggle to produce a sketch was due largely to Myrna's confusion and the terrible conflict she must have felt about identifying her own son.

"How did you recruit Rick Morehouse?"

Russ asked the question. He'd taken over for Myrna, who continued to comfort her son. Perhaps now she was giving Bob the attention he'd always craved, her sole attention.

"He molested a mental patient, a retarded girl," Bob said tonelessly.

He seemed to have detached from the events he was describing as he explained that Rick had worked as an intern in a mental ward to pay his way through grad school. He was under Bob's supervision, and Bob should have reported the offense, but never did. Instead, he took full advantage of his assistant's gratefulness and his crippling fears of the opposite sex. He bought Rick a powerful motorcycle, and he used his own research in arousal theory to convince Rick that women responded strongly to the element of surprise and to a man who could make them feel physically vulnerable.

Of course, Rick never got any of the spoils. It was Talb and his twisted fantasies that were played out in the trailer. Rick's loyalty was bought with money and bribes and the promise that soon one of the women would be his.

"Whose idea was it to frame me?" Russ asked.

Bob admitted that it was his. Jennifer was getting close to the truth with her sketches, and when Bob realized they'd brought in his own mother for questioning, he had to act. Rick Morehouse would never have been mistaken for Russ in a line-up, but Bob was familiar with eyewitness psychology through Jennifer's work, and he knew that a witness only registered one or two salient features. In this case Rick's nose was made to look broken and his brow furrowed with makeup to approximate Russ's scowl. Then, using the bike he'd taken from Russ's shed, Rick staged a random kidnapping and let the woman escape, the plan being that she would ID him as Russ.

"That was all I had to do," Bob said. "I was counting on Jennifer to do the rest with her sketch."

Jennifer didn't want to believe it. He was counting on her to help him frame Russ, and she'd stepped right into his trap. He'd used her own method against her.

"Why?" she asked him.

"Because you repeatedly failed to see that the man was beneath you, little more than a barbarian. He couldn't possibly be your consort. I proved it to you with my experiment, but you wouldn't see it."

Russ was contemptuous. "And who was her *consort?* You?"

"No," Bob said, sounding almost reflective for a moment. "There wasn't a man worthy of her — not me, certainly not you. But she failed to see that, too, so I was forced to open her eyes."

There was a terrifying menace in his observation, but the only thing on Jennifer's mind right then was his tinted glasses. "What happened to *your* eye?" she asked him. "Take off your glasses, or I'll do it for you."

"Don't!" Myrna warned. "It's evil."

Jennifer turned to the other woman. "How did it happen? Tell me and I'll leave him alone."

"He used to spy on me when I brought men home, and he swore he would do something terrible if I didn't stop. I thought he meant to hurt me, or the man, but he didn't. He hurt himself. He put out his eye with my kitchen scissors."

Jennifer shuddered, recoiling from the image. How could she have been taken in by such a sick soul? But then, so were his students taken in, hundreds of them every year, and the faculty of the university and everyone who dealt with Bob Talb. He was the classic sociopathic, narcissistic personality. There were men like him running the corporations and the country, but few of them had been deserted by their fathers and raised by women like Myrna. It took surprisingly little to turn a decent kid bad.

"What will happen to him now?" Myrna asked. She was still on the floor, kneeling next to her son.

"He'll be taken down to the department and booked," Russ said. "If there's any justice, he'll get the death penalty."

"Oh, my God, baby boy, I'm sorry."

Myrna pressed her hands to her mouth and began to rock, as if the reality of the situation had just hit her. Bob seemed barely aware that his mother was there. He struggled to get up, but before he could manage it, Russ had his hands cuffed behind his back.

"I tried to protect you," Myrna told her son. "I ran away, but they came after me, and they already knew about you. They found the trailer, and somehow they figured out that Frank Nathan was my ex-husband and your father."

Bob glared at her as if he didn't believe her, but Myrna was telling the truth. The background check on Nathan had revealed that he married Myrna Talb when she was eighteen, and that she had one child by him, a son they named Robert. She divorced Nathan after he deserted her and her child, and she took back her maiden name, tacking it onto the end of Nathan. Several years later, she married Jerry Simone. It was another short-lived union, but she kept his name because she liked the sound of it.

In short, Myrna Simone was Bob Talb's mother.

Once Russ had discovered that, the challenge became to find Myrna, who had gone into hiding when she realized that she might have to testify against her own son. She was finally tracked to a religious commune near the Oregon border, and when she realized how much they already knew, she told them the rest of it.

Myrna's first husband left her nothing but a cramped trailer and a bawling baby to raise. Her second left her with his gambling debts to pay off, and by that time, her teenage son had deserted her, too. Bob had run away from a mother who had a drug habit and who used anything and anyone, including him, to get what she needed.

Baby boy was her pet name for him when he was young, but it was a term of degradation more than endearment. She accused him of being weak and took pleasure in humiliating him when he refused to roam the valley's tourist traps and steal things for her that could be resold. As he grew older, she became seductive, manipulating him with tears and emotional bribery. She would dress provocatively and invite him to brush her long, red hair, but whenever a "real" man came into her life, she would abandon her son for days at a time.

After hearing Myrna's story, Jennifer had

begun to understand that Bob had hated her as much as he loved her. He was obsessed with her his entire life. When he became an adult, he symbolically killed her by having a tombstone inscribed and putting it on an empty grave. He then invented a new history, complete with a new mother. It was her picture he'd hung on the wall, but he was never free of Myrna. The only relief he got came from abducting women who resembled her and torturing them in the ways she tortured him. Eventually even that didn't work, so he sought his mother out after every crime and confessed to her in gruesome detail, threatening to kill her if she told. She never did. He was her only source of money and drugs.

With every strike he felt compelled to up the ante. He'd gone to psychic fairs and metaphysical shops to find his first three victims, but Sharon Myer was different. She'd come into contact with Rick Morehouse when she was canvassing BMW repair shops, and Rick had noticed her jotting down the license plate number from his bike. That made her an immediate threat — and a target — only this time Bob confessed in advance of the abduction. He told his mother he was taking a woman from her own neighborhood, someone who lived nearby. That's why Myrna Simone was out that night, hoping she could stop her son. It's also why she later left a message for Jennifer at the hotel, begging her to stop him.

"We've got him. Come on up and get him."

Russ's voice alerted Jennifer that the backup forces were on their way. He was on his cell phone, giving them the order to move in. Out in the same parking lot where she'd left her rental, there was a contingent of patrol cars that Russ had arranged for. The plan had been to catch Bob off guard, but at the same time to be prepared. There was no way to know how he might react or whether he was armed. Of course, all the necessary legal steps had been taken including obtaining a search warrant.

Jennifer went to stand by Russ as a half-dozen uniformed officers entered the office. They were there to pick up both Bob Talb and Myrna. He would be taken to the county lockup, awaiting arraignment, and she to a rehab facility, one with excellent security. They both went without a struggle, and Jennifer was grateful for that. She was even more grateful that a very long ordeal was over.

Moments later, in the deep quiet of the office, Jennifer spoke first. "I think Sharon would have liked this operation."

"She was big on teamwork," Russ agreed. "That part would have appealed to her." But then his voice changed. "Speaking of that, *I* could use some backup. You game?"

"Another case? I don't think so, Russ."

"I need help hanging a picture." Emotion flickered, shadowing his features for a moment. "It's Sharon. She's supposed to be on the Fallen Officer's Wall, and she's still in the out basket in my office."

As Jennifer gazed at him, she realized that he wasn't talking about making sure that Sharon's picture was straight. He was concerned whether he could get through it emotionally. She loved him for that. His struggles with his own tender feelings were endearing to her. They had melted her heart and always would.

"I'd be honored," she managed.

He was wearing a linen shirt with panels of black and charcoal, and Jennifer happened to know that he kept his badge in the pocket. She traced the outlines of the leather case through the material. "You're getting a little better at teamwork yourself," she said.

It was an overture, and a rather provocative one at that.

"You have no idea," he said.

"And what does that mean?"

He captured her gaze with a look that made her feel as if the floor had moved beneath her feet. But he didn't answer her question. He just smiled mysteriously, leaving her to wonder what he was up to now. Another surprise? She wasn't sure her heart could handle that.

He took her hand in his, and their fingers intertwined, locking tightly. Jennifer's breath caught hard. She felt nothing but joy in that moment, nothing but the sweetest kind of longing. For her their locked hands symbolized perfectly the kind of love she wanted, one that was equal, yet stronger when joined than apart, a partnership of the heart.

As they left the office, she had the sense that no matter what happened, this would be one of the great transitions of her life. She was leaving so much behind, and even though she didn't know exactly what lay ahead, she felt more ready for it than she ever had in her life. Maybe it was ironic that her male role models had failed her utterly, and the one man she'd been terrified to trust was the only one who'd proven to be trustworthy. She wondered if trust might be the ultimate act of faith, because if it was, then she had finally taken what felt like the biggest step of her life. She had laughed in the face of her demons, and she was ready to believe again — in someone and something other than herself.

And if there was an irony to be found in any of it, she realized, it was this: that she'd had to come all the way home — back to her beginnings — to find the man she wanted to brave the future with. She had finally chosen right. Russ Sadler might only be a reluctant hero, but he was the only one she would ever need.

Epilogue

Jennifer clicked up a flight of stairs on her way to the tenth floor. Her low-heeled sandals clattered on the cement steps, making a terrible racket, but she was late for an appointment with Kate, who had agreed to be interviewed for Jennifer's book. Breathing hard, she reached the landing between the eighth and ninth floor, and stopped short.

Someone had blocked off a section of steps with yellow crime scene tape.

How weird, was her first reaction. She continued up the steps to get a closer look, but there weren't any signs that a crime had been committed. There was no visible damage to the area, no indication of a struggle, and no blood, fortunately. She couldn't see any signs of evidence collection, either.

There didn't seem to be anyone around anywhere.

"Definitely weird," she murmured, turning around to head back down. Apparently she had a date with the elevator.

"Stop where you are!"

The command held such force that Jennifer halted and raised her hands. She turned slowly, half expecting to see an officer with his gun pointed at her. Her shock turned into a smile when she saw who it was.

Russ stood on the landing above her, his arms folded and his legs braced. He looked like a hanging judge up there, all dark shadows and skepticism.

"What's up?" she asked. Was he trying to quit coffee again?

He graced her with one of his signature scowls. "You're under arrest."

"Did I forget to water the ficus?" She grinned, but he didn't.

The crime scene tape roped off a small section of steps in the middle of the flight, and apparently Detective Sadler was the man in charge of this investigation. He unbraced himself and descended to the tape, where he continued to question her.

"Ms. Nash, do you know where you are?" he asked.

She kept waiting for the smile. "Aren't you going to read me my rights?"

"*Don't* make me ask the question again."

Wow, what a grouch. "Of course, I know where I am. I'm in Seattle. This is the Public Safety Building."

He gave her a stern look. "What *step* are you on?"

"Oh, I don't know. I didn't count." Her mouth fell open in shock, and she tried to remember the last time she hadn't automatically counted steps as she was climbing. She might have been eight or nine, maybe younger.

"I didn't count! I'm cured."

Okay, then he *almost* smiled. "You're on step one hundred and fifty, Ms. Nash, four steps below where the crime was committed."

Jennifer thought she might know the crime he was speaking of. "Can I call my attorney?"

A slow shake of his head scattered dark hair and dark vibes. "I *might* consider a plea bargain."

"Would you consider insanity? I didn't know what I was doing?"

"That's not a plea bargain. It's an excuse. You need to offer me something in exchange for my mercy and compassion, Ms. Nash." His eyes narrowed, lit by what could only have been low and wicked thoughts. "Something good."

"I'll have sex with you in the hammock whenever you want?"

"Something *lasting*, Jennifer."

"I'll have sex with you in the hammock for as long as we both shall live?"

"Something meaningful."

"We'll talk for hours after we have sex in the hammock?"

He reached inside his coat and came out with a jangling pair of handcuffs. "You're going to jail," he said.

"Wait, wait, wait! I know what the crime is."

"We *both* know what the crime is," he said disdainfully. "You stole my heart on these steps, and then you left me waiting at the altar. Now, what is your plea?"

He was right. It had better be something good. She stared up at him, struck by how vulnerable he had allowed himself to be, despite the Darth Vader pose. He needed her, and he wasn't afraid to let it be known. This was a tall, dark, and fearsome man, from his beautiful eyes to his wild heart, but he needed her. He had found a way to let her in, to let her love him . . . and God, she needed that.

A soft smile lit her face. "Can I make my plea now?"

"You'd better. A man can only hold his breath so long."

Actually, she had been holding hers, too. It spilled out now. "Will you be my husband, Russ? Will *you* marry *me?* I want to be in your hammock *and* in your life, forever."

He wet his lips. "That just might get you probation . . . for the rest of your life. Hard time with me. Soft time with me."

She ran up the steps, sandals clickety-clacking, and he ripped the yellow tape away. He pulled her into his arms with a deep groan of pleasure. "I wonder if you have any idea how hard I tried to scare you off?" he whispered.

She clung to him, and they teetered precariously on step number 154. Breathless laughter mixed with her tears. "Not hard enough," she said.

After a moment, he drew back as if to say something, but his voice was hoarse, and it took some effort to clear it.

"You blew all my theories to hell, Jennifer. My dad believed the world was divided into two groups: the snakes who betray you because that's human nature, and poisonous snakes who really enjoy betraying you. Then you came along, and I thought I could finally prove him wrong. I conducted an investigation, and I searched for evidence that you were one of the good ones. I *needed* to prove him wrong."

"And then I ran off."

Her heart burned with sadness, but he must have seen it, because he very gently cupped her face and kissed her lips.

"My dad *was* wrong," he said. "People aren't good or bad. They're just people, trying to get by and making mistakes, but most of them aren't out to hurt anyone. That's the last thing they want. You made me see that."

"It *was* the last thing I wanted. I would rather die than hurt you."

Her eyes were blurry with tears as she met his gaze. And her heart was so swollen with love that she could say nothing, do nothing, but be incredibly grateful.

"Are you crying?" he asked her. *"Don't do that."*

Now she had to clear her throat. "Did you accept my proposal of marriage, Mr. Sadler?"

He lifted her right off the steps and into his arms. She could feel the warmth and wetness of his kiss on her lips, the warmth and wetness of his tears on her face. And when he finally gave her a moment to breathe, she said, "I'll take that as a yes."

About the Author

Suzanne Forster has an academic background in clinical psychology and now puts her energies toward her writing career. A #1 bestselling author and winner of several awards, she lives with her husband in Newport Beach, California. Visit her website at www.blush.com.

The employees of Thorndike Press hope you have enjoyed this Large Print book. All our Thorndike and Wheeler Large Print titles are designed for easy reading, and all our books are made to last. Other Thorndike Press Large Print books are available at your library, through selected bookstores, or directly from us.

For information about titles, please call:

(800) 223-1244

or visit our Web site at:

www.gale.com/thorndike
www.gale.com/wheeler

To share your comments, please write:

Publisher
Thorndike Press
295 Kennedy Memorial Drive
Waterville, ME 04901